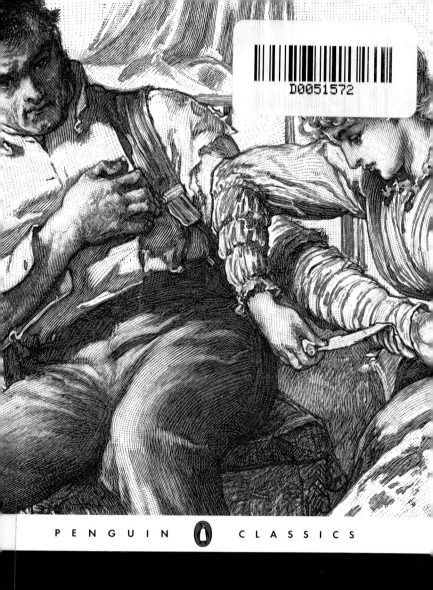

PENGUIN CLASSICS

SARAH ORNE JEWETT

A Country Doctor

PENGUIN  CLASSICS

A COUNTRY DOCTOR

SARAH ORNE JEWETT was born in 1849 into a middle-class family in South Berwick, Maine. Her father was a local physician. She graduated from Berwick Academy in 1865 and began writing seriously. Her first story appeared in 1868 in the *Atlantic Monthly*, which continued to publish her work, as did *Harper's, Scribner's*, and others. She became part of Boston's cultural elite and was good friends with her publisher James T. Fields and his wife, Annie Adams Fields. After his death in 1881, Jewett moved in with Annie, spending part of the year with her in Boston or on the Massachusetts coast and often traveling with her. Jewett's works include *Deephaven* (1877), *A Country Doctor* (1884), *The Country of the Pointed Firs* (1896), and nine volumes of short stories published between 1879 and 1899. She incurred serious injuries in 1902 after being thrown from a carriage and had to give up writing. She died in 1909.

FREDERICK WEGENER is an associate professor of English at California State University, Long Beach, and the editor of *Edith Wharton: The Uncollected Critical Writings*. His essays have appeared in *American Literature, Texas Studies in Literature and Language, Tulsa Studies in Women's Literature*, and other journals. He is working on a study of representations of medical women in the United States between 1860 and 1920.

SARAH ORNE JEWETT

A Country Doctor

Edited with an Introduction and Notes by
FREDERICK WEGENER

PENGUIN BOOKS

PENGUIN BOOKS

Published by the Penguin Group

Penguin Group (USA) Inc., 375 Hudson Street, New York, New York 10014, U.S.A.
Penguin Group (Canada), 10 Alcorn Avenue, Toronto, Ontario, Canada M4V 3B2
(a division of Pearson Penguin Canada Inc.)
Penguin Books Ltd, 80 Strand, London WC2R 0RL, England
Penguin Ireland, 25 St Stephen's Green, Dublin 2, Ireland (a division of Penguin Books Ltd)
Penguin Group (Australia), 250 Camberwell Road, Camberwell, Victoria 3124, Australia
(a division of Pearson Australia Group Pty Ltd)
Penguin Books India Pvt Ltd, 11 Community Centre, Panchsheel Park,
New Delhi - 110 017, India
Penguin Group (NZ), cnr Airborne and Rosedale Roads, Albany, Auckland 1310, New Zealand
(a division of Pearson New Zealand Ltd)
Penguin Books (South Africa) (Pty) Ltd, 24 Sturdee Avenue, Rosebank,
Johannesburg 2196, South Africa

Penguin Books Ltd, Registered Offices:
80 Strand, London WC2R 0RL, England

First published in the United States of America by Houghton, Mifflin and Company 1884
This edition with an introduction and notes by Frederick Wegener published in
Penguin Books 2005

1 3 5 7 9 10 8 6 4 2

Introduction and notes copyright © Ferderick Wegener, 2005
All rights reserved

LIBRARY OF CONGRESS CATALOGING IN PUBLICATION DATA
Jewett, Sarah Orne, 1849–1909.
A country doctor / Sarah Orne Jewett ; edited with an introduction and notes by Frederick Wegener.
p.   cm.
Includes bibliographical references.
ISBN 0 14 30.3926 1
1. Women medical students—Fiction.   2. Women physicians—Fiction.   3. Country life—Fiction.
4. New England—Fiction.   I. Wegener, Frederick, 1957–   II. Title.
PS2132.C63 2005
813'.4—dc22   2004058739

Printed in the United States of America
Set in Sabon

Contents

A COUNTRY DOCTOR

Introduction

In 1882, reflecting upon the status of women in the medical profession in the *North American Review*, the distinguished physician Mary Putnam Jacobi saw reason for hope and encouragement despite what she called "the peculiar bitterness of the opposition which has been manifested to the admission of women to medicine." As evidence that "the once continuous opposition has become intermittent," Jacobi pointed to the fact that women "are members of various medical societies, contribute to various medical journals, conduct hospitals, perform surgical operations, build up practice, and in other ways seem to conduct themselves and to be treated like other members of the medical profession." Jacobi could have cited her own career as a measure of the progress that women doctors had started to enjoy in the United States. An 1864 graduate of the pathbreaking Woman's Medical College of Pennsylvania, she had continued her education in Paris—where she attended clinics, received high honors as the first female enrollee at the École de Médecine, and briefly served as a hospital surgeon in the Commune—before returning home to join the faculty of the Woman's Medical College of the New York Infirmary for Women and Children, start a successful practice, and become one of the most prolific and scientifically informed medical writers of the day. Few at the time could have provided a more authoritative view than Jacobi of recent improvements in the woman doctor's fortunes in the United States: "That considerable numbers of women do now study medicine and support themselves by its practice, is itself a proof that the prejudice of thirty years ago has somewhat abated."[1]

In the time since the legendary Elizabeth Blackwell became the first member of her sex to receive a medical diploma in the United States in 1849, American women had indeed made great strides in the field of medicine, in the face of entrenched and often venomous hostility on the part of the medical establishment and much of the public. As of 1880, the nation's women physicians already totaled around two thousand (nearly quadrupling the number of a decade earlier) and would increase more than threefold by the second decade of the next century, when the rate at which women attended medical schools entered a steep decline that would not be significantly reversed until the 1970s. And, as their presence became more and more conspicuous, women physicians came to have an impact that reverberated well beyond their own domain, making them the object of an increasingly widespread fascination in the United States in the last third of the nineteenth century. Starting in the 1860s, for example, images of women as doctors began to circulate in works of fiction and verse, steadily accumulating into a wealth of representations that sharpened the vociferous debate under way, in both the medical and mainstream press, about one of the era's more polarizing social phenomena.

The emergence of medical women had already generated abundant imaginative response by the time Sarah Orne Jewett wrote *A Country Doctor* (1884), completing a trio of American novels about women physicians published in the space of only a few years. Preceded by *Dr. Breen's Practice* (1881), in which William Dean Howells portrays a young woman convinced of her inadequacy as a physician not long after graduating from medical school, and by Elizabeth Stuart Phelps's *Doctor Zay* (1882), which covers a year in the life of a flourishing rural female practitioner, Jewett's novel offered "a third setting forth," as one critic put it, "of the doubts and difficulties which beset a young woman who attempts the practice of medicine." Reviewers accordingly grouped *A Country Doctor* with the earlier two works in pondering "[t]he fact that such writers as Mr. Howells, Miss Phelps, and Miss Jewett should within four years so carefully study what is practically the same subject," a coincidence that amply confirmed the medical woman's noteworthiness in the United States at the time.[2]

Yet, apart from being set in New England (a region that indeed boasted the nation's largest percentage of medical women toward the end of the nineteenth century), the three novels have little in common as incarnations of the woman doctor, a figure Jewett approaches in a particularly distinctive way. Charting the maturation of an orphan adopted by the local physician of a southern Maine village, a middle-aged widower who allows her the freedom to develop unhindered and whom she reverently follows into a medical career, *A Country Doctor* represents a signal advance in the "imaging" of women in American medicine, as well as a defining moment in its author's own output. Eclipsed for decades after her death, the novel has undergone an extensive and illuminating critical reevaluation with the enlargement of the American literary canon that began in the 1970s thanks to the rediscovery of so many works by women. Now the most widely studied and discussed of Jewett's works after "A White Heron" (1886) and *The Country of the Pointed Firs* (1896), *A Country Doctor* remains nonetheless an insufficiently understood or appreciated text, more complex and provocatively forward-looking than even the growing body of scholarship on the novel might suggest.

Published in 1884, but covering a period of time that ranges from around the early 1850s through the early 1870s, *A Country Doctor* evinces a sharp awareness on Jewett's part of the growing salience of medical women and of the developments observed so incisively by Jacobi in the *North American Review* a couple of years earlier. Although Nan Prince, Jewett's protagonist, is said to have "found little encouragement [from] the interest of society in general" as she prepares to depart for medical school (where she will receive a degree that "was only a formal seal of disapproval in most persons' eyes"), it is "when she . . . remembered what renown some women physicians had won" that Nan feels emboldened once more to press ahead with her plans. The existence of such inspiring models cannot be denied even by those most bitterly opposed to her choice of a career, one of whom is later forced to acknowledge, "Of course I know that there have been some women physicians who have attained eminence. . . ." If, in Jewett's own words, "[a]ffairs must rise to a certain level before a narration of some great crisis is suggested," then the controversy ignited by the women's medical movement in the United States had already reached a stage critical enough to call forth the telling of a story like Nan's. At the same time, however, a set of far more private circumstances closely affected Jewett's work on *A Country Doctor*, which may be said to have stemmed in large part from two often noted turning points in her life that fundamentally shaped her decision to devote her first novel to the issue of women in medicine.

The principal catalyst was the sudden death in 1878 of Jewett's father, one of mid-nineteenth-century Maine's most respected physicians, on whom she openly based her characterization of Nan's guardian and mentor, Dr. John Leslie, and whose profound and pervasive influence has become one of the best-known facts of her life. In a career summarized by Jewett herself in an anonymously published obituary (reprinted here in the appendix), Theodore Herman Jewett audited lectures in medicine at Dartmouth and Harvard, attended Jefferson Medical College in Philadelphia, and returned to Maine to conduct a thriving rural practice in York County for nearly forty years. In the last year of his life, he served as president of the Maine Medical Association, delivering in that capacity an address from which his daughter liberally borrowed—incorporating several passages almost verbatim, as illustrated in some of the explanatory notes to the novel—when she composed Dr. Leslie's discussions of medical practice in the ninth chapter of *A Country Doctor*.[3] Although he seems not to have publicly commented on the question of women as doctors, the Maine Medical Association had become one of the nation's first state medical societies to admit women not long before his presidency, while Dr. Jewett's additional role as professor of obstetrics and diseases of women and children at the Medical School of Maine associated him with a specialty in which the need for women physicians had been most acutely felt for some time in the United States.[4] Yet it was more upon her intimate familiarity with his ways of thinking, and upon the depth of her attachment to him, that Jewett would have drawn in portraying an experienced rural doctor who fosters a young woman's medical aspirations while serving a community transparently identifiable with the writer's hometown of South Berwick and its environs. As she memorialized him in tracing the formative role that Dr. Leslie performs in his adopted daughter's upbringing, Jewett re-creates much of her own childhood, in which she had routinely accompanied her father on his rounds throughout the countryside, observed his exploits in ministering to patients, perused his medical books and journals, and briefly entertained the notion of seeking a career in medicine herself. Having instead channeled those energies into a literary vocation, Jewett pays tribute to her father in part by imagining herself on the road not taken, vicariously following him into the medical profession through her alter ego's experiences in *A Country Doctor*.

Yet Jewett—not only the daughter but also the granddaughter and grandniece of physicians—never entirely abandoned her early Aesculapian enthusiasms, which she continued to indulge long after establishing herself as a writer. According to one of her biographers, who notes "the satisfaction she took in prescribing medicines and tonics . . . for anyone she knew who was ailing," Jewett "retained all her life the medical knowledge she had absorbed as a girl" in her father's company.[5] Her contributions to the newsletter of an 1873 hospital fair in Portland included a trenchant and frankly opinionated essay, "Doctors and Patients," on the responsibilities of both parties to the standard therapeutic encounter. And it was not only a knowledge of medicine that she imbibed from her father; he also "ruled my early attempts at writing by the severity and simplicity of his own good taste," as she later recalled, and imparted an admonition ("Don't try to write *about* people and things, tell them just as they are!") that formed the cornerstone of Jewett's literary creed.[6] Far from merely substituting the imaginative for the medical, Jewett came to see both enterprises as closely intertwined.

More than once in *A Country Doctor*, for example, she draws distinctly aesthetic parallels to capture the essence of the healing craft, maintaining that "[t]here must be an instinct that recognizes a disease and suggests its remedy, as much as an instinct that finds the right notes and harmonies for a composer of music, or the colors for a true artist's picture," and contending that, "as the great poet tells the truths of God, and makes other souls wiser and stronger and fitter for action, so the great doctor works for the body's health." The force of such analogies would have been strengthened by experiences like one reported by F. O. Matthiessen, Jewett's kinsman and first biographer, who cites a communication in which "an old country friend of her father's spoke of how the doctor's stimulating and encouraging presence always flooded the darkest sick-rooms with light, and then added, 'You are doing the same good work in the same way, with a vastly enlarged sphere of "practice." As one of your grateful patients I send you my hearty thanks.'" [7] A remarkable diary entry penned during the first winter after her father's death indicates the extent to which Jewett thought of her own literary role as not only complementing but also in some sense completing his work: "I think if we had worked together, I with my writing and he with his insight and great thoughts which I could express for him sometimes better than he could for himself, we might have done a great deal of good and helped a great many people." [8]

It was in the long and mournful aftermath of her father's death that the second of Jewett's life-changing experiences to have a direct bearing on *A Country Doctor* commenced in 1881, the year that marked the deepening of her friendship with Annie Adams Fields. Widow of one of the nineteenth century's most distinguished American publishers, Fields had helped turn their home on Charles Street into Boston's leading literary salon by the time Jewett first met them some years earlier. Active in various important charitable and social-relief endeavors, Fields numbered the formal education and training of women as doctors among her chief causes, promoting what she called "efforts to give women a higher medical culture" in an 1878 *Harper's* essay in which she regretfully counted "only six medical colleges for women in the United States," declared that "[h]ospitals for women and children should stand high in our list of woman's work for woman," and complained that "[t]he established physicians . . . never believed much in 'women doctors.' "9 She would be reminded of their disdain two years later, when serving energetically on a committee organized to mount the latest in a series of failed attempts to gain admission for women to Harvard Medical School. A woman whose father, like Jewett's, was a physician (along with her brother), and whose nephew (again like Jewett's) would become one, Fields had thus emerged as a staunch advocate of medical women by the time she and her friend, three years before the publication of *A Country Doctor*, began living and traveling together in the arrangement that they would sustain for the rest of Jewett's life. Their relationship doubtless reinforced Jewett's understanding of the gravity of the need for women physicians in the United States. In 1890, when Fields joined the ultimately successful campaign in favor of coeducation at the college of medicine to be established at Johns Hopkins, it was surely through her involvement that Jewett also came to join the Women's Fund Committee, which solicited help in raising the initial one-hundred-thousand-dollar sum "to be offered to the Trustees for the use of the medical school, on condition that women . . . be admitted to the school, whenever it shall open, on the same terms as men."10 Later the same year, Jewett herself informed their friend John Greenleaf Whittier that Fields "had been spending two or three days in Baltimore where there has been a reception and inspection of Johns Hopkins hospital and much talk about the new medical school for women. We both tried to do something about it in the spring."11

Fields, for her part, would have quickly become aware of the early and enduring interest in medicine that Jewett had inherited from her father, remarking shortly after her death in 1909 that "many a young graduating doctor today might well envy that slip of a girl for the knowledge at first hand which had been conveyed to her impressionable mind," before adding that "her gift was undeniable, and the physicians of her acquaintance have borne testimony to her instinctive power of discernment and helpfulness."[12] That those physicians included a number of women is not surprising, given Jewett's immersion in her friend's Boston milieu, and given the increasing amount of time she spent in a city that was perhaps the friendliest to medical women, who would compose nearly 20 percent of its doctors by 1890. In a letter dated not long before she began work on *A Country Doctor*, Jewett recalled discussing with Fields "the daughter of your old friends who had studied medicine and . . . who was lost in the *Schiller* when Dr. Susan Dimock was," referring to the tragic shipwreck in which one of Boston's most promising young women physicians had perished in 1875.[13] Some years later, Jewett wrote to the poet Louise Imogen Guiney about "my friend Dr. Ella Dexter whom I like so much and who was taking care of my eyes all winter"[14] in Boston, where Dexter had a long-standing practice and became in 1889 the first woman elected a member of the New England Ophthalmological Society. Some time prior to writing *A Country Doctor*, Jewett had befriended and begun consulting another local luminary among medical women, Dr. Helen Morton, a member of the original all-female staff of attending physicians at the celebrated New England Hospital for Women and Children (which Fields described in 1878 as "an excellent hospital" operated by "[s]ome of the ablest women in their profession in this country"[15]), and soon to become one of Boston's most respected obstetricians. Once described by the writer as "touchy in her doctorly heart and more devoted in her private capacity as a friend," Morton—a graduate of the New England Female Medical College, established in Boston in 1848 as the first institution of its kind in the United States—was evidently the person to whom Jewett planned to turn for advice ("Ask Dr. Morton for process of getting degree &c.") in describing the formal stage of Nan's schooling in medicine in *A Country Doctor*.[16]

The fact that Nan doesn't begin attending a medical college until halfway into the novel, and has only just completed her studies by its end, reminds us that Jewett's title refers at least as much to Dr. Leslie as to his protégée, and less to Nan at any

point in the story than to the physician she is on the verge of becoming after she returns home from Boston and confidently
awaits her future. Such nuances differentiate *A Country Doctor*
from the full-fledged "lady-doctor" novels that had recently begun to appear in the United States and align it much more
closely with earlier texts in which a young woman—like the title character of Bayard Taylor's *Hannah Thurston* (1864) or
Ida Van Arsdel in Harriet Beecher Stowe's *My Wife and I*
(1871) or the more familiar Ruth Bolton in *The Gilded Age*
(1873)—is depicted either contemplating or embarking upon or
undertaking a medical education. (The instruction in each case,
as in Nan's, moreover, is understood to be of the orthodox or
"regular" variety, in contrast to that of Howells's "doctress"
and Phelps's, both of whom, as avowedly homeopathic physicians, practice an "irregular," sectarian brand of medicine es-
chewed by "regularly" trained medical women like those
among Jewett's friends.) What sets it apart even from those
works, however, is that Jewett's novel places its aspiring female
doctor at the center of the narrative, following her from childhood to her early twenties through each stage of her long and
conscientious preparation for a career in medicine.

As it delineates the path that carries Nan into her choice of
profession, *A Country Doctor* has been occasionally discussed
as a version or variant of the novel of formation or development.
To the extent that, in Rita Felski's words, "[t]he narrative of education or apprenticeship . . . is for the most part unavailable to
the nineteenth-century heroine," one would in fact be hard
pressed to come up with an earlier work of American fiction in
which the *Bildungsroman* is so fully and thoroughly appropri-
ated by a writer of Jewett's sex, or adapted more effectively to
the task of capturing the developmental trajectory of a female
rather than a male protagonist. As Nan advances through each
of the life-phases typically experienced by the traditionally male
Bildungsheld—youthful display of aptitude, the awakening to
a sense of vocation, interludes of uncertainty and self-doubt,
the shift from a rural to an urban environment, the encounter
with various obstacles to be surmounted on the road to self-
actualization, and the reaffirmation of commitment to one's

calling—*A Country Doctor* comes to resemble those post-1960s novels exemplifying what Felski has dubbed "the contemporary narrative of female development," in which "female self-discovery and emancipation is depicted as a process of moving outward into the public realm of social engagement and activity." Nearly a century before the cultural impact of second-wave feminism in the United States would lead critics like Felski to suggest that "[t]he *Bildungsroman* . . . has acquired a new function in charting the changing self-consciousness of women accompanying their gradual entry into the public domain," Jewett had already recast the genre in exactly the same fashion, and at a time when such a maneuver would have been all the more unusual and audacious.[17]

One notes, for example, how often the narrative is punctuated by junctures that mark, as Sarah Way Sherman has observed, an abrupt widening of Nan's consciousness and vision. "Life had suddenly grown much larger," she realizes as a child at the end of her first visit to Dr. Leslie's, "and her familiar horizon had vanished and she discovered a great distance stretching far beyond the old limits." With her grandmother's death, "the first chapter of the child's life was ended," while "her horizon of future happiness constantly grew wider" after Nan's removal to the doctor's home as his ward. Likewise, once Nan definitively announces her intention of becoming a doctor, "It seemed to her as if the first volume of her life was ended" and "she had opened a gate and shut it behind her, between that day and its yesterday." Escorted by Dr. Leslie on her first visit to Boston, Nan "had ceased to belong only to the village she had left" and "became a citizen of the world at large. Her horizon had suddenly become larger, and she might have discovered more than one range of mountains which must be crossed as the years led her forward steadily, one by one." Again, "with every year's ascent," Nan and her classmates at medical school "had been thankful for the wider horizon which was spread for their eyes to see" as they near the completion of their studies. Even in girlhood, Nan already senses the beckoning of some vast, expansive domain that transcends her immediate environment. It is because "she had really become aware of a great outside world" and "welcomed the sight of any messengers," for example, that Nan so appreciates the visit of the well-traveled Dr. Ferris. After medical school, once she returns home to launch her career in earnest by training to become Dr. Leslie's copractitioner, the same impression of spaciousness and breadth greets Nan at the start of the final scene, as she finds herself "going out at the door and down toward the gateway, which opened to a pleasantly wide world beyond."

As she moves toward, and into, that larger world (the world of productive endeavor, human usefulness, and self-fulfillment), the process Nan undergoes is described throughout the narrative, again in the manner of a classic *Bildungsroman*, as an unfolding of certain preexistent tendencies and drives, or the exfoliation of some innate potential. After deciding to encourage Nan's medical predilections, Dr. Leslie himself "was conscious of a grave and sweet desire . . . to bring out what was in her own mind and capacity, and so to wisely educate her, to give her a place to work in, and wisdom to work with," an effort in which "the wise doctor simply followed as best he could the leadings of the young nature itself." Under his guidance, "the girl grew naturally year by year, reaching out half unconsciously for what belonged to her life and growth," while "her inward sympathy with a doctor's and a surgeon's work grew stronger and stronger," as if somehow arising organically from within. Identity and calling become inseparably entwined at more than one point in Nan's understanding of her own experience: "If she had been asked in later years what had decided her to study not only her profession, but any profession, it would have been hard for her to answer anything beside the truth that the belief in it had grown with herself." Once Nan secures her guardian's approval, "as the years went by, all her desire tended in one direction," oriented in a way that Dr. Ferris commends when telling Dr. Leslie, "I like your notion of her having come to this of her own accord." It is an inclination that takes on an almost phototropic quality after the period of late-adolescent aimlessness and despondency following Nan's return home from boarding school, as the childhood dream of becoming a doctor asserts itself anew, and "her former existence seemed like a fog and uncertainty of death, from which she had turned away, this time of her own accord, toward a great light of satisfaction and certain safety and helpfulness."

More than once, in retrospect, Nan comes to perceive a kind of immanence at work in this gravitation to medicine as her life's objective, a telos toward which she has been logically and inexorably progressing whether aware of it or not. Shortly before the epiphany through which medicine regains its hold on her after boarding school, Nan realizes that "she could only wait . . . for the whole influence of her character and of the preparatory years to shape and signify themselves into a simple chart and unmistakable command." Once such a coalescence occurs, "It amazed her to find the certainty take possession of her mind that her vocation had been made ready for her from the beginning," so that "it seemed to her as if she had taken every step of her life straight toward this choice of a profession." This sense of her past as having somehow continuously moved her toward a particular outcome occurs to her again once Nan rejoins Dr. Leslie in his rural practice and recapitulates the chain of events that has led to this moment of fruition: "Her early life was spreading itself out like a picture, and as she thought it over and looked back from year to year, she was more than ever before surprised to see the connection of one thing with another, and how some slight acts had been the planting of seeds which had grown and flourished long afterward."

As such passages demonstrate, Jewett employs throughout *A Country Doctor* a vocabulary that would have been long familiar to her audience from previous novelistic representations of apprenticeship, ultimately yielding a series of rationales formulated to help justify such unconventional impulses on a young woman's part. Time and again in the narrative, the study and practice of medicine are described as pursuits for which Nan exhibits a "fitness" or "bent" or "gift," or is naturally "fitted," or as "the work for which nature had meant her," while "the evidences of her unfitness for the simple duties" of a middle-class woman's customary housebound routine are what Nan becomes miserably aware of as she tries to readjust herself to life at home after boarding school. Arriving at medical college to build upon the instruction she has received from Dr. Leslie, Nan is convinced that "she had been directed toward such a purpose entirely by her singular talent," with which she has been endowed not only by nature but, through nature, by the highest determining force of all. "God had directed her at last," Nan concludes in repledging herself to her vocation, "and though the opening of her sealed orders had been long delayed, the suspense had only made her surer that she must hold fast this unspeakably great motive: something to work for with all her might as long as she lived." What Nan senses above all is characterized at one point as "a reverent desire to make the best use possible of the gifts God had certainly not made a mistake in giving her. 'If He meant I should be a doctor,' the girl told herself, 'the best thing I can do is to try to be a good one.'" The revelation that the force leading her to a career in medicine has been divinely appointed from the start is welcomed by Nan as a kind of solemnizing imprimatur: "So many things she had never understood before, now became perfectly clear and evident proofs that, outside her own preferences and choices, a wise purpose had been at work with her and for her."

Once she travels to the coastal town of Dunport after her first term in medical school, such convictions will prove vital in countering the resistance of those (among them her long-estranged aunt, one of her aunt's elderly friends, and a young admirer) who vituperatively object to Nan's interest in medicine, or to the education and training of women for most any profession at all. Whereas "plenty of people . . . are clogged and fettered with work for which they have no fitness," as she puts it, Nan can say how fortunate she is in the work that she has embraced, invoking also the teleological argument when Dr. Leslie's influence is blamed for her ambitions: "Nobody persuaded me into following such a plan; I simply grew toward it." Confronted by the redoubtable and monumentally pre-sumptuous Mrs. Fraley, who takes it upon herself to declare, "I warn you, my dear, that your notion about studying to be a doctor has shocked me very much," Nan shows even greater self-possession in maintaining that "God would not give us the same talents if what were right for men were wrong for women"—a premise on which she later elaborates when reminding George Gerry, her young suitor, that one should consider it "a splendid thing to have the use of any gift of God. It isn't for us to choose again, or wonder and dispute, but just work in our own places, and leave the rest to God." In Nan's world, there can be no more conclusive and incontrovertible defense, or any greater validation, of a pursuit like hers than the claim that it satisfies a divine mandate, which is duly advanced as the chief reason "why I made up my mind to be a physician," as she tells her opponents: "I believe that God has given me a fitness for it, and that I never could do anything else half so well." The roles that she would perform so much less effectively include, of course, those of wife and mother, for which her unsuitability is enough of a disqualification to compel Nan, even when genuinely enamored of George, to declare that "[m]ost girls have an instinct towards marrying, but mine is all against it, and God knew best when He made me care more for another fashion of life."

For some readers, Jewett's rhetoric in passages like these will appear more than a bit calculated, evoking "the nineteenth-century association of good women with nature and nature's God," as Susan K. Harris puts it, in a deliberate effort "to suggest that God may have intended good women for purposes other than domesticity." Such reasoning on Nan's behalf, with its assurance that "she is not defying the traditional woman's place in society," in another critic's words, "but instead fulfilling her own God-given possibilities," would certainly have helped Jewett deflect the opprobrium bound to greet a woman with her protagonist's aspirations at the time. One could go further, as Barbara White does, and accuse Jewett of opportunistically resorting to a sort of providential alibi not uncommon in Victorian American novels about free-spirited girls, so that "she has young Nan Prince, who is fighting for the right to a medical career, use the old religious ploy: God has given her the talent to be a doctor and it is her duty to use it." Whatever strategic element there might be in Jewett's pious appeals to nature and to God is surely to be expected, though, given a climate in which the medically educated woman would have been considered a

uniquely unpalatable or seditious figure; and it seems anachronistic to impute any contrivance or insincerity to her claim that
a divine source authorizes Nan's calling simply because "[s]uch
an argument lends powerful support for an otherwise poten-
tially deviant act."[18] In any case, insofar as "every student of
medicine," according to what Nan learns from Dr. Leslie,
"should be fitted by nature with a power of insight, a gift for
his business, for knowing what is the right thing to do, and the
right time and way to do it," and "must have this God-given
power in his own nature of using and discovering the resources
of medicine," such endowments were understood by Jewett to
be required impartially of all would-be physicians, regardless
of sex.

Of greater concern are a number of other statements that appear not only to leave essentially undisturbed but also covertly
to reinscribe the social order and sexual hierarchies purport-
edly violated by Nan's actions. Reflecting one of the dilemmas
faced by early women physicians, who "struggled valiantly to
become creditable practitioners," as Regina Morantz-Sanchez
remarks, "without either surrendering or denigrating their fem-
ininity,"[19] Jewett takes pains to emphasize Nan's "lady-like"
temperament, on which the study and practice of medicine are
not to have the proverbially "unsexing" effect often alleged by
members of the medical establishment in the United States at
the time. However unorthodox her interests and recreations,
the students at boarding school with Nan "assured themselves
that their schoolmate showed no sign of being the sort of girl
who tried to be mannish," while it is later indicated that "Nan
was anything but self-asserting, and she had no noisy fashion of
thrusting herself before the public gaze."

Much can be made, also, of the various disclaimers that assist
Nan's justification of her calling and risk diluting its impact. "I
think such things are the duty of professional men and women
only," she reassures Mrs. Fraley, with the addition of a more
troubling demurral: "I won't attempt to say that the study of
medicine is a proper vocation for women, only that I believe
more and more every year that it is the proper study for me."
Any uneasiness occasioned by the need to decline George's

proposal of marriage might not be enough to excuse or ration-
alize Nan's further concessions in declaring, "I don't know why
God should have made me a doctor, so many other things have
seemed fitter for women," and in admitting, "I know better and
better that most women are made for another sort of existence." The double standard automatically ruling out the option
of marriage for women who would undertake a professional
career is left alarmingly intact by Nan, who acknowledges,
even in the course of defending herself to Mrs. Fraley, "I know
being married . . . is a natural condition of life, which permits a
man to follow certain public careers, and forbids them to a
woman." Here again, as some have argued, Jewett seems intent
on enhancing Nan's acceptability to an audience likely to be
skeptical of women doctors by presenting her as a "special" or
"exceptional" case, and thus perhaps as an exception tacitly
proving the rule that governed relations between the sexes,
along with the place of women, in nineteenth-century America.
Because of this hedging or "hesitancy" regarding the full impli-
cations of its theme, A Country Doctor would appear to be "in
partial compliance," as Judith Bryant Wittenberg suggests,
"with some of the prevailing notions about gender, education,
and professionalism" in Jewett's era, joined by other texts
about women physicians in "managing to pay homage to the
dominant culture even as they contest it on a number of
fronts."[20]

Insofar as these paradoxes attest the ideological bind in
which Jewett would have struggled in composing a novel like A
Country Doctor, they become perhaps less a measure of timid-
ity or acquiescence on her part than of the constraints faced by
any attempt to make the figure of the woman doctor imaginable
at the time. Even so, one can be misled into overstating not only
Nan's singularity but also the extent to which conventional
precepts or preconceptions are in fact accommodated in A
Country Doctor. For one thing, uncommon as she certainly is,
Jewett's protagonist no longer seems quite so "exceptional"
even to herself once she arrives in Boston with Dr. Leslie to attend medical school, where "both our friends lost much of the
feeling that Nan was doing a peculiar thing, when they saw so

many others following the same path." As far as her personality is concerned, although "[s]he did not look strong-minded" to her classmates at boarding school, it is Nan—when Mrs. Fraley insists that "a strong-minded woman was out of place, and unwelcome everywhere"—who promptly replies, "I think it is a pity that we have fallen into a habit of using strong-mindedness as a term of rebuke." In one of her remarks to Mrs. Fraley on the matter of a woman's eligibility to become a doctor ("I am very far from believing that every girl ought to be a surgeon any more than that she ought to be an astronomer"), Nan would appear to be making the unobjectionable, commonsense point that medicine, like any occupation, is tailored only for some members of her sex and that others might be more suited to another profession, not that other women should elect no profession at all. And if Nan seems unnecessarily cautious or prudent in other responses to Mrs. Fraley, Jewett herself provided some clarification a few years later in the draft of a letter to the publisher S. S. McClure: "In writing Country Doctor I did not mean to say that the practice of medicine was the ultimatum of a woman's career. The point was that when a girl felt herself to be detailed by nature and by inspiration for any special vocation she had a divine right and obligation to follow it at all cost."[21]

Even as Nan refuses to declare that medicine is "a proper vocation" for any woman other than herself, moreover, few readers at the time would not have been startled by her temerity in also proclaiming, "It certainly cannot be the proper vocation of all women to bring up children, so many of them are dead failures at it; and I don't see why all girls should be thought failures who do not marry." A young woman of her class and background could not have espoused any sentiments more heterodox than these, making it no surprise that Nan, although "willing to acknowledge that people who are eager for reforms are apt to develop unpleasant traits," should maintain to Mrs. Fraley that "it is only because they have to fight against opposition and ignorance. When they are dead and the world is reaping the reward of their bravery and constancy, it no longer laughs, but makes statues of them, and praises them, and

thanks them in every way it can." However mild and inoffen-
sive her own demeanor might be, it is in such exalted company
that Nan in fact imagines herself as early as that uncertain first
summer between boarding school and medical school, when
"[s]he had the feeling of a reformer, a radical, and even of a political agitator, as she tried to face her stormy future" after de-
cisively resolving to become a physician.

The muted radicalism of her views, and of Jewett's, is
nowhere more discernible than in the terms in which Nan re-
jects the possibility of marriage with George Gerry, whose
courtship elicits a response that far exceeds the standard invo-
cations of nature and divinity. In part, it is the mystique of a vo-
cational imperative that reasserts itself as Nan insists to George,
"something promises me and calls me for a life that my marrying you would hinder and not help," expressing "a certainty as
sure as the stars that the only right condition of life for me is to
follow the way that everything until now has pointed out. The
great gain and purpose of my being alive is there." Her sense of
fidelity to an incompatible vocation acquires more of an edge,
however, in the astonishing candor and dread with which Nan
predicts the aftereffects of marriage to George: "I know that
the days would come when I should see, in a way that would
make me long to die, that I had lost the true direction of my life
and had misled others beside myself." The direness working its
way into such protestations suggests that something about marriage itself is what gives pause to a figure like Nan, described
late in the novel as "the woman who had been both taught and
inspired to hold fast her freedom," and as one who remains determined "to hold fast the truth that her soul must ever be her
own." For such a woman, marriage to George would be impossible because, as Nan puts it to her aunt, "it is not my whole
self longing for his love and his companionship," and because
"something tells me all the time," in her explanation to George,
"that I could not marry the whole of myself as most women
can; there is a great share of my life which could not have its
way, and could only hide itself and be sorry."

What she averts, in rejecting George's proposal, is thus a
kind of self-truncation in marriage, the giving-over-of-oneself

in toto to one's mate required of a woman by an all-consuming union in which her individuality will eventually be liquidated. Nan's vocation summons her on a path away from marriage because marriage is a path that offers no room or margin for her vocation. Compared with such a prospect, it is no wonder that a life in medicine strikes Nan as the vastly preferable alternative; and the fact that Jewett could not foresee, much less allow herself to espouse, any correction of the imbalances within marriage (or any fundamental rearrangement of the institution itself) detracts little from the boldness of Nan's actions and beliefs. It would be difficult indeed to find an earlier American novel with a female protagonist who treats the marital bond as dismissively, and even contemptuously, as Nan does in telling her aunt, when urged to accept George, "I can look forward and see something a thousand times better than being his wife, and living here in Dunport keeping his house, and trying to forget all that nature fitted me to do."

For Jewett, the stakes involved in fashioning such a heroine had to have been rather high, given some of her era's dominant storytelling codes and protocols. In *A Country Doctor*, Nan is granted, after all, a future ordinarily deemed impermissible at a time when, "[e]ven in those texts which are able to envisage a limited degree of female self-development, . . . this autonomy," as Felski observes, "is ultimately subordinated to the demands of the marriage plot, and the necessity for the heroine's integration into the familial and domestic spheres." In sparing Nan such a fate, as in its retooling of the *Bildungsroman*, Jewett's novel looks ahead to those "narrative[s] of female self-discovery" that start to become so prevalent in late-twentieth-century fiction by women, narratives "in which access to self-knowledge is seen to require an explicit refusal of the heterosexual romance plot, the framework which has traditionally defined the meaning and direction of women's lives," and in which "[m]arriage . . . is now explicitly revealed not as the endpoint of female *Bildung*, but as its very antithesis." Even more important, something not unlike the "new narrative model" that Felski derives from such texts, whereby "the otherness of the female protagonist does not result in her subsequent death or defeat," can be found already operating in *A Country Doctor*, inasmuch as Nan's claim to an emancipated life goes wholly unpunished at the end, contrary to the nineteenth-century novel-reader's expectation that "the heroine's struggle against existing constraints necessitates her symbolic or literal destruction."[22] As Nan not only pronounces marriage inherently inimical to the attainment of her goals as a doctor-in-the-making but is ultimately rewarded for her transgressions, Jewett may thus be said to have subverted, in her own quietly and unostentatiously iconoclastic way, more than one of the governing paradigms of nineteenth-century fictional narrative.

Yet the fact that Nan finds the circumscriptions of domesticity irreconcilable with her vocation is not her only, or even the most potent, motive for choosing it over a life with George. Underlying Nan's pursuit of medicine is an additional incentive that she first articulates to Mrs. Fraley: "so many persons might be better and stronger than they are now, which would make their lives very different. I do think if I can help my neighbors in this way it will be a great kindness." It is this samaritan, even missionary impetus—widely shared by many of the early women physicians in the United States—that supplies perhaps the firmest grounds on which Nan can proceed with her intention of becoming a doctor at the expense of marriage and motherhood. For devotion to a family of her own, Nan substitutes what she regards as a larger, overriding duty to the human family, informing George that "by and by I must do my part in my own way to make many homes happy instead of one; to free them from pain, and teach grown people and little children to keep their bodies free from weakness and deformities." The treatment of children, which quickly joined that of women themselves in both warranting and dominating the practice of medicine by women in the United States, particularly appeals to Nan during her first medical school term, when "nothing had seemed to rouse her ambition so greatly as her experiences at the children's hospitals." For Nan, however, that aspect of medical practice now constitutes one of humanity's ineluctable demands upon the woman physician, a demand magnified back home by a "sick child" among Dr. Leslie's patients, a "weak little creature" who "seemed to be pleading in the name of a great army of sick children, that Nan would not desert their cause; that she would go on, as she had promised them, with her search for ways that should restore their vigor and increase their fitness to take up the work of the world." Helping them do so would represent that part of the world's work to be taken up, of course, by Nan herself as a doctor. And when she determines, near the end of her turbulent post-boarding-school summer at home, that "[f]or her part it was not enough to be waited upon and made comfortable, she wanted something more, to be really of use in the world, and to do work which the world needed," it is this call to a field of service larger and broader than domestic life can provide that Nan keeps ardently in mind, and heeds.

The world in which Nan would strive so mightily to do its work is presented throughout *A Country Doctor* as one very much in flux, a world soon to be overtaken by forces enveloping her private quest in a welter of change and instability that others in the novel find most disconcerting. Recollections of her husband, who "had some queer notions about the doin's o' sperits" and "always used to be tellin' what everything was the sign of, when we was first married," lead Nan's grandmother, early on, to remark, "There's too much now we can't make sense of without addin' to it out o' our own heads," signaling a confusion produced by what the globe-trotting Dr. Ferris, on his return to the United States, describes to Dr. Leslie as "the troubles of a transition state. Now, you're neither a new country nor an old one." As conveyed by various ancillary details meticulously planted here and there in the narrative, which spans roughly twenty years, Nan's is indeed a world in the midst of transitions—from fireplaces to cookstoves, from candles and whale-oil lamps to newer forms of lighting, from the apprenticeships in which Dr. Leslie partly received his training and helped train others to more standardized modes of medical instruction, from the clinical empiricism that displaced earlier speculative, "heroic" norms of medical practice to an emergent laboratory-based scientific medicine, and from a nostalgically idealized agrarian past to the accelerating, industrial, congested Gilded Age America very much on the rise by the end of the novel. (Curiously, the nation's most gravely altering event of the period, the Civil War, is nowhere mentioned in the text.) Combined with such details, the scattered references to New England's colonial heritage—the old burial ground and nearby fortification "against the Indians" described in the first chapter, or the witch hunts of "them old Salem days" mentioned by Mrs. Thacher, or Jewett's summary of the seventeenth-century origins of Oldfields and its Congregational parish, or the eighteenth-century atmosphere of Dunport, or Dr. Ferris's irreverent homage to "you quiet descendants of the Pilgrims and Puritans" during his visit with Dr. Leslie—establish a continuum linking the historical past to an as-yet-undetermined future through the crises of a tumultuously changing present in which Nan approaches maturity.

Needless to say, the opening of a profession like medicine to women was itself symptomatic of this wider phenomenon, a shift in which Nan's own pursuit of a medical career occupies an important transitional moment. "If you were five years older," Mrs. Fraley declares, "you would never have dreamed of such a thing," while Dr. Leslie, awaiting Nan's return from Dunport toward the end of the novel, "[s]ometimes . . . wished that she were beginning a few years later, when her position could be better recognized and respected, and she would not have to fight against so much of the opposition and petty fault-finding that come from ignorance." Although the heroism of members of the pioneering generation like Elizabeth Blackwell had made the field no longer utterly inconceivable for women, Nan prepares to enter a profession in which others of her sex were not yet as numerous as they would be even by the time of Jacobi's 1882 essay, or of Jewett's writing of *A Country Doctor* itself. Nan is about to become a physician, in other words, during an interval in the medical education and training of women when the outcome of that experiment, for many observers in the United States, remained in serious doubt.

Much as he might regret the timing of Nan's entry into medicine, however, Dr. Leslie also voices a steadfast and quite breathtaking confidence that places Nan and her future endeavors in an even more sweeping context. As Nan helps to form a select company of like-minded women in replacing the domestic with the professional, "he rejoiced that his little girl . . . would be one of the earlier proofs and examples of a certain noble advance and new vantage-ground of civilization," enlarging the frontiers of a world in no way confined to Nan's own local society. Thus envisioned by Dr. Leslie as one of the agents of an impending transformation certain to occur on a vast scale, Nan becomes the embodiment not only of late-nineteenth-century America's New Woman but also of the woman of the future:

> It was seldom . . . that so typical and evident an example as this could offer itself of the class of women who are a result of natural progression and variation, not for better work, but for different work, and who are designed for certain public and social duties. But he believed this class to be one that must inevitably increase with the higher developments of civilization, and in later years, which he might never see, the love for humanity would be recognized and employed more intelligently; while now almost every popular prejudice was against his ward, then she would need no vindication.

In her guardian's ennobling vision, women doctors and other professional women will grow more numerous the more highly "civilization" itself develops, guaranteeing Nan's own triumph as her world eventually—and inevitably—catches up with her.

Such prophecies are ratified, moreover, by the authorial voice into which one finds Dr. Leslie's perspective occasionally modulating in *A Country Doctor*. Arguing that "women have not yet begun to use the best resources of their natures, having been later developed, and in many countries but recently freed from restraining and hindering influences," Jewett almost brings to mind a far more militantly progressive thinker like Charlotte Perkins Gilman in her sense of the radically global scope of the changes projected by Dr. Leslie. As she considers the "new vantage-ground of civilization" on which Dr. Leslie situates

Nan and women like her, Jewett also sees in their emergence the culmination of a movement reaching far back in time as well: "This has been anticipated through all ages by the women who, sometimes honored and sometimes persecuted, have been drawn away from home life by a devotion to public and social usefulness. It must be recognized that certain qualities are required for married, and even domestic life, which all women do not possess; but instead of attributing this to the disintegration of society, it must be acknowledged to belong to its progress." By propelling rather than impeding the free, limitless development of "undomesticated" women like Nan, and of the much-needed skills they possess, the world to which they belong will itself reciprocally and irreversibly advance.

In the visionary outlook shared by Jewett and Dr. Leslie, as its quasi-Darwinian overtones suggest, the rise of women like Nan in professions like medicine announces a new reality to which society will need to adapt if it is to continue growing and thriving, or if it is to succeed in perpetuating itself. And, by the end of the novel, it does seem as if Nan's world has at least begun to make the necessary adjustments in reckoning with the novelty that she represents. In the course of her growth, nearly everyone she knows—her neighbors, the local townspeople, Dr. Leslie's housekeeper Marilla, his colleagues among male physicians both in the vicinity and in Boston—are won over to Nan's cause and convinced of its rightness. Even someone as implacably hostile to the specter of nondomestic women as George Gerry is compelled into a reluctant admiration after witnessing the celerity and expertness with which Nan, in a now-famous scene, tends to a farmer's dislocated shoulder. Otherwise, the few who remain intransigent, like Nan's aunt or Mrs. Fraley (living as they do in a Dunport that appears frozen in time), are presented as relics of an earlier age on the cusp of being unavoidably superseded. Closer to them in disposition, Mrs. Fraley's unmarried, thinly occupied, and discontented middle-aged daughter Eunice stands uneasily between those two worlds, someone who "could not be persuaded that a woman could possibly know as much about diseases and their remedies as a man" but on whom "Nan's perfect faith and confidence" have such an effect that, "if the practice of medicine by women could be made honorable, it certainly was in able hands here, as far as an admiring friend could decide."

Before Jewett's novel, few likelier or better-equipped candidates for such a task are to be found in the imaginative representation of American medical women than Nan, whose qualifying attributes are richly specified throughout *A Country Doctor*. "She would have little trouble in making her way," the narrative makes clear after Nan returns home from medical school, "since she had the requisite qualities, natural and acquired, which secure success," qualities on which Jewett often dwells in repeatedly underscoring "Nan's persistent interest and occupation in her studies," or "her devotion to her present studies and her marked proficiency," or "Nan's diligent devotion to her course of study," or "the young girl's power of resource, and wealth of self-reliance." Feeling "a great engine of strength and ambition . . . at work with her in her plans and studies," Nan is said to display "a strange tenacity of purpose," and "a power of direction and of command," and "a capacity for hard study and patient continuance" at various stages of her apprenticeship and schooling. By the end, it is "through hard work and much study, and many sights of pain and sorrow" in the course of her training, that Nan has earned the opportunity, as a woman, to practice medicine. Her many virtues and merits are not lost even on adversaries like George, who discerns in Nan "the stern determination which wins its way at all hazards," or her aunt, who recognizes "the same strength of will and of determination which made the framework of her own character,—an iron-like firmness of structure which could not be easily shaken by the changes or opinions of other people."

Her imperviousness in this respect, as much as anything, is what enables Nan to withstand not only an encroaching world of antagonism and disapprobation but also her own occasional doubts; for "when she remembered her perfect certainty that she was doing the right thing, and remembered . . . the avenues of usefulness which lay open to her on every side, there was no real drawing back, but rather a proud certainty of her most womanly and respectable calling." Once she completes her studies, as if answering Elizabeth Stuart Phelps's spirited exhortation to the female readers of *Harper's* some years earlier ("Be a doctor? and be sure that you could be few things more womanly or more noble"[23]), Nan stands poised to make good on that promise, however many others might insist on the "unwomanliness" of the members of her sex whom she would follow, and who will in turn follow her, into medicine. A woman "stirred and claimed by the noble duties and needs of the great profession," while also "careless of the social limitations, of the lack of sympathy, even of the ridicule of the public," Nan accepts a role surrounded with an almost oracular aura toward the end of the novel, when Dr. Leslie is sure that he glimpses in his ward a spirit destined to become "the teller of new truth, a revealer of laws, and an influence for good in its capacity for teaching, as well as in its example of pure and reasonable life."

Given the era's persistent animosity toward women physicians, Jewett's critics in 1884 were surprisingly hospitable to such a glorifying treatment of her subject in *A Country Doctor*. On the whole, reviews of the novel—far from "mostly condescending or deliberately obtuse," as one biographer suggests—tended to be quite evenhanded, if not warmly receptive. Horace Scudder, one of Jewett's first and most helpful editors, was not alone in applauding, for example, "the serene good sense which characterizes the defense of the girl's position" in choosing medicine over marriage, a view shared by the critic who declared that "Miss Jewett approves her decision—and so, in fact, does the reader; . . . for she seems a delightful and appropriate figure as a country doctor." Similarly, an English reviewer observed that "Miss Jewett calls upon us to concur in Nan's decision, and, for our own part, we do concur in it heartily," on the grounds that "[a]ll women are not fitted alike to be the centre and the reigning spirit of a quiet family group or social circle." The San Francisco *Chronicle*'s even more outspokenly partisan reviewer claimed that "[t]he reader is sure to feel a deep respect for this young girl" and upheld "the admirable way in which she has defended the woman who selects a single life" by "recognizing that she can do much more good in one of the careers heretofore opened only to men than she can as wife and mother." On the woman-doctor question itself, some reviewers were either neutral or noncommittal, if not entirely silent—as if the notion of a woman studying and practicing medicine had indeed become as accustomed as Jacobi suggested two years earlier, or commonplace enough to be taken almost for granted.[24]

For her part, Jewett seems to have arrived, later in life, at a split verdict on the work. As she acknowledged to one correspondent, some twenty years after its publication, "I understand that 'The Country Doctor' is of no value as a novel, but it has many excellent ideas, for which I must thank not only my father's teaching, but my father himself."[25] Some critics had indeed found it sufficiently didactic or tendentious to be classified as another of the "novels with a purpose" quite familiar to Jewett's Victorian readership. Yet the more captious reviewers focused less on its topicality than on the compositional flaws that Jewett herself had predicted when confessing to Scudder, more than a decade earlier, "I don't believe I could write a long story. . . . I have no dramatic talent. The story would have no plot." [26] Based on a donnée apparently too slight or thin to sustain a full-length narrative, A Country Doctor did in fact strike many as "plotless" or uneventful, less a novel properly speaking than an elongation of the sort of short story or "sketch" that Jewett had begun to perfect in earlier works like Deephaven (1877) and Country By-Ways (1881). More recently, some of the very scholars who have done so much to resurrect the novel have followed its early critics by dwelling on faults in the construction of the narrative, or on the clumsiness or implausibility that they find in Jewett's management of the abortive romance between Nan and George, or on her lapses (infrequent as they are) into overt authorial commentary. However thematically resonant it has become for obvious reasons, readers of A Country Doctor still seem all too quick to concede its aesthetic deficiencies, even at the risk of prolonging the critical tradition in which the novel languished for so long.

Given a fresh, unjaundiced look, A Country Doctor will appear to need few such apologies, disclosing the skillfulness and craftsmanship of a more than unusually accomplished first novel. As Malinda Snow has astutely observed, for example, much of the narrative revolves around a series of often-extended dialogues or conversations (between, say, Nan's grandmother and the Dyer brothers' wives in the second chapter, or as in Dr. Leslie's exchanges with Dr. Ferris in the ninth, with Mrs. Graham in the following chapter, and periodically with Nan herself, or as in Nan's debates with her aunt, Mrs. Fraley, and George) through which Jewett's themes are carefully and eloquently, if perhaps over-rhetorically, articulated. Her use of such a device produces, in addition, a series of characters that are vividly individuated yet also encompass a wide range of social "types" in the world of Jewett's small-town Maine. Alongside the recurrent plant and fruit imagery that some have examined are loosely interwoven seasonal and nautical motifs captured in many of Jewett's chapter titles and forming even more intricate symbolic patterns in the rendering of Nan's experience. Structurally, it is not long after the midpoint of the narrative, aptly enough, that its setting shifts to Dunport, permitting Nan to heal the rift within her family by uniting her with her aunt but also introducing the forces of censoriousness and derision that she will have to subdue in the second half of the novel if she is to prevail in her quest to become a doctor. Perhaps most obvious is the symmetry of the novel's conclusion, when Nan retraces the path that her dying mother took in bringing her to Oldfields in her infancy in the opening chapter, and the narrative comes full circle as its heroine prayerfully welcomes the future that awaits her.

Finally, whatever misgivings Jewett herself might have had about its artistry or design, she appears to have singled out *A Country Doctor*, in an interview not long before the carriage accident that prematurely curtailed her writing life in 1902, as the one she cherished most of all of her works.[27] And it is easy to see why the novel would have retained a special place in her regard, even apart from its value as the commemoration of a much-beloved father. One may be excused for doubting that pre-twentieth-century American fiction can offer very many more searching or sympathetic accounts of a girl's steady growth into an autonomous, self-sufficient, productive citizen unencumbered by the burdens of conventional domestic life. Of crucial help in its own time in socially and culturally validating the still-controversial figure of the medical woman, *A Country Doctor* endures also as an uncommonly moving and evocative tale about the coming-of-age of a courageous, persevering, earnest young woman determined to achieve authentic selfhood in defiance of propriety and custom, and to succeed in becoming the individual she was always, in effect, going to be.

NOTES

1. Mary Putnam Jacobi, "Shall Women Practice Medicine?" *North American Review* 134 (January 1882): 53, 52.
2. "Four American Novels," *Saturday Review* (London), 30 August 1884, p. 283; "Recent Novels," *Nation*, 31 July 1884, p. 96.
3. Theodore H. Jewett, M.D., *President's Address to the Maine Medical Association, at its Annual Meeting in Portland, June 11, 1878* (Portland, Me.: Stephen Berry, 1878), a reprint of "President's Address," *Transactions of the Maine Medical Association* 6 (1878): 313–30.
4. He also offered an intriguing glimpse of his thoughts on domestic women's plight when describing "how many instances present themselves of feeble, broken women, wasted in vital power, relieved by no changes from a dull routine, and the depression of an endless, tame monotony" (Theodore H. Jewett, M.D., *Elements of Success in the Medical Profession. Introductory Lecture Delivered Before the Students of the Medical Department of Bowdoin College, February 21, 1867* [Portland, Me.: B. Thurston & Co., 1869], p. 6).
5. Paula Blanchard, *Sarah Orne Jewett: Her World and Her Work* (Reading, Mass.: Addison-Wesley, 1994), p. 158.
6. "Looking Back on Girlhood" (1892), in *The Uncollected Short Stories of Sarah Orne Jewett*, ed. Richard Cary (Waterville, Me.: Colby College Press, 1971), p. 6.
7. Francis Otto Matthiessen, *Sarah Orne Jewett* (Boston: Houghton Mifflin, 1929), pp. 55–56.
8. Blanchard, *Sarah Orne Jewett*, pp. 122–23.
9. [Annie Adams Fields], "A Glimpse at Some of Our Charities. Part II. The Employment, Education, and Protection of Women," *Harper's New Monthly Magazine* 56 (March 1878): 601, 602.

10. Alan M. Chesney, *The Johns Hopkins Hospital and the Johns Hopkins University School of Medicine*, 3 vols. (Baltimore: Johns Hopkins Press, 1943–63), 1:291; Jewett is listed, with Fields, as a member of the Boston Local Committee (1:294).

11. Jewett to John Greenleaf Whittier, 25 November 1890, Pickard-Whittier Papers, bMS Am 1844 (169), Houghton Library, Harvard University; quoted by permission of the Houghton Library, Harvard University.

12. Annie Fields, ed., *Letters of Sarah Orne Jewett* (Boston: Houghton Mifflin, 1911), pp. 5, 6.

13. Jewett to John Greenleaf Whittier, 4 April [1882], in Richard Cary, ed., " 'Yours Always Lovingly': Sarah Orne Jewett to John Greenleaf Whittier," *Essex Institute Historical Collection* 107 (1971): 425.

14. Jewett to Louise Imogen Guiney, 12 May [1899], in William L. Lucey, S.J., " 'We New Englanders . . . ': Letters of Sarah Orne Jewett to Louise Imogen Guiney," *Records of the American Catholic Historical Society of Philadelphia* 70 (March–June 1959): 63.

15. [Fields], "A Glimpse at Some of Our Charities," p. 602.

16. Quoted in Richard Cary, "Jewett to Dresel: 33 Letters," *Colby Library Quarterly* 11 (March 1975): 35 n. 1; Sarah Orne Jewett, Miscellaneous notes for the story of "A Country Doctor," Sarah Orne Jewett Papers, bMS Am 1743.7, Houghton Library, Harvard University (quoted by permission of the Houghton Library, Harvard University). For a convenient summary of Morton's estimable career by one of her trainees, see Eliza M. Mosher, "History of American Medical Women," *Medical Woman's Journal* 29 (December 1922): 334.

17. Rita Felski, *Beyond Feminist Aesthetics: Feminist Literature and Social Change* (Cambridge, Mass.: Harvard University Press, 1989), pp. 124–25, 122, 126–27, 133. For other treatments of the female *Bildungsroman*, adhering to the critical consensus on its twentieth-century provenance but suggesting useful frameworks in which to approach Jewett's novel, see Ellen Morgan, "Human-becoming: Form & Focus in the Neo-Feminist Novel," in *Images of Women in Fiction: Feminist Perspectives*, ed. Susan Koppelman Cornillon (Bowling Green, Ohio: Bowling Green University Popular Press, 1972), pp. 183–85; Annis Pratt et al., *Archetypal Patterns in Women's Fiction* (Bloomington, Ind.: Indiana University Press, 1981), pp. 13–37; and Elizabeth Abel et al., eds., *The Voyage In: Fictions of Female Development* (Hanover, N.H.: University Press of New England, 1983). Along such lines *A Country*

Doctor is surely a purer modification of the form than *Little Women* or the other contemporaneous works mentioned in Eve Kornfeld and Susan Jackson, "The Female Bildungsroman in Nineteenth-Century America: Parameters of a Vision," *Journal of American Culture* 10 (Winter 1987): 69–75, or than the earlier texts discussed in Beverly R. Voloshin, "The Limits of Domesticity: The Female *Bildungsroman* in America, 1820–1870," in *American Literature, Culture, and Ideology: Essays in Memory of Henry Nash Smith*, ed. Beverly R. Voloshin (New York: Peter Lang, 1990), pp. 93–114.

18. Susan K. Harris, *19th-Century American Women's Novels: Interpretive Strategies* (Cambridge: Cambridge University Press, 1990), pp. 202–3; Jean Carwile Masteller, "The Women Doctors of Howells, Phelps, and Jewett: The Conflict of Marriage and Career," in *Critical Essays on Sarah Orne Jewett*, ed. Gwen L. Nagel (Boston: G. K. Hall, 1984), p. 141; Barbara A. White, *Growing Up Female: Adolescent Girlhood in American Fiction* (Westport, Conn.: Greenwood Press, 1985), p. 38; Masteller, "Women Doctors," p. 142.

19. Regina Morantz-Sanchez, *Sympathy and Science: Women Physicians in American Medicine* (1985; reprint ed., Chapel Hill: University of North Carolina Press, 2000), p. 142.

20. Judith Bryant Wittenberg, "Challenge and Compliance: Textual Strategies in *A Country Doctor* and Nineteenth-Century American Women's Medical Autobiographies," in *Jewett and Her Contemporaries: Reshaping the Canon*, ed. Karen L. Kilcup and Thomas S. Edwards (Gainesville: University Press of Florida, 1999), pp. 123, 125.

21. Jewett drafted her remarks in response to a 7 June 1889 letter in which McClure had requested a short story conveying her "idea of the ideal young woman," an ideal that she then described as embodied by "a girl who means to grow in knowledge and practical efficiency and to make the most of her gifts and surroundings" (Sarah Orne Jewett Papers, bMS Am 1743.7, Houghton Library, Harvard University; quoted by permission of the Houghton Library, Harvard University).

22. Felski, *Beyond Feminist Aesthetics*, pp. 125, 122, 138, 130, 125.

23. Elizabeth Stuart Phelps, "What Shall They Do?" *Harper's New Monthly Magazine* 35 (September 1867): 523.

24. Blanchard, *Sarah Orne Jewett*, p. 189; H. E. Scudder, "Recent Fiction," *Atlantic Monthly* 54 (September 1884): 419; "Recent Fiction," *Overland Monthly* 4 (August 1884): 222; "A Spinster Heroine," *Spectator*, 18 October 1884, p. 1378; San Francisco

Chronicle, undated clipping, Sarah Orne Jewett Papers (bMS Am 1743.26 [17]), Houghton Library, Harvard University.

25. Jewett to Charles Miner Thompson, 12 October 1904, in Fields, *Letters*, p. 195.

26. Jewett to Horace E. Scudder, 13 July 1873, in *Sarah Orne Jewett Letters*, ed. Richard Cary (Waterville, Me.: Colby College Press, 1967), p. 29.

27. As reported by a journalist after visiting Jewett, "of her own productions . . . she loves and must always love 'A Country Doctor' above everything else she has written" ("Sarah Orne Jewett and Her Maine Home," Boston Sunday *Herald*, 14 July 1901, p. 35).

Suggestions for Further Reading

BIOGRAPHIES AND LETTERS

Blanchard, Paula. *Sarah Orne Jewett: Her World and Her Work*. Reading, Mass.: Addison-Wesley, 1994.

Cary, Richard. *Sarah Orne Jewett*. New York: Twayne, 1962.

————, ed. *Sarah Orne Jewett Letters*. Waterville, Me.: Colby College Press, 1967.

Fields, Annie, ed. *Letters of Sarah Orne Jewett*. Boston: Houghton Mifflin, 1911.

Frost, John Eldridge. *Sarah Orne Jewett*. Kittery Point, Me.: Gundalow Club, 1960.

Gollin, Rita K. *Annie Adams Fields: Woman of Letters*. Amherst: University of Massachusetts Press, 2002.

Matthiessen, Francis Otto. *Sarah Orne Jewett*. Boston: Houghton Mifflin, 1929.

Roman, Judith A. *Annie Adams Fields: The Spirit of Charles Street*. Bloomington: Indiana University Press, 1990.

Silverthorne, Elizabeth. *Sarah Orne Jewett: A Writer's Life*. Woodstock, N.Y.: Overview Press, 1993.

SELECTED CRITICISM

Adams, Richard. "Heir Apparent: Inheriting the Epitome in Sarah Orne Jewett's *A Country Doctor*." In *Constance Fenimore Woolson's Nineteenth Century: Essays*, edited by Victoria Brehm, pp. 67–81. Detroit: Wayne State University Press, 2001.

Bardes, Barbara, and Suzanne Gossett. *Declarations of Independence: Women and Political Power in Nineteenth-Century American Fiction.* New Brunswick, N.J.: Rutgers University Press, 1990.

Baym, Nina. *American Women of Letters and the Nineteenth-Century Sciences: Styles of Affiliation.* New Brunswick, N.J.: Rutgers University Press, 2002.

Bender, Bert. "Darwin and 'The Natural History of Doctresses': The Sex War Between Howells, Phelps, Jewett, and James." *Prospects* 18 (1993): 81–120.

Blanc, Marie-Thérèse [Th. Bentzon]. "Le Roman de la femme-médecin." In *Appreciation of Sarah Orne Jewett: 29 Interpretive Essays,* edited by Richard Cary, pp. 3–15. Waterville, Me.: Colby College Press, 1973.

Burns, Chester R. "Fictional Doctors and the Evolution of Medical Ethics in the United States, 1875–1900." *Literature and Medicine* 7 (1988): 39–55.

Campbell, Jennifer. " 'The Great Something Else': Women's Search for Meaningful Work in Sarah Orne Jewett's *A Country Doctor* and Frances E. W. Harper's *Trial and Triumph*." *Colby Quarterly* 34 (June 1998): 83–98.

Church, Joseph. "The Healing Arts of Jewett's *Country Doctor*." *Colby Quarterly* 34 (June 1998): 99–122.

Crumpacker, Laurie. "The Art of the Healer: Women in the Fiction of Sarah Orne Jewett." *Colby Library Quarterly* 19 (Sept. 1983): 155–66.

Donovan, Josephine. "Nan Prince and the Golden Apples." *Colby Library Quarterly* 22 (March 1986): 17–27.

Elder, Nancy C., and Andrew Schwarzer. "Fictional Women Physicians in the Nineteenth Century: The Struggle for Self-Identity." *Journal of Medical Humanities* 17 (1996): 165–77.

Forrey, Carolyn. "The New Woman Revisited." *Women's Studies* 2 (1974): 37–56.

Fulton, Valerie. "Rewriting the Necessary Woman: Marriage and Professionalism in James, Jewett, and Phelps." *Henry James Review* 15 (Fall 1994): 242–56.

Furst, Lilian R. *Between Doctors and Patients: The Changing Balance of Power*. Charlottesville: University Press of Virginia, 1998.

———. "Halfway Up the Hill: Doctresses in Late Nineteenth-Century American Fiction." In *Women Healers and Physicians: Climbing a Long Hill*, edited by Lilian R. Furst, pp. 221–38. Lexington: University Press of Kentucky, 1997.

Heller, Terry. "Speaking Softly to be Heard: Jewett's Feminist Reform Contributions to *The Congregationalist*, 1882–1884." *Colby Quarterly* 36 (September 2000): 209–25.

Masteller, Jean Carwile. "The Women Doctors of Howells, Phelps, and Jewett: The Conflict of Marriage and Career." In *Critical Essays on Sarah Orne Jewett*, edited by Gwen L. Nagel, pp. 135–47. Boston: G. K. Hall, 1984.

Morgan, Ellen. "The Atypical Woman: Nan Prince in the Literary Transition to Feminism." *Kate Chopin Newsletter* 2 (1976): 33–37.

Pryse, Marjorie. " 'I was country when country wasn't cool': Regionalizing the Modern in Jewett's *A Country Doctor*." *American Literary Realism* 34 (Spring 2002): 217–32.

Renza, Louis A. *"A White Heron" and the Question of Minor Literature*. Madison: University of Wisconsin Press, 1984.

Roman, Margaret. *Sarah Orne Jewett: Reconstructing Gender*. Tuscaloosa: University of Alabama Press, 1992.

Shapiro, Ann R. *Unlikely Heroines: Nineteenth-Century American Women Writers and the Woman Question*. New York: Greenwood Press, 1987.

Sherman, Sarah Way. *Sarah Orne Jewett: An American Persephone*. Hanover, N.H.: University Press of New England, 1989.

Snow, Malinda. " 'That One Talent': The Vocation as Theme in Sarah Orne Jewett's *A Country Doctor*." *Colby Library Quarterly* 16 (Sept. 1980): 138–47.

Wegener, Frederick. " 'A Line of Her Own': Henry James's 'Sturdy Little Doctress' and the Medical Woman as Literary Type in Gilded-Age America." *Texas Studies in Literature and Language* 39 (Summer 1997): 139–80.

Wilbanks, Evelyn. "The Doctor as Romantic Hero: A Study of Idealization." *Journal of the American Medical Association* 220 (3 April 1972): 54–57.

Wittenberg, Judith Bryant. "Challenge and Compliance: Textual Strategies in *A Country Doctor* and Nineteenth-Century American Women's Medical Autobiographies." In *Jewett and Her Contemporaries: Reshaping the Canon,* edited by Karen L. Kilcup and Thomas S. Edwards, pp. 123–36. Gainesville: University Press of Florida, 1999.

ON THE RISE OF WOMEN DOCTORS
IN THE UNITED STATES

Abram, Ruth J., ed. *"Send Us a Lady Physician": Women Doctors in America, 1835–1920.* New York: Norton, 1985.

Drachman, Virginia G. *Hospital with a Heart: Women Doctors and the Paradox of Separatism at the New England Hospital, 1862–1969.* Ithaca, N.Y.: Cornell University Press, 1984.

Morantz-Sanchez, Regina. *Sympathy and Science: Women Physicians in American Medicine.* New ed. Chapel Hill: University of North Carolina Press, 2000.

More, Ellen S. *Restoring the Balance: Women Physicians and the Profession of Medicine, 1850–1995.* Cambridge, Mass.: Harvard University Press, 1999.

Peitzman, Steven J., M.D. *A New and Untried Course: Woman's Medical College and Medical College of Pennsylvania, 1850–1998.* New Brunswick, N.J.: Rutgers University Press, 2000.

Walsh, Mary Roth. *"Doctors Wanted, No Women Need Apply": Sexual Barriers in the Medical Profession, 1835–1975.* New Haven, Conn.: Yale University Press, 1977.

Wells, Susan. *Out of the Dead House: Nineteenth-Century Women Physicians and the Writing of Medicine.* Madison: University of Wisconsin Press, 2001.

ON MEDICAL EDUCATION AND PRACTICE
IN NINETEENTH-CENTURY AMERICA

Duffy, John. *From Humors to Medical Science: A History of American Medicine.* 2nd ed. Urbana: University of Illinois Press, 1993.

Haller, John S., Jr. *American Medicine in Transition, 1840–1910.* Urbana: University of Illinois Press, 1981.

Kaufman, Martin. *American Medical Education: The Formative Years, 1765–1910.* Westport, Conn.: Greenwood Press, 1976.

King, Lester S., M.D. *Transformations in American Medicine: From Benjamin Rush to William Osler.* Baltimore: Johns Hopkins University Press, 1991.

Rosen, George. *The Structure of American Medical Practice, 1875–1941.* Philadelphia: University of Pennsylvania Press, 1983.

Rosenberg, Charles E. "The Therapeutic Revolution: Medicine, Meaning, and Social Change in Nineteenth-Century America." In *The Therapeutic Revolution: Essays in the Social History of American Medicine*, edited by Morris J. Vogel and Charles E. Rosenberg, pp. 3–25. Philadelphia: University of Pennsylvania Press, 1979.

Shryock, Richard Harrison. *Medicine in America: Historical Essays.* Baltimore: Johns Hopkins University Press, 1966.

Warner, John Harley. *The Therapeutic Perspective: Medical Practice, Knowledge, and Identity in America, 1820–1885.* Cambridge, Mass.: Harvard University Press, 1986.

A Note on the Text
and Acknowledgments

The Penguin Classics edition of *A Country Doctor* reprints the text of the first edition, published in 1884 by Houghton, Mifflin, and the only edition of the novel published in Jewett's lifetime. The text is printed as it appears in the first edition, with typographical errors silently corrected; spacing within contractions has been closed up throughout, but no attempt has been made to adjust any inconsistencies or irregularities in spelling, capitalization, or punctuation.

Annotating the text of *A Country Doctor* requires some familiarity with details of local history, household life in rural New England in Jewett's time, domestic architecture in nineteenth-century America, early American naval medicine, nineteenth-century medical education and practice in the United States, and other subjects on which this edition has benefited from information generously provided by others. For their help with a number of matters discussed in the explanatory notes, I am grateful to the following individuals: Jeremy Atack; Christopher Benfey; Regina Blaszczyk; Priscilla J. Brewer; Jonathan Bumas; Rachel Carley; Paul F. Coburn; Lane R. Earns; Merri McIntyre Ferrell; Zachary B. Friedenberg, M.D.; Ruth-Ann Harris; Terry Heller; Edward "Sandy" Ives; Richard Kahn, M.D.; Peter Lamont; Harold D. Langley; Bernard C. Middleton; Michael North, head of Rare Books and Early Manuscripts, History of Medicine Division, National Library of Medicine; Rick Nowell; Lincoln P. Paine; Robert Palter; Steven J. Peitzman, M.D.; Wendy Pirsig, archivist, Old Berwick Historical Society; Charles E. Rosenberg; Laurel Thatcher Ulrich; Bryan William Van Norden; Frank G. White, curator of Mechanical Arts, Old Sturbridge Village; Susan Williams; and L. Kinvin Wroth.

For their kind assistance with numerous archival inquiries and requests, my thanks go also to Melanie Benson; Jack Eckert, reference librarian, Rare Books and Special Collections, Francis A. Countway Library of Medicine, Harvard University; Tom Ford, reference assistant, and staff, Houghton Library, Harvard University; Susan L. Speaker, Historian, Digital Manuscripts Program, History of Medicine Division, National Library of Medicine, National Institutes of Health; and Barbara Williams, archivist, Archives and Special Collections on Women in Medicine, Drexel University College of Medicine. Finally, a word of gratitude to my friend Ruth Moskowitz for her kind help in conducting a rewarding tour of South Berwick, Maine, and its environs.

Work on this edition was completed with the assistance, in part, of a Scholarly and Creative Activities Award from California State University, Long Beach, and of a Publication Grant (G13LM008086-01) from the National Library of Medicine, National Institutes of Health.

A Country Doctor

CHAPTER I.
THE LAST MILE

It had been one of the warm and almost sultry days which sometimes come in November; a maligned month, which is really an epitome of the other eleven, or a sort of index to the whole year's changes of storm and sunshine. The afternoon was like spring, the air was soft and damp, and the buds of the willows had been beguiled into swelling a little, so that there was a bloom over them, and the grass looked as if it had been growing green of late instead of fading steadily. It seemed like a reprieve from the doom of winter, or from even November itself.

The dense and early darkness which usually follows such unseasonable mildness had already begun to cut short the pleasures of this spring-like day, when a young woman, who carried a child in her arms, turned from a main road of Oldfields[1] into a foot-path which led southward across the fields and pastures. She seemed sure of her way, and kept the path without difficulty, though a stranger might easily have lost it here and there, where it led among the patches of sweet-fern or bayberry bushes, or through shadowy tracts of small white-pines. She stopped sometimes to rest, and walked more and more wearily, with increasing effort; but she kept on her way desperately, as if it would not do to arrive much later at the place which she was seeking. The child seemed to be asleep; it looked too heavy for so slight a woman to carry.

The path led after a while to a more open country, there was a low hill to be climbed, and at its top the slender figure stopped and seemed to be panting for breath. A follower might have noticed that it bent its head over the child's for a moment as it stood, dark against the darkening sky. There had formerly been a defense against the Indians on this hill, which in the daytime commanded a fine view of the surrounding country, and the low earthworks or foundations of the garrison were still plainly to be seen.[2] The woman seated herself on the sunken wall in spite of the dampness and increasing chill, still holding the child, and rocking to and fro like one in despair. The child waked and began to whine and cry a little in that strange, lonely place, and after a few minutes, perhaps to quiet it, they went on their way. Near the foot of the hill was a brook,[3] swollen by the autumn rains; it made a loud noise in the quiet pasture, as if it were crying out against a wrong or some sad memory. The woman went toward it at first, following a slight ridge which was all that remained of a covered path which had led down from the garrison to the spring below at the brookside. If she had meant to quench her thirst here, she changed her mind, and suddenly turned to the right, following the brook a short distance, and then going straight toward the river itself[4] and the high uplands, which by daylight were smooth pastures with here and there a tangled apple-tree or the grassy cellar of a long vanished farmhouse.

It was night now; it was too late in the year for the chirp of any insects; the moving air, which could hardly be called wind, swept over in slow waves, and a few dry leaves rustled on an old hawthorn tree which grew beside the hollow where a house had been, and a low sound came from the river. The whole country side seemed asleep in the darkness, but the lonely woman felt no lack of companionship; it was well suited to her own mood that the world slept and said nothing to her,—it seemed as if she were the only creature alive.

A little this side of the river shore there was an old burial place, a primitive spot enough, where the graves were only marked by rough stones, and the short, sheep-cropped grass was spread over departed generations of the farmers and their wives and children.[5] By day it was in sight of the pine woods and the moving water, and nothing hid it from the great sky overhead, but now it was like a prison walled about by the barriers of night. However eagerly the woman had hurried to this place, and with what purpose she may have sought the river bank, when she recognized her surroundings she stopped for a moment, swaying and irresolute. "No, no!" sighed the child plaintively, and she shuddered, and started forward; then, as her feet stumbled among the graves, she turned and fled. It no longer seemed solitary, but as if a legion of ghosts which had been wandering under cover of the dark had discovered this intruder, and were chasing her and flocking around her and oppressing her from every side. And as she caught sight of a light in a far-away farmhouse window, a light which had been shining after her all the way down to the river, she tried to hurry toward it. The unnatural strength of terror urged her on; she retraced her steps like some pursued animal; she remembered, one after another, the fearful stories she had known of that ancient neighborhood; the child cried, but she could not answer it. She fell again and again, and at last all her strength seemed to fail her, her feet refused to carry her farther and she crept painfully, a few yards at a time, slowly along the ground. The fear of her superhuman enemies had forsaken her, and her only desire was to reach the light that shone from the looming shadow of the house.

At last she was close to it; at last she gave one great sigh, and the child fell from her grasp; at last she clutched the edge of the worn doorstep with both hands, and lay still.

CHAPTER II.

THE FARM-HOUSE KITCHEN

Indoors there was a cheerful company; the mildness of the evening had enticed two neighbors of Mrs. Thacher, the mistress of the house, into taking their walks abroad, and so, with their heads well protected by large gingham handkerchiefs, they had stepped along the road and up the lane to spend a social hour or two. John Thacher, their old neighbor's son, was known to be away serving on a jury in the county town, and they thought it likely that his mother would enjoy company. Their own houses stood side by side. Mrs. Jacob Dyer and Mrs. Martin Dyer were their names, and excellent women they were. Their husbands were twin-brothers, curiously alike and amazingly fond of each other, though either would have scorned to make any special outward demonstration of it. They were spending the evening together in brother Martin's house, and were talking over the purchase of a bit of woodland, and the profit of clearing it, when their wives had left them without any apology to visit Mrs. Thacher, as we have already seen.

This was the nearest house and only a quarter of a mile away, and when they opened the door they had found Mrs. Thacher spinning.[1]

"I must own up, I am glad to see you more 'n common," she said. "I don't feel scary at being left sole alone; it ain't that, but I have been getting through with a lonesome spell of another kind. John, he does as well as a man can, but here I be,—here I be,"—and the good woman could say no more, while her guests understood readily enough the sorrow that had found no words.

"I suppose you haven't got no news from Ad'line?" asked

Mrs. Martin bluntly. "We was speaking of her as we come along, and saying it seemed to be a pity she should'nt feel it was best to come back this winter and help you through; only one daughter, and left alone as you be, with the bad spells you are liable to in winter time—but there, it ain't her way—her ambitions ain't what they should be, that's all I can say."

"If she'd got a gift for anything special, now," continued Mrs. Jake, "we should feel it was different and want her to have a chance, but she's just like other folks for all she felt so much above farming. I don't see as she can do better than come back to the old place, or leastways to the village,[2] and fetch up the little gal to be some use. She might dressmake or do millinery work; she always had a pretty taste, and 't would be better than roving. I 'spose 't would hurt her pride,"—but Mrs. Thacher flushed at this, and Mrs. Martin came to the rescue.

"You'll think we're reg'lar Job's comforters,"[3] cried the good soul hastily, "but there, Mis' Thacher, you know we feel as if she was our own. There ain't nothing I wouldn't do for Ad'line, sick or well, and I declare I believe she'll pull through yet and make a piece of luck that'll set us all to work praising of her. She's like to marry again for all I can see, with her good looks. Folks always has their joys and calamities as they go through the world."

Mrs. Thacher shook her head two or three times with a dismal expression, and made no answer. She had pushed back the droning wool-wheel which she had been using,[4] and had taken her knitting from the shelf by the clock and seated herself contentedly, while Mrs. Jake and Mrs. Martin had each produced a blue yarn stocking from a capacious pocket, and the shining steel needles were presently all clicking together. One knitter after another would sheathe the spare needle under her apron strings, while they asked each other's advice from time to time about the propriety of "narrerin'" or whether it were not best to "widden" according to the progress their respective stockings had made. Mrs. Thacher had lighted an extra candle, and replenished the fire, for the air was chillier since the sun went down. They were all sure of a coming change of weather, and counted various signs, Mrs. Thacher's lowness of spirits among the number, while all three described various minor maladies from which they had suffered during the day, and of which the unseasonable weather was guilty.

"I can't get over the feeling that we are watchin' with somebody,"[5] said Mrs. Martin after a while, moved by some strange impulse and looking over her shoulder, at which remark Mrs. Thacher glanced up anxiously. "Something has been hanging over me all day," said she simply, and at this the needles clicked faster than ever.

"We've been taking rather a low range," suggested Mrs. Jake. "We shall get to telling over ghost stories if we don't look out, and I for one shall be sca't to go home. By the way, I suppose you have heard about old Billy Dow's experience night afore last, Mis' Thacher?"

"John being away, I ain't had nobody to fetch me the news these few days past," said the hostess. "Why what's happened to Billy now?"

The two women looked at each other: "He was getting himself home as best he could,—he owned up to having made a lively evenin' of it,—and I expect he was wandering all over the road and didn't know nothin' except that he was p'inted towards home, an' he stepped off from the high bank this side o' Dunnell's, and rolled down, over and over; and when he come to there was a great white creatur' a-standin' over him, and he thought 't was a ghost. 'T was higher up on the bank than him, and it kind of moved along down 's if 't was coming right on to him, and he got on to his knees and begun to say his Ten Commandments fast 's he could rattle 'em out. He got 'em mixed up, and when the boys heard his teeth a-chattering, they began to laugh and he up an' cleared. Dunnell's boys had been down the road a piece and was just coming home, an' 't was their old white hoss that had got out of the barn, it bein' such a mild night, an' was wandering off. They said to Billy that 't wa'n't everybody could lay a ghost so quick as he could, and they didn't 'spose he had the means so handy."

The three friends laughed, but Mrs. Thacher's face quickly lost its smile and took back its worried look. She evidently was in no mood for joking. "Poor Billy!" said she, "he was called the smartest boy in school; I rec'lect that one of the teachers urged his folks to let him go to college; but 't wa'n't no use; they hadn't the money and couldn't get it, and 't wa'n't in him to work his way as some do. He's got a master head for figur's. Folks used to get him to post books[6] you know,—but he's past that now. Good-natured creatur' as ever stept; but he always was afeard of the dark,—'seems 's if I could see him there a-repentin' and the old white hoss shakin' his head,"—and she laughed again, but quickly stopped herself and looked over her shoulder at the window.

"Would ye like the curtain drawed?" asked Mrs. Jake. But Mrs. Thacher shook her head silently, while the gray cat climbed up into her lap and laid down in a round ball to sleep.

"She's a proper cosset, ain't she?" inquired Mrs. Martin approvingly, while Mrs. Jake asked about the candles, which gave a clear light. "Be they the last you run?" she inquired, but was answered to the contrary, and a brisk conversation followed upon the proper proportions of tallow and bayberry wax,[7] and the dangers of the new-fangled oils which the village shop-keepers were attempting to introduce. Sperm oil was growing more and more dear in price and worthless in quality, and the old-fashioned lamps were reported to be past their usefulness.[8]

"I must own I set most by good candle light," said Mrs. Martin. " 'T is no expense to speak of where you raise the taller, and it's cheerful and bright in winter time. In old times when the houses were draftier they was troublesome about flickering, candles was; but land! think how comfortable we live now to what we used to! Stoves is such a convenience; the fires's so much handier. Housekeepin' don't begin to be the trial it was once."[9]

"I must say I like old-fashioned cookin' better than oven cookin'," observed Mrs. Jake. "Seems to me 's if the taste of things was all drawed up chimbly.[10] Be you going to do much for Thanksgivin', Mis' Thacher?[11] I 'spose not;" and moved by a sudden kind impulse, she added, "Why can't you and John jine with our folks? 't wouldn't put us out, and 't will be lonesome for ye."

" 'T won't be no lonesomer than last year was, nor the year

before," and Mrs. Thacher's face quivered a little as she rose and took one of the candles, and opened the trap door that covered the cellar stairs. "Now don't ye go to makin' yourself work," cried the guests. "No, don't! we ain't needin' nothin'; we was late about supper." But their hostess stepped carefully down and disappeared for a few minutes, while the cat hovered anxiously at the edge of the black pit.

"I forgot to ask ye if ye'd have some cider?" a sepulchral voice asked presently; "but I don't know now 's I can get at it. I told John I shouldn't want any whilst he was away, and so he ain't got the spiggit in yet," to which Mrs. Jake and Mrs. Martin both replied that they were no hands for that drink, unless 't was a drop right from the press, or a taste o' good hard cider towards the spring of the year;[12] and Mrs. Thacher soon returned with some slices of cake in a plate and some apples held in her apron. One of her neighbors took the candle as she reached up to put it on the floor, and when the trap door was closed again all three drew up to the table and had a little feast. The cake was of a kind peculiar to its maker, who prided herself upon never being without it; and there was some trick of her hand or a secret ingredient which was withheld when she responded with apparent cheerfulness to requests for its recipe. As for the apples, they were grown upon an old tree, one of whose limbs had been grafted with some unknown variety of fruit so long ago that the history was forgotten; only that an English gardener, many years before, had brought some cuttings from the old country, and one of them had somehow come into the possession of John Thacher's grandfather when grafted fruit was a thing to be treasured and jealously guarded.[13] It had been told that when the elder Thacher had given away cuttings he had always stolen to the orchards in the night afterward and ruined them. However, when the family had grown more generous in later years it had seemed to be without avail, for, on their neighbors' trees or their own, the English apples had proved worthless. Whether it were some favoring quality in that spot of soil or in the sturdy old native tree itself, the rich golden apples had grown there, year after year, in perfection, but nowhere else.

"There ain't no such apples as these, to my mind," said Mrs. Martin, as she polished a large one with her apron and held it up to the light, and Mrs. Jake murmured assent, having already taken a sufficient first bite.

"There's only one little bough that bears any great," said Mrs. Thacher, "but it's come to that once before, and another branch has shot up and been likely as if it was a young tree."

The good souls sat comfortably in their splint-bottomed, straight-backed chairs,[14] and enjoyed this mild attempt at a festival. Mrs. Thacher even grew cheerful and responsive, for her guests seemed so light-hearted and free from care that the sunshine of their presence warmed her own chilled and fearful heart. They embarked upon a wide sea of neighborhood gossip and parish opinions, and at last some one happened to speak again of Thanksgiving, which at once turned the tide of conversation, and it seemed to ebb suddenly, while the gray, dreary look once more overspread Mrs. Thacher's face.

"I don't see why you won't keep with our folks this year; you and John," once more suggested Mrs. Martin. " 'T ain't wuth while to be making yourselves dismal here to home; the day'll be lonesome for you at best, and you shall have whatever we've got and welcome."

" 'T won't be lonesomer this year than it was last, nor the year before that, and we've stood it somehow or 'nother," answered Mrs. Thacher for the second time, while she rose to put more wood in the stove. "Seems to me 't is growing cold; I felt a draught acrost my shoulders. These nights is dreadful chill; you feel the damp right through your bones. I never saw it darker than 't was last evenin'. I thought it seemed kind o' stived up[15] here in the kitchen, and I opened the door and looked out, and I declare I couldn't see my hand before me."

"It always kind of scares me these black nights," said Mrs. Jake Dyer. "I expect something to clutch at me every minute, and I feel as if some sort of a creatur' was travelin' right behind me when I am out door in the dark. It makes it bad havin' a wanin' moon just now when the fogs hangs so low. It al'ays seems to me as if 't was darker when she rises late towards mornin' than when she's gone altogether. I do' know why 't is."

"I rec'lect once," Mrs. Thacher resumed, "when Ad'line was a baby and John was just turned four year old, their father had gone down river in the packet,[16] and I was expectin' on him home at supper time, but he didn't come; 't was late in the fall, and a black night as I ever see. Ad'line was taken with something like croup, and I had an end o' candle in the candlestick that I lighted, and 't wa'n't long afore it was burnt down, and I went down cellar to the box where I kep' 'em, and if you will believe it, the rats had got to it, and there wasn't a week[17] o' one left. I was near out anyway. We didn't have this cookstove then, and I cal'lated I could make up a good lively blaze, so I come up full o' scold as I could be, and then I found I'd burnt up all my dry wood. You see, I thought certain he'd be home and I was tendin' to the child'n, but I started to go out o' the door and found it had come on to rain hard, and I said to myself I wouldn't go out to the woodpile and get my clothes all damp, 'count o' Ad'line, and the candle end would last a spell longer, and he'd be home by that time. I hadn't a least o' suspicion but what he was dallying round up to the Corners,[18] 'long o' the rest o' the men, bein' 't was Saturday night, and I was some put out about it, for he knew the baby was sick, and I hadn't nobody with me. I set down and waited, but he never come, and it rained hard as I ever see it, and I left his supper standin' right in the floor, and then I begun to be distressed for fear somethin' had happened to Dan'l, and I set to work and cried, and the candle end give a flare and went out, and by 'n' by the fire begun to get low and I took the child'n and went to bed to keep warm; 't was an awful cold night, considerin' 't was such a heavy rain, and there I laid awake and thought I heard things steppin' about the room, and it seemed to me as if 't was a week long before mornin' come, and as if I'd got to be an old woman. I did go through with everything that night. 'T was that time Dan'l broke his leg, you know; they was takin' a deck load of oak knees down by the packet,[19] and one on 'em rolled down from the top of the pile and struck him just below the knee. He was poling,[20] for there wan't a breath o' wind, and he always felt certain there was somethin' mysterious about it. He'd had a good deal worse knocks than that seemed to be, as only left a black and blue spot, and he said he never see a deck load o' timber piled securer. He had some queer notions about the doin's o' sperits, Dan'l had; his old Aunt Parser was to blame for it. She lived with his father's folks, and used to fill him and the rest o' the child'n with all sorts o' ghost stories and stuff. I used to tell him she'd a' be'n hung for a witch if she'd lived in them old Salem days. He always used to be tellin' what every-thing was the sign of, when we was first married, till I laughed him out of it. It made me kind of notional. There's too much now we can't make sense of without addin' to it out o' our own heads."

Mrs. Jake and Mrs. Martin were quite familiar with the story of the night when there were no candles and Mr. Thacher had broken his leg, having been present themselves early in the morning afterward, but they had listened with none the less in-terest. These country neighbors knew their friends' affairs as well as they did their own, but such an audience is never impa-tient. The repetitions of the best stories are signal events, for ordinary circumstances do not inspire them. Affairs must rise to a certain level before a narration of some great crisis is sug-gested, and exactly as a city audience is well contented with hearing the plays of Shakespeare over and over again, so each man and woman of experience is permitted to deploy their well-known but always interesting stories upon the rustic stage.

"I must say I can't a-bear to hear anything about ghosts after sundown," observed Mrs. Jake, who was at times somewhat troubled by what she and her friends designated as "narves." "Daytimes I don't believe in 'em 'less it's something creepy more 'n common, but after dark it scares me to pieces. I do' know but I shall be afeared to go home," and she laughed un-easily. "There! when I get through with this needle I believe I won't knit no more. The back o' my neck is all numb."

"Don't talk o' goin' home yet awhile," said the hostess, look-ing up quickly as if she hated the thought of being left alone again. " 'T is just on the edge of the evenin'; the nights is so long now we think it's bedtime half an hour after we've got lit up. 'T was a good lift havin' you step over to-night. I was really a-dreadin' to set here by myself," and for some minutes nobody spoke and the needles clicked faster than ever. Suddenly there was a strange sound outside the door, and they stared at each other in terror and held their breath, but nobody stirred. This was no familiar footstep; presently they heard a strange little cry, and still they feared to look, or to know what was waiting outside. Then Mrs. Thacher took a candle in her hand, and, still hesitating, asked once, "Who is there?" and, hearing no answer, slowly opened the door.

CHAPTER III.

AT JAKE AND MARTIN'S

In the mean time, the evening had been much enjoyed by the brothers who were spending it together in Martin Dyer's kitchen. The houses stood side by side, but Mr. Jacob Dyer's youngest daughter, the only one now left at home, was receiving a visit from her lover, or, as the family expressed it, the young man who was keeping company with her, and her father, mindful of his own youth, had kindly withdrawn. Martin's children were already established in homes of their own, with the exception of one daughter who was at work in one of the cotton factories at Lowell in company with several of her acquaintances.[1] It has already been said that Jake and Martin liked nobody's company so well as their own. Their wives had a time-honored joke about being comparatively unnecessary to their respective partners, and indeed the two men had a curiously dependent feeling toward each other. It was the close sympathy which twins sometimes have each to each, and had become a byword among all their acquaintances. They were seldom individualized in any way, and neither was able to distinguish himself, apparently, for one always heard of the family as Jake and Martin's folks, and of their possessions, from least to greatest, as belonging to both brothers. The only time they had ever been separated was once in their early youth, when Jake had been fired with a desire to go to sea; but he deserted the coastwise schooner[2] in the first port and came home, because he could not bear it any longer without his brother. Martin had no turn for seafaring, so Jake remained ashore and patiently made a farmer of himself for love's sake, and in spite of a great thirst for adventure that had never ceased to fever his blood. It was astonishing how much they found to say to each other when one considers that their experiences were almost constantly the same; but nothing contented them better than an uninterrupted evening spent in each other's society, and as they hoed corn or dug potatoes, or mowed, or as they drove to the Corners,[3] sitting stiffly upright in the old-fashioned thorough-braced wagon,[4] they were always to be seen talking as if it were the first meeting after a long separation. But, having taken these quiet times for the discussion of all possible and impossible problems, they were men of fixed opinions, and were ready at a moment's warning to render exact decisions. They were not fond of society as a rule; they found little occasion for much talk with their neighbors, but used as few words as possible. Nobody was more respected than the brothers. It was often said of them that their word was their bond, and as they passed from youth to middle age, and in these days were growing to look like elderly men, they were free from shame or reproach, though not from much good-natured joking and friendly fun. Their farm had been owned in the family since the settlement of the country, and the house which Martin occupied was very old. Jake's had been built for him when he was married, from timber cut in their own woodlands, and after thirty years of wear it looked scarcely newer than its companion. And when it is explained that they had married sisters, because, as people said, they even went courting together, it will be easy to see that they had found life more harmonious than most people do. Sometimes the wife of one brother would complain that her sister enjoyed undue advantages and profits from the estate, but there was rarely any disagreement, and Mrs. Jake was mistress of the turkeys and Mrs. Martin held sway over the hens, while they divided the spoils amiably at Thanksgiving time when the geese were sold.[5] If it were a bad year for turkeys, and the tender young were chilled in the wet grass, while the hens flourished steadily the season through, Mrs. Jake's spirits drooped and she became envious of the good fortune which flaunted itself before her eyes, but on the whole, they suffered and enjoyed together, and found no fault with their destinies. The two wives, though the affection between them was of an ordinary sort, were apt to form a league against the brothers, and this prevented a more troublesome rivalry which might have existed between the households.

Jake and Martin were particularly enjoying the evening. Some accident had befallen the cooking-stove, which the brothers had never more than half approved, it being one of the early patterns, and a poor exchange for the ancient methods of cookery in the wide fireplace.[6] "The women" had had a natural desire to be equal with their neighbors, and knew better than their husbands did the difference this useful invention had made in their every-day work. However, this one night the conservative brothers could take a mild revenge; and when their wives were well on their way to Mrs. Thacher's they had assured each other that, if the plaguey thing were to be carried to the Corners in the morning to be exchanged or repaired, it would be as well to have it in readiness, and had quickly taken down its pipes and lifted it as if it were a feather[7] to the neighboring woodshed. Then they hastily pried away a fireboard which closed the great fireplace, and looked smilingly upon the crane and its pothooks and the familiar iron dogs which had been imprisoned there in darkness for many months.[8] They brought in the materials for an old-fashioned fire, backlog, forestick, and crowsticks,[9] and presently seated themselves before a crackling blaze. Martin brought a tall, brown pitcher of cider from the cellar and set two mugs beside it on the small table, and for some little time they enjoyed themselves in silence, after which Jake remarked that he didn't know but they'd got full enough of a fire for such a mild night, but he wished his own stove and the new one too could be dropped into the river for good and all.

They put the jug of cider between the andirons, and then, moved by a common impulse, drew their chairs a little farther from the mounting flames, before they quenched their thirst from the mugs.

"I call that pretty cider," said Martin; " 't is young yet, but it has got some weight a'ready, and 't is smooth. There's a sight o' difference between good upland fruit and the sposhy[10] apples

that grows in wet ground. An' I take it that the bar'l has an influence: some bar'ls kind of wilt cider and some smarten it up,
and keep it hearty. Lord! what stuff some folks are willin' to set
before ye! 't ain't wuth the name o' cider, nor no better than the
rensin's[11] of a vinegar cask."

"And then there's weather too," agreed Mr. Jacob Dyer,
"had ought to be took into consideration. Git your apples just
in the right time—not too early to taste o' the tree, nor too late
to taste o' the ground, and just in the snap o' time as to
ripeness', on a good sharp day with the sun a-shining; have 'em
into the press and what comes out is *cider*. I think if we've had
any fault in years past, 't was puttin' off makin' a little too late.
But I don't see as this could be beat. I don't know 's you feel like
a pipe, but I believe I'll light up," and thereupon a good portion
of black-looking tobacco was cut and made fine in each of the
hard left hands, and presently the clay pipes were touched off
with a live coal, and great clouds of smoke might have been
seen to disappear under the edge of the fire-place, drawn
quickly up the chimney by the draft of the blazing fire.

Jacob pushed back his chair another foot or two, and Martin
soon followed, mentioning that it was getting hot, but it was
well to keep out the damp.

"What set the women out to go traipsin' up to Thacher's
folks?" inquired Jacob, holding his cider mug with one hand
and drumming it with the finger ends of the other.

"I had an idee that they wanted to find out if anything had
been heard about Ad'line's getting home for Thanksgiving," answered Martin, turning to look shrewdly at his brother. "Women
folks does suffer if there's anything goin' on they can't find out
about. 'Liza said she was going to invite Mis' Thacher and John
to eat a piece o' our big turkey, but she didn't s'pose they'd
want to leave. Curi's about Ad'line, ain't it? I expected when
her husband died she'd be right back here with what she'd got;
at any rate, till she'd raised the child to some size. There'd be no
expense here to what she'd have elsewhere, and here's her
ma'am beginnin' to age. She can't do what she used to, John
was tellin' of me; and I don't doubt 't 'as worn upon her more 'n
folks thinks."

"I don't lay no great belief that John'll get home from court," said Jacob Dyer. "They say that court's goin' to set till Christmas maybe; there's an awful string o' cases on the docket.[12] Oh, 't was you told me, wa'n't it? Most like they'll let up for a couple o' days for Thanksgivin', but John mightn't think 't was wuth his while to travel here and back again 'less he had something to do before winter shets down. Perhaps they'll prevail upon the old lady, I wish they would, I'm sure; but an only daughter forsakin' her so, 't was most too bad of Ad'line. She al'ays had dreadful high notions when she wa'n't no more 'n a baby; and, good conscience, how she liked to rig up when she first used to come back from Lowell! Better ha' put her money out to interest."

"I believe in young folks makin' all they can o' theirselves," announced Martin, puffing hard at his pipe and drawing a little farther still from the fireplace, because the scorching red coals had begun to drop beneath the forestick. "I've give my child'n the best push forrard I could, an' you've done the same. Ad'line had a dreadful cravin' to be somethin' more 'n common; but it don't look as if she was goin' to make out any great. 'T was unfortunate her losin' of her husband, but I s'pose you've heard hints that they wa'n't none too equal-minded. She'd a done better to have worked on a while to Lowell and got forehanded, and then married some likely young fellow and settled down here, or to the Corners if she didn't want to farm it. There was Jim Hall used to be hanging round, and she'd been full as well off to-day if she'd took him, too. 'T ain't no use for folks to marry one that's of another kind and belongs different. It's like two fiddles that plays different tunes,—you can't make nothin' on't, no matter if both on em's trying their best, 'less one on 'em beats the other down entirely and has all the say, and ginerally 't is the worst one does it. Ad'line's husband wa'n't nothin' to boast of from all we can gather, but they didn't think alike about nothin'. She could 'a' done well with him if there'd been more of *her*. I don't marvel his folks felt bad: Ad'line didn't act right by 'em."

"Nor they by her," said the twin brother. "I tell ye Ad'line would have done 'em credit if she'd been let. I seem to think how 't was with her; When she was there to work in the shop she thought 't would be smart to marry him and then she'd be a lady for good and all. And all there was of it, she found his folks felt put out and hurt, and instead of pleasing 'em up and doing the best she could, she didn't know no better than to aggravate 'em. She was wrong there, but I hold to it that if they'd pleased her up a little and done well by her, she'd ha' bloomed out, and fell right in with their ways. She's got outward ambitions enough, but I view it she was all a part of his foolishness to them; I dare say they give her the blame o' the whole on't. Ad'line ought to had the sense to see they had some right on their side. Folks say he was the smartest fellow in his class to college."

"Good King Agrippy![13] how hot it does git," said Jake rising indignantly, as if the fire alone were to blame. "I must shove back the cider agin or 't will bile over, spite of everything. But 't is called unwholesome to get a house full o' damp in the fall o' the year; 't will freeze an' thaw in the walls all winter. I must git me a new pipe if we go to the Corners to-morrow. I s'pose I've told ye of a pipe a man had aboard the schooner that time I went to sea?"

Martin gave a little grumble of assent.

" 'T was made o' some sort o' whitish stuff like clay, but 't wa'n't shaped like none else I ever see and it had a silver trimmin' round it; 't was very light to handle and it drawed most excellent. I al'ays kind o' expected he may have stole it; he was a hard lookin' customer, a Dutchman or from some o' them parts o' the earth. I wish while I was about it I'd gone one trip more."

"Was it you was tellin' me that Ad'line was to work again in Lowell? I shouldn't think her husband's folks would want the child to be fetched up there in them boardin' houses"[14]—

"Belike they don't," responded Jacob, "but when they get Ad'line to come round to their ways o' thinkin' now, after what's been and gone, they'll have cause to thank themselves. She's just like her gre't grandsir Thacher; you can see she's made out o' the same stuff. You might ha' burnt him to the stake, and he'd stick to it he liked it better 'n hanging and al'ays meant to die that way. There's an awful bad streak in them

Thachers, an' you know it as well as I do. I expect there'll be bad and good Thachers to the end o' time. I'm glad for the old lady's sake that John ain't one o' the drinkin' ones. Ad'line'll give no favors to her husband's folks, nor take none. There's plenty o' wrongs to both sides, but as I view it, the longer he'd lived the worse 't would been for him. She was a well made, pretty lookin' girl, but I tell ye 't was like setting a laylock bush to grow beside an ellum tree,[15] and expecting of 'em to keep together. They wa'n't mates. He'd had a different fetchin' up, and he *was* different, and I wa'n't surprised when I come to see how things had turned out,—I believe I shall have to set the door open a half a minute, 't is gettin' dreadful"—but there was a sudden flurry outside, and the sound of heavy footsteps, the bark of the startled cur, who was growing very old and a little deaf, and Mrs. Martin burst into the room and sank into the nearest chair, to gather a little breath before she could tell her errand. "For God's sake what's happened?" cried the men.

They presented a picture of mingled comfort and misery at which Mrs. Martin would have first laughed and then scolded at any other time. The two honest red faces were well back toward the farther side of the room from the fire, which still held its own; it was growing toward low tide in the cider jug and its attendant mugs, and the pipes were lying idle. The mistress of the old farm-house did not fail to notice that high treason had been committed during her short absence, but she made no comment upon the fireplace nor on anything else, and gasped as soon as she could that one of the men must go right up to the Corners for the doctor and hurry back with him, for 't was a case of life and death.

"Mis' Thacher?" "Was it a shock?"[16] asked the brothers in sorrowful haste, while Mrs. Martin told the sad little story of Adeline's having come from nobody knew where, wet and forlorn, carrying her child in her arms. She looked as if she were in the last stages of a decline. She had fallen just at the doorstep and they had brought her in, believing that she was dead. "But while there's life, there's hope," said Mrs. Martin, "and I'll go back with you if you'll harness up. Jacob must stop to look after this gre't fire or 't will burn the house down," and this was the punishment which befell Jacob, since nothing else would have kept him from also journeying toward the Thacher house.

A little later the bewildered horse had been fully wakened and harnessed; Jacob's daughter and her lover had come eagerly out to hear what had happened; Mrs. Martin had somehow found a chance amidst all the confusion to ascend to her garret in quest of some useful remedies in the shape of herbs, and then she and her husband set forth on their benevolent errands. Martin was very apt to look on the dark side of things, and it was a curious fact that while the two sisters were like the brothers, one being inclined to despondency and one to enthusiasm, the balance was well kept by each of the men having chosen his opposite in temperament. Accordingly, while Martin heaved a great sigh from time to time and groaned softly, "Pore gal— pore gal!" his partner was brimful of zealous eagerness to return to the scene of distress and sorrow which she had lately left. Next to the doctor himself, she was the authority on all medical subjects for that neighborhood, and it was some time since her skill had been needed.

"Does the young one seem likely?"[17] asked Martin with solemn curiosity.

"Fur 's I could see," answered his wife promptly, "but nobody took no great notice of it. Pore Ad'line catched hold of it with such a grip as she was comin' to that we couldn't git it away from her and had to fetch 'em in both to once. Come urge the beast along, Martin, I'll give ye the partic'lars to-morrow, I do' know 's Ad'line's livin' now. We got her right to bed 's I told you, and I set right off considerin' that I could git over the ground fastest of any. Mis' Thacher of course wouldn't leave and Jane's heavier than I be." Martin's smile was happily concealed by the darkness; his wife and her sister had both grown stout steadily as they grew older, but each insisted upon the other's greater magnitude and consequent incapacity for quick movement. A casual observer would not have been persuaded that there was a pound's weight of difference between them.

Martin Dyer meekly suggested that perhaps he'd better go in a minute to see if there was anything Mis' Thacher needed, but

Eliza, his wife, promptly said that she didn't want anything but the doctor as quick as she could get him, and disappeared up the short lane while the wagon rattled away up the road. The white mist from the river clung close to the earth, and it was impossible to see even the fences near at hand, though overhead there were a few dim stars. The air had grown somewhat softer, yet there was a sharp chill in it, and the ground was wet and sticky under foot. There were lights in the bedroom and in the kitchen of the Thacher house, but suddenly the bedroom candle flickered away and the window was darkened. Mrs. Martin's heart gave a quick throb, perhaps Adeline had already died. It might have been a short-sighted piece of business that she had gone home for her husband.

CHAPTER IV.

LIFE AND DEATH

The sick woman had refused to stay in the bedroom after she had come to her senses. She had insisted that she could not breathe, and that she was cold and must go back to the kitchen. Her mother and Mrs. Jake had wrapped her in blankets and drawn the high-backed wooden rocking chair close to the stove, and here she was just established when Mrs. Martin opened the outer door. Any one of less reliable nerves would have betrayed the shock which the sight of such desperate illness must have given. The pallor, the suffering, the desperate agony of the eyes, were far worse than the calmness of death, but Mrs. Martin spoke cheerfully, and even when her sister whispered that their patient had been attacked by a hæmorrhage, she manifested no concern.

"How long has this be'n a-goin' on, Ad'line? Why didn't you come home before and get doctored up? You're all run down." Mrs. Thacher looked frightened when this questioning began, but turned her face toward her daughter, eager to hear the answer.

"I've been sick off and on all summer," said the young woman, as if it were almost impossible to make the effort of speaking. "See if the baby's covered up warm, will you, Aunt 'Liza?"

"Yes, dear," said the kind-hearted woman, the tears starting to her eyes at the sound of the familiar affectionate fashion of speech which Adeline had used in her childhood. "Don't you worry one mite; we're going to take care of you and the little gal too;" and then nobody spoke, while the only sound was the difficult breathing of the poor creature by the fire. She seemed like one dying, there was so little life left in her after her piteous homeward journey. The mother watched her eagerly with a mingled feeling of despair and comfort; it was terrible to have a child return in such sad plight, but it was a blessing to have her safe at home, and to be able to minister to her wants while life lasted.

They all listened eagerly for the sound of wheels, but it seemed a long time before Martin Dyer returned with the doctor. He had been met just as he was coming in from the other direction, and the two men had only paused while the tired horse was made comfortable, and a sleepy boy dispatched with the medicine for which he had long been waiting. The doctor's housekeeper had besought him to wait long enough to eat the supper which she had kept waiting, but he laughed at her and shook his head gravely, as if he already understood that there should be no delay. When he was fairly inside the Thacher kitchen, the benefaction of his presence was felt by every one. It was most touching to see the patient's face lose its worried look, and grow quiet and comfortable as if here were some one on whom she could entirely depend. The doctor's greeting was an every-day cheerful response to the women's welcome, and he stood for a minute warming his hands at the fire as if he had come upon a commonplace errand. There was something singularly self-reliant and composed about him; one felt that he was the wielder of great powers over the enemies, disease and pain, and that his brave hazel eyes showed a rare thoughtfulness and foresight. The rough driving coat which he had thrown off revealed a slender figure with the bowed shoulders of an untiring scholar. His head was finely set and scholarly, and there was that about him which gave certainty, not only of his sagacity and skill, but of his true manhood, his mastery of himself. Not only in this farm-house kitchen, but wherever one might place him, he instinctively took command, while from his great knowledge of human nature he could understand and help many of his patients whose ailments were not wholly physical. He seemed to read at a glance the shame and sorrow of the young woman who had fled to the home of her childhood, dying and worse than defeated, from the battle-field of life. And in this first moment he recognized with dismay the effects of that passion for strong drink which had been the curse of more than one of her ancestors. Even the pallor and the purifying influence of her mortal illness could not disguise these unmistakable signs.

"You can't do me any good, doctor," she whispered. "I shouldn't have let you come if it had been only that. I don't care how soon I am out of this world. But I want you should look after my little girl," and the poor soul watched the physician's face with keen anxiety as if she feared to see a shadow of unwillingness, but none came.

"I will do the best I can," and he still held her wrist, apparently thinking more of the fluttering pulse than of what poor Adeline was saying.

"That was what made me willing to come back," she continued, "you don't know how close I came to not doing it either. John will be good to her, but she will need somebody that knows the world better by and by. I wonder if you couldn't show me how to make out a paper giving you the right over her till she is of age? She must stay here with mother, long as she wants her. 'T is what I wish I had kept sense enough to do; life hasn't been all play to me;" and the tears began to roll quickly down the poor creature's thin cheeks. "The only thing I care about is leaving the baby well placed, and I want her to have a good chance to grow up a useful woman. And most of all to keep her out of *their* hands, I mean her father's folks. I hate 'em, and he cared more for 'em than he did for me, long at the last of it. . . . I could tell you stories!"—

"But not to-night, Addy," said the doctor gravely, as if he were speaking to a child. "We must put you to bed and to sleep, and you can talk about all these troublesome things in the morning. You shall see about the papers too, if you think best. Be a good girl now, and let your mother help you to bed." For the resolute spirit had summoned the few poor fragments of vitality that were left, and the sick woman was growing more and more excited. "You may have all the pillows you wish for, and sit up in bed if you like, but you mustn't stay here any longer," and he gathered her in his arms and quickly carried her to the next room. She made no resistance, and took the medicine which Mrs. Martin brought, without a word. There was a blazing fire now in the bedroom fire-place, and, as she lay still, her face took on a satisfied, rested look. Her mother sat beside her, tearful, and yet contented and glad to have her near, and the others whispered together in the kitchen. It might have been the last night of a long illness instead of the sudden, startling entrance of sorrow in human shape. "No," said the doctor, "she cannot last much longer with such a cough as that, Mrs. Dyer. She has almost reached the end of it. I only hope that she will go quickly."

And sure enough; whether the fatal illness had run its natural course, or whether the excitement and the forced strength of the evening before had exhausted the small portion of strength that was left, when the late dawn lighted again those who watched, it found them sleeping, and one was never to wake again in the world she had found so disappointing to her ambitions, and so untrue to its fancied promises.

The doctor had promised to return early, but it was hardly daylight before there was another visitor in advance of him. Old Mrs. Meeker, a neighbor whom nobody liked, but whose favor everybody for some reason or other was anxious to keep, came knocking at the door, and was let in somewhat reluctantly by Mrs. Jake, who was just preparing to go home in order to send one or both the brothers to the village and to acquaint John Thacher with the sad news of his sister's death. He was older than Adeline, and a silent man, already growing to be elderly in his appearance. The women had told themselves and each other that he would take this sorrow very hard, and Mrs. Thacher had said sorrowfully that she must hide her daughter's poor worn clothes, since it would break John's heart to know she had come home so beggarly. The shock of so much trouble was stunning the mother; she did not understand yet, she kept telling the kind friends who sorrowed with her, as she busied herself with the preparations for the funeral. "It don't seem as if 't was Addy," she said over and over again, "but I feel safe about her now, to what I did," and Mrs. Jake and Mrs. Martin,

good helpful souls and brimful of compassion, went to and fro
with their usual diligence almost as if this were nothing out of
the common course of events.

Mrs. Meeker had heard the wagon go by and had caught the
sound of the doctor's voice, her house being close by the road,
and she had also watched the unusual lights. It was annoying to
the Dyers to have to answer questions, and to be called upon to
grieve outwardly just then, and it seemed disloyal to the dead
woman in the next room to enter upon any discussion of her affairs. But presently the little child, whom nobody had thought
of except to see that she still slept, waked and got down from
the old settle where she had spent the night, and walked with
unsteady short footsteps toward her grandmother, who caught
her quickly and held her fast in her arms. The little thing looked
puzzled, and frowned, and seemed for a moment unhappy, and
then the sunshine of her good nature drove away the clouds and
she clapped her hands and laughed aloud, while Mrs. Meeker
began to cry again at the sight of this unconscious orphan.

"I'm sure I'm glad she can laugh," said Mrs. Martin. "She'll
find enough to cry about later on; I foresee she'll be a great deal
o' company to you, Mis' Thacher."

"Though 't ain't every one that has the strength to fetch up a
child after they reach your years," said Mrs. Meeker, mourn-
fully. "It's anxious work, but I don't doubt strength will be
given you. I s'pose likely her father's folks will do a good deal
for her,"—and the three women looked at each other, but neither took it upon herself to answer.

All that day the neighbors and acquaintances came and went
in the lane that led to the farm-house. The brothers Jake and
Martin made journeys to and from the village. At night John
Thacher came home from court with as little to say as ever, but,
as everybody observed, looking years older. Young Mrs.
Prince's return and sudden death were the only subjects worth
talking about in all the country side, and the doctor had to run
the usual gauntlet of questions from all his outlying patients
and their families. Old Mrs. Thacher looked pale and excited,
and insisted upon seeing every one who came to the house, with
evident intention to play her part in this strange drama with ex-

actness and courtesy. A funeral in the country is always an era
in a family's life; events date from it and centre in it. There are
so few circumstances that have in the least a public nature that
these conspicuous days receive all the more attention.

But while death seems far more astonishing and unnatural in
a city, where the great tide of life rises and falls with little apparent regard to the sinking wrecks, in the country it is not so.
The neighbors themselves are those who dig the grave and carry
the dead, whom they or their friends have made ready, to the
last resting-place. With all nature looking on,—the leaves that
must fall, and the grass of the field that must wither and be
gone when the wind passes over,[1]—living closer to life and in
plainer sight of death, they have a different sense of the mysteries of existence. They pay homage to Death rather than to the
dead; they gather from the lonely farms by scores because there
is a funeral, and not because their friend is dead; and the day of
Adeline Prince's burial, the marvelous circumstances, with
which the whole town was already familiar, brought a great
company together to follow her on her last journey.

The day was warm and the sunshine fell caressingly over the
pastures as if it were trying to call back the flowers. By afternoon there was a tinge of greenness on the slopes and under the
gnarled apple-trees, that had been lost for days before, and the
distant hills and mountains, which could be seen in a circle
from the high land where the Thacher farm-house stood, were
dim and blue through the Indian summer haze. The old men
who came to the funeral wore their faded winter overcoats and
clumsy caps all ready to be pulled down over their ears if the
wind should change; and their wives were also warmly
wrapped, with great shawls over their rounded, hard-worked
shoulders; yet they took the best warmth and pleasantness into
their hearts, and watched the sad proceedings of the afternoon
with deepest interest. The doctor came hurrying toward home
just as the long procession was going down the pasture, and he
saw it crossing a low hill; a dark and slender column with here
and there a child walking beside one of the elder mourners. The
bearers went first with the bier; the track was uneven, and the
procession was lost to sight now and then behind the slopes. It

was forever a mystery; these people might have been a company of Druid worshipers,[2] or of strange northern priests and their people, and the doctor checked his impatient horse as he watched the retreating figures at their simple ceremony. He could not help thinking what strange ways this child of the old farm had followed, and what a quiet ending it was to her wandering life. "And I have promised to look after the little girl," he said to himself as he drove away up the road.

It was a long walk for the elderly people from the house near the main highway to the little burying-ground. In the earliest days of the farm the dwelling-place was nearer the river, which was then the chief thoroughfare; and those of the family who had died then were buried on the level bit of upland ground high above the river itself. There was a wide outlook over the country, and the young pine trees that fringed the shore sang in the south wind, while some great birds swung to and fro overhead, watching the water and the strange company of people who had come so slowly over the land. A flock of sheep had ventured to the nearest hillock of the next pasture, and stood there fearfully, with upraised heads, as if they looked for danger.

John Thacher had brought his sister's child all the way in his arms, and she had clapped her hands and laughed aloud and tried to talk a great deal with the few words she had learned to say. She was very gay in her baby fashion; she was amused with the little crowd so long as it did not trouble her. She fretted only when the grave, kind man, for whom she had instantly felt a great affection, stayed too long by that deep hole in the ground and wept as he saw a strange thing that the people had carried all the way, put down into it out of sight. When he walked on again, she laughed and played; but after they had reached the empty gray house, which somehow looked that day as if it were a mourner also, she shrank from all the strangers, and seemed dismayed and perplexed, and called her mother eagerly again and again. This touched many a heart. The dead woman had been more or less unfamiliar of late years to all of them; and there were few who had really grieved for her until her little child had reminded them of its own loneliness and loss.

That night, after the house was still, John Thacher wrote to acquaint Miss Prince, of Dunport,[3] with his sister's death and to say that it was her wish that the child should remain with them during its minority. They should formally appoint the guardian whom she had selected; they would do their best by the little girl. And when Mrs. Thacher asked if he had blamed Miss Prince, he replied that he had left that to her own conscience.

In the answer which was quickly returned, there was a plea for the custody of the child, her mother's and her own namesake, but this was indignantly refused. There was no love lost between the town and the country household, and for many years all intercourse was at an end. Before twelve months were past, John Thacher himself was carried down to the pasture burying-ground, and his old mother and the little child were left to comfort and take care of each other as best they could in the lonely farm-house.

CHAPTER V.

A SUNDAY VISIT

In the gray house on the hill, one spring went by and another, and it seemed to the busy doctor only a few months from the night he first saw his ward before she was old enough to come soberly to church with her grandmother. He had always seen her from time to time, for he had often been called to the farm or to the Dyers and had watched her at play. Once she had stopped him as he drove by to give him a little handful of blue violets, and this had gone straight to his heart, for he had been made too great a bugbear to most children to look for any favor at their hands. He always liked to see her come into church on Sundays, her steps growing quicker and surer as her good grandmother's became more feeble. The doctor was a lonely man in spite of his many friends, and he found himself watching for the little brown face that, half-way across the old meeting-house,[1] would turn round to look for him more than once during the service. At first there was only the top of little Nan Prince's prim best bonnet or hood to be seen, unless it was when she stood up in prayer-time, but soon the bright eyes rose like stars above the horizon of the pew railing, and next there was the whole well-poised little head, and the tall child was possessed by a sense of propriety, and only ventured one or two discreet glances at her old friend.

The office of guardian was not one of great tasks or of many duties, though the child's aunt had insisted upon making an allowance for her of a hundred dollars a year, and this was duly acknowledged and placed to its owner's credit in the savings bank of the next town. Her grandmother Thacher always refused to spend it, saying proudly that she had never been beholden to Miss Prince and she never meant to be, and while she lived the aunt and niece should be kept apart. She would not say that her daughter had never been at fault, but it was through the Princes all the trouble of her life had come.

Dr. Leslie was mindful of his responsibilities, and knew more of his ward than was ever suspected. He was eager that the best district school teacher[2] who could be found should be procured for the Thacher and Dyer neighborhood, and in many ways he took pains that the little girl should have all good things that were possible. He only laughed when her grandmother complained that Nan would not be driven to school, much less persuaded, and that she was playing in the brook, or scampering over the pastures when she should be doing other things. Mrs. Thacher, perhaps unconsciously, had looked for some trace of the father's good breeding and gentlefolk fashions, but this was not a child who took kindly to needlework and pretty clothes. She was fearlessly friendly with every one; she did not seem confused even when the minister came to make his yearly parochial visitation,[3] and as for the doctor, he might have been her own age, for all humility she thought it necessary to show in the presence of this chief among her elders and betters. Old Mrs. Thacher gave little pulls at her granddaughter's sleeves when she kept turning to see the doctor in sermon-time, but she never knew how glad he was, or how willingly he smiled when he felt the child's eyes watching him as a dog's might have done, forcing him to forget the preaching altogether and to attend to this dumb request for sympathy. One blessed day Dr. Leslie had waited in the church porch and gravely taken the child's hand as she came out; and said that he should like to take her home with him; he was going to the lower part of the town late in the afternoon and would leave her then at the farm-house.

"I was going to ask you for something for her shoulder," said Grandmother Thacher, much pleased, "she'll tell you about it, it was a fall she had out of an apple-tree,"—and Nan looked up with not a little apprehension, but presently tucked her small hand inside the doctor's and was more than ready to go with him. "I thought she looked a little pale," the doctor said, to which Mrs. Thacher answered that it was a merciful Providence who had kept the child from breaking her neck, and then, being at the foot of the church steps, they separated. It had been a great trial to the good woman to give up the afternoon service, but she was growing old, as she told herself often in those days, and felt, as she certainly looked, greatly older than her years.

"I feel as if Anna was sure of one good friend, whether I stay with her or not," said the grandmother sorrowfully, as she drove toward home that Sunday noon with Jacob Dyer and his wife. "I never saw the doctor so taken with a child before. 'T was a pity he had to lose his own, and his wife too; how many years ago was it? I should think he'd be lonesome, though to be sure he isn't in the house much. Marilla Thomas keeps his house as clean as a button and she has been a good stand-by for him, but it always seemed sort o' homesick there ever since the day I was to his wife's funeral. She made an awful sight o' friends considering she was so little while in the place. Well I'm glad I let Nanny wear her best dress; I set out not to, it looked so much like rain."

Whatever Marilla Thomas's other failings might have been, she certainly was kind that day to the doctor's little guest. It would have been a hard-hearted person indeed who did not enter somewhat into the spirit of the child's delight. In spite of its being the first time she had ever sat at any table but her grandmother's, she was not awkward or uncomfortable, and was so hungry that she gave pleasure to her entertainers in that way if no other. The doctor leaned back in his chair and waited while the second portion of pudding slowly disappeared, though Marilla could have told that he usually did not give half time enough to his dinner and was off like an arrow the first possible minute. Before he took his often interrupted afternoon nap, he inquired for the damaged shoulder and requested a detailed account of the accident; and presently they were both laughing heartily at Nan's disaster, for she owned that she had chased and treed a stray young squirrel, and that a mossy branch of one of the old apple-trees in the straggling orchard had failed to bear even so light a weight as hers. Nan had come to the ground because she would not loose her hold of the squirrel, though he had slipped through her hands after all as she carried him towards home. The guest was proud to become a patient, especially as the only remedy that was offered was a very comfortable handful of sugar-plums. Nan had never owned so many at once, and in a transport of gratitude and affection she lifted her face to kiss so dear a benefactor.

Her eyes looked up into his, and her simple nature was so unconscious of the true dangers and perils of this world, that his very heart was touched with compassion, and he leagued himself with the child's good angel to defend her against her enemies.

And Nan took fast hold of the doctor's hand as they went to the study. This was the only room in the house which she had seen before; and was so much larger and pleasanter than any she knew elsewhere that she took great delight in it. It was a rough place now, the doctor thought, but always very comfortable, and he laid himself down on the great sofa with a book in his hand, though after a few minutes he grew sleepy and only opened his eyes once to see that Nan was perched in the largest chair with her small hands folded, and her feet very far from the floor. "You may run out to see Marilla, or go about the house anywhere you like; or there are some picture-papers on the table," the doctor said drowsily, and the visitor slipped down from her throne and went softly away.

She had thought the study a very noble room until she had seen the dining-room, but now she wished for another look at the pictures there and the queer clock, and the strange, grand things on the sideboard. The old-fashioned comfort of the house was perfect splendor to the child, and she went about on tiptoe up stairs and down, looking in at the open doors, while she lingered wistfully before the closed ones. She wondered at the great bedsteads with their high posts and dimity hangings, and at the carpets, and the worthy Marilla watched her for a moment as she stood on the threshold of the doctor's own room. The child's quick ear caught the rustle of the housekeeper's Sunday gown; she whispered with shining eyes that she thought the house was beautiful. Did Marilla live here all the time?

"Bless you, yes!" replied Marilla, not without pride, though she added that nobody knew what a sight of care it was.

"I suppose y'r aunt in Dunport lives a good deal better than this;" but the child only looked puzzled and did not answer, while the housekeeper hurried away to the afternoon meeting, for which the bell was already tolling.

The doctor slept on in the shaded study, and after Nan had grown tired of walking softly about the house, she found her way into the garden. After all, there was nothing better than being out of doors, and the apple-trees seemed most familiar and friendly, though she pitied them for being placed so near each other. She discovered a bench under a trellis where a grape-vine and a clematis were tangled together, and here she sat down to spend a little time before the doctor should call her. She wished she could stay longer than that one short afternoon; perhaps some time or other the doctor would invite her again. But what could Marilla have meant about her aunt? She had no aunts except Mrs. Jake and Mrs. Martin; Marilla must well know that their houses were not like Dr. Leslie's; and little Nan built herself a fine castle in Spain, of which this unknown aunt was queen. Certainly her grandmother had now and then let fall a word about "your father's folks"—by and by they might come to see her!

The grape leaves were waving about in the warm wind, and they made a flickering light and shade upon the ground. The clematis was in bloom, and its soft white plumes fringed the archway of the lattice work. As the child looked down the garden walk it seemed very long and very beautiful to her. Her grandmother's flower-garden had been constantly encroached upon by the turf which surrounded it, until the snowberry bush, the London pride, the tiger-lilies, and the crimson phlox were like a besieged garrison.

Nan had already found plenty of wild flowers in the world; there were no entertainments provided for her except those the fields and pastures kindly spread before her admiring eyes. Old Mrs. Thacher had been brought up to consider the hard work of this life, and though she had taken her share of enjoyment as she went along, it was of a somewhat grim and sober sort. She believed that a certain amount of friskiness was as necessary to young human beings as it is to colts, but later both must be harnessed and made to work. As for pleasure itself she had little notion of that. She liked fair weather, and certain flowers were to her the decorations of certain useful plants, but if she had known that her grand-daughter could lie down beside the anemones and watch them move in the wind and nod their heads, and afterward look up into the blue sky to watch the great gulls above the river, or the sparrows flying low, or the crows who went higher, Mrs. Thacher would have understood almost nothing of such delights, and thought it a very idle way of spending one's time.

But as Nan sat in the old summer-house[4] in the doctor's garden, she thought of many things that she must remember to tell her grandmother about this delightful day. The bees were humming in the vines, and as she looked down the wide garden-walk it seemed like the broad aisle in church, and the congregation of plants and bushes all looked at her as if she were in the pulpit. The church itself was not far away, and the windows were open, and sometimes Nan could hear the preacher's voice, and by and by the people began to sing, and she rose solemnly, as if it were her own parishioners in the garden who lifted up their voices. A cheerful robin began a loud solo in one of Dr. Leslie's cherry-trees, and the little girl laughed aloud in her make-believe meeting-house, and then the gate was opened and shut, and the doctor himself appeared, strolling along, and smiling as he came.

He was looking to the right and left at his flowers and trees, and once he stopped and took out his pocket knife to trim a straying branch of honeysuckle, which had wilted and died. When he came to the summer-house, he found his guest sitting there demurely with her hands folded in her lap. She had gathered some little sprigs of box and a few blossoms of periwinkle and late lilies of the valley, and they lay on the bench beside her. "So you did not go to church with Marilla?" the doctor said. "I dare say one sermon a day is enough for so small a person as you." For Nan's part, no sermon at all would have caused little sorrow, though she liked the excitement of the Sunday drive to the village. She only smiled when the doctor spoke, and gave a little sigh of satisfaction a minute afterward when he seated himself beside her.

"We must be off presently," he told her. "I have a long drive to take before night. I would let you go with me, but I am afraid I should keep you too long past your bedtime."

The little girl looked in his kind face appealingly; she could not bear to have the day come to an end. The doctor spoke to her as if she were grown up and understood everything, and this pleased her. It is very hard to be constantly reminded that one is a child, as if it were a crime against society. Dr. Leslie, unlike many others, did not like children because they were children; he now and then made friends with one, just as he added now and then to his narrow circle of grown friends. He felt a certain responsibility for this little girl, and congratulated himself upon feeling an instinctive fondness for her. The good old minister had said only that morning that love is the great motive power, that it is always easy to do things for those whom we love and wish to please, and for this reason we are taught to pray for love to God, and so conquer the difficulty of holiness. "But I must do my duty by her at any rate," the doctor told himself. "I am afraid I have forgotten the child somewhat in past years, and she is a bright little creature."

"Have you been taking good care of yourself?" he added aloud. "I was very tired, for I was out twice in the night taking care of sick people. But you must come to see me again some day. I dare say you and Marilla have made friends with each other. Now we must go, I suppose," and Nan Prince, still silent,—for the pleasure of this time was almost too great,— took hold of the doctor's outstretched hand, and they went slowly up the garden walk together. As they drove slowly down the street they met the people who were coming from church, and the child sat up very straight in the old gig, with her feet on the doctor's medicine-box, and was sure that everybody must be envying her. She thought it was more pleasant than ever that afternoon, as they passed through the open country outside the village; the fields and the trees were marvelously green, and the distant river was shining in the sun. Nan looked anxiously for the gray farm-house for two or three minutes before they came in sight of it, but at last it showed itself, standing firm on the hillside. It seemed a long time since she had left home in the morning, but this beautiful day was to be one of the landmarks of her memory. Life had suddenly grown much larger, and her familiar horizon had vanished and she discovered a great distance stretching far beyond the old limits. She went gravely into the familiar kitchen, holding fast the bits of box and the periwinkle flowers, quite ready to answer her grandmother's questions, though she was only too certain that it would be impossible to tell any one the whole dear story of that June Sunday.

A little later, as Marilla came sedately home, she noticed in the driveway some fresh hoof-marks which pointed toward the street, and quickly assured herself that they could not have been made very long before. "I wonder what the two of 'em have been doing all the afternoon?" she said to herself. "She's a little lady, that child is; and it's a burnin' shame she should be left to run wild. I never set so much by her mother's looks as some did, but growin' things has blooms as much as they have roots and prickles—and even them Thachers will flower out once in a while."

CHAPTER VI.

IN SUMMER WEATHER

One morning Dr. Leslie remembered an old patient whom he liked to go to see now and then, perhaps more from the courtesy and friendliness of the thing than from any hope of giving professional assistance. The old sailor, Captain Finch, had long before been condemned as unseaworthy, having suffered for many years from the effects of a bad fall on shipboard. He was a cheerful and wise person, and the doctor was much attached to him, besides knowing that he had borne his imprisonment with great patience, for his life on one of the most secluded farms of the region, surrounded by his wife's kinsfolk, who were all landsmen, could hardly be called anything else. The doctor had once made a voyage to Fayal[1] and from thence to England in a sailing-vessel, having been somewhat delicate in health in his younger days, and this made him a more intelligent listener to the captain's stories than was often available.

Dr. Leslie had brought his case of medicines from mere force of habit, but by way of special prescription he had taken also a generous handful of his best cigars, and wrapped them somewhat clumsily in one of the large sheets of letter-paper which lay on his study table near by. Also he had stopped before the old sideboard in the carefully darkened dining-room, and taken a bottle of wine from one of its cupboards. "This will do him more good than anything, poor old fellow," he told himself, with a sudden warmth in his own heart and a feeling of grateful pleasure because he had thought of doing the kindness.

Marilla called eagerly from the kitchen window to ask where he was going, putting her hand out hastily to part the morning-glory vines, which had climbed their strings and twisted their stems together until they shut out the world from their planter's sight. But the doctor only answered that he should be back at dinner time, and settled himself comfortably in his carriage, smiling as he thought of Marilla's displeasure. She seldom allowed a secret to escape her, if she were once fairly on the scent of it, though she grumbled now, and told herself that she only cared to know for the sake of the people who might come, or to provide against the accident of his being among the missing in case of sudden need. She found life more interesting when there was even a small mystery to be puzzled over. It was impossible for Dr. Leslie to resist teasing his faithful handmaiden once in a while, but he did it with proper gravity and respect, and their friendship was cemented by these sober jokes rather than torn apart.

The horse knew as well as his master that nothing of particular importance was in hand, and however well he always caught the spirit of the occasion when there was need for hurry, he now jogged along the road, going slowly where the trees cast a pleasant shade, and paying more attention to the flies than to anything else. The doctor seemed to be in deep thought, and old Major understood that no notice was to be taken of constant slight touches of the whip which his master held carelessly. It had been hot, dusty weather until the day and night before, when heavy showers had fallen; the country was looking fresh, and the fields and trees were washed clean at last from the white dust that had powdered them and given the farms a barren and discouraged look.

They had come in sight of Mrs. Thacher's house on its high hillside, and were just passing the abode of Mrs. Meeker, which was close by the roadside in the low land. This was a small, weather-beaten dwelling, and the pink and red hollyhocks showed themselves in fine array against its gray walls. Its mistress's prosaic nature had one most redeeming quality in her love for flowers and her gift in making them grow, and the doctor forgave her many things for the sake of the bright little garden in the midst of the sandy lands which surrounded her garden with their unshaded barrenness. The road that crossed these was hot in summer and swept by bitter winds in winter. It was like a bit of desert dropped by mistake among the green farms and spring-fed forests that covered the rest of the river uplands.

No sentinel was ever more steadfast to his duty in time of war and disorder than Mrs. Meeker, as she sat by the front window, from which she could see some distance either way along the crooked road. She was often absent from her own house to render assistance of one sort or another among her neighbors, but if she were at home it was impossible for man, woman, or child to go by without her challenge or careful inspection. She made couriers of her neighbors, and sent these errand men and women along the country roads or to the village almost daily. She was well posted in the news from both the village and the country side, and however much her acquaintances scolded about her, they found it impossible to resist the fascination of her conversation, and few declined to share in the banquet of gossip which she was always ready to spread. She was quick witted, and possessed of many resources and much cleverness of a certain sort; but it must be confessed that she had done mischief in her day, having been the murderer of more than one neighbor's peace of mind and the assailant of many a reputation. But if she were a dangerous inmate of one's household, few were so attractive or entertaining for the space of an afternoon visit, and it was usually said, when she was seen approaching, that she would be sure to have something to tell. Out in the country, where so many people can see nothing new from one week's end to the other, it is, after all, a great pleasure to have the latest particulars brought to one's door, as a townsman's newspaper is.

Mrs. Meeker knew better than to stop Dr. Leslie if he were going anywhere in a hurry; she had been taught this lesson years ago; but when she saw him journeying in such a leisurely way some instinct assured her of safety, and she came out of her door like a Jack-in-the-box, while old Major, only too ready for a halt, stood still in spite of a desperate twitch of the reins, which had as much effect as pulling at a fish-hook which has made fast to an anchor. Mrs. Meeker feigned a great excitement.

"I won't keep you but a moment," she said, "but I want to hear what you think about Mis' Thacher's chances."

"Mrs. Thacher's?" repeated the doctor, wonderingly. "She's doing well, isn't she? I don't suppose that she will ever be a young woman again."

"I don't know why, but I took it for granted that you was goin' there," explained Mrs. Meeker, humbly. "She has seemed to me as if she was failing all summer. I was up there last night, and I never said so to her, but she had aged dreadfully. I wonder if it's likely she's had a light shock?[2] Sometimes the fust one's kind o' hidden; comes by night or somethin', and folks don't know till they begins to feel the damage of it."

"She hasn't looked very well of late," said the doctor. For once in his life he was willing to have a friendly talk, Mrs. Meeker thought, and she proceeded to make the most of her opportunity.

"I think the care of that girl of Ad'line's has been too much for her all along," she announced, "she's wild as a hawk, and a perfect torment. One day she'll come strollin' in and beseechin' me for a bunch o' flowers, and the next she'll be here after dark scarin' me out o' my seven senses. She rigged a tick-tack here the other night against the window, and my heart was in my mouth. I thought 't was a warnin' much as ever I thought anything in my life; the night before my mother died 't was in that same room and against that same winder there came two or three raps, and my sister Drew and me we looked at each other, and turned cold all over, and mother set right up in bed the next night and looked at that winder and then laid back dead. I was all sole alone the other evenin',—Wednesday it was,—and when I heard them raps I mustered up, and went and put my head out o' the door, and I couldn't see nothing, and when I went back, knock—knock, it begun again, and I went to the door and harked. I hoped I should hear somebody or 'nother comin' along the road, and then I heard somethin' a rus'lin' amongst the sunflowers and hollyhocks, and then there was a titterin', and come to find out 't was that young one. I chased her up the road till my wind give out, and I had to go and set on the stone wall, and come to. She won't go to bed till she's a mind to. One

night I was up there this spring, and she never come in until after nine o'clock, a dark night, too; and the pore old lady was in
distress, and thought she'd got into the river. I says to myself
there wa'n't no such good news. She told how she'd be'n up
into Jake an' Martin's oaks, trying to catch a little screech owl.
She belongs with wild creatur's, I do believe,—just the same
natur'. She'd better be kept to school, 'stead o' growin' up this
way; but she keeps the rest o' the young ones all in a brile,[3] and
this last teacher wouldn't have her there at all. She'd toll off
half the school into the pasture at recess time, and none of 'em
would get back for half an hour."

"What's a tick-tack? I don't remember," asked the doctor,
who had been smiling now and then at this complaint.

"They tie a nail to the end of a string, and run it over a bent
pin stuck in the sash, and then they get out o' sight and pull,
and it clacks against the winder, don't ye see? Ain't it surprisin'
how them devil's tricks gets handed down from giniration to
giniration, while so much that's good is forgot," lamented Mrs.
Meeker, but the doctor looked much amused.

"She's a bright child," he said, "and not over strong. I don't
believe in keeping young folks shut up in the school-houses all
summer long."

Mrs. Meeker sniffed disapprovingly. "She's tougher than ellum roots. I believe you can't kill them peakèd-looking young
ones. She'll run like a fox all day long and live to see us all
buried. I can put up with her pranks; 't is of pore old Mis'
Thacher I'm thinkin'. She's had trouble enough without adding
on this young 'scape-gallows.[4] You had better fetch her up to be
a doctor," Mrs. Meeker smilingly continued, "I was up there
yisterday, and one of the young turkeys had come hoppin' and
quawkin' round the doorsteps with its leg broke, and she'd
caught it and fixed it off with a splint before you could say Jack
Robi'son.[5] She told how it was the way you'd done to Jim Finch
that fell from the hay-rigging[6] and broke his arm over to Jake
an' Martin's, haying time."

"I remember she was standing close by, watching everything I
did," said the doctor, his face shining with interest and pleasure. "I shall have to carry her about for clerk.[7] Her father stud-

ied medicine you know. It is the most amazing thing how people inherit"—but he did not finish his sentence and pulled the
reins so quickly that the wise horse knew there was no excuse
for not moving forward.

Mrs. Meeker had hoped for a longer interview. "Stop as you
come back, won't you?" she asked. "I'm goin' to pick you some
of the handsomest poppies I ever raised. I got the seed from my
sister-in-law's cousin, she that was 'Miry[8] Gregg, and they do
beat everything. They wilt so that it ain't no use to pick 'em
now, unless you was calc'latin' to come home by the other road.
There's nobody sick about here, is there?" to which the doctor
returned a shake of the head and the information that he should
be returning that way about noon. As he drove up the hill he assured himself with great satisfaction that he believed he hadn't
told anything that morning which would be repeated all over
town before night, while his hostess returned to her house quite
dissatisfied with the interview, though she hoped for better fortune on Dr. Leslie's return.

For his part, he drove on slowly past the Thacher farm-
house, looking carefully about him, and sending a special
glance up the lane in search of the invalid turkey. "I should like
to see how she managed it," he told himself half aloud. "If she
shows a gift for such things I'll take pains to teach her a lesson
or two by and by when she is older. . . . Come Major, don't go
to sleep on the road!" and in a few minutes the wagon was out
of sight, if the reader had stood in the Thacher lane, instead of
following the good man farther on his errand of mercy and
good fellowship.

At that time in the morning most housekeepers were busy in
their kitchens, but Mrs. Thacher came to stand in her doorway,
and shaded her forehead and eyes with her hand from the
bright sunlight, as she looked intently across the pastures toward the river. She seemed anxious and glanced to and fro
across the fields, and presently she turned quickly at the sound
of a footstep, and saw her young grand-daughter coming from
the other direction round the corner of the house. The child was
wet and a little pale, though she evidently had been running.

"What have you been doin' now?" asked the old lady fret-fully. "I won't have you gettin' up in the mornin' before I am awake and stealin' out of the house. I think you are drowned in the river or have broken your neck fallin' out of a tree. Here it is after ten o'clock. I've a mind to send you to bed, Nanny; who got you out of the water, for in it you've been sure enough?"

"I got out myself," said the little girl. "It was deep, though," and she began to cry, and when she tried to cover her eyes with her already well-soaked little apron, she felt quite broken-hearted and unnerved, and sat down dismally on the doorstep.

"Come in, and put on a dry dress," said her grandmother, not unkindly; "that is, if there's anything but your Sunday one fit to be seen. I've told you often enough not to go playin' in the river, and I've wanted you more than common to go out to Jake and Martin's to borrow me a little cinnamon. You're a real trial this summer. I believe the bigger you are the worse you are. Now just say what you've been about. I declare I shall have to go and have a talk with the doctor, and he'll scold you well. I'm gettin' old and I can't keep after you; you ought to consider me some. You'll think of it when you see me laying dead, what a misery you've be'n. No schoolin' worth namin';" grumbled Mrs. Thacher, as she stepped heavily to and fro in the kitchen, and the little girl disappeared within the bed-room. In a few minutes, however, her unusual depression was driven away by the comfort of dry garments, and she announced triumphantly that she had found a whole flock of young wild ducks, and that she had made a raft and chased them about up and down the river, until the raft had proved unseaworthy, and she had fallen through into the water. Later in the day somebody came from the Jake and Martin homesteads to say that there must be no more pulling down of the ends of the pasture fences. The nails had easily let go their hold of the old boards, and a stone had served our heroine for a useful shipwright's hammer, but the young cattle had strayed through these broken barriers and might have done great damage if they had been discovered a lit-tle later,—having quickly hied themselves to a piece of carefully cultivated land. The Jake and Martin families regarded Nan with a mixture of dread and affection. She was bringing a new element into their prosaic lives, and her pranks afforded them a bit of news almost daily. Her imagination was apt to busy itself in inventing tales of her unknown aunt, with which she entertained a grandchild of Martin Dyer, a little girl of nearly her own age. It seemed possible to Nan that any day a carriage drawn by a pair of prancing black horses might be seen turning up the lane, and that a lovely lady might alight and claim her as her only niece. Why this event had not already taken place the child never troubled herself to think, but ever since Marilla had spoken of this aunt's existence, the dreams of her had been growing longer and more charming, until she seemed fit for a queen, and her unseen house a palace. Nan's playmate took pleasure in repeating these glowing accounts to her family, and many were the head-shakings and evil forebodings over the untruthfulness of the heroine of this story. Little Susan Dyer's only aunt, who was well known to her, lived as other people did in a comparatively plain and humble house, and it was not to be wondered at that she objected to hearing continually of an aunt of such splendid fashion. And yet Nan tried over and over again to be in some degree worthy of the relationship. She must not be too unfit to enter upon more brilliant surroundings whenever the time should come,—she took care that her pet chickens and her one doll should have high-sounding names, such as would seem proper to the aunt, and, more than this, she took a careful survey of the house whenever she was coming home from school or from play, lest she might come upon her distinguished relative unawares. She had asked her grandmother more than once to tell her about this mysterious kinswoman, but Mrs. Thacher proved strangely uncommunicative, fearing if she answered one easy question it might involve others that were more difficult.

The good woman grew more and more anxious to fulfil her duty to this troublesome young housemate; the child was strangely dear and companionable in spite of her frequent naughtiness. It seemed, too, as if she could do whatever she undertook, and as if she had a power which made her able to use and unite the best traits of her ancestors, the strong capabilities which had been illy balanced or allowed to run to waste in others. It might be said that the materials for a fine specimen of humanity accumulate through several generations, until a child appears who is the heir of all the family wit and attractiveness and common sense, just as one person may inherit the worldly wealth of his ancestry.

CHAPTER VII.

FOR THE YEARS TO COME

Late one summer afternoon Dr. Leslie was waked from an unusually long after-dinner nap by Marilla's footsteps along the hall. She remained standing in the doorway, looking at him for a provoking length of time, and finally sneezed in her most obtrusive and violent manner. At this he sat up quickly and demanded to be told what was the matter, adding that he had been out half the night before, which was no news to the faithful housekeeper.

"There, I'm sure I didn't mean to wake you up," she said, with an apparent lack of self-reproach. "I never can tell whether you are asleep or only kind of drowsin'. There was a boy here just now from old Mis' Cunningham's over on the b'ilin' spring road. They want you to come over quick as convenient. She don't know nothin', the boy said."

"Never did," grumbled the doctor. "I'll go, toward night, but I can't do her any good."

"An' Mis' Thacher is out here waitin' too, but she says if you're busy she'll go along to the stores and stop as she comes back. She looks to me as if she was breakin' up," confided Marilla in a lower tone.

"Tell her I'm ready now," answered the doctor in a more cordial tone, and though he said half to himself and half to Marilla that here was another person who expected him to cure old age, he spoke compassionately, and as if his heart were heavy with the thought of human sorrow and suffering. But he greeted Mrs. Thacher most cheerfully, and joked about Marilla's fear of a fly, as he threw open the blinds of the study window which was best shaded from the sun.

Mrs. Thacher did indeed look changed, and the physician's quick eyes took note of it, and, as he gathered up some letters and newspapers which had been strewn about just after dinner, he said kindly that he hoped she had no need of a doctor. It was plain that the occasion seemed an uncommon one to her. She wore her best clothes, which would not have been necessary for one of her usual business trips to the village, and it seemed to be difficult for her to begin her story. Dr. Leslie, taking a purely professional view of the case, began to consider what form of tonic would be most suitable, whether she had come to ask for one or not.

"I want to have a good talk with you about the little gell; Nanny, you know;" she said at last, and the doctor nodded, and, explaining that there seemed to be a good deal of draught through the room, crossed the floor and gently shut the door which opened into the hall. He smiled a little as he did it, having heard the long breath outside which was the not unfamiliar signal of Marilla's presence. If she were curious, she was a discreet keeper of secrets, and the doctor had more than once indulged her in her sinful listening by way of friendliness and reward. But this subject promised to concern his own affairs too closely, and he became wary of the presence of another pair of ears. He was naturally a man of uncommon reserve, and most loyal in keeping his patients' secrets. If clergymen knew their congregations as well as physicians do, the sermons would be often more closely related to the parish needs. It was difficult for the world to understand why, when Dr. Leslie was anything but prone to gossip, Marilla should have been possessed of such a wealth of knowledge of her neighbors' affairs. Strange to say this wealth was for her own miserly pleasure and not to be distributed, and while she often proclaimed with exasperating triumph that she had known for months some truth just discovered by others, she was regarded by her acquaintances as if she were a dictionary written in some foreign language; immensely valuable, but of no practical use to themselves. It was sometimes difficult not to make an attempt to borrow from her store of news, but nothing delighted her more than to be so approached, and to present impenetrable barriers of discretion to the enemy.

"How is Nanny getting on?" the doctor asked. "She looks stronger than she did a year ago."

"Dear me, she's wild as ever," answered Mrs. Thacher, trying to smile; "but I've been distressed about her lately, night and day. I thought perhaps I might see you going by. She's gettin' to be a great girl, doctor, and I ain't fit to cope with her. I find my strength's a-goin', and I'm old before my time; all my folks was rugged and sound long past my age, but I've had my troubles,—you don't need I should tell you that! Poor Ad'line always give me a feelin' as if I was a hen that has hatched ducks. I never knew exactly how to do for her, she seemed to see everything so different, and Lord only knows how I worry about her, and al'ays did, thinkin' if I'd seen clearer how to do my duty her life might have come out sort of better. And it's the same with little Anna; not that she's so prone to evil as some; she's a lovin'-hearted child if ever one was born, but she's a piece o' mischief; and it may come from her father's folks and their ways o' livin', but she's made o' different stuff, and I ain't fit to make answer for her, or for fetchin' of her up. I come to ask if you won't kindly advise what's best for her. I do' know 's anything's got to be done for a good spell yet. I mind what you say about lettin' her run and git strong, and I don't check her. Only it seemed to me that you might want to speak about her sometimes and not do it for fear o' wronging my judgment. I declare I haven't no judgment about what's reasonable for her, and you're her guardeen, and there's the money her father's sister has sent her; 't would burn my fingers to touch a cent of it, but by and by if you think she ought to have schoolin' or anything else you must just say so."

"I think nothing better could have been done for the child than you have done," said Dr. Leslie warmly. "Don't worry yourself, my good friend. As for books, she will take to them of her own accord quite soon enough, and in such weather as this I think one day in the fields is worth five in the school-house. I'll do the best I can for her."

Mrs. Thacher's errand had not yet been told, though she fumbled in her pocket and walked to the open window to look for the neighbor's wagon by which she was to find conveyance home, before she ventured to say anything more. "I don't know 's my time'll come for some years yet," she said at length, falteringly, "but I have had it borne in upon my mind a good many ways this summer that I ain't going to stay here a gre't while. I've been troubled considerable by the same complaints that carried my mother off, and I'm built just like her. I don't feel no concern for myself, but it's goin' to leave the child without anybody of her own to look to. There's plenty will befriend her just so long as she's got means, and the old farm will sell for something besides what she's got already, but that ain't everything, and I can't seem to make up my mind to havin' of her boarded about. If 't was so your wife had lived I should know what I'd go down on my knees to her to do, but I can't ask it of you to be burdened with a young child a-growin' up."

The doctor listened patiently, though just before this he had risen and begun to fill a small bottle at the closet shelves, which were stocked close to their perilous edges with various drugs.[1] Without turning to look at his patient he said, "I wish you would take five or six drops of this three times a day, and let me see you again within a week or two." And while the troubled woman turned to look at him with half-surprise, he added, "Don't give yourself another thought about little Nan. If anything should happen to you, I shall be glad to bring her here, and to take care of her as if she were my own. I always have liked her, and it will be as good for me as for her. I would not promise it for any other child, but if you had not spoken to-day, I should have found a way to arrange with you the first chance that came. But I'm getting to be an old fellow myself," he laughed. "I suppose if I get through first[2] you will be friendly to Marilla?" and Mrs. Thacher let a faint sunbeam of a smile shine out from the depths of the handkerchief with which she was trying to stop a great shower of tears. Marilla was not without her little vanities, and being thought youthful was one of the chief desires of her heart.

So Mrs. Thacher went away lighter hearted than she came.

She asked the price of the vial of medicine, and was answered that they would talk about that another time; then there was a little sober joking about certain patients who never paid their doctor's bills at all because of a superstition that they would immediately require his aid again.[3] Dr. Leslie stood in his study doorway and watched her drive down the street with Martin Dyer. It seemed to him only a year or two since both the man and woman had been strong and vigorous; now they both looked shrunken, and there was a wornness and feebleness about the bodies which had done such good service. "Come and go," said the doctor to himself, "one generation after another. Getting old! all the good old-fashioned people on the farms; I never shall care so much to be at the beck and call of their grandchildren, but I must mend up these old folks and do the best I can for them as long as they stay; they're good friends to me. Dear me, how it used to fret me when I was younger to hear them always talking about old Doctor Wayland and what he used to do; and here I am the old doctor myself!" And then he went down the gravel walk toward the stable with a quick, firm step, which many a younger man might have envied, to ask for a horse. "You may saddle him," he directed. "I am only going to old Mrs. Cunningham's, and it is a cool afternoon."

Dr. Leslie had ridden less and less every year of his practice; but, for some reason best known to himself, he went down the village street at a mad pace. Indeed, almost everybody who saw him felt that it was important to go to the next house to ask if it were known for what accident or desperate emergency he had been called away.

CHAPTER VIII.

A GREAT CHANGE

Until the autumn of this year, life had seemed to flow in one steady, unchanging current. The thought had not entered little Nan Prince's head that changes might be in store for her, for, ever since she could remember, the events of life had followed each other quietly, and except for the differences in every-day work and play, caused by the succession of the seasons, she was not called upon to accommodate herself to new conditions. It was a gentle change at first: as the days grew shorter and the house and cellar were being made ready for winter, her grandmother seemed to have much more to do than usual, and Nan must stay at home to help. She was growing older at any rate; she knew how to help better than she used; she was anxious to show her grandmother how well she could work, and as the river side and the windy pastures grew less hospitable, she did not notice that she was no longer encouraged to go out to play for hours together to amuse herself as best she might, and at any rate keep out of the way. It seemed natural enough now that she should stay in the house, and be entrusted with some regular part of the business of keeping it. For some time Mrs. Thacher had kept but one cow, and early in November, after a good offer for old Brindle had been accepted, it was announced to Nan's surprise that the young cow which was to be Brindle's successor need not be bought until spring; she would be a great care in winter time, and Nan was to bring a quart of milk a day from Jake and Martin's. This did not seem an unpleasant duty while the mild weather lasted; if there came a rainy day, one of the kind neighbors would leave the little pail on his way to the village before the young messenger had started out.

Nan could not exactly understand at last why Mrs. Jake and Mrs. Martin always asked about her grandmother every morning with so much interest and curiosity, or why they came oftener and oftener to help with the heavy work. Mrs. Thacher had never before minded her occasional illnesses so much, and some time passed before Nan's inexperienced eyes and fearless young heart understood that the whole atmosphere which overhung the landscape of her life had somehow changed, that another winter approached full of mystery and strangeness and discomfort of mind, and at last a great storm was almost ready to break into the shelter and comfort of her simple life. Poor Nan! She could not think what it all meant. She was asked many a distressing question, and openly pitied, and heard her future discussed, as if her world might come to an end any day. The doctor had visited her grandmother from time to time, but always while she was at school, until vacation came, and poor Mrs. Thacher grew too feeble to enter into even a part of the usual business of the farm-house.

One morning, as Nan was coming back from the Dyer farm with the milk, she met Mrs. Meeker in the highway. This neighbor and our heroine were rarely on good terms with each other, since Nan had usually laid herself under some serious charge of wrong-doing, and had come to believe that she would be disapproved in any event, and so might enjoy life as she chose, and revel in harmless malice.

The child could not have told why she shrank from meeting her enemy so much more than usual, and tried to discover some refuge or chance for escape; but, as it was an open bit of the road, and a straight way to the lane, she could have no excuse for scrambling over the stone wall and cutting short the distance. However, her second thought scorned the idea of running away in such cowardly fashion, and not having any recent misdemeanor on her conscience, she went forward unflinchingly.

Mrs. Meeker's tone was not one of complaint, but of pity, and insinuating friendliness. "How's your grandma to-day?" she asked, and Nan, with an unsympathetic answer of "About the same," stepped bravely forward, resenting with all her young soul the discovery that Mrs. Meeker had turned and was walking alongside.

"She's been a good, kind grandma to you, hain't she?" said this unwelcome companion, and when Nan had returned a wondering but almost inaudible assent, she continued, "She'll be a great loss to you, I can tell you. You'll never find nobody to do for you like her. There, you won't realize nothing about it till you've got older 'n you be now; but the time'll come when"— and her sharp voice faltered; for Nan had turned to look full in her face, had stopped still in the frozen road, dropped the pail unconsciously and given a little cry, and in another moment was running as a chased wild creature does toward the refuge of its nest. The doctor's horse was fastened at the head of the lane, and Nan knew at last, what any one in the neighborhood could have told her many days before, that her grandmother was going to die. Mrs. Meeker stared after her with a grieved sense of the abrupt ending of the coveted interview, then she recovered her self-possession, and, picking up the forsaken pail, stepped lightly over the ruts and frozen puddles, following Nan eagerly in the hope of witnessing more of such extraordinary behavior, and with the design of offering her services as watcher[1] or nurse in these last hours. At any rate the pail and the milk, which had not been spilt, could not be left in the road.

So the first chapter of the child's life was ended in the early winter weather. There was a new unsheltered grave on the slope above the river, the farm-house door was shut and locked, and the light was out in the kitchen window. It had been a landmark to those who were used to driving along the road by night, and there were sincere mourners for the kindly woman who had kept a simple faith and uprightness all through her long life of trouble and disappointment. Nan and the cat had gone to live in the village, and both, being young, had taken the change with serenity; though at first a piteous sorrow had been waked in the child's heart, a keen and dreadful fear of the future. The past seemed so secure and pleasant, as she looked back, and now she was in the power of a fateful future which had begun with something like a whirlwind that had swept over her, leaving nothing unchanged. It seemed to her that this was to be incessant, and that being grown up was to be at the mercy of sorrow and uncertainty. She was pale and quiet during her last days in the old home, answering questions and obeying directions mechanically; but usually sitting in the least visited part of the kitchen, watching the neighbors as they examined her grandmother's possessions, and properly disposed of the contents of the house. Sometimes a spark flew from her sad and angry eyes, but she made no trouble, and seemed dull and indifferent. Late in the evening Dr. Leslie carried her home with him through the first heavy snow-storm of the year, and between the excitement of being covered from the fast-falling flakes, and so making a journey in the dark, and of keeping hold of the basket which contained the enraged kitten, the grief at leaving home was not dwelt upon.

When she had been unwound from one of the doctor's great cloaks, and her eyes had grown used to the bright light in the dining-room, and Marilla had said that supper had been waiting half an hour, and she did not know how she should get along with a black cat, and then bustled about talking much faster than usual, because the sight of the lonely child had made her ready to cry, Nan began to feel comforted. It seemed a great while ago that she had cried at her grandmother's funeral. If this were the future it was certainly very welcome and already very dear, and the time of distress was like a night of bad dreams between two pleasant days.

It will easily be understood that no great change was made in Dr. Leslie's house. The doctor himself and Marilla were both well settled in their habits, and while they cordially made room for the little girl who was to be the third member of the household, her coming made little difference to either of her elders. There was a great deal of illness that winter, and the doctor was more than commonly busy; Nan was sent to school, and discovered the delight of reading one stormy day when her guardian had given her leave to stay at home, and she had found his own old copy of Robinson Crusoe[2] looking most friendly

and inviting in a corner of one of the study shelves. As for
school, she had never liked it, and the village school gave her far
greater misery than the weather-beaten building at the cross-
roads[3] ever had done. She had known many of the village children by sight, from seeing them in church, but she did not
number many friends among them, even after the winter was
nearly gone and the days began to grow brighter and less cold,
and the out-of-door games were a source of great merriment in
the playground. Nan's ideas of life were quite unlike those held
by these new acquaintances, and she could not gain the least interest in most of the other children, though she grew fond of
one boy who was a famous rover and fisherman, and after one
of the elder girls had read a composition which fired our heroine's imagination, she worshiped this superior being from a
suitable distance, and was her willing adorer and slave. The
composition was upon The Moon, and when the author proclaimed the fact that this was the same moon which had looked
down upon Abraham, Isaac, and Jacob, little Nan's eyes had
opened wide with reverence and awe, and she opened the doors
of her heart and soul to lofty thought and high imagination.
The big girl, who sat in the back seat and glibly recited amazing lessons in history, and did sums which entirely covered the
one small blackboard, was not unmindful of Nan's admiration,
and stolidly accepted and munched the offerings of cracked
nuts, or of the treasured English apples which had been brought
from the farm and kept like a squirrel's hoard in an archway of
the cellar by themselves. Nan cherished an idea of going back
to the farm to live by herself as soon as she grew a little older,
and she indulged in pleasing day-dreams of a most charming
life there, with frequent entertainments for her friends, at
which the author of the information about the moon would be
the favored guest, and Nan herself, in a most childish and
provincial fashion, the reigning queen. What did these new
town-acquaintances know of the strawberries which grew in
the bit of meadow, or the great high-bush blackberries by one
of the pasture walls, and what would their pleasure be when
they were taken down the river some moonlight night and
caught sight of a fire blazing on a distant bank, and went

nearer to find a sumptuous feast which Nan herself had arranged? She had been told that her aunt—that mysterious and beneficent aunt—had already sent her money which was lying idle in the bank until she should need to spend it, and her imaginary riches increased week by week, while her horizon of future happiness constantly grew wider.

The other children were not unwilling at first to enter upon an inquisitive friendship with the new-comer; but Marilla was so uncongenial to the noisy visitors, and so fastidious in the matter of snowy and muddy shoes, that she was soon avoided. Nan herself was a teachable child and gave little trouble, and Marilla sometimes congratulated herself because she had reserved the violent objections which had occurred to her mind when the doctor had announced, just before Mrs. Thacher's death, that his ward would henceforth find a home in his house.

Marilla usually sat in the dining-room in the evening, though she was apt to visit the study occasionally, knitting in hand, to give her opinions, or to acquaint herself with various events of which she thought the doctor would be likely to have knowledge. Sometimes in the colder winter nights, she drew a convenient light-stand close beside the kitchen stove and refused to wander far from such comfortable warmth. Now that she had Nan's busy feet to cover, there was less danger than ever that she should be left without knitting-work, and she deeply enjoyed the child's company, since Nan could give innocent answers to many questions which could never be put to elder members of the Dyer and Thacher neighborhood. Mrs. Meeker was apt to be discussed with great freedom, and Nan told long stories about her own childish experiences, which were listened to and encouraged, and matched with others even longer and more circumstantial by Marilla. The doctor, who was always reading when he could find a quiet hour for himself, often smiled as he heard the steady sound of voices from the wide kitchen, and he more than once took a few careful steps into the dining-room, and stood there shaking with laughter at the character of the conversation. Nan, though eager to learn, and curious about many things in life and nature, at first found her school lessons difficult, and sometimes came appealingly to him

for assistance, when circumstances had made a temporary ending of her total indifference to getting the lessons at all. For this
and other reasons she sometimes sought the study, and drew a
small chair beside the doctor's large one before the blazing fire
of the black birch logs; and then Marilla in her turn would venture upon the neutral ground between study and kitchen, and
smile with satisfaction at the cheerful companionship of the
tired man and the idle little girl who had already found her way
to his lonely heart. Nan had come to another home; there was
no question about what should be done with her and for her,
but she was made free of the silent old house, and went on
growing taller, and growing dearer, and growing happier day
by day. Whatever the future might bring, she would be sure to
look back with love and longing to the first summer of her village life, when, seeing that she looked pale and drooping, the
doctor, to her intense gratification, took her away from school.
Presently, instead of having a ride out into the country as an occasional favor, she might be seen every day by the doctor's side,
as if he could not make his morning rounds without her; and in
and out of the farm-houses she went, following him like a little
dog, or, as Marilla scornfully expressed it, a briar at his heels;[4]
sitting soberly by when he dealt his medicines and gave advice,
listening to his wise and merry talk with some, and his helpful
advice and consolation to others of the country people. Many
of these acquaintances treated Nan with great kindness; she
half belonged to them, and was deeply interesting for the sake
of her other ties of blood and bonds of fortune, while she took
their courtesy with thankfulness, and their lack of notice with
composure. If there were a shiny apple offered she was glad,
but if not, she did not miss it, since her chief delight was in being the doctor's assistant and attendant, and her eyes were always watching for chances when she might be of use. And one
day, coming out from a bedroom, the doctor discovered, to his
amusement, that her quick and careful fingers had folded the
papers of some powders which he had left unfolded on the
table. As they drove home together in the bright noon sunshine,
he said, as if the question were asked for the sake of joking a
little, "What are you going to do when you grow up, Nan?" to

which she answered gravely, as if it were the one great question of her life, "I should like best to be a doctor." Strangely enough there flitted through the doctor's mind a remembrance of the day when he had talked with Mrs. Meeker, and had looked up the lane to see the unlucky turkey whose leg had been put into splints. He had wished more than once that he had taken pains to see how the child had managed it; but old Mrs. Thacher had reported the case to have been at least partially successful.

Nan had stolen a look at her companion after the answer had been given, but had been pleased and comforted to find that he was not laughing at her, and at once began a lively picture of becoming famous in her chosen profession, and the valued partner of Dr. Leslie, whose skill everybody praised so heartily. He should not go out at night, and she would help him so much that he would wonder how he ever had been able to manage his wide-spread practice alone. It was a matter of no concern to her that Marilla had laughed when she had been told of Nan's intentions, and had spoken disrespectfully of women doctors; and the child's heart was full of pride and hope. The doctor stopped his horse suddenly to show Nan some flowers which grew at the roadside, some brilliant cardinals, and she climbed quickly down to gather them. There was an unwritten law that they should keep watch, one to the right hand, and the other to the left, and such treasures of blossoms or wild fruit seldom escaped Nan's vision.[5] Now she felt as if she had been wrong to let her thoughts go wandering, and her cheeks were almost as bright as the scarlet flowers themselves, as she clambered back to the wagon seat. But the doctor was in deep thought, and had nothing more to say for the next mile or two. It had become like a bad-case day suddenly and without apparent reason; but Nan had no suspicion that she was the patient in charge whose welfare seemed to the doctor to be dependent upon his own decisions.

CHAPTER IX

AT DR. LESLIE'S

That evening Dr. Leslie made signs that he was not to be interrupted, and even shut the study doors, to which precaution he seldom resorted. He was evidently disturbed when an hour later a vigorous knocking was heard at the seldom-used front entrance, and Marilla ushered in with anything but triumph an elderly gentleman who had been his college classmate. Marilla's countenance wore a forbidding expression, and as she withdrew she took pains to shut the door between the hall and dining-room with considerable violence. It was almost never closed under ordinary circumstances, but the faithful housekeeper was impelled to express her wrath in some way, and this was the first that offered itself. Nan was sitting peacefully in the kitchen playing with her black cat and telling herself stories no doubt, and was quite unprepared for Marilla's change of temper. The bell for the Friday evening prayer-meeting was tolling its last strokes and it was Marilla's habit to attend that service. She was apt to be kept closely at home, it must be acknowledged, and this was one of her few social indulgences. Since Nan had joined the family and proved that she could be trusted with a message, she had been left in charge of the house during this coveted hour on Friday evenings.

Marilla had descended from her room arrayed for church going, but now her bonnet was pulled off as if that were the prime offender, and when the child looked wonderingly around the kitchen, she saw the bread-box brought out from the closet and put down very hard on a table, while Marilla began directly afterward to rattle at the stove.

"I'd like to say to some folks that we don't keep hotel,"

grumbled the good woman, "I wish to my heart I'd stepped right out o' the front door and gone straight to meetin' and left them there beholdin' of me. Course he hasn't had no supper, nor dinner neither like 's not, and if men are ever going to drop down on a family unexpected it's always Friday night when everything's eat up that ever was in the house. I s'pose, after I bake double quantities to-morrow mornin', he'll be drivin' off before noon-time, and treasure it up that we never have nothin' decent to set before folks. Anna, you've got to stir yourself and help, while I get the fire started up; lay one o' them big dinner napkins over the red cloth, and set a plate an' a tea-cup, for as for laying the whole table over again, I won't and I shan't. There's water to cart upstairs and the bed-room to open, but Heaven be thanked I was up there dustin' to-day, and if ever you set a mug of flowers into one o' the spare-rooms again and leave it there a week or ten days to spile, I'll speak about it to the doctor. Now you step out o' my way like a good girl. I don't know whether you or the cat's the worst for gettin' before me when I'm in a drive. I'll set him out somethin' to eat, and then I'm goin' to meetin' if the skies fall."

Nan meekly obeyed directions, and with a sense of guilt concerning the deserted posies went to hover about the study door after the plates were arranged, instead of braving further the stormy atmosphere of the kitchen. Marilla's lamp had shone in so that there had been light enough in the dining-room, but the study was quite dark except where there was one spark at the end of the doctor's half-finished cigar, which was alternately dim and bright like the revolving lantern of a lighthouse.

At that moment the smoker rose, and with his most considerate and conciliatory tone asked Marilla for the study lamp, but Nan heard, and ran on tiptoe and presently brought it in from the kitchen, holding it carefully with both hands and walking slowly. She apparently had no thought beyond her errand, but she was brimful of eagerness to see the unexpected guest; for guests were by no means frequent, and since she had really become aware of a great outside world beyond the boundaries of Oldfields she welcomed the sight of any messengers.

Dr. Leslie hastily pushed away some books from the lamp's

place; and noticing that his visitor looked at Nan with surprise, quickly explained that this little girl had come to take care of him, and bade Nan speak to Dr. Ferris. Whereupon her bravery was sorely tried, but not overcome, and afterward she sat down in her own little chair, quite prepared to be hospitable. As she heard a sound of water being poured into a pitcher in the best room upstairs, she was ready to laugh if there had been anybody to laugh with, and presently Marilla appeared at the door with the announcement that there was some tea waiting in the dining-room, after which and before anybody had thought of moving, the side gate clacked resolutely, and Marilla, looking more prim and unruffled than usual, sped forth to the enjoyment of her Friday evening privileges.

Nan followed the gentlemen to the dining-room not knowing whether she were wanted or not, but feeling quite assured when it was ascertained that neither sugar nor teaspoons had been provided. The little feast looked somewhat meagre, and the doctor spoke irreverently of his housekeeper and proceeded to abstract a jar of her best strawberry jam from the convenient store-closet, and to collect other articles of food which seemed to him to be inviting, however inappropriate to the occasion. The guest would have none of the jam, but Dr. Leslie cut a slice of the loaf of bread for himself and one for Nan, though it had already waned beyond its last quarter, and nobody knew what would happen if there were no toast at breakfast time. Marilla would never know what a waste of jam was spread upon these slices either, but she was a miser only with the best preserves, and so our friends reveled in their stolen pleasure, and were as merry together as heart could wish.

Nan thought it very strange when she found that the doctor and his guest had been at school together, for the stranger seemed so old and worn. They were talking about other classmates at first, and she sat still to listen, until the hour of Marilla's return drew near and Dr. Leslie prudently returned to his own uninvaded apartment. Nan was told, to her sorrow, that it was past her bedtime and as she stopped to say good-night, candle in hand, a few moments afterward, the doctor stooped to kiss her with unusual tenderness, and a little later, when she was safe in her small bedroom and under the coverlet which was Marilla's glory, having been knit the winter before in an intricate pattern, she almost shook with fear at the sound of its maker's vengeful footsteps in the lower room. It is to be hoped that the influence of the meeting had been very good, and that one of its attendants had come home equal to great demands upon her fortitude and patience. Nan could not help wishing she had thought to put away the jam, and she wondered how Marilla would treat them all in the morning. But, to do that worthy woman justice, she was mild and considerate, and outdid herself in the breakfast that was set forth in the guest's honor, and Dr. Ferris thought he could do no less than to add to his morning greeting the question why she was not growing old like the rest of them, which, though not answered, was pleasantly received.

The host and guest talked very late the night before, and told each other many things. Dr. Leslie had somewhat unwillingly undertaken the country practice which had grown dearer to him with every year, but there were family reasons why he had decided to stay in Oldfields for a few months at least, and though it was not long before he was left alone, not only by the father and mother whose only child he was, but by his wife and child, he felt less and less inclination to break the old ties and transplant himself to some more prominent position of the medical world. The leisure he often had at certain seasons of the year was spent in the studies which always delighted him, and little by little he gained great repute among his professional brethren. He was a scholar and a thinker in other than medical philosophies, and most persons who knew anything of him thought it a pity that he should be burying himself alive, as they were pleased to term his devotion to his provincial life. His rare excursions to the cities gave more pleasure to other men than to himself, however, in these later years, and he laughingly proclaimed himself to be growing rusty and behind the times to Dr. Ferris, who smiled indulgently, and did not take the trouble to contradict so untrue and preposterous an assertion.

If one man had been a stayer at home; a vegetable nature, as Dr. Leslie had gone on to say, which has no power to change its locality or to better itself by choosing another and more adequate or stimulating soil; the other had developed the opposite extreme of character, being by nature a rover. From the medical school he had entered at once upon the duties of a naval appointment, and after he had become impatient of its routine of practice and its check upon his freedom, he had gone, always with some sufficient and useful object, to one far country after another. Lately he had spent an unusual number of consecutive months in Japan, which was still unfamiliar even to most professional travelers,[1] and he had come back to America enthusiastic and full of plans for many enterprises which his shrewd, but not very persistent brain had conceived. The two old friends were delighted to see each other, but they took this long-deferred meeting as calmly as if they were always next-door neighbors. It was a most interesting thing that while they led such different lives and took such apparently antagonistic routes of progression, they were pretty sure to arrive at the same conclusion, though it might appear otherwise to a listener who knew them both slightly.

"And who is the little girl?" asked Dr. Ferris, who had refused his entertainer's cigars and produced a pipe from one pocket, after having drawn a handful of curious small jade figures from another and pushed them along the edge of the study table, without comment, for his friend to look at. Some of them were so finely carved that they looked like a heap of grotesque insects struggling together as they lay there, but though Dr. Leslie's eyes brightened as he glanced at them, he gave no other sign of interest at that time, and answered his guest's question instead.

"She is a ward of mine," he said; "she was left quite alone by the death of her grandmother some months ago, and so I brought her here."

"It isn't often that I forget a face," said Dr. Ferris, "but I have been trying to think what association I can possibly have with that child. I remember at last; she looks like a young assistant surgeon who was on the old frigate Fortune with me just before I left the service. I don't think he was from this part of the country though; I never heard what became of him."

"I dare say it was her father; I believe he made a voyage or two," said Dr. Leslie, much interested. "Do you know anything more about him? you always remember everything, Ferris."

"Yes," answered the guest, slowly puffing away at his pipe. "Yes, he was a very bright fellow, with a great gift at doctoring, but he was wilful, full of queer twists and fancies, the marry in haste and repent at his leisure[2] sort of young man."

"Exactly what he did, I suppose," interrupted the host. "Only his leisure was fortunately postponed to the next world, for the most part; he died very young."

"I used to think it a great pity that he had not settled himself ashore in a good city practice," continued Dr. Ferris. "He had a great knack at pleasing people and making friends, and he was always spoiling for want of work. I was ready enough to shirk my part of that, you may be sure, but if you start with a reasonably healthy set of men, crew and officers, and keep good discipline, and have no accidents on the voyage, an old-fashioned ship-master's kit of numbered doses is as good as anything on board a man-of-war[3] in time of peace. You have mild cases that result from over-heating or over-eating, and sometimes a damaged finger to dress, or a tooth to pull. I used to tell young Prince that it was a pity one of the men wouldn't let himself be chopped to pieces and fitted together again to give us a little amusement."

"That's the name," announced Nan's guardian with great satisfaction. "This is a very small world; we are all within hail of each other. I dare say when we get to Heaven there will not be a stranger to make friends with."

"I could give you more wonderful proofs of that than you would be likely to believe," responded the surgeon. "But tell me how you happened to have anything to do with the child; did Prince wander into this neighborhood?"

"Not exactly, but he fell in love with a young girl who was brought up on one of the farms just out of the village. She was a strange character, a handsome creature, with a touch of foolish ambition, and soon grew impatient of the routine of home life. I believe that she went away at first to work in one of the factories in Lowell,[4] and afterward she drifted to Dunport, where young Prince's people lived, and I dare say it was when he came home from that very voyage you knew of that he saw her and married her. She worked in a dressmaker's shop, and worked very well too, but she had offended his sister to begin with, one day when she was finding fault with some work that had been done for her, and so there was no end of trouble, and the young man had a great battle at home, and the more he was fought the less inclined he was to yield, and at last off he went to be married, and never came home again until he died. It was a wretched story; he only lived two years, and they went from one place to another, and finally the end came in some Western town. He had not been happy with his wife, and they quarreled from time to time, and he asked to be brought back to Dunport and buried. This child was only a baby, and the Princes begged her mother to give her up, and used every means to try to make friends, and to do what was right. But I have always thought there was blame on both sides. At any rate the wife was insolent and unruly, and went flinging out of the house as soon as the funeral was over. I don't know what became of them for a while, but it always seemed to me as if poor Adeline must have had a touch of insanity, which faded away as consumption developed itself. Her mother's people were a fine, honest race, self-reliant and energetic, but there is a very bad streak on the other side. I have heard that she was seen begging somewhere, but I am not sure that it is true; at any rate she would neither come here to her own home nor listen to any plea from her husband's family, and at last came back to the farm one night like a ghost, carrying the child in her arms across the fields; all in rags and tatters, both of them. She confessed to me that she had meant to drown herself and little Nan together. I could never understand why she went down so fast. I know that she had been drinking. Some people might say that it was the scorn of her husband's relatives, but that is all nonsense, and I have no doubt she and the young man might have done very well if this hadn't spoiled all their chances at the outset. She was quite unbalanced and a strange, wild creature, very handsome in her girlhood, but morally undeveloped. It was impossible not to have a liking for her. I remember her when she was a baby."

"And yet people talk about the prosaic New England life!" exclaimed Dr. Ferris. "I wonder where I could match such a story as that, though I dare say that you know a dozen others. I tell you, Leslie, that for intense, self-centred, smouldering volcanoes of humanity, New England cannot be matched the world over. It's like the regions in Iceland that are full of geysers.[5] I don't know whether it is the inheritance from those people who broke away from the old countries, and who ought to be matched to tremendous circumstances of life, but now and then there comes an amazingly explosive and uncontrollable temperament that goes all to pieces from its own conservation and accumulation of force. By and by you will have all blown up,—you quiet descendants of the Pilgrims and Puritans, and have let off your superfluous wickedness like blizzards; and when the blizzards of each family have spent themselves you will grow dull and sober, and all on a level, and be free from the troubles of a transition state. Now, you're neither a new country nor an old one. You ought to see something of the older civilizations to understand what peace of mind is. Unless some importation of explosive material from the westward stirs them up, one century is made the pattern for the next. But it is perfectly wonderful what this climate does for people who come to it,—a south of Ireland fellow, for instance, who has let himself be rained on and then waited for the sun to dry him again, and has grubbed a little in a bit of ground, just enough to hint to it that it had better be making a crop of potatoes for him. I always expect to see the gorse and daisies growing on the old people's heads to match the cabins. But they come over here and forget their idleness, and in a week or two the east winds are making them work, and thrashing them if they are slow, worse than any slave-driver who ever cracked his whip-lash.[6] I wonder how you stand it; I do, indeed! I can't take an afternoon nap or have my coffee in bed of a morning without thinking I must put into port at the next church to be preached at."

Dr. Leslie laughed a little and shook his head gently. "It's very well for you to talk, Ferris," he said, "since you have done more work than any man I know. And I find this neighborhood entirely placid; one bit of news will last us a fortnight. I dare say Marilla will let everybody know that you have come to town, and have explained why she was ten minutes late, even to the minister."

"How about the little girl herself?" asked the guest presently; "she seems well combined, and likely,⁷ as they used to say when I was a boy."

Dr. Leslie resumed the subject willingly: "So far as I can see, she has the good qualities of all her ancestors without the bad ones. Her mother's mother was an old fashioned country woman of the best stock. Of course she resented what she believed to be her daughter's wrongs, and refused to have anything to do with her son-in-law's family, and kept the child as carefully as possible from any knowledge of them. Little Nan was not strong at first, but I insisted that she should be allowed to run free out of doors. It seems to me that up to seven or eight years of age children are simply bundles of inheritances, and I can see the traits of one ancestor after another; but a little later than the usual time she began to assert her own individuality, and has grown capitally well in mind and body ever since. There is an amusing trace of the provincial self-reliance and self-respect and farmer-like dignity, added to a quick instinct, and tact and ready courtesy, which must have come from the other side of her ancestry. She is more a child of the soil than any country child I know, and yet she would not put a city household to shame. She has seen nothing of the world of course, but you can see she isn't like the usual village school-girl. There is one thing quite remarkable. I believe she has grown up as naturally as a plant grows, not having been clipped back or forced in any unnatural direction. If ever a human being were untrammeled and left alone to see what will come of it, it is this child. And I will own I am very much interested to see what will appear later."

The navy surgeon's eyes twinkled at this enthusiasm, but he asked soberly what seemed to be our heroine's bent, so far as could be discovered, and laughed outright when he was gravely told that it was a medical bent; a surprising understanding of things pertaining to that most delightful profession.

"But you surely don't mean to let her risk her happiness in

following that career?" Dr. Ferris inquired with feigned anxiety for his answer. "You surely aren't going to sacrifice that innocent creature to a theory! I know it's a theory; last time I was here, you could think of nothing but hypnotism[8] or else the action of belladonna in congestion and inflammation of the brain;"[9] and he left his very comfortable chair suddenly, with a burst of laughter, and began to walk up and down the room. "She has no relatives to protect her, and I consider it a shocking case of a guardian's inhumanity. Grown up naturally indeed! I don't doubt that you supplied her with Bell's 'Anatomy'[10] for a picture-book and made her say over the names of the eight little bones of her wrist, instead of 'This little pig went to market.' "

"I only hope that you'll live to grow up yourself, Ferris," said his entertainer, "you'll certainly be an ornament to your generation. What a boy you are! I should think you would feel as old as Methuselah by this time, after having rattled from one place to the next all these years. Don't you begin to get tired?"

"No, I don't believe I do," replied Dr. Ferris, lending himself to this new turn of the conversation, but not half satisfied with the number of his jokes. "I used to be afraid I should, and so I tried to see everything I could of the world before my enthusiasm began to cool. And as for rattling to the next place, as you say, you show yourself to be no traveler by nature, or you wouldn't speak so slightingly. It is extremely dangerous to make long halts. I could cry with homesickness at the thought of the towns I have spent more than a month in; they are like the people one knows; if you see them once, you go away satisfied, and you can bring them to mind afterward, and think how they looked or just where it was you met them,—out of doors or at the club. But if you live with those people, and get fond of them, and have a thousand things to remember, you get more pain than pleasure out of it when you go away. And one can't be everywhere at once, so if you're going to care for things tremendously, you had better stay in one town altogether. No, give me a week or two, and then I've something calling me to the next place; somebody to talk with or a book to see, and off I go. Yet, I've done a good bit of work in my day after all. Did you see that paper of mine in the 'Lancet' about some ex periments I made when I was last in India with those tree-growing jugglers?[11] and I worked out some curious things about the mathematics of music on this last voyage home! Why, I thought it would tear my heart in two when I came away. I should have grown to look like the people, and you might have happened to find a likeness of me on a tea plate[12] after another year or two. I made all my plans one day to stay another winter, and next day at eleven o'clock I was steaming down the harbor. But there was a poor young lad I had taken a liking for, an English boy, who was badly off after an accident and needed somebody to look after him. I thought the best thing I could do was to bring him home. Are you going to fit your ward for general practice or for a specialty?"[13]

"I don't know; that'll be for the young person herself to decide," said Dr. Leslie good-humoredly. "But she's showing a real talent for medical matters. It is quite unconscious for the most part, but I find that she understands a good deal already, and she sat here all the afternoon last week with one of my old medical dictionaries. I couldn't help looking over her shoulder as I went by, and she was reading about fevers, if you please, as if it were a story-book. I didn't think it was worth while to tell her we understood things better nowadays, and didn't think it best to bleed as much as old Dr. Rush recommended."[14]

"You're like a hen with one chicken,[15] Leslie," said the friend, still pacing to and fro. "But seriously, I like your notion of her having come to this of her own accord. Most of us are grown in the shapes that society and family preference and prejudice fasten us into, and don't find out until we are well toward middle life that we should have done a great deal better at something else. Our vocations are likely enough to be illy chosen, since few persons are fit to choose them for us, and we are at the most unreasonable stage of life when we choose them for ourselves. And what the Lord made some people for, nobody ever can understand; some of us are for use and more are for waste, like the flowers. I am in such a hurry to know what the next world is like that I can hardly wait to get to it. Good heavens! we live here in our familiar fashion, going at a jog-trot pace round our little circles, with only a friend or two to speak with who understand us, and a pipe and a jack-knife and a few books and some old clothes, and please ourselves by thinking we know the universe! Not a soul of us can tell what it is that sends word to our little fingers to move themselves back and forward."

"We're sure of two things at any rate," said Dr. Leslie, "love to God and love to man. And though I have lived here all my days, I have learned some truths just as well as if I had gone about with you, or even been to the next world and come back. I have seen too many lives go to pieces, and too many dissatisfied faces, and I have heard too many sorrowful confessions from these country death-beds I have watched beside, one after another, for twenty or thirty years. And if I can help one good child to work with nature and not against it, and to follow the lines marked out for her, and she turns out useful and intelligent, and keeps off the rocks of mistaking her duty, I shall be more than glad. I don't care whether it's a man's work or a woman's work; if it is hers I'm going to help her the very best way I can. I don't talk to her of course; she's much too young; but I watch her and mean to put the things in her way that she seems to reach out for and try to find. She is going to be very practical, for her hands can almost always work out her ideas already. I like to see her take hold of things, and I like to see her walk and the way she lifts her feet and puts them down again. I must say, Ferris, there is a great satisfaction in finding a human being once in a while that has some use of itself."

"You're right!" said Dr. Ferris; "but don't be disappointed when she's ten years older if she picks out a handsome young man and thinks there is nothing like housekeeping. Have you taken a look at my pocketful of heathen idols there yet? I don't think you've ever seen their mates."

The stayer at home smiled as if he understood his friend's quiet bit of pleasantry, and reached for one of the treasures, but folded it in his hand without looking at it and seemed to be lost in meditation. The surgeon concluded that he had had enough exercise and laid himself down on the wide sofa at the end of the room, from whence he could watch his companion's face. He clasped his hands under his head and looked eager and interested. He had grown to have something of the appearance of a foreigner, as people often do who have spent much time in eastern countries. The two friends were silent for some minutes, until an impatient voice roused Dr. Leslie from his reflections.

"It always makes me covet my neighbor's wits when I see you!" announced the wanderer. "If I settled myself into a respectable practice I should be obliged to march with the army of doctors who carry a great array of small weapons, and who find out what is the matter with their patients after all sorts of experiment and painstaking analysis, and comparing the results of their thermometers and microscopes with scientific books of reference. After I have done all that, you know, if I have had good luck I shall come to exactly what you can say before you have been with a sick man five minutes. You have the true gift for doctoring, you need no medical dictator, and whatever you study and whatever comes to you in the way of instruction simply ministers to your intuition. It grows to be a wonderful second-sight in such a man as you. I don't believe you investigate a case and treat it as a botanist does a strange flower, once a month. You know without telling yourself what the matter is, and what the special difference is, and the relative dangers of this case and one apparently just like it across the street, and you could do this before you were out of the hospitals.[16] I remember you!" and after a few vigorous puffs of smoke he went on; "It is all very well for the rest of the men to be proud of their book learning, but they don't even try to follow nature, as Sydenham did, who followed no man.[17] I believe such study takes one to more theory and scientific digest rather than to more skill. It is all very well to know how to draw maps when one gets lost on a dark night, or even to begin with astronomical calculations and come down to a chemical analysis of the mud you stand in, but hang me if I wouldn't rather have the instinct of a dog who can go straight home across a bit of strange country. A man has no right to be a doctor if he doesn't simply make everything bend to his work of getting sick people well, and of trying to remedy the failures of strength that come from misuse or inheritance or ignorance. The anatomists and the pathologists have their place, but we must look to the living to learn the laws of life, not to the dead.[18] A wreck shows you where the reef is, perhaps, but not how to manage a ship in the offing. The men who make it their business to write the books and the men who make it their business to follow them aren't the ones for successful practice."[19]

Dr. Leslie smiled, and looked over his shoulder at his beloved library shelves, as if he wished to assure the useful volumes of his continued affection and respect, and said quietly, as if to beg the displeased surgeon's patience with his brethren: "They go on, poor fellows, studying the symptoms and never taking it in that the life power is at fault. I see more and more plainly that we ought to strengthen and balance the whole system, and aid nature to make the sick man well again.[20] It is nature that does it after all, and diseases are oftener effects of illness than causes.[21] But the young practitioners must follow the textbooks a while until they have had enough experience to open their eyes to observe and have learned to think for themselves.[22] I don't know which is worse; too much routine or no study at all. I was trying the other day to count up the different treatments of pneumonia that have been in fashion in our day; there must be seven or eight, and I am only afraid the next thing will be a sort of skepticism and contempt of remedies.[23] Dr. Johnson said long ago that physicians were a class of men who put bodies of which they knew little into bodies of which they knew less, but certainly this isn't the fault of the medicines altogether; you and I know well enough they are often most stupidly used.[24] If we blindly follow the medical dictators, as you call them, and spend our treatment on the effects instead of the causes, what success can we expect?[25] We do want more suggestions from the men at work, but I suppose this is the same with every business. The practical medical men are the juries who settle all the theories of the hour, as they meet emergencies day after day."[26]

"The men who have the true gift for their work," said Dr. Ferris impatiently. "I hadn't the conscience to go on myself, that's why I resigned, you know. I can talk about it, but I am not a good workman. But if there are going to be doctors in the next world, I wish I might be lucky enough to be equal to such a heavenly business. You thought I didn't care enough about the profession to go on, but it wasn't so. Do push your little girl ahead if she has the real fitness. I suppose it is a part of your endowment that you can distinguish the capacities and tendencies of health as well as illness; and there's one thing certain, the world cannot afford to do without the workmen who are masters of their business by divine right."

Dr. Leslie was looking at the jade-stone gods. "I suppose the poor fellows who chipped out these treasures of yours may have thought they were really putting a visible piece of Heaven within their neighbors' reach," he said. "We can't get used to the fact that whatever truly belongs to the next world is not visible in this, and that there is idol-making and worshiping forever going on. When we let ourselves forget to educate our faith and our spiritual intellects, and lose sight of our relation and dependence upon the highest informing strength, we are trying to move our machinery by some inferior motive power. We worship our tools and beg success of them instead of remembering that we are all apprentices to the great Master of our own and every man's craft. It is the great ideas of our work that we need, and the laws of its truths. We shall be more intelligent by and by about making the best of ourselves; our possibilities are infinitely beyond what most people even dream. Spiritual laziness and physical laziness together keep us just this side of sound sleep most of the time. Perhaps you think it is a proper season for one at least?"

"Dear me, no!" said Dr. Ferris, who was evidently quite wide awake. "Do you remember how well Buckle says that the feminine intellect is the higher, and that the great geniuses of the world have possessed it? The gift of intuition reaches directly towards the truth, and it is only reasoning by deduction that can take flight into the upper air of life and certainty. You remember what he says about that?"[27]

"Yes," said Dr. Leslie. "Yes, it isn't a thing one easily forgets. But I have long believed that the powers of Christ were but the higher powers of our common humanity. We recognize them dimly now and then, but few of us dare to say so yet. The world moves very slowly, doesn't it? If Christ were perfect man, He could hardly tell us to follow Him and be like Him, and yet know all the while that it was quite impossible, because a difference in his gifts made his character an unapproachable one to ours. We don't amount to anything, simply because we won't understand that we must receive the strength of Heaven into our souls; that it depends upon our degree of receptivity, and our using the added power that comes in that way; not in our taking our few tools, and our self-esteem and satisfaction with ourselves, and doing our little tricks like dancing dogs; proud because the other dogs can do one less than we, or only bark and walk about on their four legs. It is our souls that make our bodies worth anything, and the life of the soul doesn't come from its activity, or any performance of its own. Those things are only the results and the signs of life, not the causes of it."

"Christ in us, the hope of glory,"[28] said the other doctor gravely, "and Christ's glory was his usefulness and gift for helping others; I believe there's less quackery in our profession than any other, but it is amazing how we bungle at it. I wonder how you will get on with your little girl? If people didn't have theories of life of their own, or wouldn't go exactly the wrong way, it would be easier to offer assistance; but where one person takes a right direction of his own accord, there are twenty who wander to and fro."

"I may as well confess to you," he continued presently, "that I have had a *protégé* myself, but I don't look for much future joy in watching the development of my plots. He has taken affairs into his own hands, and I dare say it is much better for him, for if I had caught him young enough, I should have wished him to run the gauntlet of all the professions, not to speak of the arts and sciences. He was a clever young fellow; I saw him married the day before I left England. His wife was the daughter of a curate, and he the younger son of a younger son, and it was a love affair worth two or three story-books. It came to be a question of money alone. I had known the boy the year before in Bombay and chanced to find him one day in the Marine Hospital at Nagasaki.[29] We had been up into the interior together. He was recommended to me as a sort of secretary and assistant and knew more than I did about most things. When he caught sight of me he cried like a baby, and I sat down and heard what the trouble was, for I had let him go off with some-body who could give him a good salary,—a government man of position, and I thought poor Bob would be put in the way of something better. Dear me, the climate was killing him before my eyes, and I took passage for both of us on the next day's steamer. When I got him home I turned my bank account into a cheque and tucked it into his pocket, and told him to marry his wife and settle down and be respectable and forget such a wan-dering old fellow as I."

The listener made a little sound of mingled admiration and disgust.

"So you're the same piece of improvidence as ever! I wonder if you worked your passage over to Boston, or came as a stow-away? Well, I'm glad to give you house-room,[30] and, to tell the truth, I was wondering how I should get on tomorrow without somebody to help me in a piece of surgery.[31] My neighbors are not very skillful, but they're good men every one of them, un-less it's old Jackson, who knows no more about the practice of medicine than a turtle knows about the nearest fixed star. Fer-ris! I don't wonder at your giving away the last cent you had in the world, I only wonder that you had a cent to give. I hope the young man was grateful, that's all, only I'm not sure I like his taking it."

"He thought I had enough more, I dare say. He said so much I couldn't stand his nonsense. He'll use it better than I could," said the guest briefly. "As I said, I couldn't bring him up; in the first place I haven't the patience, and beside, it wouldn't be just to him. But you must let me know how you get on with your project; I shall make you a day's visit once in six months."

"That'll be good luck," responded the cheerful host. "Now that I am growing old I find I wish for company oftener; just the right man, you know, to come in for an hour or two late in the evening to have a cigar, and not say a word if he doesn't feel like it."

The two friends were very comfortable together; the succes-sive cigars burnt themselves out slowly, and the light of the great lamp was bright in the room. Here and there a tinge of red shone out on the backs of the books that stood close together in the high cases. There was an old engraving or two, and in one corner a solemn bronze figure of Dante, thin and angular, as if he had risen from his coffin to take a last look at this world. Marilla had often spoken of him disrespectfully, and had suggested many other ornaments which might be brought to take his place, but the doctor had never acted upon her suggestions. From the corner of one book-case there hung a huge wasp's nest, and over the mantel-shelf, which was only wide enough for some cigar boxes and a little clock and a few vials of medicines, was a rack where three or four riding whips and a curious silver bit and some long-stemmed pipes found unmolested quarters; and in one corner were some walking sticks and a fishing rod or two which had a very ancient unused look. There was a portrait of Dr. Leslie's grandfather opposite the fireplace; a good-humored looking old gentleman who had been the most famous of the Oldfields ministers. The study-table was wide and long, but it was well covered with a miscellaneous array of its owner's smaller possessions, and the quick-eyed visitor smiled as he caught sight of Nan's new copy of Miss Edgeworth's "Parent's Assistant"[32] lying open and face downward on the top of an instrument case.

Marilla did not hear the doctor and his guest tramp up to bed until very late at night, and though she had tried to keep awake she had been obliged to take a nap first and then wake up again to get the benefit of such an aggravating occasion. "I'm not going to fret myself trying to make one of my baked omelets in the morning," she assured herself, "they'll keep breakfast waiting three quarters of an hour, and it would fall flat sure 's the world, and the doctor's got to ride to all p'ints of the compass to-morrow, too."

CHAPTER X.

ACROSS THE STREET

It would be difficult to say why the village of Oldfields should have been placed in the least attractive part of the township, if one were not somewhat familiar with the law of growth of country communities. The first settlers, being pious kindred of the Pilgrims, were mindful of the necessity of a meeting-house,[1] and the place for it was chosen with reference to the convenience of most of the worshipers. Then the parson was given a parsonage and a tract of glebe land[2] somewhere in the vicinity of his pulpit, and since this was the centre of social attraction, the blacksmith built his shop at the nearest cross-road. And when some enterprising citizen became possessed of an idea that there were traders enough toiling to and fro on the rough highways to the nearest larger village to make it worth his while to be an interceptor, the first step was taken toward a local centre of commerce, and the village was fairly begun. It had not yet reached a remarkable size, though there was a time-honored joke because an enthusiastic old woman had said once, when four or five houses and a new meeting-house were being built all in one summer, that she expected now that she might live to see Oldfields a seaport town. There had been a great excitement over the second meeting-house, to which the conservative faction had strongly objected, but, after the radicals had once gained the day, other innovations passed without public challenge.[3] The old First Parish Church was very white and held aloft an imposing steeple, and strangers were always commiserated if they had to leave town without the opportunity of seeing its front by moonlight.[4] Behind this, and beyond a green which had been the playground of many generations of boys and girls, was a long row of horse-sheds, where the farmers' horses enjoyed such part of their Sunday rest as was permitted them after bringing heavy loads of rural parishioners to their public devotions. The Sunday church-going was by no means so carefully observed in these days as in former ones, when disinclination was anything but a received excuse. In Parson Leslie's—the doctor's grandfather's—day, it would have condemned a man or woman to the well-merited reproof of their acquaintances. And indeed most parishioners felt deprived of a great pleasure when, after a week of separation from society, of a routine of prosaic farm-work, they were prevented from seeing their friends parade into church, from hearing the psalm-singing and the sermon, and listening to the news afterward. It was like going to mass and going to the theatre and the opera, and making a round of short calls, and having an outing in one's own best clothes to see other people's, all rolled into one; beside which, there was (and is) a superstitious expectation of good luck in the coming week if the religious obligations were carefully fulfilled. So many of the old ideas of the efficacy of ecclesiasticism still linger, most of them by no means unlawfully. The elder people of New England are as glad to have their clergyman visit them in their last days as if he granted them absolution and extreme unction.[5] The old traditions survive in our instincts, although our present opinions have long since ticketed many thoughts and desires and customs as out of date and quite exploded.

We go so far in our vigorous observance of the first commandment, and our fear of worshiping strange gods,[6] that sometimes we are in danger of forgetting that we must worship God himself. And worship is something different from a certain sort of constant church-going, or from even trying to be conformers and to keep our own laws and our neighbors'.

Because an old-fashioned town like Oldfields grows so slowly and with such extreme deliberation, is the very reason it seems to have such a delightful completeness when it has entered fairly upon its maturity. It is possessed of kindred virtues to a winter pear, which may be unattractive during its preparatory stages, but which takes time to gather from the ground and from the air a pleasant and rewarding individuality and sweetness. The towns which are built in a hurry can be left in a hurry without a bit of regret, and if it is the fate or fortune of the elder villages to find themselves the foundation upon which modern manufacturing communities rear their thinly built houses and workshops, and their quickly disintegrating communities of people, the weaknesses of these are more glaring and hopeless in the contrast. The hurry to make money and do much work, and the ambition to do good work, war with each other, but, as Longfellow has said, the lie is the hurrying second-hand of the clock, and the truth the slower hand that waits and marks the hour.[7] The New England that built itself houses a hundred years ago was far less oppressed by competition and by other questions with which the enormous increase of population is worrying its younger citizens. And the overgrown Oldfields that increase now, street by street, were built then a single steady sound-timbered house at a time, and all the neighbors watched them rise, and knew where the planks were sawn, and where the chimney bricks were burnt.[8]

In these days when Anna Prince was young and had lately come to live in the doctor's square house, with the three peaked windows in the roof, and the tall box borders and lilac bushes in its neat front yard, Oldfields was just beginning to wake from a fifty years' architectural sleep, and rub its eyes, and see what was thought about a smart little house with a sharp gabled roof, and much scalloping of its edges, which a new storekeeper had seen fit to build.[9] There was one long street which had plenty of room on either side for most of the houses, and where it divided, each side of the First Parish Church, it became the East road and the West road,[10] and the rest of the dwellings strayed off somewhat undecidedly toward the world beyond. There were a good many poplars in the front yards, though their former proud ranks were broken in many places, so that surviving veterans stood on guard irregularly before the houses, where usually one or two members of the once busy households were also left alone. Many of the people who lived in the village had outlying land and were farmers of it, but beside the doctor's there were some other households which the land supported indirectly, either through professions or because some kind ancestors had laid by enough money for his children and grandchildren. The ministers were both excellent men; but Dr. Leslie was the only man who looked far ahead or saw much or cared much for true success. In Titian's great Venetian picture of the Presentation of the Virgin, while the little maiden goes soberly up the steps of the temple, in the busy crowd beneath only one man is possessed by the thought that something wonderful is happening, and lifts his head, forgetting the buyers and sellers and gossipers, as his eyes follow the sacred sight.[11] Life goes on everywhere like that fragment of it in the picture, but while the man who knows more than his fellows can be found in every company, and sees the light which beckons him on to the higher meanings and better gifts, his place in society is not always such a comfortable and honored one as Dr. Leslie's. What his friends were apt to call his notions were not of such aggressive nature that he was accused of outlawry, and he was apt to speak his mind uncontradicted and undisturbed. He cared little for the friction and attrition, indeed for the inspiration, which one is sure to have who lives among many people, and which are so dear and so helpful to most of us who fall into ruts if we are too much alone. He loved his friends and his books, though he understood both as few scholars can, and he cared little for social pleasure, though Oldfields was, like all places of its size and dignity, an epitome of the world. One or two people of each class and rank are as good as fifty, and, to use the saying of the doctor's friend, old Captain Finch: "Human nature is the same the world over."

Through the long years of his solitary life, and his busy days as a country practitioner, he had become less and less inclined to take much part in what feeble efforts the rest of the townspeople made to entertain themselves. He was more apt to loiter along the street, stopping here and there to talk with his neighbors at their gates or their front-yard gardening, and not infrequently asked some one who stood in need of such friendliness to take a drive with him out into the country. Nobody was grieved at remembering that he was a repository of many secrets;

he was a friend who could be trusted always, though he was one who had been by no means slow to anger or unwilling at times to administer rebuke.

One Sunday afternoon, late in November, while the first snow-storm of the year was beginning, Dr. Leslie threw down a stout French medical work of high renown[12] as if it had failed to fulfil its mission of being instructive first and interesting afterward. He rose from his chair and stood looking at the insulted volume as if he had a mind to apologize and try again, but kept his hands behind him after all. It was thinly dressed in fluttering paper covers, and was so thick and so lightly bound that it had a tendency to divide its material substance into parts, like the seventhlies and eighthlies of an old-fashioned sermon. "Those fellows must be in league with the book-binders over here," grumbled the doctor. "I must send word to that man in New York to have some sort of cover put on these things before they come down."[13] Then he lifted the book again and poised it on one hand, looking at its irregular edges, and reflecting at length that it would be in much better condition if he had not given it a careless crushing in the corner of his carriage the day before. It had been sunshiny, pleasant weather, and he had taken Nan for a long drive in the Saturday half-holiday. He had decided, before starting, that she should manage the reins and he would think over one or two matters and read a while; it had been a great convenience lately that Nan understood the responsibility of a horse and carriage. He was finding her a more and more useful little companion. However, his studies and reflections had been postponed until some other time, for Nan had been very eager to talk about some of her lessons in which it seemed his duty to take an interest. The child seemed stronger and better that autumn than he had ever known her, and her mind had suddenly fastened itself upon certain of her studies. She seemed very quick and very accurate, the doctor thought, and the two traits do not always associate themselves.

He left the table and walked quickly to the west window, and, clasping his hands behind him, stood looking out into the front yard and the street beyond. The ground was already white and he gave a little sigh, for winter weather is rarely a source of happiness to a doctor, although this member of the profession was not made altogether sorrowful by it. He sometimes keenly enjoyed a hard tramp of a mile or two when the roads were so blocked and the snow so blinding that he left his horse in some sheltering barn on his way to an impatient sufferer.

A little way down the street on the other side was a house much like his own, with a row of tall hemlocks beside it, and a front fence higher and more imposing than his, with great posts at the gateway, which held slender urns aloft with funereal solemnity. The doctor's eyesight was not far from perfect, and he looked earnestly at the windows of one of the lower rooms and saw a familiar sight enough; his neighbor Mrs. Graham's face in its accustomed quarter of the sash. Dr. Leslie half smiled as the thought struck him that she always sat so exactly in the same place that her white cap was to be seen through the same lower window-pane. "Most people would have moved their chairs about until they wore holes in the floor," he told himself, and then remembered how many times he had gone to look over at his placid friend, in her favorite afternoon post of ob-servation. He was strongly attached to her, and he reminded himself that she was growing old and that he must try to see her oftener. He valued her companionship, more because he knew it was always ready for him, than because he always availed himself of it, but the sense of mutual dependence made them very familiar to each other when they did meet and had time for a bit of quiet talk.

Dr. Leslie suddenly turned; he had watched long enough to make sure that Mrs. Graham was alone; her head had not moved for many minutes; and at first he was going out of the front door, from some instinct he would hardly have been will-ing to acknowledge, but he resolutely turned and went out to the dining-room, to tell Marilla, after his usual professional custom of giving notice of his whereabouts, that he was going to Mrs. Graham's. A prompt inquiry came from the kitchen to know if anything ailed her, to which the doctor returned a scornful negative and escaped through the side-door which gave entrance both to the study and the dining-room. There was the

usual service at Marilla's meeting-house, but she had not ventured out to attend it, giving the weather and a grumbling
toothache for her reasons, though she concealed the fact that
the faithless town milliner had disappointed her about finishing
her winter bonnet. Marilla had begun life with certain opinions
which she had never changed, though time and occasion had
lessened the value of some of them. She liked to count herself
among those who are persecuted for conscience's sake, and was
immensely fond of an argument and of having it known that
she was a dissenter from the First Parish Church.

Mrs. Graham looked up with surprise from her book to see
the doctor coming in from the street, and, being helplessly
lame, sat still, and put out her hand to greet him, with a very
pleased look on her face. "Is there anything the matter with
me?" she asked. "I have begun to think you don't care to associate with well people; you don't usually go to church in the afternoon either, so you haven't taken refuge here because Mr.
Talcot is ill. I must say that I missed hearing the bell; I shall lose
myself altogether by the middle of the week. One must have
some landmarks."

"Marilla complained yesterday that she was all at sea because her apple pies gave out[14] a day too soon. She put the
bread to rise the wrong night, and everything went wrong
about the sweeping.[15] It has been a week of great domestic
calamity with us, but Nan confided to me this morning that
there was some trouble with our bonnet into the bargain. I had
forgotten it was time for that," said the doctor, laughing. "We
always have a season of great anxiety and disaster until the
bonnet question is settled. I keep out of the way as much as I
can. Once I tried to be amusing, and said it was a pity the
women did not follow their grandmothers' fashion and make a
good Leghorn[16] structure last ten years and have no more trouble about it; but I was assured that there wasn't a milliner now
living who could set such an arrangement going."

"Marilla's taste is not what one might call commonplace,"
said Mrs. Graham, with a smile. "I think her summer head-
covering was a little the most remarkable we have had yet. She
dresses so decently otherwise, good soul!"

"It was astonishing," said the doctor gravely, as he stood before the fire thinking how pleasant the room looked; almost as familiar as his own study, with its heavy mahogany furniture and two old portraits and few quaint ornaments. Mrs. Graham's geraniums were all flourishing and green and even in bloom, unlike most treasures of their kind. There was a modern element in the room also,—some pretty cushions and other bits of embroidery; for Mrs. Graham had some grandchildren who were city born and bred, and who made little offerings to her from time to time. On the table near her and between the front windows were many new books and magazines, and though the two neighbors kept up a regular system of exchange, the doctor went nearer to see what might be found. There were a few minutes of silence, and he became conscious that Mrs. Graham was making up her mind to say something, but when she spoke it was only to ask if there were anything serious the matter with the minister.

"Oh, no," said the doctor, "he's a dyspeptic, nervous soul, too conscientious! and when the time arrives for the sacrifice of pigs,[17] and his whole admiring parish vie with each other to offer spare-ribs on that shrine, it goes hard with the poor man."

This was worth hearing, but Mrs. Graham was a little sorry that she had let such a good chance go by for saying something that was near her heart, so presently she added, "I am sorry that poor Marilla hasn't a better gift at personal decoration. It seems a pity to let her disfigure that pretty child with such structures in the way of head-gear. I was so glad when that abominable great summer hat was laid by for the season."

"It was pretty bad," the doctor agreed, in a provokingly indifferent tone, whereupon Mrs. Graham's interest was rekindled, and saying to herself that the poor man did not know the danger and foolishness of such carelessness, she ventured another comment.

"So much depends upon giving a child's taste the right direction."

Dr. Leslie had taken up a magazine, and seemed to have found something that pleased him, but he at once laid it down and glanced once or twice at his hostess, as if he hoped for future instructions. "You see I don't know anything about it, and Nan doesn't think of her clothes at all, so far as I can tell, and so poor Marilla has to do the best she can," he said mildly.

"Oh dear, yes," answered Mrs. Graham, not without impatience. "But the child's appearance is of some importance, and since a dollar or two doesn't make any difference to you, she should be made to look like the little lady that she is. Dear old Mrs. Thacher would turn in her grave, for she certainly had a simple good taste that was better than this. Marilla became the easy prey of that foolish little woman who makes bonnets on the East road. She has done more to deprave the ideas of our townspeople than one would believe, and they tell you with such pleasure that she used to work in New York, as if that settled the question. It is a comfort to see old Sally Turner and Miss Betsy Milman go by in their decent dark silk bonnets that good Susan Martin made for them. If I could go out to-morrow I believe I would rather hunt for a very large velvet specimen of her work, which is somewhere upstairs in a big bandbox, than trust myself to these ignorant hands. It is a great misfortune to a town if it has been disappointed in its milliner. You are quite at her mercy, and, worse than all, liable to entire social misapprehension when you venture far from home."

"So bonnets are not a question of free will and individual responsibility?" asked the doctor soberly. "I must say that I have wondered sometimes if the women do not draw lots for them. But what shall I do about the little girl? I am afraid I do her great injustice in trying to bring her up at all—it needs a woman's eye."

"Your eye is just as good as anybody's," responded Mrs. Graham quickly, lest the doctor should drift into sad thought about his young wife who had been so long dead and yet seemed always a nearer and dearer living presence to him. He was apt to say a word or two about her and not answer the next question which was put to him, and presently go silently away,—but to-day Mrs. Graham had important business in hand.

"My daughter will be here next week," she observed, presently, "and I'm sure that she will do any shopping for you in Boston with great pleasure. We might forestall Marilla's plans. You could easily say when you go home that you have spoken to me about it. I think it would be an excellent opportunity now, while the East Road establishment is in disfavor," and when the doctor smiled and nodded, his friend and hostess settled herself comfortably in her chair, and felt that she had gained a point.

The sunshine itself could hardly have made that south parlor look pleasanter. There was a log in the fire that was wet, and singing gently to itself, as if the sound of the summer rustlings and chirpings had somehow been stored away in its sap, and above it were some pieces of drier white birch, which were sending up a yellow conflagration to keep the marauding snow-flakes from coming down the chimney. The geraniums looked brighter than by daylight, and seemed to hold their leaves toward the fireplace as if they were hands; and were even leaning out a little way themselves and lifting their blossoms like torches, as if they were a reserve force, a little garrison of weaker soldiers who were also enemies of the cold. The gray twilight was gathering out of doors; the trees looked naked and defenceless, as one saw them through the windows. Mrs. Graham tapped the arms of her chair gently with the tips of her fingers, and in a few minutes the doctor closed the book he was looking over and announced that the days were growing very short. There was something singularly pleasant to both the friends in their quiet Sunday afternoon companionship.

"You used to pay me a Sunday visit every week," said the old lady, pleased to find that her guest still lingered. "I don't know why, but I always have a hope that you will find time to run over for half an hour. I said to myself yesterday that a figure of me in wax would do just as well as anything nowadays. I get up and dress myself, and make the journey down-stairs, and sit here at the window and have my dinner and go through the same round day after day. If it weren't for a certain amount of expense it incurs, and occupation to other people, I think it would be of very little use. However, there are some people still left who need me. Who is it says—Béranger perhaps—that to love benefits one's self, and to inspire love benefits others.[18] I like to think that the children and grandchildren have the old place to think of and come back to. I can see that it is a great bond between them all, and that is very good. I begin to feel like a very old woman; it would be quite different, you know, if I were active and busy out of doors, and the bustling sort of person for which nature intended me. As it is, my mind is bustling enough for itself and its body both."

"Well," said the doctor, laughing a little, "what is it now?"

"The little girl," answered Mrs. Graham, gravely. "I think it is quite time she knew something of society. Don't tell yourself that I am notional and frivolous; I know you have put a great deal of hope and faith and affection into that child's career. It would disappoint you dreadfully if she were not interesting and harmonious to people in general. It seems a familiar fact now that she should have come to live with you, that she should be growing up in your house; but the first thing we know she will be a young lady instead of an amusing child, and I think that you cannot help seeing that a great deal of responsibility belongs to you. She must be equipped and provisioned for the voyage of life; she must have some resources."

"But I think she has more than most children."

"Yes, yes, I dare say. She is a bright little creature, but her brightness begins to need new things to work upon. She does very well at school now, I hear, and she minds very well and is much less lawless than she used to be; but she is like a candle that refuses to burn, and is satisfied with admiring its candlestick. She is quite the queen of the village children in one way, and in another she is quite apart from them. I believe they envy her and look upon her as being of another sort, and yet count her out of half their plans and pleasures, and she runs home, not knowing whether to be pleased or hurt, and pulls down half a dozen of your books and sits proudly at the window. Her poor foolish mother had some gifts, but she went adrift very soon, and I should teach Nan her duty to her neighbor, and make her take in the idea that she owes something to the world beside following out her own most satisfying plans. When I was a young woman it was a most blessed discovery to me—though I was not any quicker at making it than other people, perhaps,—that, beside being happy myself and valuable to myself,

I must fit myself into my place in society. We are seldom left to work alone, you know. No, not even you. I know too much about you to believe that. And it isn't enough that we are willing to talk about ourselves. We must learn to understand the subjects of the day that everybody talks about, and to make sure of a right to stand upon the highest common ground wherever we are. Society is a sort of close corporation, and we must know its watchwords, and keep an interest in its interests and affairs. I call a gentleman the man who, either by birth or by nature, belongs to the best society. There may be bad gentlemen and good gentlemen, but one must feel instinctively at home with a certain class, representatives of which are likely to be found everywhere.

"And as for Nan, you will be disappointed if she does not understand a little later your own way of looking at things. She mustn't grow up full of whims and indifferences. I am too fond of you to look forward calmly to your being disappointed, and I do believe she will be a most lovely, daughterly, friendly girl, who will keep you from being lonely as you grow older, and be a great blessing in every way. Yet she has a strange history, and is in a strange position. I hope you will find a good school for her before very long."

This was said after a moment's pause, and with considerable hesitation, and Mrs. Graham was grateful for the gathering darkness which sheltered her, and not a little surprised at the doctor's answer.

"I have been thinking of that," he said quickly, "but it is a great puzzle at present and I am thankful to say, I think it is quite safe to wait a year or two yet. You and I live so much apart from society that we idealize it a good deal, though you are a stray-away bit of it. We too seldom see the ideal gentleman or lady; we have to be contented with keeping the ideal in our minds, it seems to me, and saying that this man is gentlemanly, and that woman ladylike. But I do believe in aiming at the best things, and turning this young creature's good instincts and uncommon powers into the proper channels instead of letting her become singular and self-centred because she does not know enough of people of her own sort."

Mrs. Graham gave a little sound of approval that did not stand for any word in particular: "I wonder if her father's people will ever make any claim to her? She said something about her aunt one day; I think it was to hear whatever I might answer. It seemed to me that the poor child had more pleasure in this unknown possession than was worth while; she appeared to think of her as a sort of fairy godmother who might descend in Oldfields at any moment."

"I did not know she thought of her at all," announced the doctor, somewhat dismayed. "She never has talked about her aunt to me. I dare say that she has been entertained with the whole miserable story."

"Oh, no," answered Mrs. Graham, placidly. "I don't think that is likely, but it is quite reasonable that the child should be aware of some part of it by this time. The Dyer neighbors are far from being reticent, good creatures, and they have little to remember that approaches the interest and excitement of that time. Do you know anything about Miss Prince nowadays? I have not heard anything of her in a long while."

"She still sends the yearly remittance, which I acknowledge and put into the savings-bank as I always have done. When Nan came to me I advised Miss Prince that I wished to assume all care of her and should be glad if she would give me entire right to the child, but she took no notice of the request. It really makes no practical difference. Only," and the doctor became much embarrassed, "I must confess that I have a notion of letting her study medicine by and by if she shows a fitness for it."

"Dear, dear!" said the hostess, leaning forward so suddenly that she knocked two or three books from the corner of the table, and feeling very much excited. "John Leslie, I can't believe it! but my dear man used to say you thought twice for everybody else's once. What can have decided you upon such a plan?"

"How happened the judge to say that?" asked the doctor, trying to scoff, but not a little pleased. "I'm sure I can't tell you, Mrs. Graham, only the idea has grown of itself in my mind, as all right ideas do, and everything that I can see seems to favor it. You may think that it is too early to decide, but I see plainly that

Nan is not the sort of girl who will be likely to marry. When a man or woman has that sort of self-dependence and unnatural self-reliance, it shows itself very early. I believe that it is a mistake for such a woman to marry. Nan's feeling toward her boy-playmates is exactly the same as toward the girls she knows. You have only to look at the rest of the children together to see the difference; and if I make sure by and by, the law of her nature is that she must live alone and work alone, I shall help her to keep it instead of break it, by providing something else than the business of housekeeping and what is called a woman's natural work, for her activity and capacity to spend itself upon."

"But don't you think that a married life is happiest?" urged the listener, a good deal shocked at such treason, yet somewhat persuaded by its truth.

"Yes," said Dr. Leslie, sadly. "Yes indeed, for most of us. We could say almost everything for that side, you and I; but a rule is sometimes very cruel for its exceptions; and there is a life now and then which is persuaded to put itself in irons by the force of custom and circumstances, and from the lack of bringing reason to bear upon the solving of the most important question of its existence. Of course I don't feel sure yet that I am right about Nan, but looking at her sad inheritance from her mother, and her good inheritances from other quarters, I cannot help feeling that she might be far more unhappy than to be made ready to take up my work here in Oldfields when I have to lay it down. She will need a good anchor now and then. Only this summer she had a bad day of it that made me feel at my wits' end. She was angry with one of the children at school, and afterward with Marilla because she scolded her for not keeping better account of the family times and seasons, and ran away in the afternoon, if you please, and was not heard from until next morning at breakfast time. She went to the old place and wandered about the fields as she used, and crept into some shelter or other. I dare say that she climbed in at one of the windows of the house, though I could not make quite sure without asking more questions than I thought worth while. She came stealing in early in the morning, looking a little pale and wild, but she hasn't played such a prank since. I had a call to the next town and Marilla had evidently been awake all night. I got home early in the morning myself, and was told that it was supposed I had picked up Nan on the road and carried her with me, so the blame was all ready for my shoulders unless we had both happened to see the young culprit strolling in at the gate. I was glad she had punished herself, so that there was no need of my doing it, though I had a talk with her a day or two afterward, when we were both in our right minds. She is a good child enough."

"I dare say," remarked Mrs. Graham drily, "but it seems to me that neither of you took Marilla sufficiently into account. That must have been the evening that the poor soul went to nearly every house in town to ask if there were any stray company to tea. Some of us could not help wondering where the young person was finally discovered. She has a great fancy for the society of Miss Betsy Milman and Sally Turner at present, and I quite sympathize with her. I often look over there and see the end of their house with that one little square window in the very peak of it spying up the street, and wish I could pay them a visit myself and hear a bit of their wise gossip. I quite envy Nan her chance of going in and being half forgotten as she sits in one of their short chairs listening and watching. They used to be great friends of her grandmother's. Oh no; if I could go to see them they would insist upon my going into the best room, and we should all be quite uncomfortable. It is much better to sit here and think about them and hear their flat-irons creak away over the little boys' jackets and trousers."

"I must confess that I have my own clothes mended there to this day," said the doctor. "Marilla says their mending is not what it used to be, too, but it is quite good enough. As for that little window, I hardly ever see it without remembering the day of your aunt Margaret's funeral. I was only a boy and not deeply afflicted, but of course I had my place in the procession and was counted among the mourners, and as we passed the Milman place I saw the old lady's face up there just filling the four small panes. You know she was almost helpless, and how she had got up into the little garret I cannot imagine, but she was evidently determined to inspect the procession as it went down the burying-ground lane. It was a pity they did not cut the window beneath it in the lower room in her day. You know what an odd face she had; I suppose it was distorted by disease and out of all shape it ever knew; but I can see it now, framed in with its cap border and the window as if there were no more of her."

"She really was the most curious old creature; it more than accounts for Mrs. Turner's and Miss Betsy's love for a piece of news," said Mrs. Graham, who was much amused. "But I wish we understood the value of these old news-loving people. So much local history and tradition must die with every one of them if we take no pains to save it. I hope you are wise about getting hold of as much as possible. You doctors ought to be our historians, for you alone see the old country folks familiarly and can talk with them without restraint."

"But we haven't time to do any writing," the guest replied. "That is why our books amount to so little for the most part. The active men, who are really to be depended upon as practitioners, are kept so busy that they are too tired to use the separate gift for writing, even if they possess it, which many do not. And the literary doctors, the medical scholars, are a different class, who have not had the experience which alone can make their advice reliable. I mean of course in practical matters, not anatomy and physiology. But we have to work our way and depend upon ourselves, we country doctors, to whom a consultation is more or less a downfall of pride. Whenever I hear that an old doctor is dead I sigh to think what treasures of wisdom are lost instead of being added to the general fund. That was one advantage of putting the young men with the elder practitioners; many valuable suggestions were handed down in that way." [19]

"I am very well contented with my doctor," said Mrs. Graham, with enthusiasm, at this first convenient opportunity. "And it is very wise of you all to keep up our confidence in the face of such facts as these. You can hardly have the heart to scold any more about the malpractice of patients when we believe in you so humbly and so ignorantly. You are always safe though, for our consciences are usually smarting under the remembrance of some transgression which might have hindered you if it did not. Poor humanity," she added in a tone of compassion. "It has to grope its way through a deal of darkness."

The doctor sighed, but he was uncommonly restful and comfortable in the large arm-chair before the fender. It was quite dark out of doors now, and the fire gave all the light that was in the room. Presently he roused himself a little to say " 'Poor humanity,' indeed! And I suppose nobody sees the failures and miseries as members of my profession do. There will be more and more sorrow and defeat as the population increases and competition with it. It seems to me that to excel in one's work becomes more and more a secondary motive; to do a great deal and be well paid for it ranks first. One feels the injury of such purposes even in Oldfields."

"I cannot see that the world changes much. I often wish that I could, though surely not in this way," said the lame woman from her seat by the window, as the doctor rose to go away. "I find my days piteously alike, and you do not know what a pleasure this talk has been. It satisfies my hungry mind and gives me a great deal to think of; you would not believe what an appetite I had. Oh, don't think I need any excuses, it is a great pleasure to see you drive in and out of the gate, and I like to see your lamp coming into the study, and to know that you are there and fond of me. But winter looked very long and life very short before you came in this afternoon. I suppose you have had enough of society for one day, so I shall not tell you what I mean to have for tea, but next Sunday night I shall expect you to come and bring your ward. Will you please ring, so that Martha will bring the lights? I should like to send Nan a nice letter to read which came yesterday from my little granddaughter in Rome. I shall be so glad when they are all at home again. She is about Nan's age, you know; I must see to it that they make friends with each other. Don't put me on a dusty top shelf again and forget me for five or six weeks," laughed the hostess, as her guest protested and lingered a minute still before he opened the door.

"You won't say anything of my confidences?" at which Mrs. Graham shakes her head with satisfactory gravity, though if

Doctor Leslie had known she was inwardly much amused, and assured herself directly that she hoped to hear no more of such plans; how could he tell that the girl herself would agree to them, and whether Oldfields itself would favor Nan as his own successor and its medical adviser? But John Leslie was a wise, far-seeing man, with a great power of holding to his projects. He really must be kept to his promise of a weekly visit; she was of some use in the world after all, so long as these unprotected neighbors were in it, and at any rate she had gained her point about the poor child's clothes.

As for the doctor, he found the outer world much obscured by the storm, and hoped that nobody would need his services that night, as he went stumbling home though the damp and clogging snow underfoot. He felt a strange pleasure in the sight of a small, round head at the front study window between the glass and the curtain, and Nan came to open the door for him, while Marilla, whose unwonted Sunday afternoon leisure seemed to have been devoted to fragrant experiments in cookery, called in pleased tones from the dining-room that she had begun to be afraid he was going to stay out to supper. It was somehow much more homelike than it used to be, the doctor told himself, as he pushed his feet into the slippers which had been waiting before the fire until they were in danger of being scorched. And before Marilla had announced with considerable ceremony that tea was upon the table, he had assured himself that it had been a very pleasant hour or two at Mrs. Graham's, and it was the best thing in the world for both of them to see something of each other. For the little girl's sake he must try to keep out of ruts, and must get hold of somebody outside his own little world.

But while he called himself an old fogy and other impolite names he was conscious of a grave and sweet desire to make the child's life a successful one,—to bring out what was in her own mind and capacity, and so to wisely educate her, to give her a place to work in, and wisdom to work with, so far as he could; for he knew better than most men that it is the people who can do nothing who find nothing to do, and the secret of happiness in this world is not only to be useful, but to be forever elevating one's uses. Some one must be intelligent for a child until it is ready to be intelligent for itself, and he told himself with new decision that he must be wise in his laws for Nan and make her keep them, else she never would be under the grace of any of her own.

CHAPTER XI.

NEW OUTLOOKS

Dr. Leslie held too securely the affection of his townspeople to be in danger of losing their regard or respect, yet he would have been half pained and half amused if he had known how foolishly his plans, which came in time to be his ward's also, were smiled and frowned upon in the Oldfields houses. Conformity is the inspiration of much second-rate virtue. If we keep near a certain humble level of morality and achievement, our neighbors are willing to let us slip through life unchallenged. Those who anticipate the opinions and decisions of society must expect to be found guilty of many sins.

There was not one of the young village people so well known as the doctor's little girl, who drove with him day by day, and with whom he kept such delightful and trustful companionship. If she had been asked in later years what had decided her to study not only her profession, but any profession, it would have been hard for her to answer anything beside the truth that the belief in it had grown with herself. There had been many reasons why it seemed unnecessary. There was every prospect that she would be rich enough to place her beyond the necessity of self-support. She could have found occupation in simply keeping the doctor's house and being a cordial hostess in that home and a welcome guest in other people's. She was already welcome everywhere in Oldfields, but in spite of this, which would have seemed to fill the hearts and lives of other girls, it seemed to her like a fragment of her life and duty; and when she had ordered her housekeeping and her social duties, there was a restless readiness for a more absorbing duty and industry; and, as the years went by, all her desire tended in one direction. The one thing she cared most to learn increased its attraction continually, and though one might think the purpose of her guardian had had its influence and moulded her character by its persistence, the truth was that the wise doctor simply followed as best he could the leadings of the young nature itself, and so the girl grew naturally year by year, reaching out half unconsciously for what belonged to her life and growth; being taught one thing more than all, that her duty must be followed eagerly and reverently in spite of the adverse reasons which tempted and sometimes baffled her. As she grew older she was to understand more clearly that indecision is but another name for cowardice and weakness; a habit of mind that quickly increases its power of hindrance. She had the faults that belonged to her character, but these were the faults of haste and rashness rather than the more hopeless ones of obstinacy or a lack of will and purpose.

The Sunday evening tea-drinking with Mrs. Graham, though somewhat formidable at first to our heroine, became quickly one of her dearest pleasures, and led to a fast friendship between the kind hostess and her young guest. Soon Nan gave herself eagerly to a plan of spending two or three evenings a week across the way for the purpose of reading aloud, sometimes from books she did not understand, but oftener from books of her own choice. It was supposed to be wholly a kindness on the young girl's part, and Mrs. Graham allowed the excuse of a temporary ailment of her own strong and useful eyes to serve until neither she nor Nan had the least thought of giving up their pleasant habit of reading together. And to this willing listener Nan came in time with her youthful dreams and visions of future prosperities in life, so that presently Mrs. Graham knew many things which would have surprised the doctor, who on the other hand was the keeper of equally amazing and treasured confidences of another sort. It was a great pleasure to both these friends, but most especially to the elderly woman, that Nan seemed so entirely satisfied with their friendship. The busy doctor, who often had more than enough to think and worry about, sometimes could spare but little time to Nan for days together, but her other companion was always waiting for her, and the smile was always ready by way of greeting when the child looked eagerly up at the parlor window. What stories of past days and memories of youth and of long-dead friends belonging to the dear lady's own girlhood were poured into Nan's delighted ears! She came in time to know Mrs. Graham's own immediate ancestors, and the various members of her family with their fates and fortunes, as if she were a contemporary, and was like another grandchild who was a neighbor and beloved crony, which real blessing none of the true grandchildren had ever been lucky enough to possess. She formed a welcome link with the outer world, did little Nan, and from being a cheerful errand-runner, came at last to paying friendly visits in the neighborhood to carry Mrs. Graham's messages and assurances. And from all these daily suggestions of courtesy and of good taste and high breeding, and helpful fellowship with good books, and the characters in their stories which were often more real and dear and treasured in her thoughts than her actual fellow townsfolk, Nan drew much pleasure and not a little wisdom; at any rate a direction for which she would all her life be thankful. It would have been surprising if her presence in the doctor's house had not after some time made changes in it, but there was no great difference outwardly except that she gathered some trifling possessions which sometimes harmonized, and as often did not, with the household gods of the doctor and Marilla. There was a shy sort of intercourse between Nan and Mrs. Graham's grandchildren, but it was not very valuable to any of the young people at first, the country child being too old and full of experience to fellowship with the youngest, and too unversed in the familiar machinery of their social life to feel much kinship with the eldest.

It was during one of these early summer visits, and directly after a tea-party which Marilla had proudly projected on Nan's account, that Dr. Leslie suddenly announced that he meant to go to Boston for a few days and should take Nan with him. This event had long been promised, but had seemed at length like the promise of happiness in a future world, reasonably certain, but a little vague and distant. It was a more important thing than anybody understood, for a dear and familiar chapter of life was ended when the expectant pair drove out of the village on their way to the far-off railway station,[1] as another had been closed when the door of the Thacher farm-house had been shut and padlocked, and Nan had gone home one snowy night to live with the doctor. The weather at any rate was different now, for it was early June, the time when doctors can best give themselves a holiday;[2] and though Dr. Leslie assured himself that he had little wish to take the journey, he felt it quite due to his ward that she should see a little more of the world, and happily due also to certain patients and his brother physicians that he should visit the instrument-makers' shops, and some bookstores; in fact there were a good many important errands to which it was just as well to attend in person. But he watched Nan's wide-open, delighted eyes, and observed her lack of surprise at strange sights, and her perfect readiness for the marvelous, with great amusement. He was touched and pleased because she cared most for what had concerned him; to be told where he lived and studied, and to see the places he had known best, roused most enthusiasm. An afternoon in a corner of the reading-room at the Athenæum library,[3] in which he had spent delightful hours when he was a young man, seemed to please the young girl more than anything else. As he sat beside the table where he had gathered enough books and papers to last for many days, in his delight at taking up again his once familiar habit, Nan looked on with sympathetic eyes, or watched the squirrels in the trees of the quiet Granary Burying Ground,[4] which seemed to her like a bit of country which the noisy city had caught and imprisoned. Now that she was fairly out in the world she felt a new, strange interest in her mysterious aunt, for it was this hitherto unknown space outside the borders of Oldfields to which her father and his people belonged. And as a charming old lady went by in a pretty carriage, the child's gaze followed her wistfully as she and the doctor were walking along the street. With a sudden blaze of imagination she had wished those pleasant eyes might have seen the likeness to her father, of which she had been sometimes told, and that the carriage had been hurried back, so that the long estrangement might be ended. It was a strange thing that, just afterward, Dr. Leslie had, with much dismay, caught sight of the true aunt; for Miss Anna Prince of Dunport had also seen fit to make one of her rare visits to Boston. She looked dignified and stately, but a little severe, as she went down the side street away from them. Nan's quick eyes had noticed already the difference between the city people and the country folks, and would have even recognized a certain provincialism in her father's sister. The doctor had only seen Miss Prince once many years before, but he had known her again with instinctive certainty, and Nan did not guess, though she was most grateful for it, why he reached for her hand, and held it fast as they walked together, just as he always used to do when she was a little girl. She was not yet fully grown, and she never suspected the sudden thrill of dread, and consciousness of the great battle of life which she must soon begin to fight, which all at once chilled the doctor's heart. "It's a cold world, a cold world," he had said to himself. "Only one thing will help her through safely, and that is her usefulness. She shall never be either a thief or a beggar of the world's favor if I can have my wish." And Nan, holding his hand with her warm, soft, childish one, looked up in his face, all unconscious that he thought with pity how unaware she was of the years to come, and of their difference to this sunshine holiday. "And yet I never was so happy at her age as I am this summer," the doctor told himself by way of cheer.

They paid some visits together to Dr. Leslie's much-neglected friends, and it was interesting to see how, for the child's sake, he resumed his place among these acquaintances to whom he had long been linked either personally in times past, or by family ties. He was sometimes reproached for his love of seclusion and cordially welcomed back to his old relations, but as often found it impossible to restore anything but a formal intercourse of a most temporary nature. The people for whom he cared most, all seemed attracted to his young ward, and he noted this with pleasure, though he had not recognized the fact that he had been, for the moment, basely uncertain whether his judgment of her worth would be confirmed. He laughed at the insinuation that he had made a hermit or an outlaw of himself; he would have been still more amused to hear one of his old friends say that this was the reason they had seen so little of him in late years, and that it was a shame that a man of his talent and many values to the world should be hiding his light under the Oldfields bushel,[5] and all for the sake of bringing up this child. As for Nan, she had little to say, but kept her eyes and ears wide open, and behaved herself discreetly. She had ceased to belong only to the village she had left; in these days she became a citizen of the world at large. Her horizon had suddenly become larger, and she might have discovered more than one range of mountains which must be crossed as the years led her forward steadily, one by one.

There is nothing so interesting as to be able to watch the change and progress of the mental and moral nature, provided it grows eagerly and steadily. There must be periods of repose and hibernation like the winter of a plant, and in its springtime the living soul will both consciously and unconsciously reach out for new strength and new light. The leaves and flowers of action and achievement are only the signs of the vitality that works within.

CHAPTER XII.

AGAINST THE WIND

During the next few years, while Nan was growing up, Old-fields itself changed less than many country towns of its size. Though some faces might be missed or altered, Dr. Leslie's household seemed much the same, and Mrs. Graham, a little thinner and older, but more patient and sweet and delightful than ever, sits at her parlor window and reads new books and old ones, and makes herself the centre of much love and happiness. She and the doctor have grown more and more friendly, and they watch the young girl's development with great pride: they look forward to her vacations more than they would care to confess even to each other; and when she comes home eager and gay, she makes both these dear friends feel young again. When Nan is not there to keep him company, Dr. Leslie always drives, and has grown more careful about the comfort of his carriages, though he tells himself with great pleasure that he is really much more youthful in his feelings than he was twenty years before, and does not hesitate to say openly that he should have been an old fogy by this time if it had not been for the blessing of young companionship. When Nan is pleased to command, he is always ready to take long rides and the two saddles are brushed up, and they wonder why the bits are so tarnished, and she holds his horse's bridle while he goes in to see his patients, and is ready with merry talk or serious questions when he reappears. And one dark night she listens from her window to the demand of a messenger, and softly creeps down stairs and is ready to take her place by his side, and drive him across the hills as if it were the best fun in the world, with the frightened country-boy clattering behind on his bare-backed steed. The moon rises late and they come home just before day-break, and though the doctor tries to be stern as he says he cannot have such a piece of mischief happen again, he wonders how the girl knew that he had dreaded for once in his life the drive in the dark, and had felt a little less strong than usual.

Marilla still reigns in noble state. She has some time ago accepted a colleague after a preliminary show of resentment, and Nan has little by little infused a different spirit into the house-keeping; and when her friends come to pay visits in the vacations they find the old home a very charming place, and fall quite in love with both the doctor and Mrs. Graham before they go away. Marilla always kept the large east parlor for a sacred shrine of society, to be visited chiefly by herself as guardian priestess; but Nan has made it a pleasanter room than anybody ever imagined possible, and uses it with a freedom which appears to the old housekeeper to lack consideration and respect. Nan makes the most of her vacations, while the neighbors are all glad to see her come back, and some of them are much amused because in summer she still clings to her childish impatience at wearing any head covering, and no matter how much Marilla admires the hat which is decorously worn to church every Sunday morning, it is hardly seen again, except by chance, during the week, and the brown hair is sure to be faded a little before the summer sunshine is past. Nan goes about visiting when she feels inclined, and seems surprisingly unchanged as she seats herself in one of the smoke-browned Dyer kitchens, and listens eagerly to whatever information is offered, or answers cordially all sorts of questions, whether they concern her own experiences or the world's in general. She has never yet seen her father's sister, though she still thinks of her, and sometimes with a strange longing for an evidence of kind feeling and kinship which has never been shown. This has been chief among the vague sorrows of her girlhood. Yet once when her guardian had asked if she wished to make some attempt at intercourse or conciliation, he had been answered, with a scorn and decision worthy of grandmother Thacher herself, that it was for Miss Prince to make advances if she ever wished for either the respect or affection of her niece. But the young girl has clung with touching affection to the memory and association of her childhood, and again and again sought in every season of the year the old playgrounds and familiar corners of the farm, which she has grown fonder of as the months go by. The inherited attachment of generations seems to have been centred in her faithful heart.

It must be confessed that the summer which followed the close of her school-life was, for the most part, very unsatisfactory. Her school-days had been more than usually pleasant and rewarding, in spite of the sorrows and disappointments and unsolvable puzzles which are sure to trouble thoughtful girls of her age. But she had grown so used at last to living by rules and bells that she could not help feeling somewhat adrift without them. It had been so hard to put herself under restraint and discipline after her free life in Oldfields that it was equally hard for a while to find herself at liberty; though, this being her natural state, she welcomed it heartily at first, and was very thankful to be at home. It did not take long to discover that she had no longer the same desire for her childish occupations and amusements; they were only incidental now and pertained to certain moods, and could not again be made the chief purposes of her life. She hardly knew what to do with herself, and sometimes wondered what would become of her, and why she was alive at all, as she longed for some sufficient motive of existence to catch her up into its whirlwind. She was filled with energy and a great desire for usefulness, but it was not with her, as with many of her friends, that the natural instinct toward marriage, and the building and keeping of a sweet home-life, ruled all other plans and possibilities. Her best wishes and hopes led her away from all this, and however tenderly she sympathized in other people's happiness, and recognized its inevitableness, for herself she avoided unconsciously all approach or danger of it. She was trying to climb by the help of some other train of experiences to whatever satisfaction and success were possible for her in this world. If she had been older and of a different nature, she might have been told that to climb up any other way toward a shelter from the fear of worthlessness, and mistake, and reproach, would be to prove herself in most people's eyes a thief and a robber.[1] But in these days she was not fit to reason much about her fate; she could only wait for the problems to make themselves understood, and for the whole influence of her character and of the preparatory years to shape and signify themselves into a simple chart and unmistakable command. And until the power was given to "see life steadily and see it whole,"[2] she busied herself aimlessly with such details as were evidently her duty, and sometimes following the right road and often wandering from it in willful impatience, she stumbled along more or less unhappily. It seemed as if everybody had forgotten Nan's gift and love for the great profession which was her childish delight and ambition. To be sure she had studied anatomy and physiology with eager devotion in the meagre text-books at school, though the other girls had grumbled angrily at the task. Long ago, when Nan had confided to her dearest cronies that she meant to be a doctor, they were hardly surprised that she should determine upon a career which they would have rejected for themselves. She was not of their mind, and they believed her capable of doing anything she undertook. Yet to most of them the possible and even probable marriage which was waiting somewhere in the future seemed to hover like a cloudy barrier over the realization of any such unnatural plans.

They assured themselves that their school-mate showed no sign of being the sort of girl who tried to be mannish and to forsake her natural vocation for a profession. She did not look strong-minded; besides she had no need to work for her living, this ward of a rich man, who was altogether the most brilliant and beautiful girl in school. Yet everybody knew that she had a strange tenacity of purpose, and there was a lack of pretension, and a simplicity that scorned the deceits of school-girl existence. Everybody knew too that she was not a commonplace girl, and her younger friends made her the heroine of their fondest anticipations and dreams. But after all, it seemed as if everybody, even the girl herself, had lost sight of the once familiar idea. It was a natural thing enough that she should have become expert in rendering various minor services to the patients in Dr. Leslie's absence, and sometimes assist him when no other person was at hand. Marilla became insensible at the sight of the least dangerous of wounds, and could not be trusted to suggest the most familiar household remedy, after all her years of association with the practice of medicine, and it was considered lucky that Nan had some aptness for such services. In her childhood she had been nicknamed "the little doctor," by the household and even a few familiar friends, but this was apparently outgrown, though her guardian had more than once announced in sudden outbursts of enthusiasm that she already knew more than most of the people who tried to practice medicine. They once in a while talked about some suggestion or discovery which was attracting Dr. Leslie's attention, but the girl seemed hardly to have gained much interest even for this, and became a little shy of being found with one of the medical books in her hand, as she tried to fancy herself in sympathy with the conventional world of school and of the every-day ideas of society. And yet her inward sympathy with a doctor's and a surgeon's work grew stronger and stronger, though she dismissed reluctantly the possibility of following her bent in any formal way, since, after all, her world had seemed to forbid it. As the time drew near for her school-days to be ended, she tried to believe that she should be satisfied with her Oldfields life. She was fond of reading, and she had never lacked employment, besides, she wished to prove herself an intelligent companion to Dr. Leslie, whom she loved more and more dearly as the years went by. There had been a long time of reserve between her childish freedom of intercourse with him and the last year or two when they had begun to speak freely to each other as friend to friend. It was a constant surprise and pleasure to the doctor when he discovered that his former plaything was growing into a charming companion who often looked upon life from the same standpoint as himself, and who had her own outlooks upon the world, from whence she was able to give him by no means worthless intelligence; and after the school-days were over he was not amazed to find how restless and dissatisfied the girl was; how impossible it was for her to content herself with following the round of household duties which were supposed to content young women of her age and station. Even if she tried to pay visits or receive them from her friends, or to go on with her studies, or to review some text-book of which she had been fond, there was no motive for it; it all led to nothing; it began for no reason and ended in no use, as she exclaimed one day most dramatically. Poor Nan hurried through her house business, or neglected it, as the case might be, greatly to Marilla's surprise and scorn, for the girl had always proved herself diligent and interested in the home affairs. More and more she puzzled herself and everybody about her, and as the days went by she spent them out of doors at the old farm, or on the river, or in taking long rides on a young horse; a bargain the doctor had somewhat repented before he found that Nan was helped through some of her troubled hours by the creature's wildness and fleetness. It was very plain that his ward was adrift, and at first the doctor suggested farther study of Latin or chemistry, but afterward philosophically resigned himself to patience, feeling certain that some indication of the right course would not be long withheld, and that a wind from the right quarter would presently fill the flapping sails of this idle young craft and send it on its way.

One afternoon Nan went hurrying out of the house just after dinner, and the doctor saw that her face was unusually troubled. He had asked her if she would like to drive with him to a farm just beyond the Dyers' later in the day, but for a wonder she had refused. Dr. Leslie gave a little sigh as he left the table, and presently watched her go down the street as he stood by the window. It would be very sad if the restlessness and discord of her poor mother should begin to show themselves again; he could not bear to think of such an inheritance.

But Nan thought little of anybody else's discomforts as she hurried along the road; she only wished to get to the beloved farm, and to be free there from questions, and from the evidences of her unfitness for the simple duties which life seemed offering her with heartless irony. She was not good for anything after all, it appeared, and she had been cheating herself. This was no life at all, this fretful idleness; if only she had been trained as boys are, to the work of their lives! She had hoped that Dr. Leslie would help her; he used to talk long ago about her studying medicine, but he must have forgotten that, and the girl savagely rebuked society in general for her unhappiness. Of course she could keep the house, but it was kept already; any one with five senses and good health like hers could prove herself able to do any of the ordinary work of existence. For her part it was not enough to be waited upon and made comfortable, she wanted something more, to be really of use in the world, and to do work which the world needed.

Where the main road turned eastward up the hills, a foot-path, already familiar to the reader, shortened the distance to the farm, and the young girl quickly crossed the rude stile and disappeared among the underbrush, walking bareheaded with the swift steps of a creature whose home was in some such place as this. Often the dry twigs, fallen from the gray lower branches of the pines, crackled and snapped under her feet, or the bushes rustled backed again to their places after she pushed against them in passing; she hurried faster and faster, going first through the dense woods and then out into the sunlight. Once or twice in the open ground she stopped and knelt quickly on the soft turf or moss to look at a little plant, while the birds which she startled came back to their places directly, as if they had been quick to feel that this was a friend and not an enemy, though disguised in human shape. At last Nan reached the moss-grown fence of the farm and leaped over it, and fairly ran to the river-shore, where she went straight to one of the low-growing cedars, and threw herself upon it as if it were a couch. While she sat there, breathing fast and glowing with bright color, the river sent a fresh breeze by way of messenger, and the old cedar held its many branches above her and around her most comfortably, and sheltered her as it had done many times before. It need not have envied other trees the satisfaction of climbing straight upward in a single aspiration of growth.

And presently Nan told herself that there was nothing like a good run. She looked to and fro along the river, and listened to the sheep-bell which tinkled lazily in the pasture behind her.

She looked over her shoulder to see if a favorite young birch tree had suffered no harm, for it grew close by the straight-edged path in which the cattle came down to drink. So she rested in the old playground, unconscious that she had been fol-lowing her mother's footsteps, or that fate had again brought her here for a great decision. Years before, the miserable, suffer-ing woman, who had wearily come to this place to end their lives, had turned away that the child might make her own choice between the good and evil things of life. Though Nan told herself that she must make it plain how she could spend her time in Oldfields to good purpose and be of most use at home, and must get a new strength for these duties, a decision sud-denly presented itself to her with a force of reason and necessity the old dream of it had never shown. Why should it not be a re-ality that she studied medicine?

The thought entirely possessed her, and the glow of excite-ment and enthusiasm made her spring from the cedar boughs and laugh aloud. Her whole heart went out to this work, and she wondered why she had ever lost sight of it. She was sure this was the way in which she could find most happiness. God had directed her at last, and though the opening of her sealed or-ders[3] had been long delayed, the suspense had only made her surer that she must hold fast this unspeakably great motive: something to work for with all her might as long as she lived. People might laugh or object. Nothing should turn her aside, and a new affection for kind and patient Dr. Leslie filled her mind. How eager he had been to help her in all her projects so far, and yet it was asking a great deal that he should favor this; he had never seemed to show any suspicion that she would not live on quietly at home like other girls; but while Nan told her-self that she would give up any plan, even this, if he could con-vince her that it would be wrong, still her former existence seemed like a fog and uncertainty of death, from which she had turned away, this time of her own accord, toward a great light of satisfaction and certain safety and helpfulness. The doctor would know how to help her; if she only could study with him that would be enough; and away she went, hurrying down the river-shore as if she were filled with a new life and happiness.

She startled a brown rabbit from under a bush, and made him a grave salutation when he stopped and lifted his head to look at her from a convenient distance. Once she would have stopped and seated herself on the grass to amaze him with courteous attempts at friendliness, but now she only laughed again, and went quickly down the steep bank through the junipers and then hurried along the pebbly margin of the stream toward the village. She smiled to see lying side by side a flint arrowhead and a water-logged bobbin that had floated down from one of the mills,⁴ and gave one a toss over the water, while she put the other in her pocket. Her thoughts were busy enough, and though some reasons against the carrying out of her plan ventured to assert themselves, they had no hope of carrying the day, being in piteous minority, though she considered them one by one. By and by she came into the path again, and as she reached the stile she was at first glad and then sorry to see the doctor coming along the high road from the Donnell farm. She was a little dismayed at herself because she had a sudden disinclination to tell this good friend her secret.

But Dr. Leslie greeted her most cheerfully, giving her the reins when she had climbed into the wagon, and they talked of the weather and of the next day's plans as they drove home together. The girl felt a sense of guilt and a shameful lack of courage, but she was needlessly afraid that her happiness might be spoiled by a word from that quarter.

That very evening it was raining outside, and the doctor and Nan were sitting in the library opposite each other at the study-table, and as they answered some letters in order to be ready for the early morning post, they stole a look at each other now and then. The doctor laid down his pen first, and presently, as Nan with a little sigh threw hers into the tray beside it, he reached forward to where there was one of the few uncovered spaces of the dark wood of the table and drew his finger across it. They both saw the shining surface much more clearly, and as the dusty finger was held up and examined carefully by its owner, the girl tried to laugh, and then found her voice trembling as she said: "I believe I haven't forgotten to put the table in order before. I have tried to take care of the study at any rate."

"Nan dear, it isn't the least matter in the world!" said Dr. Leslie. "I think we are a little chilly here this damp night; suppose you light the fire? At any rate it will clear away all those envelopes and newspaper wrappers," and he turned his armchair so that it faced the fireplace, and watched the young girl as she moved about the room. She lifted one of the large sticks and stood it on one end at the side of the hearth, and the doctor noticed that she did it less easily than usual and without the old strength and alertness. He had sprung up to help her just too late, but she had indignantly refused any assistance with a half pettishness that was not a common mood with her.

"I don't see why Jane or Marilla, or whoever it was, put that heavy log on at this time of the year," said Dr. Leslie, as if it were a matter of solemn consequence. By this time he had lighted a fresh cigar, and Nan had brought her little wooden chair from some corner of the room where it had always lived since it came with her from the farm. It was a dear old-fashioned little thing, but quite too small for its owner, who had grown up tall and straight, but who had felt a sudden longing to be a child again, as she quietly took her place before the fire.

"That log?" she said, "I wonder if you will never learn that we must not burn it? I saw Marilla myself when she climbed the highest woodpile at the farther end of the wood-house for it. I suppose all the time I have been away you have been remorselessly burning up the show logs. I don't wonder at her telling me this very morning that she was born to suffer, and suffer she supposed she must. We never used to be allowed to put papers in the fireplace, but you have gained ever so many liberties. I wonder if Marilla really thinks she has had a hard life?" the girl said, in a different tone.

"I wonder if you think yours is hard too?" asked the doctor.

And Nan did not know at first what to say. The bright light of the burning papers and the pine-cone kindlings suddenly faded out and the study seemed dark and strange by contrast; but the doctor did not speak either; he only bent towards her presently, and put his hand on the top of the girl's head and stroked the soft hair once or twice, and then gently turned it until he could see Nan's face.

Her eyes met his frankly as ever, but they were full of tears. "Yes," she said; "I wish you would talk to me. I wish you would give me a great scolding. I never needed it so much in my life. I meant to come home and be very good, and do everything I could to make you happy, but it all grows worse every day. I thought at first I was tired with the last days of school, but it is something more than that. I don't wish in the least that I were back at school, but I can't understand anything; there is something in me that wants to be busy, and can't find anything to do. I don't mean to be discontented; I don't want to be anywhere else in the world."

"There is enough to do," answered the doctor, as placidly as possible, for this was almost the first time he had noticed distinctly the mother's nature in her daughter; a restless, impatient, miserable sort of longing for The Great Something Else, as Dr. Ferris had once called it. "Don't fret yourself, Nan, yours is a short-lived sorrow; for if you have any conscience at all about doing your work you will be sure enough to find it."

"I think I have found it at last, but I don't know whether any one else will agree with me," half whispered poor Nan; while the doctor, in spite of himself, of his age, and experience, and sympathy, and self-control, could not resist a smile. "I hate to talk about myself or to be sentimental, but I want to throw my whole love and life into whatever there is waiting for me to do, and—I began to be afraid I had missed it somehow. Once I thought I should like to be a teacher, and come back here when I was through school and look after the village children. I had such splendid ideas about that, but they all faded out. I went into the school-house one day, and I thought I would rather die than be shut up there from one week's end to another."

"No," said Dr. Leslie, with grave composure. "No, I don't feel sure that you would do well to make a teacher of yourself."

"I wish that I had known when school was over that I must take care of myself, as one or two of the girls meant to do, and sometimes it seems as if I ought," said Nan, after a silence of a few minutes, and this time it was very hard to speak. "You have been so kind, and have done so much for me; I supposed at first there was money enough of my own, but I know now."

"Dear child!" the doctor exclaimed, "you will never know, unless you are left alone as I was, what a blessing it is to have somebody to take care of and to love; I have put you in the place of my own little child, and have watched you grow up here, with more thankfulness every year. Don't ever say another word to me about the money part of it. What had I to spend money for? And now I hear you say all these despairing things; but I am an old man, and I take them for what they are worth. You have a few hard months before you, perhaps, but before you know it they will be over with. Don't worry yourself; look after Marilla a little, and that new handmaid, and drive about with me. To-morrow I must be on the road all day, and, to tell the truth, I must think over one or two of my cases before I go to bed. Won't you hand me my old prescription book? I was trying to remember something as I came home."

Nan, half-comforted, went to find the book, while Dr. Leslie, puffing his cigar-smoke very fast, looked up through the cloud abstractedly at a new ornament which had been placed above the mantel shelf since we first knew the room. Old Captain Finch had solaced his weary and painful last years by making a beautiful little model of a ship, and had left it in his will to the doctor. There never was a more touching gift, this present owner often thought, and he had put it in its place with reverent hands. A comparison of the two lives came stealing into his mind, and he held the worn prescription-book a minute before he opened it. The poor old captain waiting to be released, stranded on the inhospitable shore of this world, and eager Nan, who was sorrowfully longing for the world's war to begin. "Two idle heroes," thought Dr. Leslie, "and I neither wished to give one his discharge nor the other her commission;" but he said aloud, "Nan, we will take a six o'clock start in the morning, and go down through the sandy plains before the heat begins. I am afraid it will be one of the worst of the dog-days."

"Yes," answered Nan eagerly, and then she came close to the doctor, and looked at him a moment before she spoke, while her face shone with delight. "I am going to be a doctor, too! I have thought it would be the best thing in the world ever since I can remember. The little prescription-book was the match that lit the fire! but I have been wishing to tell you all the evening."

"We must ask Marilla," the doctor began to say, and tried to add, "What *will* she think?" but Nan hardly heard him, and did not laugh at his jokes. For she saw by his face that there was no need of teasing. And she assured herself that if he thought it was only a freak of which she would soon tire, she was quite willing to be put to the proof.

Next morning, for a wonder, Nan waked early, even before the birds had quite done singing, and it seemed a little strange that the weather should be clear and bright, and almost like June, since she was a good deal troubled.

She felt at first as if there were some unwelcome duty in her day's work, and then remembered the early drive with great pleasure, but the next minute the great meaning and responsibility of the decision she had announced the evening before burst upon her mind, and a flood of reasons assailed her why she should not keep to so uncommon a purpose. It seemed to her as if the first volume of life was ended, and as if it had been deceitfully easy, since she had been led straight-forward to this point. It amazed her to find the certainty take possession of her mind that her vocation had been made ready for her from the beginning. She had the feeling of a reformer, a radical, and even of a political agitator, as she tried to face her stormy future in that summer morning loneliness. But by the time she had finished her early breakfast, and was driving out of the gate with the doctor, the day seemed so much like other days that her trouble of mind almost disappeared. Though she had known instinctively that all the early part of her life had favored this daring project, and the next few years would hinder it if they could, still there was something within her stronger than any doubts that could possibly assail her. And instead of finding everything changed, as one always expects to do when a great change has happened to one's self, the road was so familiar, and the condition of the outer world so harmonious, that she hardly understood that she had opened a gate and shut it behind her, between that day and its yesterday. She held the reins, and the doctor was apparently in a most commonplace frame of mind. She wished he would say something about their talk of the night before, but he did not. She seemed very old to herself, older than she ever would seem again, perhaps, but the doctor had apparently relapsed into their old relations as guardian and child. Perhaps he thought she would forget her decision, and did not know how much it meant to her. He was quite provoking. He hurried the horse himself as they went up a somewhat steep ascent, and as Nan touched the not very fleet steed with the whip on the next level bit of road, she was reminded that it was a very hot morning and that they had a great way to drive. When she asked what was the matter with the patient they were on their way to see, she was answered abruptly that he suffered from a complication of disorders, which was the more aggravating because Nan had heard this answer laughed at as being much used by old Dr. Jackson, who was usually unwilling or unable to commit himself to a definite opinion. Nan fancied herself at that minute already a member of the profession, and did not like to be joked with in such a fashion, but she tried to be amused, which generosity was appreciated by her companion better than she knew.

Dr. Leslie was not much of a singer, but he presently lifted what little voice he had, and began to favor Nan with a not very successful rendering of "Bonny Doon."[5] Every minute seemed more critical to the girl beside him, and she thought of several good ways to enter upon a discussion of her great subject, but with unusual restraint and reserve let the moments and the miles go by until the doctor had quickly stepped down from the carriage and disappeared within his patient's door. Nan's old custom of following him had been neglected for some time, since she had found that the appearance of a tall young woman had quite a different effect upon a household from that of a little child. She had formed the habit of carrying a book with her on the long drives, though she often left it untouched while she walked up and down the country roads, or even ventured upon excursions as far afield as she dared, while the doctor made his visit, which was apt to be a long one in the lonely country houses. This morning she had possessed herself of a square, thin volume which gave lists and plates of the nerve system of the human body. The doctor had nearly laughed aloud when he caught sight of it, and when Nan opened it with decision and gravity and read the first page slowly, she was conscious of a lack of interest in her subject. She had lost the great enthusiasm of the night before, and felt like the little heap of ashes which such a burning and heroic self might well have left.

Presently she went strolling down the road, gathering some large leaves on her way, and stopped at the brook, where she pulled up some bits of a strange water-weed, and made them into a damp, round bundle with the leaves and a bit of string. This was a rare plant which they had both noticed the day before, and they had taken some specimens then, Nan being at this time an ardent botanist, but these had withered and been lost, also, on the way home.

Dr. Leslie was in even less of a hurry than usual, and when he came out he looked very much pleased. "I never was more thankful in my life," he said eagerly, as soon as he was within convenient distance. "That poor fellow was at death's door yesterday, and when I saw his wife and little children, and thought his life was all that stood between them and miserable destitution, it seemed to me that I *must* save it! This morning he is as bright as a dollar, but I have been dreading to go into that house ever since I left it yesterday noon. They didn't in the least know how narrow a chance he had. And it isn't the first time I have been chief mourner. Poor souls! they don't dread their troubles half so much as I do. He will have a good little farm here in another year or two, it only needs draining to be excellent land, and he knows that." The doctor turned and looked back over the few acres with great pleasure. "Now we'll go and see about old Mrs. Willet, though I don't believe there's any great need of it. She belongs to one of two very bad classes of patients. It makes me so angry to hear her cough twice as much as need be. In your practice," he continued soberly, "you must remember that there is danger of giving too strong doses to such a sufferer, and too light ones to the friends who insist there is nothing the matter with them. I wouldn't give much for a doctor who can't see for himself in most cases, but not always,—not always."

The doctor was in such a hospitable frame of mind that nobody could have helped telling him anything, and happily he made an excellent introduction for Nan's secret by inquiring how she had got on with her studies, but she directed his attention to the wet plants in the bottom of the carriage, which were complimented before she said, a minute afterward, "Oh, I wonder if I shall make a mistake? I was afraid you would laugh at me, and think it was all nonsense."

"Dear me, no," replied the doctor. "You will be the successor of Mrs. Martin Dyer, and the admiration of the neighborhood;" but changing his tone quickly, he said: "I am going to teach you all I can, just as long as you have any wish to learn. It has not done you a bit of harm to know something about medicine, and I believe in your studying it more than you do yourself. I have always thought about it. But you are very young; there's plenty of time, and I don't mean to be hurried; you must remember that,—though I see your fitness and peculiar adaptability a great deal better than you can these twenty years yet. You will be growing happier these next few years at any rate, however impossible life has seemed to you lately."

"I suppose there will be a great many obstacles," reflected Nan, with an absence of her usual spirit.

"Obstacles! Yes," answered Dr. Leslie, vigorously. "Of course there will be; it is climbing a long hill to try to study medicine or to study anything else. And if you are going to fear obstacles you will have a poor chance at success. There are just as many reasons as you will stop to count up why you should not do your plain duty, but if you are going to make anything of yourself you must go straight ahead, taking it for granted that there will be opposition enough, but doing what is right all the same. I suppose I have repeated to you fifty times what old Friend Meadows[6] told me years ago; he was a great success at money-making, and once I asked him to give me some advice about a piece of property. 'Friend Leslie,' says he, 'thy own opinion is the best for thee; if thee asks ten people what to do, they will tell thee ten things, and then thee doesn't know as much as when thee set out,'" and Dr. Leslie, growing very much in earnest, reached forward for the whip. "I want you to be a good woman, and I want you to be all the use you can," he said. "It seems to me like stealing, for men and women to live in the world and do nothing to make it better. You have thought a great deal about this, and so have I, and now we will do the best we can at making a good doctor of you. I don't care whether people think it is a proper vocation for women or not. It seems to me that it is more than proper for you, and God has given you a fitness for it which it is a shame to waste. And if you ever hesitate and regret what you have said, you won't have done yourself any harm by learning how to take care of your own health and other people's."

"But I shall never regret it," said Nan stoutly. "I don't believe I should ever be fit for anything else, and you know as well as I that I must have something to do. I used to wish over and over again that I was a boy, when I was a little thing down at the farm, and the only reason I had in the world was that I could be a doctor, like you."

"Better than that, I hope," said Dr. Leslie. "But you mustn't think it will be a short piece of work; it will take more patience than you are ready to give just now, and we will go on quietly and let it grow by the way, like your water-weed here. If you don't drive a little faster, Sister Willet may be gathered[7] before we get to her;" and this being a somewhat unwise and hysterical patient, whose recovery was not in the least despaired of, Dr. Leslie and his young companion were heartlessly merry over her case.

The doctor had been unprepared for such an episode; outwardly, life had seemed to flow so easily from one set of circumstances to the next, and the changes had been so gradual and so natural. He had looked forward with such certainty to Nan's future, that it seemed strange that the formal acceptance of such an inevitable idea as her studying medicine should have troubled her so much.

Separated as he was from the groups of men and women who are responsible for what we call the opinion of society, and independent himself of any fettering conventionalities, he had grown careless of what anybody might say. He only hoped, since his ward had found her proper work, that she would hold to it, and of this he had little doubt. The girl herself quickly lost sight of the fancied difficulty of making the great decision, and, as is usually the case, saw all the first objections and hindrances fade away into a dim distance, and grow less and less noticeable. And more than that, it seemed to her as if she had taken every step of her life straight toward this choice of a profession. So many things she had never understood before, now became perfectly clear and evident proofs that, outside her own preferences and choices, a wise purpose had been at work with her and for her. So it all appeared more natural every day, and while she knew that the excitement and formality of the first very uncomfortable day or two had proved her freedom of choice, it seemed the more impossible that she should have shirked this great commission and trust for which nature had fitted her.

CHAPTER XIII.

A STRAIGHT COURSE

The next year or two was spent in quiet life at home. It was made evident that, beside her inclination and natural fitness for her chosen work, our student was also developing the other most important requisite, a capacity for hard study and patient continuance. There had been as little said as possible about the plan, but it was not long before the propriety of it became a favorite subject of discussion. It is quite unnecessary, perhaps, to state that everybody had his or her own opinion of the wisdom of such a course, and both Dr. Leslie and his ward suffered much reproach and questioning, as the comments ranged from indignation to amusement. But it was as true of Nan's calling, as of all others, that it would be her own failure to make it respected from which any just contempt might come, and she had thrown herself into her chosen career with such zeal, and pride, and affectionate desire to please her teacher, that the small public who had at first jeered or condemned her came at last to accepting the thing as inevitable and a matter of course, even if they did not actually approve. There was such a vigorous determination in the minds of the doctor and his pupil that Nan should not only be a doctor but a good one, that anything less than a decided fitness for the profession would have doomed them both to disappointment, even with such unwearied effort and painstaking. In the earlier years of his practice Dr. Leslie had been much sought as an instructor, but he had long since begun to deny the young men who had wished to be his students,[1] though hardly one had ever gone from the neighborhood of Oldfields who did not owe much to him for his wise suggestions and practical help.

He patiently taught this eager young scholar day by day, and gave her, as fast as he could, the benefit of the wisdom which he had gained through faithful devotion to his business and the persistent study of many years. Nan followed step by step, and, while becoming more conscious of her own ignorance and of the uncertainties and the laws of the practice of medicine with every week's study, knew better and better that it is resource, and bravery, and being able to think for one's self, that make a physician worth anything. There must be an instinct that recognizes a disease and suggests its remedy, as much as an instinct that finds the right notes and harmonies for a composer of music, or the colors for a true artist's picture, or the results of figures for a mathematician. Men and women may learn these callings from others; may practice all the combinations until they can carry them through with a greater or less degree of unconsciousness of brain and fingers; but there is something needed beside even drill and experience; every student of medicine should be fitted by nature with a power of insight, a gift for his business, for knowing what is the right thing to do, and the right time and way to do it; must have this God-given power in his own nature of using and discovering the resources of medicine without constant reliance upon the books or the fashion. Some men use their ability for their own good and renown, and some think first of the good of others, and as the great poet tells the truths of God, and makes other souls wiser and stronger and fitter for action, so the great doctor works for the body's health, and tries to keep human beings free from the failures that come from neglect and ignorance, and ready to be the soul's instrument of action and service in this world. It is not to keep us from death, it is no superstitious avoidance of the next life, that should call loudest for the physician's skill; but the necessity of teaching and remedying the inferior bodies which have come to us through either our ancestors' foolishness or our own. So few people know even what true and complete physical life is, much less anything of the spiritual existence that is already possible, and so few listen to what the best doctors are trying their best to teach. While half-alive people think it no wrong to bring into the world human beings with even less vitality than themselves, and take no pains to keep the simplest laws of health, or to teach their children to do so, just so long there will be plenty of sorrow of an avoidable kind, and thousands of shipwrecked, and failing, and inadequate, and useless lives in the fullest sense of the word. How can those who preach to the soul hope to be heard by those who do not even make the best of their bodies? but alas, the convenience and easiness, or pleasure, of the present moment is allowed to become the cause of an endless series of terrible effects, which go down into the distance of the future, multiplying themselves a thousandfold.

The doctor told Nan many curious things as they drove about together: certain traits of certain families, and how the Dyers were of strong constitution, and lived to a great age in spite of severe illnesses and accidents and all manner of unfavorable conditions; while the Dunnells, who looked a great deal stronger, were sensitive, and deficient in vitality, so that an apparently slight attack of disease quickly proved fatal.[2] And so Nan knew that one thing to be considered was the family, and another the individual variation, and she began to recognize the people who might be treated fearlessly, because they were safe to form a league with against any ailment, being responsive to medicines, and straightforward in their departure from or return to a state of health; others being treacherous and hard to control; full of surprises, and baffling a doctor with their feints and follies of symptoms; while all the time Death himself was making ready for a last, fatal siege; these all being the representatives of types which might be found everywhere. Often Dr. Leslie would be found eagerly praising some useful old-fashioned drugs which had been foolishly neglected by those who liked to experiment with newer remedies and be "up with the times," as they called their not very intelligent dependence upon the treatment in vogue at the moment among the younger men of certain cliques, to some of whom the brilliant operation was more important than its damaging result. There was, even in those days, a haphazard way of doctoring, in which the health of the patient was secondary to the promotion of new theories, and the young scholar who could write a puzzlingly technical paper too often outranked the old practitioner who conquered some malignant disorder single-handed, where even the malpractice of the patient and his friends had stood like a lion in the way.[3]

But Dr. Leslie was always trying to get at the truth, and nobody recognized more clearly the service which the reverent and truly progressive younger men were rendering to the profession. He added many new publications to his subscription list, and gleaned here and there those notes which he knew would be helpful, and which were suited to the degree of knowledge which his apprentice had already gained. It is needless to say what pleasure it gave him, and what evening talks they had together; what histories of former victories and defeats and curious discoveries were combined, like a bit of novel-reading, with Nan's diligent devotion to her course of study. And presently the girl would take a step or two alone, and even make a visit by herself to see if anything chanced to be needed when a case was progressing favorably, and with the excuse of the doctor's business or over-fatigue. And the physicians of the neighboring towns, who came together occasionally for each other's assistance, most of whom had known Nan from her childhood, though at first they had shrunk from speaking of many details of their professional work in her hearing, and covered their meaning, like the ostriches' heads, in the sand of a Latin cognomen, were soon set at their ease by Nan's unconsciousness of either shamefacedness or disgust, and one by one grew interested in her career, and hopeful of her success.

It is impossible to describe the importance of such experiences as these in forming the character of the young girl's power of resource, and wealth of self-reliance and practical experience. Sometimes in houses where she would have felt at least liberty to go only as spectator and scholar of medicine, Dr. Leslie insisted upon establishing her for a few days as chief nurse and overseer, and before Nan had been at work many months her teacher found her of great use, and grew more proud and glad day by day as he watched her determination, her enthusiasm, and her excellent progress. Over and over again he said to himself, or to her, that she was doing the work for which nature had meant her, and when the time came for her to go away from Oldfields, it seemed more impossible than it ever had before that he should get on without her, at home, or as an independent human being, who was following reverently in the path he had chosen so many years before. For her sake he had reached out again toward many acquaintances from whom he had drifted away, and he made many short journeys to Boston or to New York, and was pleased at his hearty welcome back to the medical meetings he had hardly entered during so many years. He missed not a few old friends, but he quickly made new ones. He was vastly pleased when the younger men seemed glad to hear him speak, and it was often proved that either through study or experience he had caught at some fresh knowledge of which his associates were still ignorant. He had laughingly accused himself of being a rusty country doctor and old fogy who had not kept up with the times; but many a letter followed him home, with thanks for some helpful suggestion or advice as to the management of a troublesome case. He was too far away to give room for any danger of professional jealousy, or for the infringement of that ever lengthening code of etiquette so important to the sensitive medical mind.[4] Therefore he had only much pleasure and a fine tribute of recognition and honor, and he smiled more than once as he sat in the quiet Oldfields study before the fire, and looked up at Captain Finch's little ship, and told Nan of his town experiences, not always omitting, though attempting to deprecate, the compliments, in some half-hour when they were on peculiarly good terms with each other. And Nan believed there could be no better doctor in the world, and stoutly told him so, and yet listened only half-convinced when he said that he had a great mind to go to town and open an office, and make a specialty of treating diseases of the heart, since everybody had a specialty nowadays.[5] He never felt so ready for practice as now, but Nan somehow could not bear the thought of his being anywhere but in his home. For herself, she would have been ready to venture anything if it would further her ever-growing purpose; but that Dr. Leslie should begin a new career or contest with the world seemed impossible. He was not so strong as he used to be, and he was already famous among his fellows. She would help him with his work by and by even more than now, and her own chosen calling of a country doctor was the dearer to her, because he had followed it so gallantly before her loving and admiring eyes. But Dr. Leslie built many a castle in the air, with himself and a great city practice for tenants, and said that it would be a capital thing for Nan; she could go on with it alone by and by. It was astonishing how little some of the city doctors knew; they relied upon each other too much; they should all be forced to drive over hill and dale, and be knocked about in a hard country practice for eight or ten years before they went to town. "Plenty of time to read their books in June and January," the doctor would grumble to himself, and turn to look fondly at the long rows of his dear library acquaintances, his Braithwaites and Lancets,[6] and their younger brothers, beside the first new Sydenham Society's books, with their clumsy blot of gilding.[7] And he would stand sometimes with his hands behind him and look at the many familiar rows of brown leather-covered volumes, most of them delightfully worn with his own use and that of the other physicians whose generous friend and constant instructor he had been through years of sometimes stormy but usually friendly intercourse and association.

When people in general had grown tired of discussing this strange freak and purpose of the doctor and his ward, and had become familiar with Nan's persistent interest and occupation in her studies, there came a time of great discontent to the two persons most concerned. For it was impossible to disguise the fact that the time had again come for the girl to go away from home. They had always looked forward to this, and directed much thought and action toward it, and yet they decided with great regret upon setting a new train of things in motion.

While it was well enough and useful enough that Nan should go on with her present mode of life, they both had a wider outlook, and though with the excuse of her youthfulness they had put off her departure as long as possible, still almost without any discussion it was decided that she must enter the medical school to go through with its course of instruction formally, and receive its authority to practice her profession.[8] They both felt that this held a great many unpleasantnesses among its store of benefits. Nan was no longer to be shielded and protected and guided by some one whose wisdom she rarely questioned, but must make her own decisions instead, and give from her own bounty, and stand in her lot and place. Her later school-days were sure to be more trying than her earlier ones, as they carried her into deeper waters of scholarship, and were more important to her future position before the public.

If a young man plans the same course, everything conspires to help him and forward him, and the very fact of his having chosen one of the learned professions gives him a certain social preëminence and dignity. But in the days of Nan's student life it was just the reverse. Though she had been directed toward such a purpose entirely by her singular talent, instead of by the motives of expediency which rule the decisions of a large proportion of the young men who study medicine,[9] she found little encouragement either from the quality of the school[10] or the interest of society in general. There were times when she actually resented the prospect of the many weeks which she must spend in listening to inferior instruction before gaining a diploma, which was only a formal seal of disapproval in most persons' eyes. And yet, when she remembered her perfect certainty that she was doing the right thing, and remembered what renown some women physicians had won, and the avenues of usefulness which lay open to her on every side, there was no real drawing back, but rather a proud certainty of her most womanly and respectable calling, and a reverent desire to make the best use possible of the gifts God had certainly not made a mistake in giving her. "If He meant I should be a doctor," the girl told herself, "the best thing I can do is to try to be a good one."

So Nan packed her boxes and said good-by to Mrs. Graham, who looked wistful and doubtful, but blessed her most heartily, saying she should miss her sadly in the winter. And Marilla, who had unexpectedly reserved her opinion of late, made believe that she was very busy in the pantry, just as she had done when Nan was being launched for boarding-school. She shook her own floury hands vigorously, and offered one at last, muffled in her apron, and wished our friend good luck, with considerable friendliness, mentioning that she should be glad if Nan would say when she wrote home what shapes they seemed to be wearing for bonnets in the city, though she supposed they would be flaunting for Oldfields anyway. The doctor was going too, and they started for the station much too early for the train, since Dr. Leslie always suffered from a nervous dread of having an unavoidable summons to a distant patient at the last moment.

And when the examinations were over, and Nan had been matriculated,[11] and the doctor had somewhat contemptuously overlooked the building and its capabilities, and had compared those students whom he saw with his remembrance of his own class, and triumphantly picked out a face and figure that looked hopeful here and there; he told himself that like all new growths it was feeble yet, and needed girls like his Nan, with high moral purpose and excellent capacity, who would make the college strong and to be respected. Not such doctors as several of whom he reminded himself, who were disgracing their sex, but those whose lives were ruled by a pettiness of detail, a lack of power, and an absence of high aim.[12] Somehow both our friends lost much of the feeling that Nan was doing a peculiar thing, when they saw so many others following the same path. And having seen Nan more than half-settled in her winter quarters, and knowing that one or two of her former school friends had given her a delighted and most friendly welcome, and having made a few visits to the people whom he fancied would help her in one way or another, Dr. Leslie said goodby, and turned his face homeward, feeling more lonely than he had felt in a great many years before. He thought about Nan a great deal on the journey, though he had provided himself with some most desirable new books. He was thankful he had been able to do a kind turn for one of the most influential doctors, who had cheerfully promised to put some special advantages in Nan's way; but when he reached home the house seemed very empty, and he missed his gay companion as he drove along the country roads. After the days began to grow longer, and the sun brighter, such pleasant letters came from the absent scholar, that the doctor took heart more and more, and went over to Mrs. Graham with almost every fresh bit of news. She smiled, and listened, and applauded, and one day said with delightful cordiality that she wished there were more girls who cared whether their lives really amounted to anything. But not every one had a talent which was such a stimulus as Nan's.

"Nothing succeeds like success," rejoined the doctor cheerfully, "I always knew the child would do the best she could."

CHAPTER XIV

MISS PRINCE OF DUNPORT

While all these years were passing, Miss Anna Prince the elder was living quietly in Dunport, and she had changed so little that her friends frequently complimented her upon such continued youthfulness. She had by no means forgotten the two greatest among the many losses and sorrows of her life, but the first sharp pain of them was long since over with. The lover from whom she had parted for the sake of a petty misunderstanding had married afterward and died early; but he had left a son of whom Miss Prince was very proud and fond; and she had given him the place in her heart which should have belonged to her own niece. When she thought of the other trial, she believed herself, still, more sinned against than sinning, and gave herself frequent assurances that it had been impossible to act otherwise at the time of her brother's death and his wife's strange behavior afterward. And she had persuaded her conscience to be quiet, until at last, with the ideal of a suspicious, uncongenial, disagreeable group of rustics in her mind, she thought it was well ordered by Heaven that she had been spared any closer intercourse.

Miss Prince was a proud and stately woman of the old New England type: more colonial than American perhaps, and quite provincial in her traditions and prejudices. She was highly respected in her native town, where she was a prominent figure in society. Nobody was more generous and kind or public spirited, as her friends often said, and young George Gerry was well-rewarded, though he gave her great pleasure by his evident affection and interest. He liked to pay frequent visits to his old friend, and to talk with her. She had been a very attractive girl long ago, and the best of her charms had not faded yet; the young man was always welcomed warmly, and had more than once been helped in his projects. His mother was a feeble woman, who took little interest in anything outside her own doors; and he liked himself better as he sat in Miss Prince's parlor than anywhere else. We are always fond of the society of our best selves, and though he was popular with the rest of his townspeople, he somehow could not help trying always to be especially agreeable to Miss Prince.

Although she was apparently free from regrets, and very well satisfied with life, even her best friends did not know how lonely her life had seemed to her, or how sadly hurt she had been by the shame and sorrow of her only brother's marriage. The thought of his child and of the impossibility of taking her to her heart and home had been like a nightmare at first, and yet Miss Prince lacked courage to break down the barriers, and to at least know the worst. She kept the two ideas of the actual niece and the ideal one whom she might have loved so much distinct and separate in her mind, and was divided between a longing to see the girl and a fierce dread of her sudden appearance. She had forbidden any allusion to the subject years and years before, and so had prevented herself from hearing good news as well as bad; though she had always been careful that the small yearly remittance should be promptly sent, and was impatient to receive the formal acknowledgment of it, which she instantly took pains to destroy. She sometimes in these days thought about making her will; there was no hurry about it, but it would be only fair to provide for her nearest of kin, while she was always certain that she should not let all her money and the old house with its handsome furnishings go into such unworthy hands. It was a very hard question to settle, and she thought of it as little as possible, and was sure there was nothing to prevent her living a great many years yet. She loved her old home dearly, and was even proud of it, and had always taken great care of the details of its government. She never had been foolish enough to make away with her handsome mahogany furniture, and to replace it with cheaper and less comfortable chairs and tables, as many of her neighbors had done, and had taken an obstinate satisfaction all through the years when it seemed quite out of date, in insisting upon the polishing of the fine wood and the many brass handles, and of late she had been reaping a reward for her constancy. It had been a marvel to certain progressive people that a person of her comfortable estate should be willing to reflect that there was not a marble-topped table in her house, until it slowly dawned upon them at last that she was mistress of the finest house in town.[1] Outwardly, it was painted white and stood close upon the street, with a few steep front steps coming abruptly down into the middle of the narrow sidewalk; its interior was spacious and very imposing, not only for the time it was built in the last century, but for any other time. Miss Prince's ancestors had belonged to some of the most distinguished among the colonial families, which fact she neither appeared to remember nor consented to forget; and, as often happened in the seaport towns of New England, there had been one or two men in every generation who had followed the sea. Her own father had been among the number, and the closets of the old house were well provided with rare china and fine old English crockery that would drive an enthusiastic collector to distraction. The carved woodwork of the railings and wainscotings and cornices had been devised by ingenious and patient craftsmen, and the same portraits and old engravings hung upon the walls that had been there when its mistress could first remember. She had always been so well suited with her home that she had never desired to change it in any particular. Her maids were well drilled to their duties, and Priscilla, who was chief of the staff, had been in that dignified position for many years. If Miss Prince's grandmother could return to Dunport from another world, she would hardly believe that she had left her earthly home for a day, it presented so nearly the same appearance.

But however conscientiously the effort had been made to keep up the old reputation for hospitality, it had somehow been a failure, and Miss Prince had given fewer entertainments every year. Long ago, while she was still a young woman, she had begun to wear a certain quaint and elderly manner, which might have come from association with such antiquated household gods and a desire to match well with her beloved surroundings. A great many of her early friends had died, and she was not the sort of person who can easily form new ties of intimate friendship. She was very loyal to those who were still left, and, as has been said, her interest in George Gerry, who was his father's namesake and likeness, was a very great pleasure to her. Some persons liked to whisper together now and then about the mysterious niece, who was never mentioned otherwise. But though curiosity had led to a partial knowledge of our heroine's not unfavorable aspect and circumstances, nobody ever dared to give such information to the person who should have been most interested.

This was one of the standard long stories of Dunport with which old residents liked to regale new-comers, and handsome Jack Prince was the hero of a most edifying romance, being represented as a victim of the Prince pride, as his sister had been before him. His life had been ruined, and he had begged his wretched wife at the last to bring him home to Dunport, alive or dead. The woman had treated Miss Prince with shameful impudence and had disappeared afterward. The child had been brought up with her own people, and it was understood that Miss Prince's efforts to have any connection with them were all thwarted. Lately it had become known that the girl's guardian was a very fine man and was taking a great interest in her. But the reader will imagine how this story grew and changed in different people's minds. Some persons insisted that Miss Prince had declined to see her brother's child, and others that it was denied her. It was often said in these days that Nan must be free to do as she chose, but it was more than likely that she had assumed the prejudices against her aunt with which she must have become most familiar.

As for Miss Prince herself, she had long ago become convinced that there was nothing to be done in this matter. After one has followed a certain course for some time, everything seems to persuade one that no other is possible. Sometimes she feared that an excitement and danger lurked in her future, but, after all, her days went by so calmly, and nearer things seemed so much more important than this vague sorrow and dread, that she went to and fro in the Dunport streets, and was courteous and kind in her own house, and read a sensible book now and then, and spent her time as benevolently and respectably as possible. She was indeed an admirable member of society, who had suffered very much in her youth, and those who knew her well could not be too glad that her later years were passing far less unhappily than most people's.

In the days when her niece had lately finished her first winter at the medical school,[2] Miss Prince had just freed herself from the responsibility of some slight repairs which the house had needed. She had been in many ways much more occupied than usual, and had given hardly a thought to more remote affairs. At last there had come an evening when she felt at leisure, and happily Miss Fraley, one of her earliest friends, had come to pay her a visit. The two ladies sat at the front windows of the west parlor looking out upon the street, while the hostess expressed her gratitude that the overturning of her household affairs was at an end, and that she was all in order for summer. They talked about the damage and discomfort inflicted by masons, and the general havoc which follows a small piece of fallen ceiling. Miss Prince, having made a final round of inspection just after tea, had ascertained that the last of the white dimity curtains and coverings were in their places upstairs in the bedrooms, and her love of order was satisfied. She had complimented Priscilla, and made her and the maids the customary spring present, and had returned to her evening post of observation at the parlor window just as Miss Fraley came in. She was not in the mood for receiving guests, being a trifle tired, but Eunice Fraley was a mild little creature, with a gentle, deprecatory manner which had always appealed to Miss Prince's more chivalrous nature. Besides, she knew this to be a most true and affectionate friend, who had also the gift of appearing when everything was ready for her, as the bluebirds come, and the robins, in the early days of spring.

"I wish I could say that our house was all in order but one closet," said the guest, in a more melancholy tone than usual. "I believe we are more behind-hand than ever this year. You know we have Susan's children with us for a fortnight while she goes away for a rest, and they have been a good deal of care. I think mother is getting tired of them now, though she was very eager to have a visit from them at first. She said this morning that the little girl was worse than a kitten in a fit, and she did hope that Susan wouldn't think it best to pass another week away."

Miss Prince laughed a little, and so did Miss Fraley after a moment's hesitation. She seemed to be in a somewhat sentimental and introspective mood as she looked out of the window in the May twilight.

"I so often feel as if I were not accomplishing anything," she said sadly. "It came over me to-day that here I am, really an old woman, and I am just about where I first started,—doing the same things over and over and no better than ever. I haven't the gift of style; anybody else might have done my work just as well, I am afraid; I am sure the world would have got along just as well without me. Mother has been so active, and has reached such a great age, that perhaps it hasn't been much advantage to me. I have only learned to depend upon her instead of myself. I begin to see that I should have amounted to a great deal more if I had had a home of my own. I sometimes wish that I were as free to go and come as you are, Nancy."

But Miss Prince's thoughts were pleased to take a severely practical turn: "I'm not in the least free," she answered cheerfully. "I believe you need something to strengthen you, Eunice. I haven't seen you so out of spirits for a great while. Free! why I'm tied to this house as if I were the knocker on the front door; and I certainly have a great deal of care. I put the utmost confidence in Priscilla, but those nieces of hers would be going wherever they chose, from garret to cellar, before I was ten miles away from Dunport. I have let the cook go away for a week, and Phœbe and Priscilla are alone. Phœbe is a good little creature; I only hope she won't be married within six months, for I don't know when I have liked a young girl so well. Priscilla was anxious I should take that black-eyed daughter of her brother's, and was quite hurt because I refused."

"I dare say you were right," acknowledged Miss Fraley,

though she could not exactly see the obstacles to her friend's freedom in such strong light as was expected.

"I know that it must be difficult for you sometimes," resumed the hostess presently, in a more sympathetic tone. "Your mother naturally finds it hard to give up the rule. We can't expect her to look at life as younger persons do."

"I don't expect it," said poor Miss Fraley appealingly, "and I am sure I try to be considerate; but how would you like it, to be treated as if you were sixteen instead of nearly sixty? I know it says in the Bible that children should obey their parents,[3] but there is no such commandment, that I can see, to women who are old enough to be grandmothers themselves. It does make me perfectly miserable to have everything questioned and talked over that I do; but I know I ought not to say such things. I suppose I shall lie awake half the night grieving over it. You know I have the greatest respect for mother's judgment; I'm sure I don't know what in the world I should do without her."

"You are too yielding, Eunice," said Miss Prince kindly. "You try to please everybody, and that's your way of pleasing yourself; but, after all, I believe we give everybody more satisfaction when we hold fast to our own ideas of right and wrong. There have been a great many friends who were more than willing to give me their advice in all these years that I have been living alone; but I have always made up my mind and gone straight ahead. I have no doubt I should be very impatient now of much comment and talking over; and yet there are so many times when I would give anything to see father or mother for a little while. I haven't suffered from living alone as much as some persons do, but I often feel very sad and lonely when I sit here and think about the past. Dear me! here is Phœbe with the lights, and I dare say it is just as well. I am going to ask you to go up stairs and see the fresh paint, and how ship-shape we are at last, as father used to say."

Miss Fraley rose at once, with an expression of pleasure, and the two friends made a leisurely tour of the old house which seemed all ready for a large family, and though its owner apparently enjoyed her freedom and dominion, it all looked deserted and empty to her guest. They lingered together in the wide lower hall, and parted with unusual affection. This was by no means the first hint that had been given of a somewhat fettered and disappointing home life, though Miss Fraley would have shuddered at the thought of any such report's being sent abroad.

"Send the children round to see me," said Miss Prince, by way of parting benediction. "They can play in the garden an hour or two, and it will be a change for them and for you;" which invitation was gratefully accepted, though Miss Eunice smiled at the idea of their needing a change, when they were sure to be on every wharf in town in the course of the day, and already knew more people in Dunport than she did.

The next morning Miss Prince's sense of general well-being seemed to have deserted her altogether. She was overshadowed by a fear of impending disaster and felt strangely tired and dissatisfied. But she did not believe in moping, and only assured herself that she must make the day an easy one. So, being strong against tides, as some old poet says of the whale,[4] Miss Prince descended the stairs calmly, and advised Priscilla to put off the special work that had been planned until still later in the week. "You had better ask your sister to come and spend the day with you and have a good, quiet visit," which permission Priscilla received without comment, being a person of few words; but she looked pleased, and while her mistress went down the garden walk to breathe the fresh morning air, she concocted a small omelet as an unexpected addition to the breakfast. Miss Prince was very fond of an omelet, but Priscilla, in spite of all her good qualities, was liable to occasional fits of offishness and depression, and in those seasons kept her employer, in one way or another, on short commons.[5]

The day began serenely. It was the morning for the Dunport weekly paper, which Miss Prince sat down at once to read, making her invariable reproachful remark that there was nothing in it, after having devoted herself to this duty for an hour or more. Then she mounted to the upper floor of her house to put away a blanket which had been overlooked in the spring packing of the camphor-wood chests which stood in a solemn row in the north corner of the garret. There were three dormer windows[6] in the front of the garret-roof, and one of these had been a favorite abiding-place in her youth. She had played with her prim Dutch dolls there in her childhood, and she could remember spending hour after hour watching for her father's ship when the family had begun to expect him home at the end of a long voyage. She remembered with a smile how grieved she had been because once he came into port late in the night and surprised them all early in the morning, but he had made amends by taking her back with him when he hurried on board again after a hasty greeting. Miss Prince lived that morning over again as she stood there, old and gray and alone in the world. She could see again the great weather-beaten and tar-darkened ship, and even the wizened monkey which belonged to one of the sailors. She lingered at her father's side admiringly, and felt the tears come into her eyes once more when he gave her a taste of the fiery contents of his tumbler. They were all in his cabin; old Captain Dunn and Captain Denny and Captain Peterbeck were sitting round the little table, also provided with tumblers, as they listened eagerly to the story of the voyage. The sailors came now and then for orders; Nancy thought her handsome father, with his bronzed cheeks and white forehead and curly hair, was every inch a king.[7] He was her hero, and nothing could please her so much to the end of her days as to have somebody announce, whether from actual knowledge or hearsay, that Captain Jack Prince was the best shipmaster that ever sailed out of Dunport. . . . She always was sure there were some presents stored away for herself and young Jack, her brother, in one of the lockers of the little cabin. Poor Jack! how he used to frighten her by climbing the shrouds and waving his cap from almost inaccessible heights. Poor Jack! and Miss Prince climbed the step to look down the harbor again, as if the ship were more than thirty days out from Amsterdam, and might be expected at any time if the voyage had been favorable.

The house was at no great distance from the water side, though the crowded buildings obscured the view from the lower stories. There was nothing coming in from sea but a steam-tug, which did not harmonize with these pleasant reminiscences, though as Miss Prince raised the window a fine salt breeze entered, well warmed with the May sunshine. It had the flavor of tar and the spirit of the high seas, and for a wonder there could be heard the knocking of shipwrights' hammers, which in old times were never silent in the town. As she sat there for a few minutes in the window seat, there came to her other recollections of her later girlhood, when she had stolen to this corner for the sake of being alone with her pleasant thoughts, though she had cried there many an hour after Jack's behavior had given them the sorrow they hardly would own to each other. She remembered hearing her father's angry voice down stairs. No! she would not think of that again, why should she? and she shut the window and went back to be sure that she had locked the camphor chest, and hung its key on the flat-headed rusty nail overhead. Miss Prince heard some one open and shut the front door as she went down, and in the small front room she found Captain Walter Parish, who held a high place among her most intimate friends. He was her cousin, and had become her general adviser and counselor. He sometimes called himself laughingly the ship's husband,[8] for it was he who transacted most of Miss Prince's important business, and selected her paint and shingles and her garden seeds beside, and made and mended her pens.[9] He liked to be useful and agreeable, but he had not that satisfaction in his own home, for his wife had been a most efficient person to begin with, and during his absences at sea in early life had grown entirely self-reliant. The captain joked about it merrily, but he nevertheless liked to feel that he was still important, and Miss Prince generously told him, from time to time, that she did not know how she should get on without him, and considerately kept up the fiction of not wishing to take up his time when he must be busy with his own affairs.

"How are you this fine morning, Cousin Nancy?" said the captain gallantly. "I called to say that Jerry Martin will be here to-morrow without fail. It seems he thought you would send him word when you wanted him next, and he has been working for himself. I don't think the garden will suffer, we have had so much cold weather. And here is a letter I took from the office." He handed it to Miss Prince with a questioning look; he knew the handwriting of her few correspondents almost as well as she, and this was a stranger's.

"Perhaps it is a receipt for my subscription to the"—But Miss Prince never finished the sentence, for when she had fairly taken the letter into her hand, the very touch of it seemed to send a tinge of ashen gray like some quick poison over her face. She stood still, looking at it, then flushed crimson, and sat down in the nearest chair, as if it were impossible to hold herself upright. The captain was uncertain what he ought to do.

"I hope you haven't heard bad news," he said presently, for Miss Prince had leaned back in the arm-chair and covered her eyes with one hand, while the letter was tightly held in the other.

"It is from my niece," she answered, slowly.

"You don't mean it's from Jack's daughter?" inquired the captain, not without eagerness. He never had suspected such a thing; the only explanation which had suggested itself to his mind was that Miss Prince had been investing some of her money without his advice or knowledge, and he had gone so far as to tell himself that it was just like a woman, and quite good enough for her if she had lost it. "I never thought of its being from her," he said, a little bewildered, for the captain was not a man of quick wit; his powers of reflection served him better. "Well, aren't you going to tell me what she has to say for herself?"

"She proposes to make me a visit," answered Miss Prince, trying to smile as she handed him the little sheet of paper which she had unconsciously crumpled together; but she did not give even one glance at his face as he read it, though she thought it a distressingly long time before he spoke.

"I must say that this is a very good letter, very respectful and lady-like," said the captain honestly, though he felt as if he had been expected to condemn it, and proceeded to read it through again, this time aloud:—

My dear Aunt,—I cannot think it is right that we do not know each other. I should like to go to Dunport for a day some time next month; but if you do not wish to see me you have only to tell me so, and I will not trouble you.

Yours sincerely,
Anna Prince.

"A very good handwriting, too," the captain remarked, and then gathered courage to say that he supposed Miss Prince would give her niece the permission for which she asked. "I have been told that she is a very fine girl," he ventured, as if he were poor Nan's ambassador; and at this Miss Prince's patience gave way.

"Yes, I shall ask her to come, but I do not wish anything said about it; it need not be made the talk of the town." She answered her cousin angrily, and then felt as if she had been unjust. "Do not mind me, Walter," she said; "it has been a terrible grief and trouble to me all these years. Perhaps if I had gone to see those people, and told them all I felt, they would have pitied me, and not blamed me, and so everything would have been better, but it is too late now. I don't know what sort of a person my own niece is, and I wish that I need never find out, but I shall try to do my duty."

The captain was tender-hearted, and seemed quite unmanned, but he gave his eyes a sudden stroke with his hand and turned to go away. "You will command me, Nancy, if I can be of service to you?" he inquired, and his cousin bowed her head in assent. It was, indeed, a dismal hour of the family history.

For some time Miss Prince did not move, except as she watched Captain Parish cross the street and take his leisurely way along the uneven pavement. She was almost tempted to call him back, and felt as if he were the last friend she had in the world, and was leaving her forever. But after she had allowed the worst of the miserable shock to spend itself, she summoned the stern energy for which she was famous, and going with slower steps than usual to the next room, she unlocked the desk of the ponderous secretary and seated herself to write. Before many minutes had passed the letter was folded, and sealed, and

addressed, and the next evening Nan was reading it at Oldfields. She was grateful for being asked to come on the 5th of
June to Dunport, and to stay a few days if it were convenient,
and yet her heart fell because there was not a sign of welcome
or affection in the stately fashioning of the note. It had been
hardly wise to expect it under the circumstances, the girl assured herself later, and at any rate it was kind in her aunt to answer her own short letter so soon.

CHAPTER XV

HOSTESS AND GUEST

Nan had, indeed, resolved to take a most important step. She had always dismissed the idea of having any communication with her aunt most contemptuously when she had first understood their unhappy position toward each other; but during the last year or two she had been forced to look at the relationship from a wider point of view. Dr. Leslie protested that he had always treated Miss Prince in a perfectly fair and friendly manner, and that if she had chosen to show no interest in her only niece, nobody was to blame but herself. But Nan pleaded that her aunt was no longer young; that she might be wishing that a reconciliation could be brought about; the very fact of her having constantly sent the yearly allowance in spite of Mrs. Thacher's and Dr. Leslie's unwillingness to receive it appealed to the young girl, who was glad to believe that her aunt had, after all, more interest in her than others cared to observe. She had no near relatives except Miss Prince. There were some cousins of old Mrs. Thacher's and their descendants settled in the vicinity of Oldfields; but Nan clung more eagerly to this one closer tie of kindred than she cared to confess even to her guardian. It was too late now for any interference in Dr. Leslie's plans, or usurping of his affectionate relationship; so, after he found that Nan's loyal heart was bent upon making so kind a venture, he said one day, with a smile, that she had better write a letter to her aunt, the immediate result of which we already know. Nan had been studying too hard, and suffering not a little from her long-continued city life, and though the doctor had been making a most charming plan that later in the season they should take a journey together to Canada, he said nothing about that, and told himself with a sigh that this would be a more thorough change, and even urged Nan to stay as long as she pleased in Dunport, if she found her aunt's house pleasant and everything went well. For whether Nan liked Miss Prince remained to be proved, though nobody in their senses could doubt that Miss Prince would be proud of her niece.

It was not until after Nan had fairly started that she began to feel at all dismayed. Perhaps she had done a foolish thing after all; Marilla had not approved the adventure, while at the last minute Nan had become suspicious that the doctor had made another plan, though she contented herself with the remembrance of perfect freedom to go home whenever she chose. She told herself grimly that if her aunt died she should be thankful that she had done this duty; yet when, after a journey of several hours,[1] she knew that Dunport was the next station, her heart began to beat in a ridiculous manner. It was unlike any experience that had ever come to her, and she felt strangely unequal to the occasion. Long ago she had laughed at her early romances of her grand Dunport belongings, but the memory of them lingered still, in spite of this commonplace approach to their realities, and she looked eagerly at the groups of people at the railway station with a great hope and almost certainty that she should find her aunt waiting to meet her. There was no such good fortune, which was a chill at the outset to the somewhat tired young traveler, but she beckoned a driver whom she had just ignored, and presently was shut into a somewhat antiquated public carriage and on her way to Miss Prince's house.

So this was Dunport, and in these very streets her father had played, and here her mother had become deeper and deeper involved in the suffering and tragedy which had clouded the end of her short life. It seemed to the young stranger as if she must shrink away from the curious glances that stray passers-by sent into the old carriage; and that she was going to be made very conspicuous by the newly-awakened interest in a sad story which surely could not have been forgotten. Poor Nan! she sent a swift thought homeward to the doctor's house and Mrs. Graham's; even to the deserted little place which had sheltered her good old grandmother and herself in the first years she could remember. And with strange irony came also a picture of the home of one of her schoolmates,—where the father and mother and their children lived together and loved each other. The tears started to her eyes until some good angel whispered the kind "Come back soon, Nan dear," with which Dr. Leslie had let her go away.

The streets were narrow and roughly paved in the old provincial seaport town; the houses looked a good deal alike as they stood close to the street, though here and there the tops of some fruit trees showed themselves over a high garden fence. And presently before a broad-faced and gambrel-roofed house,[2] the driver stopped his horses, and now only the front door with its bull's-eyed top-lights and shining knocker stood between Nan and her aunt. The coachman had given a resounding summons at this somewhat formidable entrance before he turned to open the carriage door, but Nan had already alighted, and stepped quickly into the hall. Priscilla directed her with some ceremony to the south parlor, and a prim figure turned away from one of the windows that overlooked the garden, and came forward a few steps. "I suppose this is Anna," the not very cordial voice began, and faltered; and then Miss Prince led her niece toward the window she had left, and without a thought of the reserve she had decided upon, pushed one of the blinds wide open, and looked again at Nan's appealing face, half eager herself, and half afraid. Then she fumbled for a handkerchief, and betook herself to the end of the sofa and began to cry: "You are so like my mother and Jack," she said. "I did not think I should be so glad to see you."

The driver had deposited Nan's box, and now appeared at the door of the parlor with Priscilla (who had quite lost her wits with excitement) looking over his shoulder. Nan sprang forward, glad of something to do in the midst of her vague discomfort, and at this sight the hostess recovered herself, and, commanding Priscilla to show Miss Prince to her room, assumed the direction of business affairs.

The best bedroom was very pleasant, though somewhat stiff and unused, and Nan was glad to close its door and find herself in such a comfortable haven of rest and refuge from the teasing details of that strange day. The wind had gone to the eastward, and the salt odor was most delightful to her. A vast inheritance of memories and associations was dimly brought to mind by that breath of the sea and freshness of the June day by the harbor side. Her heart leaped at the thought of the neighborhood of the wharves and shipping, and as she looked out at the ancient street, she told herself with a sense of great fun that if she had been a boy she would inevitably have been a surgeon in the navy. So this was the aunt whom Nan had thought about and dreamed about by day and by night, whose acquaintance had always been a waiting pleasure, and the mere fact of whose existence had always given her niece something to look forward to. She had not known until this moment what a reserved pleasure this meeting had been, and now it was over with. Miss Prince was so much like other people, though why she should not have been it would be difficult to suggest, and Nan's taste had been so educated and instructed by her Oldfields' advantages, not to speak of her later social experiences, that she felt at once that her aunt's world was smaller than her own. There was something very lovable about Miss Prince, in spite of the constraint of her greeting, and for the first time Nan understood that her aunt also had dreaded the meeting. Presently she came to the door, and this time kissed Nan affectionately. "I don't know what to say to you, I am sure," she told the girl, "only I am thankful to have you here. You must understand that it is a great event to me;" at which Nan laughed and spoke some cheerful words. Miss Prince seated herself by the other front window, and looked at her young guest with ever-growing satisfaction. This was no copy of that insolent, ill-bred young woman who had so beguiled and ruined poor Jack; she was a little lady, who did honor to the good name of the Princes and Lesters,—a niece whom anybody might be proud to claim, and whom Miss Prince could cordially entreat to make herself quite at home, for she had only been too long in coming to her own. And presently, when tea was served, the careful ordering of it, which had been meant partly to mock and astonish the girl who could not have been used to such ways of living, seemed only a fitting entertainment for so distinguished a guest. "Blood will tell," murmured Miss Prince to herself as she clinked the teacups and looked at the welcome face the other side of the table. But when they talked together in the evening, it was made certain that Nan was neither ashamed of her mother's people nor afraid to say gravely to Miss Prince that she did not know how much injustice was done to grandmother Thacher, if she believed she were right in making a certain statement. Aunt Nancy smiled, and accepted her rebuff without any show of disapproval, and was glad that the next day was Sunday, so that she could take Nan to church for the admiration of all observers. She was even sorry that she had not told young Gerry to come and pay an evening visit to her niece, and spoke of him once or twice. Her niece observed a slight self-consciousness at such times, and wondered a little who Mr. George Gerry might be.

Nan thought of many things before she fell asleep that night. Her ideas of her father had always been vague, and she had somehow associated him with Dr. Leslie, who had shown her all the fatherliness she had ever known. As for the young man who had died so long ago, if she had said that he seemed to her like a younger brother of Dr. Leslie, it would have been nearest the truth, in spite of the details of the short and disappointed life which had come to her ears. Dr. Ferris had told her almost all she knew of him, but now that she was in her own father's old home, among the very same sights he had known best, he suddenly appeared to her in a vision, as one might say, and invested himself in a cloud of attractive romance. His daughter felt a sudden blaze of delight at this first real consciousness of her kinship. Miss Prince had shown her brother's portrait early in the evening, and had even taken the trouble to light a candle and hold it high, so that Nan could see the handsome, boyish face, in which she recognized quickly the likeness to her own. "He was only thirteen then," said Miss Prince, "but he looks several years older. We all thought that the artist had made a great mistake when it was painted, but poor Jack grew to look like it. Yes, you are wonderfully like him," and she held the light near Nan's face and studied it again as she had just studied the picture. Nan's eyes filled with tears as she looked up at her father's face. The other portraits in the room were all of older people, her grandfather and grandmother and two or three ancestors, and Miss Prince repeated proudly some anecdotes of the most distinguished. "I suppose you never heard of them," she added sadly at the close, but Nan made no answer; it was certainly no fault of her own that she was ignorant of many things, and she would not confess that during the last few years she had found out everything that was possible about her father's people. She was so thankful to have grown up in Oldfields that she could not find it in her heart to rail at the fate that had kept her away from Dunport; but the years of silence had been very unlovely in her aunt.

She wondered, before she went to sleep that night, where her father's room had been, and thought she would ask Miss Prince in the morning. The windows were open, and the June air blew softly in, and sometimes swayed the curtains of the bed. There was a scent of the sea and of roses, and presently up the quiet street came the sound of footsteps and young voices. Nan said to herself that some party had been late in breaking up, and felt her heart thrill with sympathy. She had been dwelling altogether in the past that evening, and she liked to hear the revelers go by. But as they came under the windows she heard one say, "I should be afraid of ghosts in that best room of Miss Prince's," and then they suddenly became quiet, as if they had seen that the windows were open, and Nan first felt like a stranger, but next as if this were all part of the evening's strange experiences, and as if these might be her father's young companions, and she must call to them as they went by.

The next morning both the hostess and her guest waked early, and were eager for the time when they should see each other again. The beauty and quiet of the Sunday morning were very pleasant, and Nan stood for some minutes at the dining-room windows, looking out on the small paved court-yard, and the flowers and green leaves beyond the garden gate. Miss Prince's was one of the fine old houses which kept its garden behind it, well-defended from the street, for the family's own pleasure.

"Those are the same old bushes and trees which we used to play among; I have hardly changed it at all," said Miss Prince, as she came in. It must be confessed that she had lost the feeling of patroness with which she had approached her acquaintance with Nan. She was proud and grateful now, and as she saw the girl in her pretty white dress, and found her as simple and affectionate and eager to please as she had thought her the night before, she owned to herself that she had not looked for such happiness to fall into her life. And there was something about the younger Anna Prince which others had quickly recognized; a power of direction and of command. There are some natures like the Prussian blue[3] on a painter's palette, which rules all the other colors it is mixed with; natures which quickly make themselves felt in small or great companies.

Nan discovered her father's silver mug beside her plate, and was fired with a fiercer resentment than she had expected to feel again, at the sight of it. The thought of her childhood in good grandmother Thacher's farm-house came quickly to her mind, with the plain living, to her share of which she had been made a thousand times welcome; while by this richer house, of which she was also heir, such rightful trinkets and treasures had been withheld. But at the next minute she could meet Miss Prince's observant eyes without displeasure, and wisely remembered that she herself had not been responsible for the state of affairs, and that possibly her aunt had been as wronged and insulted and beaten back as she complained. So she pushed the newly-brightened cup aside with an almost careless hand, as a sort of compromise with revenge, and Miss Prince at once caught sight of it. "Dear me," she said, not without confusion, "Priscilla must have thought you would be pleased," and then faltered, "I wish with all my heart you had always had it for your own, my dear." And this was a great deal for Miss Prince to say, as any of her acquaintances could have told her nearest relative, who sat, almost a stranger, at the breakfast-table.

The elder woman felt a little light-headed and unfamiliar to herself as she went up the stairway to get ready for church. It seemed as if she had entered upon a new stage of existence, since for so many years she had resented the existence of her brother's child, and had kept up an imaginary war, in which she ardently fought for her own rights. She had brought forward reason after reason why she must maintain her position as representative of a respected family who had been shamed and disgraced and insulted by her brother's wife. Now all aggressors of her peace, real and imaginary, were routed by the appearance of this young girl upon the field of battle, which she traversed with most innocent and fearless footsteps, looking smilingly into her aunt's face, and behaving almost as if neither of them had been concerned in the family unhappiness. Beside, Nan had already added a new interest to Miss Prince's life, and as this defeated warrior took a best dress from the closet without any of the usual reflection upon so important a step, she felt a great consciousness of having been added to and enriched, as the person might who had suddenly fallen heir to an unexpected property. From this first day she separated herself as much as possible from any thought of guilt or complicity in the long estrangement. She seemed to become used to her niece's presence, and with the new relationship's growth there faded away the thought of the past times. If any one dared to hint that it was a pity this visit had been so long delayed, Miss Prince grandly ignored all personality.

Priscilla had come to the guest's room on some undeclared errand, for it had already been put in order, and she viewed with pleasure the simple arrangements for dressing which were in one place and another about the room. Priscilla had scorned the idea of putting this visitor into the best bedroom, and had had secret expectations that Miss Prince's niece would feel more at home with her than with her mistress. But Miss Anna was as much of a lady as Miss Prince, which was both pleasing and disappointing, as Priscilla hoped to solace some disrespectful feelings of her own heart by taking down Miss Nancy's pride. However, her loyalty to the house was greater than her own very small grudges, and as she pretended to have some difficulty with the fastening of the blind, she said in a whisper, "Y'r aunt'll like to have you make yourself look pretty," which was such a reminder of Marilla's affectionate worldliness that Nan had to laugh aloud. "I'm afraid I haven't anything grand enough," she told the departing housekeeper, whose pleasure it was not hard to discern.

It was with a very gratified mind that Miss Prince walked down the street with her niece and bowed to one and another of her acquaintances. She was entirely careless of what any one should say, but she was brimful of excitement, and answered several of Nan's questions entirely wrong. The old town was very pleasant that Sunday morning. The lilacs were in full bloom, and other early summer flowers in the narrow strips of front-yards or the high-fenced gardens were in blossom too, and the air was full of sweetness and delight. The ancient sea-port had gathered for itself quaint names and treasures; it was pleased with its old fashions and noble memories; its ancient bells had not lost their sweet voices, and a flavor of the past pervaded everything. The comfortable houses, the elderly citizens, the very names on the shop signs, and the worn cobblestones of the streets and flagstones of the pavements, delighted the young stranger, who felt so unreasonably at home in Dunport. The many faces that had been colored and fashioned by the sea were strangely different from those which had known an inland life only, and she seemed to have come a great deal nearer to foreign life and to the last century. Her heart softened as she wondered if her father knew that she was following his boyish footsteps, for the first time in her life, on that Sunday morning. She would have liked to wander away by herself and find her way about the town, but such a proposal was not to be thought of, and all at once Miss Nancy turned up a narrow side street toward a high-walled brick church, and presently they walked side by side up the broad aisle so far that it seemed to Nan as if her aunt were aiming for the chancel itself, and had some public ceremony in view, of a penitential nature. They were by no means early, and the girl was disagreeably aware of a little rustle of eagerness and curiosity as she took her seat, and was glad to have fairly gained the shelter of the high-backed pew as she bent her head. But Miss Prince the senior seemed calm; she said her prayer, settled herself as usual, putting the footstool in its right place and finding the psalms and the collect.[4] She then laid the prayer-book on the cushion beside her and folded her hands in her lap, before she turned discreetly to say good-morning to Miss Fraley, and exchange greetings until the clergyman made his appearance. Nan had taken the seat next the pew door, and was looking about her with great interest, forgetting herself and her aunt as she wondered that so dear and quaint a place of worship should be still left in her iconoclastic native country. She had seen nothing even in Boston like this, there were so many antique splendors about the chancel, and many mural tablets on the walls, where she read with sudden delight her own family name and the list of virtues which had belonged to some of her ancestors. The dear old place! there never had been and never could be any church like it; it seemed to have been waiting all her life for her to come to say her prayers where so many of her own people had brought their sins and sorrows in the long years that were gone. She only wished that the doctor were with her, and the same feeling that used to make her watch for him in her childhood until he smiled back again filled all her loving and grateful heart. She knew that he must be thinking of her that morning; he was not in church himself, he had planned a long drive to the next town but one, to see a dying man, who seemed to be helped only by this beloved physician's presence. There had been some talk between Dr. Leslie and Nan about a medicine which might possibly be of use, and she found herself thinking about that again and again. She had reminded the doctor of it and he had seemed very pleased. It must be longer ago than yesterday since she left Oldfields, it already counted for half a lifetime.

One listener at least was not resentful because the sermon was neither wise nor great, for she had so many things to think of; but while she was sometimes lost in her own thoughts, Nan stole a look at the thinly filled galleries now and then, and at one time was pleased with the sight of the red-cheeked cherubs which seemed to have been caught like clumsy insects and

pinned as a sort of tawdry decoration above the tablets where
the Apostle's Creed[5] and the Ten Commandments were printed
in faded gilt letters. The letter s was made long[6] in these copies
and the capitals were of an almost forgotten pattern, and after
Nan had discovered her grandfather's name in the prayer-book
she held, and had tried again to listen to the discourse, she
smiled at the discovery of a familiar face in one of the wall
pews. It somehow gave her a feeling of security as being a link
with her past experiences, and she looked eagerly again and
again until this old acquaintance, who also was a stranger and
a guest in Dunport, happened to direct a careless glance toward
her, and a somewhat dull and gloomy expression was changed
for surprised and curious recognition. When church was over at
last Miss Prince seemed to have a great deal to say to her neighbor in the next pew, and Nan stood in her place waiting until
her aunt was ready. More than one person had lingered to
make sure of a distinct impression of the interesting stranger
who had made one of the morning congregation, and Nan
smiled suddenly as she thought that it might seem proper that
she and her aunt should walk down the aisle together as if they
had been married, or as if the ceremony were finished which
she had anticipated as they came in. And Miss Prince did make
an admirable exit from the church, mustering all her self-
possession and taking stately steps at her niece's side, while she
sometimes politely greeted her acquaintances. There were flickering spots of color in her cheeks when they were again in the
sunshiny street.

"It is really the first day this summer when I have needed my
parasol," said Aunt Nancy, as she unfurled the carefully pre-
served article of her wardrobe and held it primly aloft. "I am so
sorry that our rector was absent this morning. I suppose that
you have attended an Episcopal church sometimes; I am glad
that you seem to be familiar with the service;" to which Nan
replied that she had been confirmed while she was first at
boarding-school,[7] and this seemed to give her aunt great satisfaction. "Very natural and proper, my dear," she said. "It is
one thing I have always wished when I thought of you at serious moments. But I was persuaded that you were far from such

influences, and that there would be nothing in your surroundings to encourage your inherited love of the church."

"I have always liked it best," said Nan, who seemed all at once to grow taller. "But I think one should care more about being a good woman than a good Episcopalian, Aunt Nancy."

"No doubt," said the elder woman, a little confused and dismayed, though she presently rallied her forces and justly observed that the rules of the church were a means to the end of good living, and happily, before any existing differences of opinion could be discovered, they were interrupted by a pleasant-faced young man, who lifted his hat and gracefully accepted his introduction to the younger Miss Prince.

"This is Mr. George Gerry, Anna, one of my young friends," smiled Aunt Nancy, and saying, as she walked more slowly, "You must come to see us soon, for I shall have to depend upon the younger people to make my niece's stay agreeable."

"I was looking forward to my Sunday evening visit," the wayfarer said hesitatingly; "you have not told me yet that I must not come;" which appeal was only answered by a little laugh from all three, as they separated. And Miss Prince had time to be quite eloquent in her favorite's praise before they reached home. Nan thought her first Dunport acquaintance very pleasant, and frankly said so. This seemed to be very gratifying to her aunt, and they walked toward home together by a roundabout way and in excellent spirits. It seemed more and more absurd to Nan that the long feud and almost tragic state of family affairs should have come to so prosaic a conclusion, and that she who had been the skeleton of her aunt's ancestral closet should have dared to emerge and to walk by her side through the town. After all, here was another proof of the wisdom of the old Spanish proverb, that it takes two to make a quarrel, but only one to end it.

CHAPTER XVI.

A JUNE SUNDAY

It was Miss Prince's custom to indulge herself by taking a long Sunday afternoon nap in summer, though on this occasion she spoke of it to her niece as only a short rest. She was glad to gain the shelter of her own room, and as she brushed a little dust from her handsome silk gown before putting it away she held it at arm's length and shook it almost indignantly. Then she hesitated a moment and looked around the comfortable apartment with a fierce disdain. "I wonder what gives me such a sense of importance," she whispered. "I have been making mistakes my whole life long, and giving excuses to myself for not doing my duty. I wish I had made her a proper allowance, to say the least. Everybody must be laughing at me!" and Miss Prince actually stamped her foot. It had been difficult to keep up an appearance of self-respect, but her pride had helped her in that laudable effort, and as she lay down on the couch she tried to satisfy herself with the assurance that her niece should have her rights now, and be treated justly at last.

Miss Fraley had come in to pay a brief visit on her way to Sunday-school just as they finished dinner, and had asked Nan to tea the following Wednesday, expressing also a hope that she would come sooner to call, quite without ceremony. Finding the state of affairs so pleasant, Miss Eunice ventured to say that Nan's father had been a favorite of her mother, who was now of uncommon age. Miss Prince became suddenly stern, but it was only a passing cloud, which disturbed nobody.

Nan had accepted willingly the offered apologies and gayly wished her aunt a pleasant dream, but being wide awake she gladly made use of the quiet time to send a letter home, and to stroll down the garden afterward. It all seemed so unlike what she had expected, yet her former thoughts about her aunt were much more difficult to recall as every hour went by and made the impression of actual things more distinct. Her fancied duty to a lonely old lady who mourned over a sad past seemed quite quixotic when she watched this brisk woman come and go without any hindrance of age, or, now that the first meeting was over, any appearance of former melancholy. As our friend went down the garden she told herself that she was glad to have come; it was quite right, and it was very pleasant, though there was no particular use in staying there long, and after a few days she would go away. Somehow her life seemed a great deal larger for this new experience, and she would try to repeat the visit occasionally. She wished to get Dunport itself by heart, but she had become so used to giving the best of herself to her studies, that she was a little shy of the visiting and the tea-parties and the apparently fruitless society life of which she had already learned something. "I suppose the doctor would say it is good for me," said Nan, somewhat grimly, "but I think it is most satisfactory to be with the persons whose interests and purposes are the same as one's own." The feeling of a lack of connection with the people whom she had met made life appear somewhat blank. She had already gained a certain degree of affection for her aunt; to say the least she was puzzled to account for such an implacable hostility as had lasted for years in the breast of a person so apparently friendly and cordial in her relations with her neighbors. Our heroine was slow to recognize in her relative the same strength of will and of determination which made the framework of her own character,—an iron-like firmness of structure which could not be easily shaken by the changes or opinions of other people. Miss Prince's acquaintances called her a very set person, and were shy of intruding into her secret fastnesses. There were all the traits of character which are necessary for the groundwork of an enterprising life, but Miss Prince seemed to have neither inherited nor acquired any high aims or any especial and fruitful single-heartedness, so her gifts of persistence and self-confidence had ranked themselves for the defense of a comparatively unimportant and commonplace existence. As has been said, she forbade, years before, any mention of her family troubles, and had lived on before the world as if they could be annihilated, and not only were not observable, but never had been. In a more thoughtful and active circle of social life the contrast between her rare capacity and her unnoticeable career would have been more striking. She stood as a fine representative of the old school, but it could not be justly said that she was a forward scholar, since, however sure of some of her early lessons, she was most dull and reluctant before new ones of various enlightening and uplifting descriptions.

Nan had observed that her aunt had looked very tired and spent as she went up-stairs after dinner, and understood better than she had before that this visit was moving the waters of Miss Prince's soul more deeply than had been suspected. She gained a new sympathy, and as the hours of the summer afternoon went by she thought of a great many things which had not been quite plain to her, and strolled about the garden until she knew that by heart, and had made friends with the disorderly company of ladies-delights and periwinkles which had cropped up everywhere, as if the earth were capable of turning itself into such small blossoms without anybody's help, after so many years of unvarying tuition. The cherry-trees and pear-trees had a most venerable look, and the plum-trees were in dismal mourning of black knots. There was a damp and shady corner where Nan found a great many lilies of the valley still lingering, though they had some time ago gone out of bloom in the more sunshiny garden at Oldfields. She remembered that there were no flowers in the house and gathered a great handful at last of one sort and another to carry in.

The dining-room was very dark, and Nan wished at first to throw open the blinds which had been carefully closed. It seemed too early in the summer to shut out the sunshine, but it seemed also a little too soon to interfere with the housekeeping, and so she brought two or three tall champagne glasses from a high shelf of the closet and filled them with her posies, and after putting them in their places, went back to the garden. There was a perfect silence in the house, except for the sound of the tall clock in the dining-room, and it seemed very lonely. She had taken another long look at her father's portrait, but as she shut the rusty-hinged garden gate after her, she smiled at the thought of her unusual idleness, and wondered if it need last until Tuesday, which was the day she had fixed upon for her departure. Nan wished that she dared to go away for a long walk; it was a pity she had not told her aunt of a wish to see something of the town and of the harbor-side that afternoon, but it would certainly be a little strange if she were to disappear, and very likely the long nap would soon come to an end. Being well taught in the details of gardening, she took a knife from her pocket and pruned and trained the shrubs and vines, and sang softly to herself as she thought about her next winter's study and her plans for the rest of the summer, and also decided that she would insist upon the doctor's going away with her for a journey when she reached home again.

After a little while she heard her aunt open the blinds of the garden door and call her in most friendly tones, and when she reached the house Miss Prince was in the south parlor entertaining a visitor,—Captain Walter Parish, who had gladly availed himself of some trifling excuse of a business nature, which involved the signing and sending of a paper by the early post of next day. He was going to his daughter's to tea, and it was quite a long drive to her house, so he had not dared to put off his errand, he explained, lest he should be detained in the evening. But he had been also longing to take a look at Miss Prince's guest. His wife went to another church and he dutifully accompanied her, though he had been brought up with Miss Prince at old St. Ann's.[1]

"So this is my young cousin?" said the captain gallantly, and with great simplicity and tenderness held both Nan's hands and looked full in her face a moment before he kissed her; then to Miss Prince's great discomposure and embarrassment he turned to the window and looked out without saying a word, though he drew the back of his hand across his eyes in sailor-fashion, as if he wished to make them clear while he sighted something on the horizon. Miss Prince thought it was all nonsense and would have liked to say so, though she trusted that her silence was eloquent enough.

"She brings back the past," said Captain Walter as he re-turned presently and seated himself where he could look at Nan as much as he liked. "She brings back the past."

"You were speaking of old Captain Slater," reminded Miss Prince with some dignity.

"I just came from there," said Captain Parish, with his eyes still fixed on his young relative, though it was with such a friendly gaze that Nan was growing fonder of him every minute. "They told me he was about the same as yesterday. I offered to watch with him[2] to-morrow night. And how do you like the looks of Dunport, my dear?"

Nan answered eagerly with brightening face, and added that she was longing to see more of it; the old wharves especially.

"Now that's good," said the captain; "I wonder if you would care anything about taking a stroll with me in the morning. Your aunt here is a famous housekeeper, and will be glad to get you off her hands, I dare say."

Nan eagerly accepted, and though it was suggested that Miss Prince had a plan for showing the town in the afternoon, she was promptly told that there was nothing easier than taking both these pleasant opportunities. "You would lose yourself among the old store-houses, I'm sure, Nancy," laughed the old sailor, "and you must let me have my way. It's a chance one doesn't get every day, to tell the old Dunport stories to a new listener."

Some one had opened the front door, and was heard coming along the hall. "This is very kind, George," said Miss Prince, with much pleasure, while the captain looked a little discon-certed at his young rival; he assured himself that he would make a long morning's cruise of it, next day, with this attractive sight-seer, and for once the young beaux would be at a disad-vantage; the girls of his own day used to think him one of the best of their gallants, and at this thought the captain was invin-cible. Mr. Gerry must take the second chance.

The blinds were open now, and the old room seemed very pleasant. Nan's brown hair had been blown about not a little in the garden, and as she sat at the end of the long, brass-nailed sofa, a ray of sunshine touched the glass of a picture behind her and flew forward again to tangle itself in her stray locks, so that altogether there was a sort of golden halo about her pretty head. And young Gerry thought he had never seen anything so charming. The white frock was a welcome addition to the usually sombre room, and his eyes quickly saw the flowers on the table. He knew instantly that the bouquet was none of Miss Prince's gathering.

"I hope you won't think I mean to stay as much too late as I have come too early," he laughed. "I must go away soon after tea, for I have promised to talk with the captain of a schooner which is to sail in the morning. Mr. Wills luckily found out that he could give some evidence in a case we are working up."

"The collision?" asked Captain Parish, eagerly. "I was wondering to-day when I saw the Highflyer's foremast between the buildings on Fleet Street as I went to meeting, if they were going to let her lie there and dry-rot. I don't think she's being taken proper care of. I must say I hate to see a good vessel go to ruin when there's no need of it."

"The man in charge was recommended very highly, and everything seemed to be all right when I was on board one day this week," said young Gerry, good-naturedly, and turned to explain to Nan that this vessel had been damaged by collision with another, and the process of settling the matter by litigation had been provokingly slow.

The captain listened with impatience. "I dare say she looked very well to your eyes, but I'd rather have an old shipmaster's word for it than a young lawyer's. I haven't boarded her for some weeks; I dare say 't was before the snow was gone; but she certainly needed attention then. I saw some bad-looking places in the sheathing and planking. There ought to be a coat of paint soon, and plenty of tar carried aloft besides, or there'll be a long bill for somebody to pay before she's seaworthy."

"I wish you would make a careful inspection of her," said the young man, with gratifying deference. "I don't doubt that it is necessary; I will see that you are well satisfied for your services. Of course the captain himself should have stayed there and kept charge, but you remember he was sick and had to resign. He looks feeble yet. I hope nothing will happen to him before the matter is settled up, but we are sure of the trial in September."

"She's going to be rigged with some of your red tape, I'm afraid,"[3] said Captain Parish, with great friendliness. "I don't see any reason why I can't look her over to-morrow morning, I'm obliged to you, or at least make a beginning," and he gave a most knowing nod at Nan, as if they would divide the pleasure. "I'll make the excuse of showing this young lady the construction of a good-sized merchant vessel, and then the keeper can't feel affronted. She is going to take a stroll with me along the wharves," he concluded, triumphantly. While Mr. Gerry looked wistful for a moment, and Miss Prince quickly took advantage of a pause in the conversation to ask if he knew whether anything pleasant was going forward among the young people this week. She did not wish her niece to have too dull a visit.

"Some of us are going up the river very soon," said the young man, with eager pleasure, looking at Nan. "It would be so pleasant if Miss Prince would join us. We think our Dunport supper parties of that sort would be hard to match."

"The young folks will all be flocking here by to-morrow," said the captain; and Miss Prince answered "Surely," in a tone of command, rather than entreaty. She knew very well how the news of Nan's coming must be flying about the town, and she almost regretted the fact of her own previous silence about this great event. In the mean time Nan was talking to the two gentlemen as if she had already been to her room to smooth her hair, which her aunt looked at reproachfully from time to time, though the sunshine had not wholly left it. The girl was quite unconscious of herself, and glad to have the company and sympathy of these kind friends. She thought once that if she had a brother she would like him to be of young Mr. Gerry's fashion. He had none of the manner which constantly insisted upon her remembering that he was a man and she was a girl; she could be good friends with him in the same way that she had been with some Oldfields schoolfellows, and after the captain had reluctantly taken his leave, they had a pleasant talk about out-of-door life and their rides and walks, and were soon exchanging experiences in a way that Miss Nancy smiled upon gladly. It was not to be wondered at that she could not get used to so great a change in her life. She could not feel sure yet that she no longer had a secret, and that this was the niece whom she had so many years dreaded and disclaimed. George Gerry had taken the niece's place in her affections, yet here was Anna, her own namesake, who showed plainly in so many ways the same descent as herself, being as much a Prince as herself in spite of her mother's low origin and worse personal traits, and the loutish companions to whom she had always persuaded herself poor Nan was akin. And it was by no means sure that the last of the Princes was not the best of them; she was very proud of her brother's daughter, and was more at a loss to know how to make excuses for being shortsighted and neglectful. Miss Prince hated to think that Nan had any but the pleasantest associations with her nearest relative; she must surely keep the girl's affection now. She meant to insist at any rate upon Dunport's being her niece's home for the future, though undoubtedly it would be hard at first to break with the many associations of Oldfields. She must write that very night to Dr. Leslie to thank him for his care, and to again express her regret that Anna's misguided young mother should have placed such restrictions upon the child's relations with her nearest of kin, and so have broken the natural ties of nature. And she would not stop there; she would blame herself generously and say how sorry she was that she had been governed by her painful recollections of a time she should now strive to forget. Dr. Leslie must be asked to come and join his ward for a few days, and then they would settle her plans for the future. She should give her niece a handsome allowance at any rate, and then, as Miss Prince looked across the room and forgot her own thoughts in listening to the young people's friendly talk, a sudden purpose flashed through her mind. The dream of her heart began to unfold itself slowly: could anything be so suitable, so comforting to her own mind, as that they should marry each other?

Two days before, her pleasure and pride in the manly fellow, who was almost as dear to her as an own son could be, would have been greatly shocked, but Miss Prince's heart began to beat quickly. It would be such a blessed solution of all the puzzles and troubles of her life if she could have both the young people near her through the years that remained, and when she died, or even before, they could live here in the old house, and begin a new and better order of things in the place of her own failures and shortcomings. It was all so distinct and possible in Miss Prince's mind that only time seemed necessary, and even the time could be made short. She would not put any hindrances between them and their blessed decision. As she went by them to seek Priscilla, she smoothed the cushion which Nan had leaned upon before she moved a little nearer George Gerry in some sudden excitement of the conversation, which had begun while the captain was still there, and there was a needless distance between them. Then Miss Prince let her hand rest for a minute on the girl's soft hair. "You must ask Mr. Gerry to excuse you for a few minutes, my dear, you have been quite blown about in the garden. I meant to join you there."

"It is a dear old garden," said Nan. "I can't help being almost as fond of it already as I am of ours at home;" but though Aunt Nancy's unwonted caress had been so unlike her conduct in general, this reference to Oldfields called her to her senses, and she went quickly away. She did not like to hear Nan speak in such loving fashion of a house where she had no real right.

But when Mr. George Gerry was left alone, he had pleasant thoughts come flocking in to keep him company in the ladies' stead. He had not dreamed of such a pleasure as this; who could have? and what could Aunt Nancy think of herself!

"It is such a holiday," said Nan, when tea was fairly begun, and her new friend was acknowledging an uncommon attack of hunger, and they were all merry in a sedate way to suit Miss Prince's ideas and preferences. "I have been quite the drudge this winter over my studies, and I feel young and idle again, now that I am making all these pleasant plans." For Mr. Gerry had been talking enthusiastically about some excursions he should arrange to certain charming places in the region of Dunport. Both he and Miss Prince smiled when Nan announced that she was young and idle, and a moment afterward the aunt asked doubtfully about her niece's studies; she supposed that Anna was done with schools.

Nan stopped her hand as it reached for the cup which Miss Prince had just filled. "School; yes," she answered, somewhat bewildered; "but you know I am studying medicine." This most important of all facts had been so present to her own mind, even in the excitement and novelty of her new surroundings, that she could not understand that her aunt was still entirely ignorant of the great purpose of her life.

"What do you mean?" demanded Miss Prince, coldly, and quickly explained to their somewhat amused and astonished companion, "My niece has been the ward of a distinguished physician, and it is quite natural she should have become interested in his pursuits."

"But I am really studying medicine; it is to be my profession," persisted Nan fearlessly, though she was sorry that she had spoiled the harmony of the little company. "And my whole heart is in it, Aunt Nancy."

"Nonsense, my dear," returned Miss Prince, who had recovered her self-possession partially. "Your father gave promise of attaining great eminence in a profession that was very proper for him, but I thought better of Dr. Leslie than this. I cannot understand his indulgence of such a silly notion."

George Gerry felt very uncomfortable. He had been a good deal shocked, but he had a strong impulse to rush into the field as Nan's champion, though it were quite against his conscience. She had been too long in a humdrum country-town with no companion but an elderly medical man. And after a little pause he made a trifling joke about their making the best of the holiday, and the talk was changed to other subjects. The tide was strong against our heroine, but she had been assailed before, and had no idea of sorrowing yet over a lost cause. And for once Miss Prince was in a hurry for Mr. Gerry to go away.

CHAPTER XVII

BY THE RIVER

As Nan went down the street next morning with Captain Parish, who had been most prompt in keeping his appointment, they were met by Mr. Gerry and a young girl who proved to be Captain Parish's niece and the bearer of a cordial invitation. It would be just the evening for a boat-party, and it was hoped that Miss Prince the younger would be ready to go up the river at half-past five.

"Dear me, yes," said the captain; "your aunt will be pleased to have you go, I'm sure. These idle young folks mustn't expect us to turn back now, though, to have a visit from you. We have no end of business on hand."

"If Miss Prince will remember that I was really on my way to see her," said Mary Parish pleasantly, while she looked with eager interest at the stranger. The two girls were quite ready to be friends. "We will just stop to tell your aunt, lest she should make some other plan for you," she added, giving Nan a nod that was almost affectionate. "We have hardly used the boats this year, it has been such a cold, late spring, and we hope for a very good evening. George and I will call for you," and George, who had been listening to a suggestion about the ship business, smiled with pleasure as they separated.

"Nice young people," announced the captain, who was in a sympathetic mood. "There has been some reason for thinking that they meant to take up with each other for good and all. I don't know that either of them could do better, though I like the girl best; that's natural; she's my brother's daughter, and I was her guardian; she only came of age last year. Her father and yours were boys together, younger than I am by a dozen years, both gone before me too," sighed the captain, and quickly changed so sad a subject by directing his companion's attention to one of the old houses, and telling the story of it as they walked along. Luckily they had the Highflyer all to themselves when they reached the wharf, for the keeper had gone up into the town, and his wife, who had set up a frugal housekeeping in the captain's cabin, sat in the shade of the house with her sewing, the Monday's washing having been early spread to the breeze in a corner of the main deck. She accepted Captain Parish's explanations of his presence with equanimity, and seemed surprised and amused at the young landswoman's curiosity and eagerness, for a ship was as commonplace to herself as any farm-house ashore.

"Dear me! you wouldn't know it was the same place," said the captain, in the course of his enumeration of the ropes and yards[1] and other mysterious furnishings of the old craft. "With a good crew aboard, this deck is as busy as a town every day. I don't know how I'm going below until the keeper gets back. I suppose you don't want me to show you the road to the main-to'gallant cross-trees;[2] once I knew it as well as anybody, and I could make quicker time now than most of the youngsters," and the captain gave a knowing glance aloft, while at this moment somebody crossed the gangway plank.[3] It was a broken-down old sailor, who was a familiar sight in Dunport.

"Mornin' to you, sir," and the master of the Highflyer, for the time being, returned the salute with a mixture of dignity and friendliness.

"Goin' to take command?" chuckled the bent old fellow. "I'd like to ship under ye; 't wouldn't be the first time," and he gave his hat an unsettling shake with one hand as he looked at Nan for some sign of recognition, which was quickly given.

"You've shipped under better masters than I. Any man who followed the sea with Cap'n Jack Prince had more to teach than to learn. And here's his grand-daughter before you, and does him credit too," said Captain Walter. "Anna, you won't find many of your grandfather's men about the old wharves, but here's one of the smartest that ever had hold of a hawser."[4]

"Goodsoe by name: I thank ye kindly, cap'n, but I ain't much account nowadays," said the pleased old man, trying to get the captain's startling announcement well settled in his mind. "Old Cap'n Jack Prince's grand-darter? Why Miss Nancy's never been brought to change her mind about nothing, has she?"

"It seems so," answered Nan's escort, laughing as if this were a good joke; and Nan herself could not help smiling.

"I don't believe if the old gentleman can look down at ye he begrudges the worst of his voyages nor the blackest night he ever spent on deck, if you're going to have the spending of the money. Not but what Miss Prince has treated me handsome right straight along," the old sailor explained, while the inspector, thinking this not a safe subject to continue, spoke suddenly about some fault of the galley;⁵ and after this was discussed, the eyes of the two practiced men sought the damaged mizzen mast,⁶ the rigging of which was hanging in snarled and broken lengths. When Nan asked for some account of the accident, she was told with great confidence that the Highflyer had been fouled, and that it was the other vessel's fault; at which she was no wiser than before, having known already that there had been a collision. There seemed to be room enough on the high seas, she ventured to say, or might the mischief have been done in port?

"It does seem as if you ought to know the sense of sea talk without any learning, being Cap'n Jack Prince's grand-darter," said old Goodsoe; for Captain Parish had removed himself to a little distance, and was again investigating the condition of the ship's galley, which one might suppose to have been neglected in some unforgivable way, judging from his indignant grumble.

"Fouled, we say aboard ship, when two vessels lay near enough so that they drift alongside. You can see what havick 't would make, for ten to one they don't part again till they have tore each other all to shoestrings; the yards will get locked together, and the same wind that starts one craft starts both, and first one and then t' other lifts with a wave, don't ye see, and the rigging's spoilt in a little time. I've sometimes called it to mind when I've known o' married couples that wasn't getting on. 'T is easy to drift alongside, but no matter if they was bound to the same port they'd 'a' done best alone;" and the old fellow shook his head solemnly, and was evidently selecting one of his numerous stories for Nan's edification, when his superior officer came bustling toward them.

"You might as well step down here about four o'clock; I shall have the keys then. I may want you to hold a lantern for me; I'm going into the lower hold and mean to do my work thoroughly, if I do it at all," to which Goodsoe responded "ay, ay, sir," in most seamanlike fashion and hobbled off.

"He'd have kept you there all day," whispered Captain Walter. "He always loved to talk, and now he has nothing else to do; but we are all friendly to Goodsoe. Some of us pay a little every year toward his support, but he has always made himself very useful about the wharves until this last year or two; he thought everything of your grandfather, and I knew it would please him to speak to you. It seems unfortunate that you should have grown up anywhere else than here; but I hope you'll stay now?"

"It is not very likely," said Nan coldly. She wished that the captain would go on with his stories of the former grandeur of Dunport, rather than show any desire to talk about personal matters. She had been little troubled at first by her aunt's evident disapproval the evening before of her plans for the future, for she was so intent upon carrying them out and certain that no one had any right to interfere. Still it would have been better to have been violently opposed than to have been treated like a child whose foolish whim would soon be forgotten when anything better offered itself. Nan felt much older than most girls of her years, and as if her decisions were quite as much to be respected as her aunt's. She had dealt already with graver questions than most persons, and her responsibilities had by no means been light ones. She felt sometimes as if she were separated by half a lifetime from the narrow limits of school life. Yet there was an uncommon childlikeness about her which not only misled these new friends, but many others who had known her longer. And when these listened to accounts of her devotion to her present studies and her marked proficiency, they shook their wise heads smilingly, as if they knew that the girl was innocent of certain proper and insurmountable obstacles farther on.

The air was fresh, and it was so pleasant on the wharf that the captain paced to and fro several times, while he pointed out different objects of interest along the harbor-side, and tapped the rusty anchor and the hawsers with his walking-stick as he went by. He had made some very pointed statements to the keeper's wife about the propriety of opening the hatches on such a morning as that, which she had received without comment, and wished her guests good-day with provoking equanimity. The captain did not like to have his authority ignored, but mentioned placidly that he supposed every idler along shore had been giving advice; though he wondered what Nan's grandfather and old Captain Peterbeck would have said if any one had told them this would be the only square-rigged vessel[7] in Dunport harbor for weeks at a time.

"Dear me!" he exclaimed again presently, "there's young Gerry hard at work!" and he directed his companion's attention to one of the upper windows of the buildings whose fronts had two stories on the main street, while there were five or six on the rear, which faced the river. Nan could see the diligent young man and thought it hard that any one must be drudging within doors that beautiful morning.

"He has always been a great favorite of your aunt's," said Captain Parish, confidentially, after the law student had pretended to suddenly catch sight of the saunterers, and waved a greeting which the captain exultantly returned. "We have always thought that she was likely to make him her heir. She was very fond of his father, you see, and some trouble came between them. Nobody ever knew, because if anybody ever had wit enough to keep her own counsel 't was Nancy Prince. I know as much about her affairs as anybody, and what I say to you is between ourselves. I know just how far to sail with her and when to stop, if I don't want to get wrecked on a lee shore. Your aunt has known how to take care of what she had come to her, and I've done the best I could to help her; it's a very handsome property,—very handsome indeed. She helped George Gerry to get his education, and then he had some little money left him by his father's brother,—no great amount, but enough to give him a start; he's a very smart, upright fellow, and I am glad for whatever Nancy did for him; but it didn't seem fair that he should be stepping into your rights. But I never have dared to speak up for you since one day—she wouldn't hear a word about it, that's all I have to remark," the captain concluded in a hurry, for wisdom's sake, though he longed to say more. It seemed outrageous to him at this moment that the girl at his side should have been left among strangers, and he was thankful that she seemed at last to have a good chance of making sure of her rightful possessions.

"But I haven't needed anything," she said, giving Captain Walter a grateful glance for his championship. "And Mr. Gerry is very kind and attentive to my aunt, so I am glad she has been generous to him. He seems a fine fellow, as you say," and Nan thought suddenly that it was very hard for him to have had her appear on the scene by way of rival, if he had been led to suppose that he was her aunt's heir. There were so many new things to think of, that Nan had a bewildering sense of being a stranger and a foreigner in this curiously self-centred Dunport, and a most disturbing element to its peace of mind. She wondered if, since she had not grown up here, it would not have been better to have stayed away altogether. Her own life had always been quite unvexed by any sort of social complications, and she thought how good it would be to leave this talkative and staring little world and go back to Oldfields and its familiar interests and associations. But Dunport was a dear old place, and the warm-hearted captain a most entertaining guide, and by the time their walk was over, the day seemed a most prosperous and entertaining one. Aunt Nancy appeared to be much pleased with the plan for the afternoon, and announced that she had asked some of the young people to come to drink tea the next evening, while she greeted Nan so kindly that the home-coming was particularly pleasant. As for the captain, he was unmistakably happy, and went off down the street with a gentle, rolling gait, and a smile upon his face that fairly matched the June weather, though he was more than an hour late for the little refreshment with which he and certain dignified associates commonly provided themselves at eleven o'clock in the forenoon. Life was as regular ashore as on board ship with these idle mariners of high degree. There was no definite business among them except that of occasionally settling an estate, and the forming of decided opinions upon important questions of the past and future.

The shadows had begun to grow long when the merry company of young people went up river with the tide, and Nan thought she had seldom known such a pleasure away from her own home. She begged for the oars, and kept stroke with George Gerry, pulling so well that they quickly passed the other boat. Mary Parish and the friend who made the fourth of that division of the party sat in the stern and steered with fine dexterity, and the two boats kept near each other, so that Nan soon lost all feeling of strangeness, and shared in the good comradeship to which she had been willingly admitted. It was some time since she had been on the water before, and she thought more than once of her paddling about the river in her childhood, and even regaled the company once with a most amusing mishap, at the remembrance of which she had been forced to laugh outright. The river was broad and brimful of water; it seemed high tide already, and the boats pulled easily. The fields sloped down to the river-banks, shaded with elms and parted by hedgerows like a bit of English country. The freshest bloom of the June greenness was in every blade of grass and every leaf. The birds were beginning to sing the long day to a close, and the lowing of cattle echoed from the pastures again and again across the water; while the country boats were going home from the town, sometimes with a crew of women, who seemed to have made this their regular conveyance instead of following the more roundabout highways ashore. Some of these navigators rowed with a cross-handed stroke that jerked their boats along in a droll fashion, and some were propelled by one groping oar, the sculler[8] standing at the stern as if he were trying to push his craft out of water altogether and take to the air, toward which the lifted bow pointed. And in one of the river reaches half a mile ahead, two heavy packet boats,[9] with high-peaked lateen sails,[10] like a great bird's single wing, were making all the speed they could toward port before the tide should begin to fall two hours later. The young guest of the party was very happy; she had spent so many of her childish days out of doors that a return to such pleasures always filled her with strange delight. The color was bright in her cheeks, and her half-forgotten girlishness came back in the place of the gravity and dignity that had brought of late a sedate young womanliness to her manner. The two new friends in the stern of the boat were greatly attracted to her, and merry laughter rang out now and then. Nan was so brave and handsome, so willing to be pleased, and so grateful to them for this little festivity, that they quickly became interested in each other, as girls will. The commander thought himself a fortunate fellow, and took every chance of turning his head to catch a glimpse of our heroine, though he always had a good excuse of taking his bearings or inspecting for himself some object afloat or ashore which one of the boat's company had pointed out. And Nan must be told the names of the distant hills which stood out clear in the afternoon light, and to what towns up river the packet boats were bound, and so the time seemed short before the light dory was run in among the coarse river grass and pulled up higher than seemed necessary upon the shore.

Their companions had not chosen so fleet a craft, and were five instead of four at any rate, but they were welcomed somewhat derisively, and all chattered together in a little crowd for a few minutes before they started for a bit of woodland which overhung the river on a high point. The wind rustled the oak leaves and roughened the surface of the water, which spread out into a wide inland bay. The clouds began to gather in the west and to take on wonderful colors, as if such a day must be ended with a grand ceremony, and the sun go down through banners and gay parades of all the forces of the sky. Nan had watched such sunsets from her favorite playground at the farm, and somehow the memory of those days touched her heart more tenderly than they had ever done before, and she wished for a moment that she could get away from the noisy little flock who were busy getting the supper ready, though they said eagerly what a beautiful evening it would be to go back to town, and that they must go far up the river first to meet the moonlight.

In a few minutes Nan heard some one say that water must be brought from a farm-house not far away, and quickly insisted that she should make one of the messengers, and after much discussion and remonstrance, she and young Gerry found themselves crossing the open field together. The girl had left her hat swinging from one of the low oak branches; she wondered why Mary Parish had looked at her first as if she were very fond of her, and then almost appealingly, until the remembrance of Captain Walter's bit of gossip came to mind too late to be acted upon. Nan felt a sudden sympathy, and was sorry she had not thought to share with this favorite among her new friends, the companion whom she had joined so carelessly. George Gerry had some very attractive ways. He did not trouble Nan with unnecessary attentions, as some young men had, and she told herself again, how much she liked him. They walked fast, with free, light steps, and talked as they went in a way that was very pleasant to both of them. Nan was wise to a marvel, the good fellow told himself, and yet such an amusing person. He did not know when he had liked anybody so much; he was very glad to stand well in the sight of these sweet, clear eyes, and could not help telling their owner some of the things that lay very near his heart. He had wished to get away from Dunport; he had not room there; everybody knew him as well as they knew the court-house; he somehow wanted to get to deeper water, and out of his depth, and then swim for it with the rest. And Nan listened with deep sympathy, for she also had felt that a great engine of strength and ambition was at work with her in her plans and studies.

She waited until he should have finished his confidence, to say a word from her own experience, but just then they reached the farm-house and stood together at the low door. There was a meagre show of flowers in the little garden, which the dripping eaves had beaten and troubled in the late rains, and one rose-bush was loosely caught to the clapboards here and there.

There did not seem to be anybody in the kitchen, into which

they could look through the open doorway, though they could
hear steps and voices from some part of the house beyond it;
and it was not until they had knocked again loudly that a
woman came to answer them, looking worried and pale.

"I never was so glad to see folks, though I don't know who
you be," she said hurriedly. "I believe I shall have to ask you to
go for help. My man's got hurt; he managed to get home, but
he's broke his shoulder, or any ways 't is out o' place. He was to
the pasture, and we've got some young cattle, and somehow or
'nother one he'd caught and was meaning to lead home give a
jump, and John lost his balance; he says he can't see how 't
should 'a' happened, but over he went and got jammed against
a rock before he could let go o' the rope he'd put round the crit-
ter's neck. He's in dreadful pain so 't I couldn't leave him, and
there's nobody but me an' the baby. You'll have to go to the
next house and ask them to send; Doctor Bent's always attended
of us."

"Let me see him," said Nan with decision. "Wait a minute,
Mr. Gerry, or perhaps you had better come in too," and she led
the way, while the surprised young man and the mistress of the
house followed her. The patient was a strong young fellow, who
sat on the edge of the bed in the little kitchen-bedroom, pale as
ashes, and holding one elbow with a look of complete misery,
though he stopped his groans as the strangers came in.

"Lord bless you, young man! don't wait here," he said; "tell
the doctor it may only be out o' place, but I feel as if 't was
broke."

But Nan had taken a pair of scissors from the high mantel-
piece and was making a cut in the coarse, white shirt, which
was already torn and stained by its contact with the ground,
and with quick fingers and a look of deep interest made herself
sure what had happened, when she stood still for a minute and
seemed a little anxious, and all at once entirely determined.
"Just lie down on the floor a minute," she said, and the patient
with some exclamations, but no objections, obeyed.

Nan pushed the spectators into the doorway of the kitchen,
and quickly stooped and unbuttoned her right boot, and then
planted her foot on the damaged shoulder and caught up the

hand and gave a quick pull, the secret of which nobody understood; but there was an unpleasant cluck as the bone went back into its socket; and a yell from the sufferer, who scrambled to his feet.

"I'll be hanged if she ain't set it," he said, looking quite weak and very much astonished. "You're the smartest young woman I ever see. I shall have to lay down just to pull my wits together. Marthy, a drink of water," and by the time this was brought the excitement seemed to be at an end, though the patient was a little faint, and his wife looked at Nan admiringly. Nan herself was fastening her boot again with unwonted composure. George Gerry had not a word to say, and listened to a simple direction of Nan's as if it were meant for him, and acceded to her remark that she was glad for the shoulder's sake that it did not have to wait and grow worse and worse all the while the doctor was being brought from town. And after a few minutes, when the volley of thanks and compliments could be politely cut short, the two members of the picnic party set forth with their pail of water to join their companions.

"Will you be so good as to tell me how you knew enough to do that?" asked Mr. Gerry humbly, and looking at his companion with admiration. "I should not have had the least idea."

"I was very glad it turned out so well," said Nan simply. "It was a great pleasure to be of use, they were so frightened, poor things. We won't say anything about it, will we?"

But the young man did not like to think yet of the noise the returning bone had made. He was stout-hearted enough usually; as brave a fellow as one could wish to see; but he felt weak and womanish, and somehow wished it had been he who could play the doctor. Nan hurried back bareheaded to the oak grove as if nothing had happened, though, if possible, she looked gayer and brighter than ever. And when the waiting party scolded a little at their slow pace, Miss Prince was much amused and made two or three laughing apologies for their laziness, and even ventured to give the information that they had made a pleasant call at the farm-house.

The clouds were fading fast and the twilight began to gather under the trees before they were ready to go away, and then the high tide had floated off one of the boats, which must be chased and brought back. But presently the picnickers embarked, and, as the moon came up, and the river ebbed, the boats went back to the town and overtook others on the way, and then were pulled up stream again in the favoring eddy to make the evening's pleasure longer; at last Nan was left at her door. She had managed that George Gerry should give Mary Parish his arm, and told them, as they came up the street with her from the wharf, that she had heard their voices Saturday night as they passed under her window: it was Mary Parish herself who had talked about the best room and its ghosts.

CHAPTER XVIII.

A SERIOUS TEA-DRINKING

It was very good for Nan to find herself cordially welcomed to a company of young people who had little thought of anything but amusement in the pleasant summer weather. Other young guests came to Dunport just then, and the hospitable town seemed to give itself up to their entertainment. Picnics and tea-drinkings followed each other, and the pleasure boats went up river and down river, while there were walks and rides and drives, and all manner of contrivances and excuses for spending much time together on the part of the young men and maidens. It was a good while since Nan had taken such a long holiday, though she had by no means been without the pleasures of society. Not only had she made friends easily during her school-life and her later studies, but Oldfields itself, like all such good old nests, was apt to call back its wandering fledglings when the June weather came. It delighted her more and more to be in Dunport, and though she sometimes grew impatient, wise Dr. Leslie insisted that she must not hurry home. The change was the very best thing in the world for her. Dr. Ferris had alighted for a day or two in the course of one of his wandering flights; and it seemed to the girl that since everything was getting on so well without her in Oldfields, she had better, as the doctor had already expressed it, let her visit run its course like a fever. At any rate she could not come again very soon, and since her aunt seemed so happy, it was a pity to hurry away and end these days sooner than need be. It had been a charming surprise to find herself such a desired companion, and again and again quite the queen of that little court of frolickers, because lately she had felt like one who looks on at such things, and cannot make part of them. Yet all the time that she was playing she thought of her work with growing satisfaction. By other people the knowledge of her having studied medicine was not very well received. It was considered to have been the fault of Miss Prince, who should not have allowed a whimsical country doctor to have beguiled the girl into such silly notions, and many were the shafts sped toward so unwise an aunt for holding out against her niece so many years. To be sure the child had been placed under a most restricted guardianship; but years ago, it was thought, the matter might have been rearranged, and Nan brought to Dunport. It certainly had been much better for her that she had grown up elsewhere; though, for whatever was amiss and willful in her ways, Oldfields was held accountable. It must be confessed that every one who had known her well had discovered sooner or later the untamed wildnesses which seemed like the tangles which one often sees in field-corners,[1] though a most orderly crop is taking up the best part of the room between the fences. Yet she was hard to find fault with, except by very short-sighted persons who resented the least departure by others from the code they themselves had been pleased to authorize, and who could not understand that a nature like Nan's must and could make and keep certain laws of its own.

There seemed to be a sort of inevitableness about the visit; Nan herself hardly knew why she was drifting on day after day without reasonable excuse. Her time had been most carefully ordered and spent during the last few years, and now she sometimes had an uneasy feeling and a lack of confidence in her own steadfastness. But everybody took it for granted that the visit must not come to an end. The doctor showed no sign of expecting her. Miss Prince would be sure to resent her going away, and the pleasure-makers marked one day after another for their own. It seemed impossible, and perhaps unwise, to go on with the reading she had planned, and, in fact, she had been urged to attend to her books rather by habit than natural inclination; and when the temptation to drift with the stream first made itself felt, the reasons for opposing it seemed to fade away. It was easier to remember that Dr. Leslie, and even those

teachers who knew her best at the medical school, had advised
a long vacation.

The first formal visits and entertainments were over with for
the most part, and many of the Dunport acquaintances began
to seem like old friends. There had been a little joking about
Nan's profession, and also some serious remonstrance and unwise championship which did not reach this heroine's ears. It
all seemed romantic and most unusual when anybody talked
about her story at all, and the conclusion was soon reached that
all such whims and extravagances were merely incident to the
pre-Dunportian existence, and that now the young guest had
come to her own, the responsibilities and larger field of activity
would have their influence over her plan of life. The girl herself
was disposed to talk very little about this singular fancy; it may
have been thought that she had grown ashamed of it as seen by
a brighter light, but the truth was it kept a place too near her
heart to allow her to gossip with people who had no real sympathy, and who would ask questions from curiosity alone. Miss
Eunice Fraley had taken more than one opportunity, however,
to confess her interest, though she did this with the manner of
one who dares to be a conspirator against public opinion, and
possibly the permanent welfare of society, and had avowed, beside, her own horror of a doctor's simplest duties. But poor
Miss Fraley looked at her young friend as a caged bird at a window might watch a lark's flight, and was strangely glad whenever there was a chance to spend an hour in Nan's company.

The first evening at Mrs. Fraley's had been a great success,
and Miss Prince had been vastly pleased because both the hostess and the guest had received each other's commendation.
Mrs. Fraley was, perhaps, the one person whom Miss Prince
recognized as a superior officer, and she observed Nan's unconscious and suitable good behavior with great pride. The
hostess had formerly been an undisputed ruler of the highest
social circles of Dunport society, and now in her old age, when
she could no longer be present at any public occasions, she was
still the queen of a little court that assembled in her own house.
It was true that the list of her subjects grew shorter year by
year, but the survivors remained loyal, and hardly expected, or

even desired, that any of the new-comers to the town should recognize their ruler. Nan had been much interested in the old lady's stories, and had gladly accepted an invitation to come often to renew the first conversation. She was able to give Mrs. Fraley much welcome information of the ways and fashions of other centres of civilization, and it was a good thing to make the hours seem shorter. The poor old lady had few alleviations; even religion had served her rather as a basis for argument than an accepted reliance and guide; and though she still prided herself on her selection of words, those which she used in formal conversations with the clergyman seemed more empty and meaningless than most others. Mrs. Fraley was leaving this world reluctantly; she had been well fitted by nature for social preëminence, and had never been half satisfied with the opportunities provided for the exercise of her powers. It was only lately that she had been forced to acknowledge that Time showed signs of defeating her in the projects of her life, and she had begun to give up the fight altogether, and to mourn bitterly and aggressively to her anxious and resourceless daughter. It was plain enough that the dissatisfactions and infirmities of age were more than usually great, and poor Eunice was only too glad when the younger Miss Prince proved herself capable of interesting the old friend of her family, and Mrs. Fraley took heart and suggested both informal visits and future entertainments. The prudent daughter was careful not to tell her mother of the guest's revolutionary ideas, and for a time all went well, until some unwise person, unaware of Miss Fraley's warning gestures from the other side of the sitting-room, proceeded to give a totally unnecessary opinion of the propriety of women's studying medicine. Poor Eunice expected that a sharp rebuke, followed by a day or two's disdain and general unpleasantness, would descend upon her quaking shoulders; but, to her surprise, nothing was said until the next morning, when she was bidden, at much inconvenience to the household, to invite Miss Prince and her niece to come that afternoon to drink tea quite informally.

There was a pathetic look in the messenger's faded face,—she felt unusually at odds with fortune as she glided along the street, sheltered by the narrow shadows of the high fences. Nan herself came to the door, and when she threw back the closed blinds and discovered the visitor, she drew her in with most cordial welcome, and the two friends entered the darkened south parlor, where it was cool, and sweet with the fragrance of some honeysuckle which Nan had brought in early that morning from the garden.

"Dear me," said the little woman deprecatingly. "I don't know why I came in at all. I can't stop to make a call. Mother was very desirous that you and your aunt should come over to tea this evening. It seems a good deal to ask in such hot weather, but she has so little to amuse her, and I really don't see that the weather makes much difference, she used to feel the heat very much years ago." And Miss Eunice gave a sigh, and fanned herself slowly, letting the fan which had been put into her hand turn itself quite over on her lap before it came up again. There was an air of antique elegance about this which amused Nan, who stood by the table wiping with her handkerchief some water that had dropped from the vase. A great many of the ladies in church the Sunday before had fanned themselves in this same little languishing way; she remembered one or two funny old persons in Oldfields who gave themselves airs after the same fashion.

"I think we shall both be very pleased," she answered directly, with a bit of a smile; while Miss Fraley gazed at her admiringly, and thought she had never seen the girl look so fresh and fair as she did in this plain, cool little dress. There had been more water than was at first suspected; the handkerchief was a limp, white handful, and they both laughed as it was held up. Miss Fraley insisted that she could not stay. She must go to the shops to do some errands, and hoped to meet Miss Prince who had gone that way half an hour before.

"Don't mind anything mother may say to you," she entreated, after lingering a minute, and looking imploringly in Nan's face. "You know we can't expect a person of her age to look at everything just as we do."

"Am I to be scolded?" asked Nan, serenely. "Do you know what it is about?"

"Oh, perhaps nothing," answered Miss Fraley, quickly. "I ought not to have spoken, only I fancied she was a little distressed at the idea of your being interested in medicines. I don't know anything that is more useful myself. I am sure every family needs to have some one who has some knowledge of such things; it saves calling a doctor. My sister Susan knows more than any of us, and it has been very useful to her with her large family."

"But I shouldn't be afraid to come, I think," said Nan, laughing. "Mrs. Fraley told me that she would finish that story of the diamond ring, you know, and we shall get on capitally. Really I think her stories of old times are wonderfully interesting. I wish I had a gift for writing them down whenever I am listening to her."

Miss Eunice was much relieved, and felt sure that Nan was equal to any emergency. The girl had put a strong young arm quickly round her guest's thin shoulders, and had kissed her affectionately, and this had touched the lonely little woman's very heart.

There were signs of storm in Madam Fraley's face that evening, but everybody feigned not to observe them, and Nan behaved with perilous disregard of a lack of encouragement, and made herself and the company uncommonly merry. She described the bad effect her coming had had upon her aunt's orderly house. She confessed to having left her own possessions in such confusion the evening before when she dressed again to go up the river, that Priscilla had called it a monkey's wedding, and had gone away after one scornful look inside the door. Miss Fraley dared to say that no one could mind seeing such pretty things, and even Miss Prince mentioned that her niece was not so careless as she would make them believe; while Nan begged to know if anybody had ever heard of a monkey's wedding before, and seemed very much amused.

"She called such a disarray in the kitchen one morning the monkey's wedding breakfast," said Miss Prince, as if she never had thought it particularly amusing until this minute. "Priscilla has always made use of a great many old-fashioned expressions."[2]

They had seated themselves at the tea-table; it was evident that Miss Fraley had found it a hard day, for she looked tired and worn. The mistress of the house was dressed in her best and most imposing clothes, and sat solemnly in her place. A careful observer might have seen that the best blue teacups with their scalloped edges[3] were not set forth. The occasion wore the air of a tribunal rather than that of a festival, and it was impossible not to feel a difference between it and the former tea-party.

Miss Prince was not particularly sensitive to moods and atmospheres; she happened to be in very good spirits, and talked for some time before she became entirely aware that something had gone wrong, but presently faltered, and fell under the ban, looking questioningly toward poor Eunice, who busied herself with the tea-tray.

"Nancy," said Mrs. Fraley impatiently, "I was amazed to find that there is a story going about town that your niece here is studying to be a doctor. I hope that you don't countenance any such nonsense?"

Miss Prince looked helpless and confounded, and turned her eyes toward her niece. She could only hope at such a mortifying juncture that Nan was ready to explain, or at least to shoulder the responsibility.

"Indeed she doesn't give me any encouragement, Mrs. Fraley," said Nan, fearlessly. "Only this morning she saw a work on ventilation in my room and told me it wasn't proper reading for a young woman."[4]

"I really didn't look at the title," said Miss Prince, smiling in spite of herself.

"It doesn't seem to improve the health of you young folks because you think it necessary to become familiar with such subjects," announced the irate old lady. It was her habit to take a very slight refreshment at the usual tea hour, and supplement it by a substantial lunch at bed-time, and so now she was not only at leisure herself, but demanded the attention of her guests. She had evidently prepared an opinion, and was determined to give it. Miss Eunice grew smaller and thinner than ever, and fairly shivered with shame behind the tea-tray. She looked steadily at the big sugar-bowl, as if she were thinking whether she might creep into it and pull something over her head. She never liked an argument, even if it were a good-natured one, and always had a vague sense of personal guilt and danger.

"In my time," Mrs. Fraley continued, "it was thought proper for young women to show an interest in household affairs. When I was married it was not asked whether I was acquainted with dissecting-rooms."

"But I don't think there is any need of that," replied Nan. "I think such things are the duty of professional men and women only. I am very far from believing that every girl ought to be a surgeon any more than that she ought to be an astronomer. And as for the younger people's being less strong than the old, I am afraid it is their own fault, since we understand the laws of health better than we used. 'Who breaks, pays,' you know."

It was evidently not expected that the young guest should venture to discuss the question, but rather have accepted her rebuke meekly, and acknowledged herself in the wrong. But she had the courage of her opinions, and the eagerness of youth, and could hardly bear to be so easily defeated. So when Mrs. Fraley, mistaking the moment's silence for a final triumph, said again, that a woman's place was at home, and that a strong-minded woman was out of place, and unwelcome everywhere, the girl's cheeks flushed suddenly.

"I think it is a pity that we have fallen into a habit of using strong-mindedness as a term of rebuke," she said. "I am willing to acknowledge that people who are eager for reforms are apt to develop unpleasant traits, but it is only because they have to fight against opposition and ignorance. When they are dead and the world is reaping the reward of their bravery and constancy, it no longer laughs, but makes statues of them, and praises them, and thanks them in every way it can. I think we ought to judge each other by the highest standards, Mrs. Fraley, and by whether we are doing good work."

"My day is past," said the hostess. "I do not belong to the

present, and I suppose my judgment is worth nothing to you;" and Nan looked up quickly and affectionately.

"I should like to have all my friends believe that I am doing right," she said. "I do feel very certain that we must educate people properly if we want them to be worth anything. It is no use to treat all the boys and girls as if nature had meant them for the same business and scholarship, and try to put them through the same drill, for that is sure to mislead and confuse all those who are not perfectly sure of what they want. There are plenty of people dragging themselves miserably through the world, because they are clogged and fettered with work for which they have no fitness. I know I haven't had the experience that you have, Mrs. Fraley, but I can't help believing that nothing is better than to find one's work early and hold fast to it, and put all one's heart into it."

"I have done my best to serve God in the station to which it has pleased Him to call me," said Mrs. Fraley, stiffly. "I believe that a young man's position is very different from a girl's. To be sure, I can give my opinion that everything went better when the master workmen took apprentices to their trades, and there wasn't so much schooling. But I warn you, my dear, that your notion about studying to be a doctor has shocked me very much indeed. I could not believe my ears,—a refined girl who bears an honorable and respected name to think of being a woman doctor! If you were five years older you would never have dreamed of such a thing. It lowers the pride of all who have any affection for you. If it were not that your early life had been somewhat peculiar and most unfortunate, I should blame you more; as it is, I can but wonder at the lack of judgment in others. I shall look forward in spite of it all to seeing you happily married." To which Miss Prince assented with several decided nods.

"This is why I made up my mind to be a physician," said the culprit; and though she had been looking down and growing more uncomfortable every moment, she suddenly gave her head a quick upward movement and looked at Mrs. Fraley frankly, with a beautiful light in her clear eyes. "I believe that God has given me a fitness for it, and that I never could do anything else half so well. Nobody persuaded me into following such a plan; I simply grew toward it. And I have everything to learn, and a great many faults to overcome, but I am trying to get on as fast as may be. I can't be too glad that I have spent my childhood in a way that has helped me to use my gift instead of hindering it. But everything helps a young man to follow his bent; he has an honored place in society, and just because he is a student of one of the learned professions, he ranks above the men who follow other pursuits. I don't see why it should be a shame and dishonor to a girl who is trying to do the same thing and to be of equal use in the world. God would not give us the same talents if what were right for men were wrong for women."

"My dear, it is quite unnatural you see," said the antagonist, impatiently. "Here you are less than twenty-five years old, and I shall hear of your being married next thing,—at least I hope I shall,—and you will laugh at all this nonsense. A woman's place is at home. Of course I know that there have been some women physicians who have attained eminence, and some artists, and all that. But I would rather see a daughter of mine take a more retired place. The best service to the public can be done by keeping one's own house in order and one's husband comfortable, and by attending to those social responsibilities which come in our way. The mothers of the nation have rights enough and duties enough already, and need not look farther than their own firesides, or wish for the plaudits of an ignorant public."

"But if I do not wish to be married, and do not think it right that I should be," said poor Nan at last. "If I have good reasons against all that, would you have me bury the talent God has given me, and choke down the wish that makes itself a prayer every morning that I may do this work lovingly and well? It is the best way I can see of making myself useful in the world. People must have good health or they will fail of reaching what success and happiness are possible for them; and so many persons might be better and stronger than they are now, which would make their lives very different. I do think if I can help my neighbors in this way it will be a great kindness. I won't attempt to say that the study of medicine is a proper vocation for women, only that I believe more and more every year that it is the proper study for me. It certainly cannot be the proper vocation of all women to bring up children, so many of them are dead failures at it; and I don't see why all girls should be thought failures who do not marry. I don't believe that half those who do marry have any real right to it, at least until people use common sense as much in that most important decision as in lesser ones. Of course we can't expect to bring about an ideal state of society all at once; but just because we don't really believe in having the best possible conditions, we make no effort at all toward even better ones. People ought to work with the great laws of nature and not against them."

"You don't know anything about it," said Mrs. Fraley, who hardly knew what to think of this ready opposition. "You don't know what you are talking about, Anna. You have neither age nor experience, and it is easy to see you have been associating with very foolish people. I am the last person to say that every marriage is a lucky one; but if you were my daughter I should never consent to your injuring your chances for happiness in this way."

Nan could not help stealing a glance at poor Miss Eunice, behind her fragile battlement of the tea-set, and was deeply touched at the glance of sympathy which dimly flickered in the lonely eyes. "I do think, mother, that Anna is right about single women's having some occupation," was timidly suggested. "Of course, I mean those who have no special home duties; I can see that life would not"—

"Now Eunice," interrupted the commander in chief, "I do wish you could keep an opinion of your own. You are the last person to take up with such ideas. I have no patience with people who don't know their own minds half an hour together."

"There are plenty of foolish women who marry, I'll acknowledge," said Miss Prince, for the sake of coming to the rescue. "I was really angry yesterday, when Mrs. Gerry told me that everybody was so pleased to hear that Hattie Barlow was engaged, because she was incapable of doing anything to support herself. I couldn't help feeling that if there was so little power that it had never visibly turned itself in any practical direction, she wasn't likely to be a good housekeeper. I think that is a most responsible situation, myself."

Nan looked up gratefully. "It isn't so much that people can't do anything, as that they try to do the wrong things, Aunt Nancy. We all are busy enough or ought to be; only the richest people have the most cares and have to work hardest. I used to think that rich city people did nothing but amuse themselves, when I was a little girl; but I often wonder nowadays at the wisdom and talent that are needed to keep a high social position respected in the world's eyes. It must be an orderly and really strong-minded woman who can keep her business from getting into a most melancholy tangle. Yet nobody is afraid when the most foolish girls take such duties upon themselves, and all the world cries out with fear of disaster, if once in a while one makes up her mind to some other plan of life. Of course I know being married isn't a trade: it is a natural condition of life, which permits a man to follow certain public careers, and forbids them to a woman. And since I have not wished to be married, and have wished to study medicine, I don't see what act of Parliament can punish me."

"Wait until Mr. Right comes along," said Mrs. Fraley, who had pushed back her chair from the table and was beating her foot on the floor in a way that betokened great displeasure and impatience. "I am only thankful I had my day when women were content to be stayers at home. I am only speaking for your good, and you'll live to see the truth of it, poor child!"

"I am sure she will get over this," apologized Miss Prince, after they had reached the parlor, for she found that her niece had lingered with Miss Fraley in the dining-room.

"Don't talk to me about the Princes changing their minds," answered the scornful old hostess. "You ought to know them better than that by this time." But just at that moment young Gerry came tapping at the door, and the two ladies quickly softened their excited looks and welcomed him as the most powerful argument for their side of the debate. It seemed quite a thing of the past that he should have fancied Mary Parish, and more than one whisper had been listened to that the young man was likely to have the Prince inheritance, after all. He looked uncommonly well that evening, and the elder women could not imagine that any damsel of his own age would consider him slightingly. Nan had given a little shrug of impatience when she heard his voice join the weaker ones in the parlor, and a sense of discomfort that she never had felt before came over her suddenly. She reminded herself that she must tell her aunt that very night that the visit must come to an end. She had neglected her books and her drives with the doctor altogether too long already.

CHAPTER XIX.

FRIEND AND LOVER

In these summer days the young lawyer's thoughts had often been busy elsewhere while he sat at the shaded office window and looked out upon the river. The very housekeeping on the damaged ship became more interesting to him than his law books, and he watched the keeper's wife at her various employments on deck, or grew excited as he witnessed the good woman's encounters with marauding small boys, who prowled about hoping for chances of climbing the rigging or solving the mysteries of the hold. It had come to be an uncommon event that a square-rigged vessel[1] should make the harbor of Dunport, and the elder citizens ignored the deserted wharves, and talked proudly of the days of Dunport's prosperity, convicting the railroad of its decline as much as was consistent with their possession of profitable stock. The younger people took the empty warehouses for granted, and listened to their grandparents' stories with interest, if they did not hear them too often; and the more enterprising among them spread their wings of ambition and flew away to the larger cities or to the westward. George Gerry had stayed behind reluctantly. He had neither enough desire for a more active life, nor so high a purpose that he could disregard whatever opposition lay in his way. Yet he was honestly dissatisfied with his surroundings, and thought himself hardly used by a hindering fate. He believed himself to be most anxious to get away, yet he was like a ship which will not be started out of port by anything less than a hurricane. There really were excuses for his staying at home, and since he had stopped to listen to them they beguiled him more and more, and his friends one by one commended his devotion to his mother and sisters, and sometimes forgot to sympathize with him for his disappointments as they praised him for being such a dutiful son. To be sure, he might be a great lawyer in Dunport as well as anywhere else; he would not be the first; but a more inspiring life might have made him more enthusiastic and energetic, and if he could have been winning his way faster elsewhere, and sending home good accounts of himself, not to speak of substantial aid, there is no question whether it would not have given his family greater happiness and done himself more good. He was not possessed of the stern determination which wins its way at all hazards, and so was dependent upon his surroundings for an occasional stimulus.

But Dunport was very grateful to him because he had stayed at home, and he was altogether the most prominent young man in the town. It is so easy to be thankful that one's friends are no worse that one sometimes forgets to remember that they might be better; and it would have been only natural if he thought of himself more highly than he ought to think, since he had received a good deal of applause and admiration. It is true that he had avoided vice more noticeably than he had pursued virtue; but the senior member of the firm, Mr. Sergeant, pronounced his young partner to have been a most excellent student, and not only showed the greatest possible confidence in him, but was transferring a good deal of the business to him already. Miss Prince and her old lawyer had one secret which had never been suspected, and the townspeople thought more than ever of young Mr. Gerry's ability when it was known that the most distinguished legal authority of that region had given him a share of a long-established business. George Gerry had been led to think better of himself, though it had caused him no little wonder when the proposal had been made. It was possible that Mr. Sergeant feared that there might be some alliance offered by his rivals in Dunport. To be sure, the younger firm had been making a good deal of money, but it was less respected by the leading business men. Mr. Sergeant had even conferred with his young friend one morning upon the propriety of some new investments; but Mr. Gerry had never even suspected that they were the price of his own new dignity and claim upon the public honor. Captain Walter Parish and Mr. Sergeant had both been aids and advisers of Miss Prince; but neither had ever known the condition of all her financial affairs, and she had made the most of a comfortable sense of liberty. To do young Gerry justice, he had not hesitated to express his amazement; and among his elders and betters, at any rate, he had laid his good fortune at the door of Mr. Sergeant's generosity and kindness instead of his own value.

But at certain seasons of the year, like this, there was no excitement in the office, and after an attendance at court and the proper adjustment, whether temporary or permanent, of the subsequent business, the partners had returned to a humdrum fulfilling of the minor duties of their profession, and the younger man worked at his law books when there were no deeds or affidavits to engage his attention. He thought of many things as he sat by his window; it was a great relief to the tiresomeness of the dull rooms to look at the river and at the shores and hills beyond; to notice carelessly whether the tide came in or went out. He was apt to feel a sense of dissatisfaction in his leisure moments; and now a new current was bringing all its force to bear upon him in his quiet anchorage.

He had looked upon Miss Prince as a kind adviser; he was on more intimate terms with her than with any woman he knew; and the finer traits in his character were always brought out by some compelling force in her dignity and simple adherence to her somewhat narrow code of morals and etiquette. He was grateful to her for many kindnesses; and as he had grown older and come to perceive the sentiment which had been the first motive of her affection toward him, he had instinctively responded with a mingling of gallantry and sympathy which made him, as has been already said, appear at his very best. The gossips of Dunport had whispered that he knew that it was more than worth his while to be polite to Miss Prince; but he was too manly a fellow to allow any trace of subserviency to show itself in his conduct. As often happens, he had come back to Dunport almost a stranger after his years of college life were over, and he had a mingled love and impatience for the old place. The last year had been very pleasant, however: there were a few young men whose good comrade and leader he was; his relations with his fellow-citizens were most harmonious; and as for the girls of his own age and their younger sisters, who were just growing up, he was immensely popular and admired by them. It had become a subject of much discussion whether he and Mary Parish would not presently decide upon becoming engaged to each other, until Miss Prince's long-banished niece came to put a new suspicion into everybody's mind.

Many times when George Gerry had a new proof that he had somehow fallen into the habit of walking home with the pleasant girl who was his friend and neighbor, he had told himself abruptly that there was no danger in it, and that they never could have any other feeling for each other. But he had begun to think also that she belonged to him in some vague way, and sometimes acknowledged that it might be a thing to consider more deeply by and by. He was only twenty-six, and the world was still before him,[2] but he was not very sympathetic with other people's enthusiasm over their love affairs, and wondered if it were not largely a matter of temperament, though by and by he should like to have a home of his own.

He was somewhat attracted toward Miss Prince, the younger, for her aunt's sake, and had made up his mind that he would be very attentive to her, no matter how displeasing and uninteresting she might be: it was sure to be a time of trial to his old friend, and he would help all he could to make the visit as bearable as possible. Everybody knew of the niece's existence who had known the Prince family at all, and though Miss Prince had never mentioned the unhappy fact until the day or two before her guest was expected, her young cavalier had behaved with most excellent discretion, and feigning neither surprise nor dismay, accepted the announcement in a way that had endeared him still more to his patroness.

But on the first Sunday morning, when a most admirable young lady had walked up the broad aisle of St. Ann's church,[3] and Mr. Gerry had caught a glimpse of her between the rows of heads which all looked commonplace by contrast, it seemed to begin a new era of things. This was a welcome link with the busier world outside Dunport; this was what he had missed since he had ended his college days, a gleam of cosmopolitan sunshine, which made the provincial fog less attractive than ever. He was anxious to claim companionship with this fair citizen of a larger world, and to disclaim any idea of belonging to the humdrum little circle which exaggerated its own importance. He persuaded himself that he must pay Miss Prince's guest an early visit. It was very exciting and interesting altogether; and as he watched the flicker of light in our heroine's hair as she sat on the straight sofa in her aunt's parlor on the Sunday evening, a feeling of great delight stole over him. He had known many nice girls in his lifetime, but there was something uncommonly interesting about Miss Anna Prince; besides, who could help being grateful to her for being so much nicer than anybody had expected?

And so the days went by. Nobody thought there was any objection when the junior partner of the law firm took holiday after holiday, for there was little business and Mr. Sergeant liked to keep on with his familiar routine. His old friends came to call frequently, and they had their conferences in peace, and were not inclined to object if the younger ears were being used elsewhere. Young people will be young people, and June weather does not always last; and if George Gerry were more devoted to social duties than to legal ones, it was quite natural, and he had just acquitted himself most honorably at the May term of court,⁴ and was his own master if he decided to take a vacation.

He had been amused when the announcement had been made so early in their acquaintance that Nan meant to study medicine. He believed if there were any fault, it was Dr. Leslie's, and only thought it a pity that her evident practical talents had not been under the guidance of a more sensible director. The girl's impetuous defense of her choice was very charming; he had often heard Mr. Sergeant speak of the rare insight and understanding of legal matters which his favorite daughter had possessed, and her early death had left a lonely place in the good man's heart. Miss Prince's life at Oldfields must have been very dull, especially since her boarding-school days were over. For himself he had a great prejudice against the usurpation of men's duties and prerogatives by women, and had spoken of all such assumptions with contempt. It made a difference that this attractive young student had spoken bravely on the wrong side; but if he had thought much about it he would have made himself surer and surer that only time was needed to show her the mistake. If he had gone deeper into the subject he would have said that he thought it all nonsense about women's having the worst of it in life; he had known more than one good fellow who had begun to go down hill from the day he was married, and if girls would only take the trouble to fit themselves for their indoor business the world would be a vastly more comfortable place. And as for their tinkering at the laws, such projects should be bitterly resented.

It only needed a few days to make it plain to this good fellow that the coming of one of the summer guests had made a great difference in his life. It was easy to find a hundred excuses for going to Miss Prince's, who smiled benignantly upon his evident interest in the fair stranger within her gates.[5] The truth must be confessed, however, that the episode of the lamed shoulder at the picnic party had given Mr. George Gerry great unhappiness. There was something so high and serene in Anna Prince's simplicity and directness, and in the way in which she had proved herself adequate to so unusual an occasion, that he could not help mingling a good deal of admiration with his dissatisfaction. It is in human nature to respect power; but all his manliness was at stake, and his natural rights would be degraded and lost, if he could not show his power to be greater than her own. And as the days went by, every one made him more certain that he longed, more than he had ever longed for anything before, to win her love. His heart had never before been deeply touched, but life seemed now like a heap of dry wood, which had only waited for a live coal to make it flame and leap in mysterious light, and transfigure itself from dullness into a bewildering and unaccountable glory. It was no wonder any longer that poets had sung best of love and its joys and sorrows, and that men and women, since the world began, had followed at its call. All life and its history was explained anew, yet this eager lover felt himself to be the first discoverer of the world's great secret.

It was hard to wait and to lack assurance, but while the hours when he had the ideal and the dream seemed to make him certain, he had only to go back to Miss Prince's to become doubtful and miserable again. The world did not consent to second his haste, and the persons most concerned in his affairs were stupidly slow at understanding the true state of them. While every day made the prize look more desirable, every day seemed to put another barrier between himself and Nan; and when she spoke of her visit's end it was amazing to him that she should not understand his misery. He wondered at himself more and more because he seemed to have the power of behaving much as usual when he was with his friends; it seemed impossible that he could always go on without betraying his thoughts. There was no question of any final opposition to his suit, it seemed to him; he could not be more sure than he was already of Miss Prince's willingness to let him plead his cause with her niece, so many vexed questions would be pleasantly answered; and he ventured to hope that the girl herself would be glad to spend her life in dear old Dunport, where her father's people had been honored for so many years. The good Dr. Leslie must be fast growing old, and, though he would miss his adopted child, it was reasonable that he should be glad to see her happily anchored in a home of her own, before he died. If Nan were friendless and penniless it would make no difference; but nevertheless, for her sake, it was good to remember that some one had said that Dr. Leslie, unlike most physicians, was a man of fortune.[6] And nothing remained but to win an affection which should match his own, and this impatient suitor walked and drove and spent the fleeting hours in waiting for a chance to show himself in the lists of love. It seemed years instead of weeks at last, and yet as if he had only been truly alive and free since love had made him captive. He could not fasten himself down to his work without great difficulty, though he built many a castle in Spain with his imagined wealth, and laid deep plans of study and acquirement which should be made evident as time went on.

All things seemed within his reach in these first days of his enlightenment: it had been like the rising of the sun which showed him a new world of which he was lawful master, but the minor events of his blissful existence began to conspire against him in a provoking way, and presently it was sadly forced upon his understanding that Anna Prince was either unconscious or disdainful of his affection. It could hardly be the latter, for she was always friendly and hospitable, and took his courtesies in such an unsuspecting and grateful way. There was something so self-reliant about her and so independent of any one's protection, that this was the most discouraging thing of all, for his own instinct was that of standing between her and all harm,—of making himself responsible for her shelter and happiness. She seemed to get on capitally well without him, but after all he could not help being conqueror in so just and inevitable a war. The old proverb suddenly changed from a pebble to a diamond,[7] and he thanked the philosopher more than once who had first reminded the world that faint heart ne'er won fair lady;[8] presently he grew sad, as lovers will, and became paler and less vigorous, and made his friends wonder a good deal, until they at last suspected his sweet sorrow, and ranged themselves in eager ranks upon his side, with all history and tradition in their favor.

Nan herself was not among the first to suspect that one of her new friends had proved to be a lover; she had been turned away from such suspicions by her very nature; and when she had been forced to believe in one or two other instances that she was unwillingly drawing to herself the devotion which most women unconsciously seek, she had been made most uncomfortable, and had repelled all possibility of its further progress. She had believed herself proof against such assailment, and so indeed she had been; but on the very evening of her battle for her opinions at Mrs. Fraley's she had been suddenly confronted by a new enemy, a strange power, which seemed so dangerous that she was at first overwhelmed by a sense of her own defenselessness.

She had waited with Miss Fraley, who was not quite ready to leave the dining-room with the rest, and had been much touched by her confidence. Poor Eunice had been very fond of one of her school-fellows, who had afterward entered the navy, and who had been fond of her in return. But as everybody had opposed the match, for her sake, and had placed little reliance in the young man, she had meekly given up all hope of being his wife, and he had died of yellow fever at Key West[9] soon after. "We were not even engaged you know, dear," whispered the little lady, "but somehow I have always felt in my heart that I belonged to him. Though I believe every word you said about a girl's having an independence of her own. It is a great blessing to have always had such a person as my mother to lean upon, but I should be quite helpless if she were taken away. . . . Of course I have had what I needed and what we could afford," she went on, after another pause, "but I never can get over hating to ask for money. I do sometimes envy the women who earn what they spend."

Nan's eyes flashed. "I think it is only fair that even those who have to spend their husband's or their father's money should be made to feel it is their own. If one does absolutely nothing in one's home, and is not even able to give pleasure, then I think it is stealing. I have felt so strongly about that since I have grown up, for you know Dr. Leslie, my guardian, has done everything for me. Aunt Nancy gave me money every year, but I never spent any of it until I went away to school, and then I insisted upon taking that and what my grandmother left me. But my later studies have more than used it all. Dr. Leslie is so kind to me, like an own father, and I am looking forward to my life with him most eagerly. After the next year or two I shall be at home all the time, and I am so glad to think I can really help him, and that we are interested in the same things."

Miss Eunice was a little incredulous, though she did not dare to say so. In the first place, she could not be persuaded that a woman could possibly know as much about diseases and their remedies as a man, and she wondered if even the rural inhabitants of Oldfields would cheerfully accept the change from their trusted physician to his young ward, no matter what sails of diplomas she might spread to the breeze. But Nan's perfect faith and confidence were not to be lightly disputed; and if the practice of medicine by women could be made honorable, it certainly was in able hands here, as far as an admiring friend could decide. Nan was anything but self-asserting, and she had no noisy fashion of thrusting herself before the public gaze, but everybody trusted her who knew her; she had the rare and noble faculty of inspiring confidence.

There was no excuse for a longer absence from the parlor, where Mrs. Fraley was throned in state in her high-backed chair, and was already calling the loiterers. She and Miss Prince were smiling indulgently upon the impatient young man, who was describing to them a meeting of the stockholders of the Turnpike Company,[10] of which he had last year been made secretary. A dividend had been declared, and it was larger than had been expected, and the ladies were as grateful as if he had furnished the means from his own pocket. He looked very tall and handsome and business-like as he rose to salute Miss Fraley and Nan, and presently told his real errand. He apologized for interfering with the little festival, but two or three of the young people had suddenly made a plan for going to see a play which was to be given that night in the town hall by a traveling company. Would Miss Anna Prince care to go, and Miss Fraley?

Nan hardly knew why she at once refused, and was filled with regret when she saw a look of childish expectancy on Miss Eunice's face quickly change to disappointment.

"It is too hot to shut one's self into that close place, I am afraid," she said. "And I am enjoying myself very much here, Mr. Gerry." Which was generous on Nan's part, if one considered the premeditated war which had been waged against her. Then the thought flashed through her mind that it might be a bit of good fun for her companion; and without waiting for either approval or opposition from the elder women, she said, in a different tone, "However, if Miss Fraley will go too, I will accept with pleasure; I suppose it is quite time?" and before there could be a formal dissent she had hurried the pleased daughter of the house, who was not quick in her movements, to her room, and in a few minutes, after a good deal of laughter which the presence of the escort kept anybody from even wishing to silence, the three were fairly started down the street. It was of no avail that Mrs. Fraley condemned her own judgment in not having advised Eunice to stay at home and leave the young people free, and that Miss Prince made a feeble protest for politeness' sake,—the pleasure-makers could not be called back.

Nan had really grown into a great liking for George Gerry. She often thought it would have been very good to have such a brother. But more than one person in the audience thought they had never seen a braver young couple; and the few elderly persons of discretion who had gone to the play felt their hearts thrill with sudden sympathy as our friends went far down the room to their seats. Miss Fraley was almost girlish herself, and looked so pleased and bright that everybody who cared anything about her smiled when they caught sight of her, she was so prim and neat; it was impossible for her, under any circumstances, to look anything but discreet and quaint; but as for Nan, she was beautiful with youth and health; as simply dressed as Miss Eunice, but with the gayety of a flower,—some slender, wild thing, that has sprung up fearlessly under the great sky, with only the sunshine and the wind and summer rain to teach it, and help it fulfill its destiny,—a flower that has grown with no painful effort of its own, but because God made it and kept it; that has bloomed because it has come in the course of its growth to the right time. And Miss Eunice, like a hindered little house-plant, took a long breath of delight as she sat close by her kind young friend, and felt as if somebody had set her roots free from their familiar prison.

To let God make us, instead of painfully trying to make ourselves; to follow the path that his love shows us, instead of through conceit or cowardice or mockery choosing another; to trust Him for our strength and fitness as the flowers do, simply giving ourselves back to Him in grateful service,—this is to keep the laws that give us the freedom of the city in which there is no longer any night of bewilderment or ignorance or uncertainty. So the woman who had lived a life of bondage, whose hardest task-master was herself, and the woman who had been both taught and inspired to hold fast her freedom, sat side by side: the one life having been blighted because it lacked its mate, and was but half a life in itself; while the other, fearing to give half its royalty or to share its bounty, was being tempted to cripple itself, and to lose its strait and narrow way where God had left no room for another.[11]

For as the play went on and the easily pleased audience laughed and clapped its hands, and the tired players bowed and smiled from behind the flaring foot-lights, there was one spectator who was conscious of a great crisis in her own life, which the mimicry of that evening seemed to ridicule and counterfeit. And though Nan smiled with the rest, and even talked with her neighbors while the tawdry curtain had fallen, it seemed to her that the coming of Death at her life's end could not be more strange and sudden than this great barrier which had fallen between her and her girlhood, the dear old life which had kept her so unpuzzled and safe. So this was love at last, this fear, this change, this strange relation to another soul. Who could stand now at her right hand and give her grace to hold fast the truth that her soul must ever be her own?

The only desire that possessed her was to be alone again, to make Love show his face as well as make his mysterious presence felt. She was thankful for the shelter of the crowd, and went on, wishing that the short distance to her aunt's home could be made even shorter. She had felt this man's love for her only in a vague way before, and now, as he turned to speak to her from time to time, she could not meet his eyes. The groups of people bade each other good-night merrily, though the entertainment had been a little tiresome to every one at the last, and it seemed the briefest space of time before Miss Fraley and Nan and their cavalier were left by themselves, and at last Nan and George Gerry were alone together.

For his part he had never been so happy as that night. It seemed to him that his wish was coming true, and he spoke gently enough and of the same things they might have talked about the night before, but a splendid chorus of victory was sounding in his ears; and once, as they stopped for a moment to look between two of the old warehouses at the shining river and the masts and rigging of the ship against the moon-lighted sky, he was just ready to speak to the girl at his side. But he looked at her first and then was silent. There was something in her face that forbade it,—a whiteness and a strange look in her eyes, that made him lose all feeling of comradeship or even acquaintance. "I wonder if the old Highflyer will ever go out again?" she said slowly. "Captain Parish told me some time ago that he had found her more badly damaged than he supposed. A vessel like that belongs to the high seas, and is like a prisoner when it touches shore. I believe that the stray souls that have no bodies must sometimes make a dwelling in inanimate things and make us think they are alive. I am always sorry for that ship"—

"Its guardian angel must have been asleep the night of the collision," laughed young Gerry, uneasily; he was displeased with himself the moment afterward, but Nan laughed too, and felt a sense of reprieve; and they went on again and said good night quietly on the steps of the old Prince house. It was very late for Dunport, and the door was shut, but through the bull's-eyed panes of glass overhead a faint light was shining, though it could hardly assert itself against the moonlight. Miss Prince was still down-stairs, and her niece upbraided her, and then began to give an account of the play, which was cut short by the mistress of the house; for after one eager, long look at Nan, she became sleepy and disappointed, and they said good-night; but the girl felt certain that her aunt was leagued against her, and grew sick at heart and tired as she climbed the stairs. There was a letter on the long mahogany table in the hall, and Nan stopped and looked over the railing at it wearily. Miss Prince stopped too, and said she was sorry she had forgotten,—it was from Oldfields, and in Dr. Leslie's writing. But though Nan went back for it, and kissed it more than once before she went to bed, and even put it under her pillow as a comfort and defense against she knew not what, for the first time in her life she was afraid to open it and read the kind words. That night she watched the moonlight creep along the floor, and heard the cocks crow at midnight and in the morning; the birds woke with the new day while she tried to understand the day that had gone, wondering what she must do and say when she faced the world again only a few hours later.

Sometimes she felt herself carried along upon a rushing tide, and was amazed that a hundred gifts and conditions to which she had scarcely given a thought seemed dear and necessary. Once she fancied herself in a quiet home; living there, perhaps, in that very house, and being pleased with her ordering and care-taking. And her great profession was all like a fading dream; it seemed now no matter whether she had ever loved the studies of it, or been glad to think that she had it in her power to make suffering less, or prevent it altogether. Her old ambitions were torn away from her one by one, and in their place came the hardly-desired satisfactions of love and marriage, and home-making and housekeeping, the dear, womanly, sheltered fashions of life, toward which she had been thankful to see her friends go hand in hand, making themselves a complete happiness which nothing else could match. But as the night waned, the certainty of her duty grew clearer and clearer. She had long ago made up her mind that she must not marry. She might be happy, it was true, and make other people so, but her duty was not this, and a certainty that satisfaction and the blessing of God would not follow her into these reverenced and honored limits came to her distinctly. One by one the reasons for keeping on her chosen course grew more unanswerable than ever. She had not thought she should be called to resist this temptation, but since it had come she was glad she was strong enough to meet it. It would be no real love for another person, and no justice to herself, to give up her work, even though holding it fast would bring weariness and pain and reproach, and the loss of many things that other women held dearest and best.

In the morning Nan smiled when her aunt noticed her tired look, and said that the play had been a pursuit of pleasure under difficulties. And though Miss Prince looked up in dismay, and was full of objections and almost querulous reproaches because Nan said she must end her visit within a day or two, she hoped that George Gerry would be, after all, a reason for the girl's staying. Until Nan, who had been standing by the window, looking wistfully at the garden, suddenly turned and said, gently and solemnly, "Listen, Aunt Nancy! I must be about my business;[12] you do not know what it means to me, or what I hope to make it mean to other people." And then Miss Prince knew once for all, that it was useless to hope or to plan any longer. But she would not let herself be vanquished so easily, and summoned to her mind many assurances that girls would not be too easily won, and after a short season of disapproving silence, returned to her usual manner as if there had been neither difference nor dispute.

CHAPTER XX.

ASHORE AND AFLOAT

"Your cousin Walter Parish is coming to dine with us to-day," said Miss Prince, later that morning. "He came to the Fraleys just after you went out last evening, to speak with me about a business matter, and waited to walk home with me afterward. I have been meaning to invite him here with his wife, but there doesn't seem to be much prospect of her leaving her room for some time yet, and this morning I happened to find an uncommonly good pair of young ducks. Old Mr. Brown has kept my liking for them in mind for a great many years. Your grandfather used to say that there was nothing like a duckling to his taste; he used to eat them in England, but people in this country let them get too old. He was willing to pay a great price for ducklings always; but even Mr. Brown seems to think it is a great wrong not to let them grow until Thanksgiving time,[1] and makes a great many apologies every year. It is from his farm that we always get the best lamb too; they are very nice people, the Browns, but the poor old man seems very feeble this summer. Some day I should really like to take a drive out into the country to see them, you know so well how to manage a horse. You can spare a day or two to give time for that, can't you?"

Nan was sorry to hear the pleading tone, it was so unlike her aunt's usually severe manner, and answered quickly that she should be very glad to make the little excursion. Mr. Brown had asked her to come to the farm one day near the beginning of her visit.

"You must say this is home, if you can," said Miss Prince, who was a good deal excited and shaken that morning, "and not think of yourself as a visitor any more. There are a great many things I hope you can understand, even if I have left them unsaid. It has really seemed more like home since you have been here, and less like a lodging. I wonder how I—When did you see Mr. Brown? I did not know you had ever spoken to him."

"It was some time ago," the girl answered. "I was in the kitchen, and he came to the door. He seemed very glad to see me," and Nan hesitated a moment. "He said I was like my father."

"Yes, indeed," responded Miss Prince, drearily; and the thought seized her that it was very strange that the same mistaken persistency should show itself in father and child in exactly opposite ways. If Nan would only care as much for marrying George Gerry, as her father had for marrying his wretched wife! It seemed more and more impossible that this little lady should be the daughter of such a woman; how dismayed the girl would be if she could be shown her mother's nature as Miss Prince remembered it. Alas! this was already a sorrow which no vision of the reality could deepen, and the frank words of the Oldfields country people about the bad Thachers had not been spoken fruitlessly in the ears of their last descendant.

"I am so glad the captain is coming," Nan said presently, to break the painful silence. "I do hope that he and Dr. Leslie will know each other some time, they would be such capital friends. The doctor sent his kind regards to you in last night's letter, and asked me again to say that he hoped that you would come to us before the summer is over. I should like so much to have you know what Oldfields is like." It was hard to save herself from saying "home" again, instead of Oldfields, but the change of words was made quickly.

"He is very courteous and hospitable, but I never pay visits nowadays," said Miss Prince, and thought almost angrily that there was no necessity for her making a target of herself for all those curious country-people's eyes. And then they rose and separated for a time, each being burdened less by care than thought.

The captain came early to dine, and brought with him his own and Miss Prince's letters from the post-office, together with the morning paper, which he proceeded to read. He also seemed to have a weight upon his mind, but by the time they were at table a mild cheerfulness made itself felt, and Nan summoned all her resources and was gayer and brighter than usual. Miss Prince had gone down town early in the day, and her niece was perfectly sure that there had been a consultation with Mr. Gerry. He had passed the house while Nan sat at her upper window writing, and had looked somewhat wistfully at the door as if he had half a mind to enter it. He was like a great magnet: it seemed impossible to resist looking after him, and indeed his ghost-like presence would not forsake her mind, but seemed urging her toward his visible self. The thought of him was so powerful that the sight of the young man was less strange and compelling, and it was almost a relief to have seen his familiar appearance,—the strong figure in its every-day clothes, his unstudent-like vigor, and easy step as he went by. She liked him still, but she hated love, it was making her so miserable,—even when later she told Captain Parish some delightful Oldfields stories, of so humorous a kind that he laughed long and struck the table more than once, which set the glasses jingling, and gave a splendid approval to the time-honored fun. The ducklings were amazingly good; and when Captain Walter had tasted his wine and read the silver label on the decanter, which as usual gave no evidence of the rank and dignity of the contents,[2] his eyes sparkled with satisfaction, and he turned to his cousin's daughter with impressive gravity.

"You may never have tasted such wine as that," he said. "Your grandfather, the luckiest captain who ever sailed out of Dunport, brought it home fifty years ago, and it was well ripened then. I didn't know there was a bottle of it left, Nancy," he laughed. "My dear, your aunt has undertaken to pay one of us a handsome compliment."

"Your health, cousin Walter!" said the girl quickly, lifting her own glass, and making him a little bow over the old Madeira.

"Bless your dear heart!" responded the captain; "the same good wishes to you in return, and now you must join me in my respects to your aunt. Nancy! I beg you not to waste this in pudding-sauces;[3] that's the way with you ladies."

The toast-drinking had a good effect upon the little company, and it seemed as if the cloud which had hung over it at first had been blown away. When there was no longer any excuse for lingering at the table, the guest seemed again a little ill at ease, and after a glance at his hostess, proposed to Nan that they should take a look at the garden. The old sailor had become in his later years a devoted tiller of the soil, and pleaded a desire to see some late roses which were just now in bloom. So he and Nan went down the walk together, and he fidgeted and hurried about for a few minutes before he could make up his mind to begin a speech which was weighing heavily on his conscience.

Nan was sure that something unusual was perplexing him, and answered his unnecessary questions patiently, wondering what he was trying to say.

"Dear me!" he grumbled at last, "I shall have to steer a straight course. The truth is, Nancy has been telling me that I ought to advise with you, and see that you understand what you are about with young Gerry. She has set her heart on your fancying him. I dare say you know she has treated him like a son all through his growing up; but now that you have come to your rightful place, she can't bear to have anybody hint at your going back to the other people. 'T is plain enough what he thinks about it, and I must say I believe it would be for your good. Here you are with your father's family, what is left of it; and I take no liberty when I tell you that your aunt desires this to be your home, and means to give you your father's share of the property now and the rest when she is done with it. It is no more than your rights, and I know as much as anybody about it, and can tell you that there's a handsomer fortune than you may have suspected. Money grows fast if it is let alone; and though your aunt has done a good deal for others, her expenses have been well held in hand. I must say I should like to keep you here, child," the captain faltered, "but I shall want to do what's for your happiness. I couldn't feel more earnest about that if I were your own father. You must think it over. I'm not going to beseech you: I learned long ago that 't is no use to drive a Prince."

Nan had tried at first to look unconcerned and treat the matter lightly, but this straightforward talk appealed to her much more than the suggestion and general advice which Miss Prince had implored the captain to give the night before. And now her niece could only thank him for his kindness, and tell him that by and by she would make him understand why she put aside these reasons, and went back to the life she had known before.

But a sudden inspiration made her resolution grow stronger, and she looked at Captain Parish with a convincing bravery.

"When you followed the sea," she said quickly, "if you had a good ship with a freight that you had gathered with great care and hopefulness, and had brought it almost to the market that it was suited for, would you have been persuaded to turn about and take it to some place where it would be next to useless?"

"No," said Captain Parish, "no, I shouldn't," and he half smiled at this illustration.

"I can't tell you all my reasons for not wishing to marry," Nan went on, growing very white and determined, "or all my reasons for wishing to go on with my plan of being a doctor; but I know I have no right to the one way of life, and a perfect one, so far as I can see, to the other. And it seems to me that it would be as sensible to ask Mr. Gerry to be a minister since he has just finished his law studies, as to ask me to be a wife instead of a physician. But what I used to dread without reason a few years ago, I must forbid myself now, because I know the wretched inheritance I might have had from my poor mother's people. I can't speak of that to Aunt Nancy, but you must tell her not to try to make me change my mind."

"Good God!" said the captain. "I dare say you have the right points of it; but if I were a young man 't would go hard with me to let you take your life into your own hands. It's against nature."

"No," said Nan. "The law of right and wrong must rule even love, and whatever comes to me, I must not forget that. Three years ago I had not thought about it so much, and I might not have been so sure; but now I have been taught there is only one road to take. And you must tell Aunt Nancy this."

But when they went back to the house, Miss Prince was not to be seen, and the captain hurried away lest she should make her appearance, for he did not wish just then to talk about the matter any more. He told himself that young people were very different in these days; but when he thought of the words he had heard in the garden, and remembered the pale face and the steadfast, clear-toned voice, he brushed away something like a tear. "If more people used judgment in this same decision the world would be better off," he said, and could not help reminding himself that his own niece, little Mary Parish, who was wearing a wistful countenance in these days, might by and by be happy after all. For Nan's part it was a great relief to have spoken to the kind old man; she felt more secure than before; but sometimes the fear assailed her that some unforeseen event or unreckoned influence might give her back to her indecisions, and that the battle of the night before might after all prove not to be final.

The afternoon wore away, and late in the day our heroine heard George Gerry's step coming up the street. She listened as she sat by the upper window, and found that he was giving a message for her. It was perfect weather to go up the river, he was saying; the tide served just right and would bring them home early; and Miss Prince, who was alone in the parlor, answered with pleased assurance that she was sure her niece would like to go. "Yes," said Nan, calling from the window, urged by a sudden impulse. "Yes indeed, I should like it above all things; I will get ready at once; will you carry two pairs of oars?"

There was a ready assent, but the uncertainty of the tone of it struck Anna Prince's quick ear. She seemed to know that the young man and her aunt were exchanging looks of surprise, and that they felt insecure and uncertain. It was not the yielding maiden who had spoken to her lover, but the girl who was his good comrade and cordial friend. The elder woman shook her head doubtfully; she knew well what this foreboded, and was impatient at the overthrow of her plans; yet she had full confidence in the power of Love. She had seen apparent self-reliance before, and she could not believe that her niece was invincible. At any rate nothing could be more persuasive than a twilight row upon the river, and for her part, she hoped more eagerly than ever that Love would return chief in command of the boat's young crew; and when the young man flushed a little, and looked at her appealingly, as he turned to go down the street, his friend and counselor could not resist giving him a hopeful nod. Nan was singularly frank, and free from affectations, and she might have already decided to lower her colors and yield the victory, and it seemed for a moment that it would be much more like her to do so, than to invite further contest when she was already won. Miss Prince was very kind and sympathetic when this explanation had once forced itself upon her mind; she gave the young girl a most affectionate kiss when she appeared, but at this unmistakable suggestion of pleasure and treasured hopes, Nan turned back suddenly into the shaded parlor, though Mr. Gerry was waiting outside with his favorite oars, which he kept carefully in a corner of the office.

"Dear Aunt Nancy," said the girl, with evident effort, "I am so sorry to disappoint you. I wish for your sake that I had been another sort of woman; but I shall never marry. I know you think I am wrong, but there is something which always tells me I am right, and I must follow another way. I should only wreck my life, and other people's. Most girls have an instinct towards marrying, but mine is all against it, and God knew best when He made me care more for another fashion of life. Don't make me seem unkind! I dare say that I can put it all into words better by and by, but I can never be more certain of it in my own heart than now."

"Sit down a minute," said Miss Prince, slowly. "George can wait. But, Anna, I believe that you are in love with him, and that you are doing wrong to the poor lad, and to yourself, and to me. I lost the best happiness of my life for a whim, and you wish to throw away yours for a theory. I hope you will be guided by me. I have come to love you very much, and it seems as if this would be so reasonable."

"It does make a difference to me that he loves me," confessed the girl. "It is not easy to turn away from him," she said,—still standing, and looking taller than ever, and even thin, with a curious tenseness of her whole being. "It is something that I have

found it hard to fight against, but it is not my whole self longing for his love and his companionship. If I heard he had gone
to the other side of the world for years and years, I should be
glad now and not sorry. I know that all the world's sympathy
and all tradition fight on his side; but I can look forward and
see something a thousand times better than being his wife, and
living here in Dunport keeping his house, and trying to forget
all that nature fitted me to do. You don't understand, Aunt
Nancy. I wish you could! You see it all another way." And the
tears started to the eager young eyes. "Don't you know that
Cousin Walter said this very day that the wind which sets one
vessel on the right course may set another on the wrong?"

"Nonsense, my dear," said the mistress of the house. "I don't
think this is the proper time for you to explain yourself at any
rate. I dare say the fresh air will do you good and put everything
right too. You have worked yourself into a great excitement
over nothing. Don't go out looking so desperate to the poor fellow; he will think strangely of it;" and the girl went out
through the wide hall, and wished she were far away from all
this trouble.

Nan had felt a strange sense of weariness, which did not leave
her even when she was quieted by the fresh breeze of the river-
shore, and was contented to let her oars be stowed in the bottom
of the boat, and to take the comfortable seat in the stern. She
pulled the tiller ropes[4] over her shoulders, and watched her
lover's first strong strokes, which had quickly sent them out into
the stream, beyond the course of a larger craft which was coming toward the wharf. She wished presently that she had chosen
to row, because they would not then be face to face; but, strange
to say, since this new experience had come to her, she had not
felt so sure of herself as now, and the fear of finding herself too
weak to oppose the new tendency of her life had lessened since
her first recognition of it the night before. But Nan had fought a
hard fight, and had grown a great deal older in those hours of
the day and night. She believed that time would make her even
more certain that she had done right than she could be now in

the heat of the battle, but she wished whatever George Gerry meant to say to her might be soon over with.

They went slowly up the river, which was now quite familiar to the girl who had come to it a stranger only a few weeks before. She liked out-of-door life so well that this country-side of Dunport was already more dear to her than to many who had seen it bloom and fade every year since they could remember. At one moment it seemed but yesterday that she had come to the old town, and at the next she felt as if she had spent half a lifetime there, and as if Oldfields might have changed unbearably since she came away.

Sometimes the young oarsman kept in the middle of the great stream, and sometimes it seemed pleasanter to be near the shore. The midsummer flowers were coming into blossom, and the grass and trees had long since lost the brilliance of their greenness, and wore a look of maturity and completion, as if they had already finished their growth. There was a beautiful softness and harmony of color, a repose that one never sees in a spring landscape. The tide was in, the sun was almost down, and a great, cloudless, infinite sky arched itself from horizon to horizon. It had sent all its brilliance to shine backward from the sun,—the glowing sphere from which a single dazzling ray came across the fields and the water to the boat. In a moment more it was gone, and a shadow quickly fell like that of a tropical twilight; but the west grew golden, and one light cloud, like a floating red feather, faded away upward into the sky. A later bright glow touched some high hills in the east, then they grew purple and gray, and so the evening came that way slowly, and the ripple of the water plashed and sobbed against the boat's side; and presently in the midst of the river's inland bay, after a few last eager strokes, the young man drew in his oars, letting them drop with a noise which startled Nan, who had happened to be looking over her shoulder at the shore.

She knew well enough that he meant to put a grave question to her now, and her heart beat faster and she twisted the tiller cords around her hands unconsciously.

"I think I could break any bonds you might use to keep

yourself away from me," he said hurriedly, as he watched her. "I am not fit for you, only that I love you. Somebody told me you meant to go away, and I could not wait any longer before I asked you if you would give yourself to me."

"No, no!" cried Nan, "dear friend, I must not do it; it would all be a mistake. You must not think of it any more. I am so sorry, I ought to have understood what was coming to us, and have gone away long ago."

"It would have made no difference," said the young man, almost angrily. He could not bear delay enough even for speech at that moment; he watched her face desperately for a look of assurance; he leaned toward her and wondered why he had not risked everything, and spoken the evening before when they stood watching the ship's mast, and Nan's hands were close enough to be touched. But the miserable knowledge crept over him that she was a great deal farther away from him than half that small boat's length, and as she looked up at him again, and shook her head gently, a great rage of love and shame at his repulse urged him to plead again. "You are spoiling my life," he cried. "You do not care for that, but without you I shall not care for anything."

"I would rather spoil your life in this way than in a far worse fashion," said Nan sadly. "I will always be your friend, but if I married you I might seem by and by to be your enemy. Yes, you will love somebody else some day, and be a great deal happier than I could have made you, and I shall be so glad. It does not belong to me."

But this seemed too scornful and cold-hearted. "Oh, my love is only worth that to you," the lover said. "You shall know better what it means. I don't want you for my friend, but for my own to keep and to have. It makes me laugh to think of your being a doctor and going back to that country town to throw yourself away for the fancies and silly theories of a man who has lived like a hermit. It means a true life for both of us if you will only say you love me, or even let me ask you again when you have thought of it more. Everybody will say I am in the right."

"Yes, there are reasons enough for it, but there is a better reason against it. If you love me you must help me do what is best," said Nan. "I shall miss you and think of you more than you know when I am away. I never shall forget all these pleasant days we have been together. Oh George!" she cried, in a tone that thrilled him through and through, "I hope you will be friends with me again by and by. You will know then I have done right because it is right and will prove itself. If it is wrong for me I couldn't really make you happy; and over all this and beyond it something promises me and calls me for a life that my marrying you would hinder and not help. It isn't that I shouldn't be so happy that it is not easy to turn away even from the thought of it; but I know that the days would come when I should see, in a way that would make me long to die, that I had lost the true direction of my life and had misled others beside myself. You don't believe me, but I cannot break faith with my duty. There are many reasons that have forbidden me to marry, and I have a certainty as sure as the stars that the only right condition of life for me is to follow the way that everything until now has pointed out. The great gain and purpose of my being alive is there; and I must not mind the blessings that I shall have to do without."

He made a gesture of impatience and tried to interrupt her, but she said quickly, as if to prevent his speaking: "Listen to me. I can't help speaking plainly. I would not have come with you this afternoon, only I wished to make you understand me entirely. I have never since I can remember thought of myself and my life in any way but unmarried,—going on alone to the work I am fit to do. I do care for you. I have been greatly surprised and shaken because I found how strongly something in me has taken your part, and shown me the possibility of happiness in a quiet life that should centre itself in one man's love, and within the walls of his home. But something tells me all the time that I could not marry the whole of myself as most women can; there is a great share of my life which could not have its way, and could only hide itself and be sorry. I know better and better that most women are made for another sort of existence, but by and by I must do my part in my own way to make many homes happy instead of one; to free them from pain, and teach grown people and little children to keep their bodies free from weakness and deformities. I don't know why God should have made me a doctor, so many other things have seemed fitter for women; but I see the blessedness of such a useful life more and more every year, and I am very thankful for such a trust. It is a splendid thing to have the use of any gift of God. It isn't for us to choose again, or wonder and dispute, but just work in our own places, and leave the rest to God."

The boat was being carried downward by the ebbing tide, and George Gerry took the oars again, and rowed quietly and in silence. He took his defeat unkindly and drearily; he was ashamed of himself once, because some evil spirit told him that he was losing much that would content him, in failing to gain this woman's love. It had all been so fair a prospect of worldly success, and she had been the queen of it. He thought of himself growing old in Mr. Sergeant's dusty office, and that this was all that life could hold for him. Yet to be was better than to have. Alas! if he had been more earnest in his growth, it would have been a power which this girl of high ideals could have been held and mastered by. No wonder that she would not give up her dreams of duty and service, since she had found him less strong than such ideals. The fancied dissatisfaction and piteousness of failure which she would be sure to meet filled his heart with dismay; yet, at that very next moment, resent it as he might, the certainty of his own present defeat and powerlessness could not be misunderstood. Perhaps, after all, she knew what was right; her face wore again the look he had feared to disturb the night before, and his whole soul was filled with homage in the midst of its sorrow, because this girl, who had been his merry companion in the summer holidays, so sweet and familiar and unforgetable in the midst of the simple festivals, stood nearer to holier things than himself, and had listened to the call of God's messengers to whom his own doors had been ignorantly shut. And Nan that night was a soul's physician, though she had been made to sorely hurt her patient before the new healthfulness could well begin.

They floated down the river and tried to talk once or twice, but there were many spaces of silence, and as they walked along the paved streets, they thought of many things. An east wind was blowing in from the sea, and the elm branches were moving restlessly overhead. "It will all be better to-morrow," said Nan, as they stood on the steps at last. "You must come to see Aunt Nancy very often after I have gone, for she will be lonely. And do come in the morning as if nothing had been spoken. I am so sorry. Good-night, and God bless you," she whispered; and when she stood inside the wide doorway, in the dark, she listened to his footsteps as he went away down the street. They were slower than usual, but she did not call him back.

CHAPTER XXI.

AT HOME AGAIN

In Oldfields Dr. Leslie had outwardly lived the familiar life to which his friends and patients had long since accustomed themselves; he had seemed a little preoccupied, perhaps, but if that were observed, it was easily explained by his having one or two difficult cases to think about. A few persons suspected that he missed Nan, and was, perhaps, a little anxious lest her father's people in Dunport should claim her altogether. Among those who knew best the doctor and his ward there had been an ardent championship of Nan's rights and dignity, and a great curiosity to know the success of the visit. Dr. Leslie had answered all questions with composure, and with a distressing meagreness of details; but at length Mrs. Graham became sure that he was not altogether free from anxiety, and set her own quick wits at work to learn the cause. It seemed a time of great uncertainty, at any rate. The doctor sometimes brought one of Nan's bright, affectionate letters for his neighbor to read, and they agreed that this holiday was an excellent thing for her, but there was a silent recognition of the fact that this was a critical time in the young girl's history; that it either meant a new direction of her life or an increased activity in the old one. Mrs. Graham was less well than usual in these days, and the doctor found time to make more frequent visits than ever, telling himself that she missed Nan's pleasant companionship, but really wishing as much to receive sympathy as to give it. The dear old lady had laughingly disclaimed any desire to summon her children or grandchildren, saying that she was neither ill enough to need them, nor well enough to enjoy them; and so in the beautiful June weather the two old friends became strangely dear to each other, and had many a long talk which the cares of the world or their own reserve had made them save until this favoring season.

The doctor was acknowledged to be an old man at last, though everybody still insisted that he looked younger than his age, and could not doubt that he had half a lifetime of usefulness before him yet. But it makes a great difference when one's ambitions are transferred from one's own life to that of a younger person's; and while Dr. Leslie grew less careful for himself, trusting to the unconscious certainty of his practiced skill, he pondered eagerly over Nan's future, reminding himself of various hints and suggestions, which must be added to her equipment. Sometimes he wished that she were beginning a few years later, when her position could be better recognized and respected, and she would not have to fight against so much of the opposition and petty fault-finding that come from ignorance; and sometimes he rejoiced that his little girl, as he fondly called her, would be one of the earlier proofs and examples of a certain noble advance and new vantage-ground of civilization. This has been anticipated through all ages by the women who, sometimes honored and sometimes persecuted, have been drawn away from home life by a devotion to public and social usefulness. It must be recognized that certain qualities are required for married, and even domestic life, which all women do not possess; but instead of attributing this to the disintegration of society, it must be acknowledged to belong to its progress.

So long as the visit in Dunport seemed to fulfill its anticipated purpose, and the happy guest was throwing aside her cares and enjoying the merry holiday and the excitement of new friendships and of her uncommon position, so long the doctor had been glad, and far from impatient to have the visit end. But when he read the later and shorter letters again and again in the vain hope of finding something in their wording which should explain the vague unhappiness which had come to him as he had read them first, he began to feel troubled and dismayed. There was something which Nan had not explained; something was going wrong. He was sure that if it were anything he could set right, that she would have told him. She had always done so;

but it became evident through the strange sympathy which made him conscious of the mood of others that she was bent upon fighting her way alone.

It was a matter of surprise, and almost of dismay to him early one morning, when he received a brief note from her which told him only that she should be at home late that afternoon. It seemed to the wise old doctor a day of most distressing uncertainty. He tried to make up his mind to accept with true philosophy whatever decision she was bringing him. "Nan is a good girl," he told himself over and over again; "she will try to do right." But she was so young and so generous, and whether she had been implored to break the old ties of home life and affection for her aunt's sake, or whether it was a newer and stronger influence still which had prevailed, waited for explanation. Alas, as was written once, it is often the higher nature that yields, because it is the most generous. The doctor knew well enough the young girl's character. He knew what promises of growth and uncommon achievement were all ready to unfold themselves,—for what great uses she was made. He could not bear the thought of her being handicapped in the race she had been set to run. Yet no one recognized more clearly than he the unseen, and too often unconsidered, factor which is peculiar to each soul, which prevents any other intelligence from putting itself exactly in that soul's place, so that our decisions and aids and suggestions are never wholly sufficient or available for those even whom we love most. He went over the question again and again; he followed Nan in his thoughts as she had grown up,—unprejudiced, unconstrained as is possible for any human being to be. He remembered that her heroes were the great doctors,[1] and that her whole heart had been stirred and claimed by the noble duties and needs of the great profession. She had been careless of the social limitations, of the lack of sympathy, even of the ridicule of the public. She had behaved as a bird would behave if it were assured by beasts and fishes that to walk and to swim were the only proper and respectable means of getting from place to place. She had shown such rare insight into the principles of things; she had even seemed to him, as he watched her, to have anticipated experience, and he could not help believing that it was within her power to add much to the too small fund of certainty, by the sure instinct and aim of her experiment. It counted nothing whether God had put this soul into a man's body or a woman's. He had known best, and He meant it to be the teller of new truth, a revealer of laws, and an influence for good in its capacity for teaching, as well as in its example of pure and reasonable life.

But the old doctor sighed, and told himself that the girl was most human, most affectionate; it was not impossible that, in spite of her apparent absence of certain domestic instincts, they had only lain dormant and were now awake. He could not bear that she should lose any happiness which might be hers; and the tender memory of the blessed companionship which had been withdrawn from his mortal sight only to be given back to him more fully as he had lived closer and nearer to spiritual things, made him shrink from forbidding the same sort of fullness and completion of life to one so dear as Nan. He tried to assure himself that while a man's life is strengthened by his domestic happiness, a woman's must either surrender itself wholly, or relinquish entirely the claims of such duties, if she would achieve distinction or satisfaction elsewhere. The two cannot be taken together in a woman's life as in a man's. One must be made of lesser consequence, though the very natures of both domestic and professional life need all the strength which can be brought to them. The decision between them he knew to be a most grave responsibility, and one to be governed by the gravest moral obligations, and the unmistakable leadings of the personal instincts and ambitions. It was seldom, Dr. Leslie was aware, that so typical and evident an example as this could offer itself of the class of women who are a result of natural progression and variation, not for better work, but for different work, and who are designed for certain public and social duties. But he believed this class to be one that must inevitably increase with the higher developments of civilization, and in later years, which he might never see, the love for humanity would be recognized and employed more intelligently; while now almost every popular prejudice was against his ward, then she would need no vindication. The wielder of ideas has always a certain advantage over the depender upon facts; and though the two classes of minds by no means inevitably belong, the one to women, and the other to men,[2] still women have not yet begun to use the best resources of their natures, having been later developed, and in many countries but recently freed from restraining and hindering influences.

The preservation of the race is no longer the only important question; the welfare of the individual will be considered more and more. The simple fact that there is a majority of women in any centre of civilization means that some are set apart by nature for other uses and conditions than marriage. In ancient times men depended entirely upon the women of their households to prepare their food and clothing,—and almost every man in ordinary circumstances of life was forced to marry for this reason; but already there is a great change. The greater proportion of men and women everywhere will still instinctively and gladly accept the high duties and helps of married life; but as society becomes more intelligent it will recognize the fitness of some persons, and the unfitness of others, making it impossible for these to accept such responsibilities and obligations, and so dignify and elevate home life instead of degrading it.

It had been one thing to act from conviction and from the promptings of instinct while no obstacles opposed themselves to his decisions, and quite another thing to be brought face to face with such an emergency. Dr. Leslie wished first to be able to distinctly explain to himself his reasons for the opinions he held; he knew that he must judge for Nan herself in some measure; she would surely appeal to him; she would bring this great question to him, and look for sympathy and relief in the same way she had tearfully shown him a wounded finger in her childhood. He seemed to see again the entreating eyes, made large with the pain which would not show itself in any other way, and he felt the rare tears fill his own eyes at the thought. "Poor little Nan," he said to himself, "she has been hurt in the great battle, but she is no skulking soldier." He would let her tell her story, and then give her the best help he could; and so when the afternoon shadows were very long across the country, and the hot summer day was almost done, the doctor drove down the wide street and along East Road to the railroad station. As he passed a group of small houses he looked at his watch and found that there was more than time for a second visit to a sick child whose illness had been most serious and perplexing at first, though now she was fast recovering. The little thing smiled as her friend came in, and asked if the young lady were coming to-morrow, for Dr. Leslie had promised a visit and a picture-book from Nan, whom he wished to see and understand the case. They had had a long talk upon such ailments as this just before she went away, and nothing had seemed to rouse her ambition so greatly as her experiences at the children's hospitals[3] the winter before. Now, this weak little creature seemed to be pleading in the name of a great army of sick children, that Nan would not desert their cause; that she would go on, as she had promised them, with her search for ways that should restore their vigor and increase their fitness to take up the work of the world. And yet, a home and children of one's very own,—the doctor, who had held and lost this long ago, felt powerless to decide the future of the young heart which was so dear to him.

Nan saw the familiar old horse and carriage waiting behind the station, and did not fail to notice that the doctor had driven to meet her himself. He almost always did, but her very anxiety to see him again had made her doubtful. The train had hardly stopped before she was standing on the platform and had hastily dropped her checks[4] into the hand of the nearest idle boy, who looked at them doubtfully, as if he hardly dared to hope that he had been mistaken for the hackman. She came quickly to the side of the carriage; the doctor could not look at her, for the horse had made believe that some excitement was necessary, and was making it difficult for the welcome passenger to put her foot on the step. It was all over in a minute. Nan sprang to the doctor's side and away they went down the road. He had caught a glimpse of her shining eyes and eager face as she had hurried toward him, and had said, "Well done!" in a most cheerful and every-day fashion, and then for a minute there was silence.

"Oh, it is so good to get home," said the girl, and her companion turned toward her; he could not wait to hear her story.

"Yes," said Nan, "it is just as well to tell you now. Do you remember you used to say to me when I was a little girl, 'If you know your duty, don't mind the best of reasons for not doing it'?" And the doctor nodded. "I never thought that this reason would come to me for not being a doctor," she went on, "and at first I was afraid I should be conquered, though it was myself who fought myself. But it came to me clearer than ever after a while. I think I could have been fonder of some one than most people are of those whom they marry, but the more I cared for him the less I could give him only part of myself; I knew that was not right. Now that I can look back at it all I am so glad to have had those days; I shall work better all my life for having been able to make myself so perfectly sure that I know my way."

The unconsidered factor had asserted itself in the doctor's favor. He gave the reins to Nan and leaned back in the carriage, but as she bent forward to speak to a friend whom they passed she did not see the look that he gave her.

"I am sure you knew what was right," he said, hastily. "God bless you, dear child!"

Was this little Nan, who had been his plaything? this brave young creature, to whose glorious future all his heart and hopes went out. In his evening it was her morning, and he prayed that God's angels should comfort and strengthen her and help her to carry the burden of the day. It is only those who can do nothing who find nothing to do, and Nan was no idler; she had come to her work as Christ came to his, not to be ministered unto but to minister.[5]

The months went by swiftly, and through hard work and much study, and many sights of pain and sorrow, this young student of the business of healing made her way to the day when some of her companions announced with melancholy truth that they had finished their studies.[6] They were pretty sure to be accused of having had no right to begin them, or to take such trusts and responsibilities into their hands. But Nan and many of her friends had gladly climbed the hill so far, and with every year's ascent had been thankful for the wider horizon which was spread for their eyes to see.

Dr. Leslie in his quiet study almost wished that he were beginning life again, and sometimes in the twilight, or in long and lonely country drives, believed himself ready to go back twenty years so that he could follow Nan into the future and watch her successes. But he always smiled afterward at such a thought. Twenty years would carry him back to the time when his ward was a little child, not long before she came to live with him. It was best as God had planned it. Nobody had watched the child's development as he had done, or her growth of character, of which all the performances of her later years would be to him only the unnecessary proofs and evidences. He knew that she would be faithful in great things, because she had been faithful in little things, and he should be with her a long time yet, perhaps. God only knew.

There was a great change in the village; there were more small factories now which employed large numbers of young women, and though a new doctor had long ago come to Oldfields who had begun by trying to supersede Dr. Leslie, he had ended by longing to show his gratitude some day for so much help and kindness. More than one appointment had been offered the heroine of this story in the city hospitals. She would have little trouble in making her way since she had the requisite qualities, natural and acquired, which secure success. But she decided for herself that she would neither do this, nor carry out yet the other plan of going on with her studies at some school across the sea. Zurich held out a great temptation,[7] but there was time enough yet, and she would spend a year in Oldfields with the doctor, studying again with him, since she knew better than ever before that she could find no wiser teacher. And it was a great pleasure to belong to the dear old town, to come home to it with her new treasures, so much richer than she had gone away that beside medicines and bandages and lessons in general hygiene for the physical ails of her patients, she could often be a tonic to the mind and soul; and since she was trying to be good, go about doing good in Christ's name to the halt and maimed and blind in spiritual things.

Nobody sees people as they are and finds the chance to help poor humanity as a doctor does. The decorations and deceptions of character must fall away before the great realities of pain and death. The secrets of many hearts and homes must be told to this confessor, and sadder ailments than the text-books name are brought to be healed by the beloved physicians. Teachers of truth and givers of the laws of life, priests and ministers,— all these professions are joined in one with the gift of healing, and are each part of the charge that a good doctor holds in his keeping.[8]

One day in the beginning of her year at Oldfields, Nan, who had been very busy, suddenly thought it would be well to give herself a holiday; and with a sudden return of her old sense of freedom was going out at the door and down toward the gateway, which opened to a pleasantly wide world beyond. Marilla had taken Nan's successes rather reluctantly, and never hesitated to say that she only hoped to see her well married and settled before she died; though she was always ready to defend her course with even virulence to those who would deprecate it. She now heard Nan shut the door, and called at once from an upper window to know if word had been left where she was going, and the young practitioner laughed aloud as she answered, and properly acknowledged the fetter of her calling.

The leaves were just beginning to fall, and she pushed them about with her feet, and sometimes walked and sometimes ran lightly along the road toward the farm. But when she reached it, she passed the lane and went on to the Dyer houses. Mrs. Jake was ailing as usual, and Nan had told the doctor before she came out that she would venture another professional visit in his stead. She was a great help to him in this way, for his calls to distant towns had increased year by year, and he often found it hard to keep his many patients well in hand.

The old houses had not changed much since she first knew them, and neither they nor their inmates were in any danger of being forgotten by her; the old ties of affection and association grew stronger instead of weaker every year. It pleased and amused the old people to be reminded of the days when Nan was a child and lived among them, and it was a great joy to her to be able to make their pain and discomfort less, and be their interpreter of the outside world.

It was a most lovely day of our heroine's favorite weather. It has been said that November is an epitome of all the months of the year, but for all that, no other season can show anything so beautiful as the best and brightest November days. Nan had spent her summer in a great hospital, where she saw few flowers save human ones, and the warmth and inspiration of this clear air seemed most delightful. She had been somewhat tempted by an offer of a fine position in Canada, and even Dr. Leslie had urged her acceptance, and thought it an uncommonly good chance to have the best hospital experience and responsibility,[9] but she had sent the letter of refusal only that morning. She could not tell yet what her later plans might be; but there was no place like Oldfields, and she thought she had never loved it so dearly as that afternoon.

She looked in at Mrs. Martin's wide-open door first, but finding the kitchen empty, went quickly across to the other house, where Mrs. Jake was propped up in her rocking-chair and began to groan loudly when she saw Nan; but the tonic of so gratifying a presence soon had a most favorable effect. Benignant Mrs. Martin was knitting as usual, and the three women sat together in a friendly group and Nan asked and answered questions most cordially.

"I declare I was sort of put out with the doctor for sending you down here day before yesterday instead of coming himself," stated Mrs. Jake immediately, "but I do' know 's I ever had anything do me so much good as that bottle you gave me."

"Of course!" laughed Nan. "Dr. Leslie sent it to you himself. I told you when I gave it to you."

"Well now, how you talk!" said Mrs. Jake, a little crestfallen. "I begin to find my hearing fails me by spells. But I was bound to give you the credit, for all I've stood out against your meddling with a doctor's business."

Nan laughed merrily. "I am going to steal you for my patient," she answered, "and try all the prescriptions on your case first."

"Land, if you cured her up 't would be like stopping the leaks in a basket," announced Mrs. Martin with a beaming smile, and clicking her knitting-needles excitedly. "She can't hear of a complaint anywheres about but she thinks she's got the mate to it."

"I don't seem to have anything fevery about me," said Mrs. Jake, with an air of patient self-denial; and though both her companions were most compassionate at the thought of her real sufferings, they could not resist the least bit of a smile. "I declare you've done one first-rate thing, if you're never going to do any more," said Mrs. Jake, presently. " 'Liza here's been talking for some time past, about your straightening up the little boy's back,—the one that lives down where Mis' Meeker used to live you know,—but I didn't seem to take it in till he come over here yisterday forenoon. Looks as likely[10] as any child, except it many be he's a little stunted. When I think how he used to creep about there, side of the road, like a hopper-toad, it does seem amazin'!"

Nan's eyes brightened. "I have been delighted about that. I saw him running with the other children as I came down the road. It was a long bit of work, though. The doctor did most of it; I didn't see the child for months, you know. But he needs care yet; I'm going to stop and have another talk with his mother as I go home."

"She's a pore shiftless creature," Mrs. Martin hastened to say. "There, I thought o' the doctor, how he'd laugh, the last time I was in to see her; her baby was sick, and she sent up to know if I'd lend her a variety of herbs, and I didn't know but she might p'isen it, so I stepped down with something myself. She begun to flutter about like she always does, and I picked my way acrost the kitchen to the cradle. 'There,' says she, 'I have been laying out all this week to go up to the Corners[11] and git me two new chairs.' 'I should think you had plenty of chairs now,' said I, and she looked at me sort of surprised, and says she, 'There ain't a chair in this house but what's full.' "

And Nan laughed as heartily as could have been desired before she asked Mrs. Jake a few more appreciative questions about her ailments, and then rose to go away. Mrs. Martin fol-

lowed her out to the gate; she and Nan had always been very
fond of each other, and the elder woman pointed to a field not
far away where the brothers were watching a stubble-fire,
which was sending up a thin blue thread of smoke into the still
air.[12] "They were over in your north lot yisterday," said Mrs.
Martin. "They're fullest o' business nowadays when there's
least to do. They took it pretty hard when they first had to come
down to hiring help, but they kind of enjoy it now. We're all
old folks together on the farm, and not good for much. It don't
seem but a year or two since your poor mother was playing
about here, and then you come along, and now you're the last o'
your folks out of all the houseful of 'em I knew. I'll own up
sometimes I've thought strange of your fancy for doctoring, but
I never said a word to nobody against it, so I haven't got anything to take back as most folks have. I couldn't help thinking
when you come in this afternoon and sat there along of us, that
I'd give a good deal to have Mis' Thacher step in and see you
and know what you've made o' yourself. She had it hard for a
good many years, but I believe 't is all made up to her; I do certain."

Nan meant to go back to the village by the shorter way of the
little foot-path, but first she went up the grass-grown lane toward the old farm-house. She stood for a minute looking about
her and across the well-known fields, and then seated herself on
the door-step, and stayed there for some time. There were two
or three sheep near by, well covered and rounded by their soft
new winter wool, and they all came as close as they dared and
looked at her wonderingly. The narrow path that used to be
worn to the door-step had been overgrown years ago with the
short grass, and in it there was a late little dandelion with
hardly any stem at all. The sunshine was warm, and all the
country was wrapped in a thin, soft haze.

She thought of her grandmother Thacher, and of the words
that had just been said; it was beginning to seem a very great
while since the days of the old farm-life, and Nan smiled as she
remembered with what tones of despair the good old woman
used to repeat the well-worn phrase, that her grandchild would
make either something or nothing. It seemed to her that she had

brought all the success of the past and her hopes for the future to the dear old place that afternoon. Her early life was spreading itself out like a picture, and as she thought it over and looked back from year to year, she was more than ever before surprised to see the connection of one thing with another, and how some slight acts had been the planting of seeds which had grown and flourished long afterward. And as she tried to follow herself back into the cloudy days of her earliest spring, she rose without knowing why, and went down the pastures toward the river. She passed the old English apple-tree, which still held aloft a flourishing bough. Its fruit had been gathered, but there were one or two stray apples left, and Nan skillfully threw a stick at these by way of summons.

Along this path she had hurried or faltered many a time. She remembered her grandmother's funeral, and how she had walked, with an elderly cousin whom she did not know, at the head of the procession, and had seen Martin Dyer's small grandson peeping like a rabbit from among the underbrush near the shore. Poor little Nan! she was very lonely that day. She had been so glad when the doctor had wrapped her up and taken her home.

She saw the neighborly old hawthorn-tree that grew by a cellar, and stopped to listen to its rustling and to lay her hand upon the rough bark. It had been a cause of wonder once, for she knew no other tree of the kind. It was like a snow-drift when it was in bloom, and in the grass-grown cellar she had spent many an hour, for there was a good shelter from the wind and an excellent hiding-place, though it seemed very shallow now when she looked at it as she went by.

The burying-place was shut in by a plain stone wall, which she had long ago asked the Dyers to build for her, and she leaned over it now and looked at the smooth turf of the low graves. She had always thought she would like to lie there too when her work was done. There were some of the graves which she did not know, but one was her poor young mother's, who had left her no inheritance except some traits that had won Nan many friends; all her evil gifts had been buried with her, the neighbors had said, when the girl was out of hearing, that very afternoon.

There was a strange fascination about these river uplands; no place was so dear to Nan, and yet she often thought with a shudder of the story of those footprints which had sought the river's brink, and then turned back. Perhaps, made pure and strong in a better world, in which some lingering love and faith had given her the true direction at last, where even her love for her child had saved her, the mother had been still taking care of little Nan and guiding her. Perhaps she had helped to make sure of the blessings her own life had lost, of truth and whiteness of soul and usefulness; and so had been still bringing her child in her arms toward the great shelter and home, as she had toiled in her fright and weakness that dark and miserable night toward the house on the hill.

And Nan stood on the shore while the warm wind that gently blew her hair felt almost like a hand, and presently she went closer to the river, and looked far across it and beyond it to the hills. The eagles swung to and fro above the water, but she looked beyond them into the sky. The soft air and the sunshine came close to her; the trees stood about and seemed to watch her; and suddenly she reached her hands upward in an ecstasy of life and strength and gladness. "O God," she said, "I thank thee for my future."

Explanatory Notes

CHAPTER I.
THE LAST MILE

1. *Oldfields:* Historically, "Old Fields"—so named because of the cornfields abandoned there by local Native American tribes-people—refers to Maine's earliest colonial domain, an area first occupied by English settlers around 1630 at the southernmost end of what later became the town of Berwick, located near the New Hampshire border at the convergence of the Great Works River and the Salmon Falls River (chief branch of the Piscataqua River, which flows into the Atlantic Ocean near Portsmouth roughly twelve miles downstream). In the novel, "Oldfields" represents Jewett's hometown of South Berwick, the oldest of three communities into which Berwick was divided in 1814, and a village just north of the site of the original English settlement, which then consisted principally of farmlands.

2. *a defense against the Indians . . . still plainly to be seen:* Probably Spencer's garrison, one of numerous garrison houses each erected by a leading family of the colonial English settlement at Old Fields as a refuge during attacks in King Philip's War and the French and Indian Wars.

3. *a brook:* Hamilton Brook, coursing inland from the Salmon Falls River in the Old Fields area of South Berwick.

4. *the river itself:* As in the Salmon Falls River, bordering South Berwick and the Old Fields area.

5. *an old burial place . . . wives and children:* The Old Fields Burying Ground, dating from the seventeenth century, is located near the intersection of Vine Street and Brattle Street in South Berwick.

CHAPTER II.
THE FARM-HOUSE KITCHEN

1. *found Mrs. Thacher spinning:* In northern New England, spinning wheels continued to be used in rural households through the middle decades of the nineteenth century.

2. *the village:* i.e., of "Oldfields," denoting South Berwick, Maine; see chapter 1, note 1.

3. *Job's comforters:* "I have heard many such things: miserable comforters are ye all" (Job 16:2).

4. *the droning wool-wheel which she had been using:* When in operation, the steel spindle in a "wool wheel," or large walking wheel (by contrast to the smaller "flax wheel"), vibrated as it was turned, generating at full speed a humming or droning sound often referred to in that era as the spinning wheel's "song."

5. *watchin' with somebody:* Staying awake or holding vigil by the bedside of someone gravely ill or dead.

6. *post books:* Keep accounts, as in a ledger.

7. *tallow and bayberry wax:* When boiled in water, bayberries shed a green waxlike coating, which was often blended with tallow, or hard animal fat, in the making of candles.

8. *dangers of the new-fangled oils . . . past their usefulness:* By the 1850s, sperm oil—derived from a cavity in the heads of sperm whales—had become too scarce and costly for common use; initial replacements like camphene (alcohol mixed with turpentine), although more economical, were generally considered unsafe. Whale-oil lamps and tallow candles remained the chief sources of household illumination in the United States before the introduction of kerosene, or "coal oil," around the time of the Civil War.

9. *Stoves is such a convenience . . . the trial it was once:* Cookstoves had increasingly replaced open wood fireplaces even in many rural areas of the northeast as of the 1840s and 1850s, making for dramatic improvements in efficiency in heating and food preparation, and sparing women like Mrs. Dyer a great deal of time and labor.

10. *chimbly:* Colloquial for "chimney."

11. *Be you going to do much for Thanksgivin', Mis' Thacher?:* Although it would not be declared a national holiday until Abraham Lincoln first proclaimed one for the last Thursday of November in 1863, Thanksgiving had of course been celebrated in New England on a late-autumn Thursday since colonial times.

12. *I forgot to ask ye . . . a taste o' good hard cider towards the spring of the year:* Cider, once the quintessential New England

household beverage, would have been made by farmers each autumn out of apples ground or mashed to a pulp and then passed through a wooden cider press in order to draw out the juice, known as "sweet cider." The juice would then be stored for the winter months in large wooden barrels on the earthen floor of a farmer's cellar, where it gradually fermented into "hard cider." Widespread in early New England, cider-making reached a high point in its popularity in the United States as of the middle of the nineteenth century.

13. *a thing to be treasured and jealously guarded:* Since early settlers tended to bring seeds rather than cuttings with them from England, the occasional cutting that survived the ocean voyage long enough to be grafted onto an indigenous tree could prove especially valuable in colonial New England. By the nineteenth century, the grafting of apple (as well as other fruit) trees in New England had been practiced successfully for quite some time.

14. *their splint-bottomed, straight-backed chairs:* One of the most common chair designs in eighteenth- and nineteenth-century America, with the seat made of splint (strips of wood drawn, in the northeast, principally from black ash trees) in a basket-weave pattern. Such chairs were inexpensive and largely unadorned, used most often in work spaces, particularly the kitchen.

15. *stived up:* Cramped, stifling.

16. *in the packet:* As in packet boat, a vessel typically used to convey goods or passengers, for example, between two points at regular intervals.

17. *week:* i.e., wick (of a candle).

18. *the Corners:* In New England, the name often colloquially used to denote a small local village or town center where churches, the post office, a country store, and shops were clustered. In South Berwick, Jewett's home faced the center of town, where the gathering places that Mrs. Thacher has in mind would have been located.

19. *a deck load of oak knees down by the packet:* Pile or stack of logs, consisting in this case of pieces of oak having a natural angular bend, fastened together on a packet boat for transport. Lumbering had become one of the leading industries in Maine by the middle of the nineteenth century, when loggers in Jewett's region of the state would typically float or drive felled timber down the Piscataqua River or its branches from forested areas to the sawmills or to market. The industry would have been crucial to the prosperous shipowning enterprise operated in Berwick "[f]or many years" by Jewett's paternal grandfather, whom she later re-

membered "buying large quantities of timber from the north-
ward and eastward, and sending it down the river and so to sea"
("Looking Back on Girlhood" [1892], in *The Uncollected Short
Stories of Sarah Orne Jewett*, ed. Richard Cary [Waterville, Me.:
Colby College Press, 1971], p. 4). As Daniel Thacher's experience attests, the "drive" downriver often proved to be a lumber-
man's most difficult and hazardous task.

20. *poling:* Lumbermen used a pick-pole to guide or prod logs downriver or, as apparently in this case, to navigate the craft on which
logs were piled.

CHAPTER III.
AT JAKE AND MARTIN'S

1. *at Lowell . . . with several of her acquaintances:* Starting in the
late 1820s, the prospect of good wages, decent living and working conditions, and personal independence had drawn thousands
of young, unmarried, mostly rural New England women to work
in the cotton mills of Lowell, Massachusetts, which rapidly became the home of the nation's textile industry as well as the
largest manufacturing center of mid-nineteenth-century America.
The "mill-girls" of Lowell, many of them literarily gifted, became renowned both in the United States and overseas.

2. *coastwise schooner:* The principal ship (usually a two-masted
sailing vessel) engaged in trade between the West Indies and ports
along the New England coast during this period.

3. *the Corners:* See chapter 2, note 18.

4. *the old-fashioned thorough-braced wagon:* By the 1840s, the
body of most carriages of this sort would no longer have been
supported by leather straps, or "thoroughbraces," which provided one of the earliest forms of suspension for such vehicles.

5. *at Thanksgiving time when the geese were sold:* Although turkey
had started to become popularly associated with the holiday earlier in the nineteenth century, other forms of fresh game like
geese or duck were still frequently served at Thanksgiving dinners in New England.

6. *Some accident . . . in the wide fireplace:* Despite the widely
touted advantages of cookstoves, many Americans (particularly
men) continued to prefer the traditional open-fire hearth until
late in the nineteenth century.

7. *lifted it as if it were a feather:* Since early cookstoves weighed several hundred pounds, it would have been a sign of the Dyer

brothers' strength as rugged Yankee farmers that they could move one so easily.

8. *they hastily pried away . . . imprisoned there in darkness for many months:* Before a cookstove could be installed properly, the kitchen fireplace usually had to be boarded up, in this case hiding along with it utensils like a "crane" (an upright revolving axle with horizontal arms from which a pot or kettle could be suspended over the flames) or "iron dogs," a pair of andirons placed on each side of a fireplace to support the burning wood.

9. *backlog, forestick, and crowsticks:* Large log usually placed at the back of a fireplace; the front stick resting on andirons in a wood fire; a form of "brush" providing additional kindling in farmhouses.

10. *sposhy:* Soft, wet.

11. *rensin's:* i.e., "rinsings."

12. *I don't lay no great belief . . . on the docket:* In nineteenth-century Maine's lower courts, which convened in each county seat or other major population center, jurors heard a full term's worth of cases; a term lasting several days to a couple of weeks and ending sometime before Christmas would not have been unusual.

13. *Good King Agrippy!:* Used in such an exclamation perhaps in avoidance of a more blasphemous oath or expletive, the name meant here is perhaps that of Herod Agrippa II, known as Agrippa, son of the equally Rome-friendly but more popular Herod Agrippa I (king of Judea from A.D. 37 to 44), appointed king of Chalcis in southern Lebanon in A.D. 50, and the ruler before whom Paul testified about his conversion (Acts 25–26). (Suggested by Terry Heller, ed., *A Country Doctor*, by Sarah Orne Jewett [Sarah Orne Jewett Text Project, 1997–2004], http://www.public.coe.edu/~theller/soj/acd/acdo3.html.) In rural Maine, the terminal "a" in proper nouns would usually have been pronounced "y."

14. *in them boardin' houses:* Because so many of the young women who worked in the cotton factories in Lowell, Massachusetts, had moved there from distant parts of New England, proprietors established an initially attractive and comfortable network of boardinghouses (as well as medical services, a lending library, and other amenities). By the mid-1840s, however, both living and working conditions had badly deteriorated for Lowell's famous "mill-girls" as a result of overcrowding in the boardinghouses, a "speed up" in production, and the reduction of wages.

15. *a laylock bush . . . an ellum tree:* i.e., a lilac bush and an elm tree.

16. *a shock:* Northern New England colloquialism, derived from Scots dialect, for a paralytic stroke or seizure.

17. *likely:* Promising in appearance and character; giving an impression of strength and vigor.

CHAPTER IV.
LIFE AND DEATH

1. *the grass of the field . . . the wind passes over:* "As for man, his days are as grass: as a flower of the field, so he flourisheth. / For the wind passeth over it, and it is gone; and the place thereof shall know it no more" (Psalms 103:15–16).

2. *a company of Druid worshipers:* Druids, a class of ancient Celtic priests and teachers, were said to have typically performed rites in forest clearings.

3. *Dunport:* Jewett's fictional name for what is evidently meant to represent Portsmouth, New Hampshire.

CHAPTER V.
A SUNDAY VISIT

1. *the old meeting-house:* See chapter 10, note 3.

2. *the best district school teacher:* Shortly after becoming a state in 1820, Maine had adopted a district system governing the operation of elementary or "common" schools, with each town authorized to determine the number of school districts in which it was to be divided, and teachers appointed in each division by a district agent. As of the 1850s, the number of separate districts varied greatly from town to town and totaled over four thousand statewide, resulting in many problems that led to severe criticism of the district system, which would be abolished in Maine in 1893.

3. *his yearly parochial visitation:* Among his pastoral duties, Dr. Leslie's local clergyman would have tried to visit each household in his parish at least once a year, engaging principally in prayer, counsel, and religious instruction.

4. *the old summer-house:* Typically, a simple rustic structure placed in a garden or park to provide a cool, shady spot in hot weather.

CHAPTER VI.
IN SUMMER WEATHER

1. *Fayal:* Faial, one of the islands of the Azores, located in the north Atlantic Ocean nearly a thousand miles west of Portugal.
2. *shock:* See chapter 3, note 16.
3. *all in a brile:* In a mess, in confusion; evidently a Newfoundland dialect term, from "broil."
4. *'scape-gallows:* Rascal, scoundrel; pronounced "scapegallus."
5. *before you could say Jack Robi'son:* Of uncertain origin, the English expression "faster than you can say Jack Robinson" dates from at least the late eighteenth century.
6. *the hay-rigging:* Framework projecting from the sides of a wagon on which hay would be transported on a farm after being gathered, usually in midsummer.
7. *clerk:* Pupil, student.
8. *'Miry:* As in "Almira."

CHAPTER VII.
FOR THE YEARS TO COME

1. *a small bottle . . . with various drugs:* Particularly in rural areas of the United States, where few towns had pharmacies or apothecaries, most nineteenth-century physicians dispensed drugs themselves to their patients.
2. *get through first:* i.e., precede her in death.
3. *a little sober joking . . . would immediately require his aid again:* In mid-nineteenth-century America, successfully collecting fees owed by patients had become one of the chief difficulties of a physician's practice.

CHAPTER VIII.
A GREAT CHANGE

1. *watcher:* See chapter 2, note 5.
2. *his own old copy of Robinson Crusoe:* Although not originally intended for children, the classic 1719 text by Daniel Defoe (1660–1731), English novelist, had been familiar children's reading material since the late eighteenth century.
3. *the weather-beaten building at the cross-roads:* Jewett appears to be referring to a schoolhouse that stood at this time at the intersection of Brattle Street and Old South Road, near that of Old

Fields Road and Vine Street, in the original Old Fields area below
South Berwick.

4. *she might been seen every day . . . a briar at his heels:* As Jewett
would later recall of her own youth, "my father was always ready
to let me be his companion in long drives about the country"
when visiting his patients: "I used to follow him about silently,
like an undemanding little dog, content to follow at his heels"
("Looking Back on Girlhood" [1892], in *The Uncollected Short
Stories of Sarah Orne Jewett*, ed. Richard Cary [Waterville, Me.:
Colby College Press, 1971], p. 6).

5. *The doctor stopped his horse . . . Nan's vision:* Many nineteenth-
century American physicians were amateur naturalists, cultivat-
ing an interest in botany or other aspects of natural history; the
hobby would have been especially popular among rural practitioners, in part as a diversion on long drives in the countryside
between one patient's home and another.

CHAPTER IX.
AT DR. LESLIE'S

1. *still unfamiliar even to most professional travelers:* Although
Commodore Matthew C. Perry's famous arrival in Tokyo Bay in
1854 had recently opened Japan to American visitors, travel there
would not become fashionable until after 1876, when displays at
Philadelphia's Centennial Exhibition (which Jewett twice attended) launched the late-nineteenth-century "Japan craze" in the
United States.

2. *marry in haste and repent at his leisure:* Proverbial expression
first appearing in English in the early seventeenth century, perhaps most familiar from act 5 of *The Old Bachelor* (1693), by
William Congreve (1670–1729), English playwright: "Marry'd
in haste, we may repent at leisure" (line 356).

3. *ship-master's kit of numbered doses . . . a man-of-war:* Unlike
naval ships, American merchant vessels and whalers typically did
not have physicians on board in the nineteenth century, carrying
instead a chest with medicine bottles each identified by number
and correlated with particular symptoms in the accompanying instructions that the ship's captain, or another officer, would follow in treating any of the crew's ailments.

4. *one of the factories in Lowell:* See chapter 3, note 1.

5. *regions in Iceland that are full of geysers:* Since the late eighteenth century, Iceland had become renowned to travelers for its

network of hot springs periodically spouting water and vapor, particularly in the area east of Reykjavík surrounding the "Great Geysir," from which the English word is derived.

6. *a south of Ireland fellow . . . cracked his whip-lash:* By the middle of the nineteenth century, southern Ireland had become increasingly associated with Roman Catholicism, by contrast to the more Protestant north. The ethnic typecasting in which Dr. Ferris indulges here would have been all the more unfortunate in light of the fact that the potato blight resulting in the Great Famine of 1845–48 had accelerated emigration from Ireland to the United States, particularly to New England, where anti-Irish-Catholic sentiments soared in the following decade. Testimony of Irish male immigrants at the time does suggest that many thought that, if they had worked as hard in Ireland as they did in the United States, they need never have emigrated (perhaps forgetting the dire economic conditions back home).

7. *likely:* See chapter 3, note 17.

8. *hypnotism:* In the second quarter of the nineteenth century, some American physicians became fascinated by the therapeutic possibilities of hypnotism, or mesmerism, associated with Friedrich Anton Mesmer (1734–1815), a Swabian practitioner whose thinking had recently been promulgated in the United States.

9. *the action of belladonna in congestion and inflammation of the brain:* "Belladonna," a drug extracted from the leaves and root of the plant of that name, had been discussed more than once along the same lines by Jewett's father, who cited what he called "the beneficial results of belladonna in cerebral congestion" two years after presenting an entire paper on the subject (Theodore H. Jewett, M.D., *President's Address to the Maine Medical Association, at its Annual Meeting in Portland, June 11, 1878* [Portland, Me.: Stephen Berry, 1878], p. 9; *Belladonna in Congestion of the Brain. A paper read before the Maine Medical Association, June, 1876* [Portland, Me.: Stephen Berry, 1876]).

10. *Bell's "Anatomy":* Published in four volumes between 1797 and 1804, *The Anatomy of the bones, muscles and joints* (later reissued as *The Anatomy of the Human Body*), by John Bell (1763–1820), an eminent Scots surgeon, with the assistance of his brother, Sir Charles Bell (1774–1842), an anatomist and pioneer in the study of neurology, was for decades a standard text on the subject.

11. *in the "Lancet" . . . those tree-growing jugglers:* Founded in 1823 and published weekly in London, *The Lancet* remains one

of the most prestigious English-language medical journals; first reported by seventeenth-century travelers to India, the famous mango trick—performed by Indian "jugglers," or street magicians, who allegedly conjured a mango tree to sprout within a brief period of time from a stick planted in the ground, or from seeds in a mound of soil covered with a cloth—attracted renewed interest among Westerners in the middle decades of the nineteenth century.

12. *a likeness of me on a tea plate:* Ceramics decorated with images of notable personages had become quite popular in England by the middle of the nineteenth century, after new processes such as transfer-printing enabled manufacturers to reproduce portraits on objects like china for a large market.

13. *for general practice or for a specialty?:* By the 1850s, specialization, or "specialism," had begun to emerge in American medical training and practice and would become increasingly prominent after the Civil War.

14. *to bleed as much as old Dr. Rush recommended:* Bloodletting, or "bleeding," epitomized the "heroic" therapies influentially advocated by Benjamin Rush (1746–1813), the illustrious early American physician whose drastic, aggressively interventionist forms of treatment were on the decline in medical practice in the United States by the middle of the nineteenth century.

15. *like a hen with one chicken:* Displaying excessive or single-minded fussiness or concern about a particular matter.

16. *before you were out of the hospitals:* Since most medical colleges in the United States did not offer clinical instruction or require hospital attendance until later in the nineteenth century, the fact that Dr. Leslie's course of study had included such training would have been a mark of the high quality of his education in medicine.

17. *to follow nature, as Sydenham did, who followed no man:* Thomas Sydenham (1624–89), a physician celebrated as "the English Hippocrates" and known for his independence of orthodox medical doctrine in his own time, emphasized clinical experience and the observation of nature in the treatment of disease. Dr. Ferris, in effect, is quoting Jewett's father, who acknowledged "SYDENHAM, the father of English medicine," and once castigated various eminent doctors of the recent past on the grounds that "[t]hey did not follow nature, like SYDENHAM, who followed no man. He investigated and thought for himself, and his name will be honored throughout all time" (Theodore H. Jewett, M.D., *President's Address*, pp. 13, 17).

18. *The anatomists and the pathologists . . . not to the dead:* Dr. Ferris refers to one result of the influence of the so-called Paris Clinical School, which had revolutionized medicine earlier in the nineteenth century by demonstrating the value of postmortem examinations, among other innovative procedures. Between 1820 and 1860, hundreds of American medical students and physicians visited Paris to study in its clinics, returning home to disseminate what they had learned. Some practitioners, like Dr. Ferris, remained ambivalent about the results of such teachings, whose proponents struck them as largely disengaged from their traditional function as healers and as therefore contributing little to therapeutic practice. Here Jewett duplicates much of the phrasing in which her father had counseled that "pathology . . . has been made too much the all-in-all, to the neglect of rational and skillful practice," and that "a dead body is one thing, a live body is another. We must look to the living chiefly to learn the laws of life, not to the dead" (Theodore H. Jewett, M.D., *President's Address*, pp. 11, 12–13).

19. *The men who make it their business . . . aren't the ones for successful practice:* Dr. Ferris again closely echoes Jewett's father, who once suggested to his colleagues, "We are all too much governed by our text books," contending that "[m]any of them . . . are written by scholarly rather than by practical men, who can often teach learnedly but not practice successfully" (Theodore H. Jewett, M.D., *President's Address*, p. 14). By the 1860s, according to historians, many practitioners had indeed begun to disparage medical textbooks, but more because they tended to be doctrinairely conservative or out of date on, say, therapeutic matters.

20. *They go on, poor fellows . . . the sick man well again:* In the second third of the nineteenth century, many physicians in the United States began to subscribe to the notion of the healing power of nature and to exalt nature's curative capacities, arguing that some diseases could not be therapeutically affected through "heroic" medical practices (i.e., "bleeding," purging, or excessive drugging) but were "self-limiting" and would thus tend toward a cure spontaneously on their own, with minimal intervention. (It was a principle espoused by Jewett's father, who demanded that "the profession learn not to administer medicines in cases where nature is perfectly capable of restoring the patient" and that "we . . . do not, with egotistic wisdom, try to teach nature to work according to our notions" [Theodore H. Jewett, M.D.,

President's Address, pp. 18, 19].) For the process of natural healing to succeed, many physicians also considered it important to
maintain the body's "vital power" (what Dr. Leslie calls "the life
power"), a concept reflecting the survival of an earlier "holistic"
view of the body, in which disease or illness was thought to bring
about a systemic imbalance corrected by reestablishing the "balance" that represented the body's "natural" state. Jewett's father
had likewise derived "the essence of all diseases" from the fact
"that the life power is at fault," while complaining about "how
little aid [is given] to nature to strengthen and balance the system
and to improve the malcondition—to nature, which really always
restores the sick to health" (*President's Address*, p. 12).

21. *diseases are oftener effects of illness than causes:* Although somewhat opaque about the nature and relationships of the entities involved, such a remark, like that of Jewett's father in maintaining
that "[d]iseases themselves have been altogether too much regarded as causes of illness, when really they are effects," is perhaps clarified by his additional claim about the dangers of
"regard[ing] any one symptom in any disease as the origin of the
illness" (Theodore H. Jewett, M.D., *President's Address*, pp. 11,
18). Both he and Dr. Leslie thus seem to identify "diseases" with
"symptoms" as the observable phenomena manifesting the "illness" that would have been considered the primary causal agent
or disturbance in the body.

22. *But the young practitioners . . . think for themselves:* "Of
course," as Dr. Jewett had also acknowledged, "junior physicians
must follow the books until their eyes are opened by experience,
and their judgment sufficiently matured to think for themselves"
(*President's Address*, p. 14).

23. *the different treatments of pneumonia . . . contempt of remedies:*
Jewett's father had cited the use of around half a dozen therapies
in declaring, "I am astonished, when I look back at the ideas and
treatment that have been in fashion in my own time, as to pneumonia"; as a result of this sort of variability, "Skepticism as to
the use of remedies is now the rule," leading him to insist that
"when medicines are administered rationally in cases proper for
their use, we shall have less scepticism as to their worth"
(Theodore H. Jewett, M.D., *President's Address*, pp. 16, 8, 18).
By the late 1850s and 1860s, according to historians, therapeutics as a branch of medicine—left static or stagnant by the emphasis on empirical observation that triumphed under the
influence of the Paris Clinical School—had entered something of

a crisis in the eyes of many physicians, who would have agreed with Dr. Jewett's complaints that "[t]herapeutics have been most lamentably neglected" and "have not been studied sufficiently in connection with clinical education" (*President's Address*, pp. 8, 10). Like Dr. Leslie, Jewett's father seems to be trying to stake out a middle ground between the milder, more moderate application of drugs, or "remedies," that had supplanted traditional "heroic" measures (once the concept of self-limited diseases, or of the restorative power of nature, took hold) and an increasingly skeptical attitude toward drugs that came to be known, in its more extreme or radical form, as "therapeutic nihilism." It was to that position, which had some powerful adherents in the medical world by the end of the nineteenth century, that Jewett herself objected as late as 1906, somewhat exaggerating its impact when she remarked, after rereading his 1878 address to the Maine Medical Association, "I was . . . interested to find how much my father had anticipated of the condition of things now in 'practice,' and especially the contempt of remedies, with which I have but little patience. It seems as if there *were* such a thing as Therapeutics, and as if it were just as ignorant to take too little medicine as to take too much" (Jewett to Sarah Wheelwright, Sunday [1906], in *Letters of Sarah Orne Jewett*, ed. Annie Fields [Boston: Houghton Mifflin, 1911], p. 217).

24. *Dr. Johnson said . . . most stupidly used:* The full epigram ("Doctors are men who prescribe medicine of which they know little to cure diseases of which they know less in bodies of which they know nothing") is commonly attributed not to Samuel Johnson (1709–84), English critic and lexicographer, but to Voltaire, born François-Marie Arouet (1694–1778), French Enlightenment *philosophe* and wit. Jewett's father made the same misattribution when quoting the line before similarly concluding, "If ill success follows the exhibition of medicines, most surely it is not the fault of the medicines. There is something in the way they are used" (Theodore H. Jewett, M.D., *President's Address*, p. 10).

25. *spend our treatment . . . can we expect?:* "Treatment has been generally expended upon these effects [of illness] rather than the causes. The results have been unsatisfactory, no matter what has been the theory entertained or the medicines prescribed" (Theodore H. Jewett, M.D., *President's Address*, p. 11).

26. *The practical medical men . . . emergencies day after day:* Jewett here recalls her father's assertion that "[w]e need reports from . . . the class of independent thinkers who have met many

an emergency successfully, men who are not wholly followers of the text books and the theories of the passing hour," and that "[t]he practical medical men are the juries who sooner or later settle forever all theories" (Theodore H. Jewett, M.D., *President's Address*, pp. 17–18).

27. *Do you remember how well Buckle says . . . what he says about that?:* Paraphrase of the argument in "The Influence of Women on the Progress of Knowledge," a lecture delivered at the Royal Institution of Great Britain, in London, on March 19, 1858, by Henry Thomas Buckle (1821–62), best known in his time as the author of *History of Civilization in England* (1857–61). Contending that "women naturally prefer the deductive method [of reasoning] to the inductive" (which he identifies with the male intellect) in part because "they possess more of what is called intuition," Buckle posits "a spiritual, a poetic, and for aught we know a spontaneous and uncaused element in the human mind, which ever and anon, suddenly and without warning, gives us a glimpse and a forecast of the future, and urges us to seize truth as it were by anticipation." In his overt "gendering" of the division of intellectual labor, it is their association with that element and with the "ideal method" of intuition-based deduction that accounts for what Buckle described as "the incalculable service women have rendered to the progress of knowledge." Among "the great geniuses" referred to by Dr. Ferris, Newton and Goethe are mentioned as exemplifying "the triumph of the deductive method" and thus the influence of women's "habits of mind." Buckle's lecture, which appears to have stirred considerable interest at the time, was published in the April 1858 issue of *Fraser's Magazine* and reprinted in his *Essays* (1863) and again in *Miscellaneous and Posthumous Works of Henry Thomas Buckle* (1872).

28. *Christ in us, the hope of glory:* See Colossians 1:27.

29. *the Marine Hospital at Nagasaki:* Dr. Ferris appears to be referring to the teaching hospital established in Nagasaki by a Dutch naval surgeon in 1861; residents or guests of the foreign settlement there were among those treated at the hospital, which represented a turning point in the introduction of Western medicine in Japan.

30. *house-room:* Lodgings; room or accommodations for a guest.

31. *to help me in a piece of surgery:* At the time, most surgeries—limited to amputations, the draining of abscesses, or the removal

of tumors—were performed in a patient's home, especially in rural areas where hospitals remained scarce.

32. *Miss Edgeworth's "Parent's Assistant":* The Parent's Assistant; or, Stories for Children (1796), a widely popular collection of tales by the Anglo-Irish novelist and children's writer Maria Edgeworth (1767–1849), appeared in several editions in England and the United States through the middle of the nineteenth century.

CHAPTER X.
ACROSS THE STREET

1. *the necessity of a meeting-house:* The first meetinghouse in the colonial Old Fields area was built around 1660, near the intersection of Brattle Street and Old South Road, and abandoned by the start of the eighteenth century.

2. *glebe land:* Parcel of land set aside for the use of the local ministry, as in the one hundred and fifty acres assigned to Berwick parish in 1669.

3. *There had been a great excitement . . . without public challenge:* Jewett appears to be conflating various aspects of local history involving the First Parish (Congregational) Church, which opened in 1702 at the site of the original Old Fields meetinghouse and moved into a new, larger structure nearby in 1752, evidently after some debate about where it should be situated. Its distant location became a problem as the community expanded inland and grew in population, until a new meetinghouse opened in the mid-1820s in South Berwick village, near the center of town, where it is now known as the First Parish Federated Church. (At the time, some worshipers chose not to leave the original congregation, which remained at the Old Fields site for another decade.) By "the old meeting-house," where Nan—who "liked the excitement of the Sunday drive to the village" from her grandmother's farm—is described in the fifth chapter as habitually looking out for Dr. Leslie, Jewett has in mind this most recent structure, in which her family had its own pew.

4. *The old First Parish Church . . . its front by moonlight:* Referring here again to the structure erected in South Berwick in the mid-1820s, Jewett later described "the meeting-house of the old First Church and Parish" as "a most tasteful building," distinguished by "its handsome front with the three doors and Corinthian columns, its high panelled pews, gallery, great mahogany pulpit,

and . . . its beautiful windows of the best hand-made sash-work" ("The Old Town of Berwick," *New England Magazine* 10 [July 1894]: 605, 606).

5. *absolution and extreme unction:* In other words, the remission of sins involved in "penance" and the "last rites," both sacraments performed by priests in the Roman Catholic Church rather than by Protestant ministers.

6. *the first commandment . . . strange gods:* "Thou shalt have no other gods before me" (Exodus 20:3).

7. *the lie . . . that waits and marks the hour:* ". . . The nimble lie / Is like the second-hand upon a clock; / We see it fly, while the hour-hand of truth / Seems to stand still, and yet it moves unseen, / And wins at last, for the clock will not strike / Till it has reached the goal": lines from scene 5 of *Michael Angelo: A Fragment* (1883), posthumously published work of dramatic verse by Henry Wadsworth Longfellow (1807–82), celebrated American poet.

8. *where the chimney bricks were burnt:* Bricks, molded out of clay and then "fired," or vitrified, in kilns operated in brickyards, had been used almost exclusively in the construction of chimneys during the colonial era in New England, where houses were otherwise usually built of wood or rough stone, rather than brick, until the early 1800s.

9. *a smart little house . . . had seen fit to build:* Jewett is describing a cottage built in the English or rural Gothic style, one of the first Victorian modes of domestic architecture to come into vogue by the 1850s, succeeding the classicism of the Greek Revival style that had been favored in New England since the early nineteenth century.

10. *the East road and the West road:* Now Academy Street and Main Street in South Berwick.

11. *In Titian's great Venetian picture . . . follow the sacred sight:* The *Presentation of the Virgin in the Temple* (c. 1534–38), by Titian, born Tiziano Vecellio (c. 1488–1576), renowned Italian Renaissance painter, occupies a wall in the Gallerie dell'Accademia, formerly the Scuola della Carita, in Venice.

12. *French medical work of high renown:* As a result of the influence of the Paris Clinical School on American medicine (see chapter 9, note 18), French medical texts either in the original or in English translation circulated widely among informed physicians in the United States in the middle decades of the nineteenth century.

13. *It was thinly dressed . . . some sort of cover put on these things before they come down:* Until well into the twentieth century,

publishers in France usually issued books in flimsy paper "wrappers" to booksellers, whose customers were expected to take their purchases to a binder themselves for cloth binding. As Jewett recalled in a letter not long after publishing *A Country Doctor*, "Father had a great quantity of paper-covered literature of a most professional sort. . . . I suppose some of these old French and English books would make any doctor happy" (quoted in Francis Otto Matthiessen, *Sarah Orne Jewett* [Boston: Houghton Mifflin, 1929], pp. 75–76).

14. *gave out:* i.e., "ran out," or became depleted; originally a nineteenth-century Americanism referring to the exhaustion of one's supply of a particular item or product.

15. *the sweeping:* Possibly a reference to the removal of coals and ash after heating a beehive oven to prepare it for baking bread.

16. *Leghorn:* A fine, plaited straw derived from wheat grown in the region of Tuscany after which it was named, Leghorn remained popular in the nineteenth century in the making of bonnets for spring and summer wear.

17. *the sacrifice of pigs:* Dr. Leslie refers to the annual pig-killing, a custom observed in the winter months in rural areas like northern New England, where a family's pig would be slaughtered, eaten, stored, shared or exchanged with neighbors, or, as in this instance, presented as a gift to one's clergyman.

18. *Who is it says . . . to inspire love benefits others:* "Aimer, aimer, c'est être utile à soi; / Se faire aimer, c'est être utile aux autres," lines from "Le Suicide" (1833), by Pierre-Jean de Béranger (1780–1857), French Romantic poet and chansonnier. In earlier signs of their value to her, Jewett had transcribed the same lines, in slightly modified English ("To love is to be useful to yourself; to cause love is to be useful to others"), at the end of one of her diaries and also in a commonplace book (Sarah Orne Jewett, Diary 1871–1879 and Collections of extracts and poems from other authors, Sarah Orne Jewett Papers, bMS Am 1743.1 [341] and bMS Am 1743.26 [13], Houghton Library, Harvard University; quoted by permission of the Houghton Library, Harvard University).

19. *That was one advantage . . . in that way:* From the colonial era until well into the nineteenth century, men seeking a career in medicine first apprenticed themselves for a certain number of years to an older, experienced physician who served as a preceptor. (During the first half of the nineteenth century, when medical schools began proliferating in the United States, an apprenticeship of three years would have been typically a prerequisite for

admission.) Dr. Leslie's convictions on this score repeat those of Jewett's father: "I have reason to believe that students in olden times, who accompanied their masters to the sick room and assisted in the care of patients, enjoyed a better opportunity for information than do many now" (Theodore H. Jewett, M.D., *President's Address to the Maine Medical Association, at its Annual Meeting in Portland, June 11, 1878* [Portland, Me.: Stephen Berry, 1878], p. 10).

CHAPTER XI.
NEW OUTLOOKS

1. *the far-off railway station:* South Berwick Junction, a couple of miles away from the village center, and the depot where the local train originating in Portland connected with the train to Boston operated in that era by the Boston & Maine Railroad.

2. *for it was early June . . . a holiday:* Perhaps because a physician's practice would start to become much busier with the incidence of fevers and other heat-related ailments (especially in children) during the summer months.

3. *at the Athenæum library:* Founded in 1807, the Boston Athenaeum had become a center of intellectual life in the city by the middle of the nineteenth century, housing one of the nation's five largest libraries at the time.

4. *the quiet Granary Burying Ground:* The famous cemetery, located next to Boston's Park Street Church on the site of a colonial-era grain storehouse, contains the graves of Paul Revere, John Hancock, Samuel Adams, and other luminaries of the American revolution.

5. *hiding his light under the Oldfields bushel:* In Christ's words from the sermon on the mount, "Neither do men light a candle, and put it under a bushel, but on a candlestick; and it giveth light unto all that are in the house. / Let your light so shine before men, that they may see your good works, and glorify your Father which is in heaven" (Matthew 5:15–16).

CHAPTER XII.
AGAINST THE WIND

1. *to climb up any other way . . . a thief and a robber:* Allusion to one of Christ's parables, which begins, "Verily, verily, I say unto you, He that entereth not by the door into the sheepfold, but

climbeth up some other way, the same is a thief and a robber" (John 10:1).

2. *to "see life steadily and see it whole":* Paraphrase of the famous tribute to the ancient Greek dramatist Sophocles, "Who saw life steadily, and saw it whole" (line 12), in "To a Friend" (1849), by Matthew Arnold (1822–88), English poet and critic.

3. *sealed orders:* Instructions not to be opened until a designated time, or until one has arrived at a certain place (as on a ship).

4. *a water-logged bobbin . . . one of the mills:* Cylinder or spindle that would have been used in the manufacturing of textiles at a nearby factory like the Salmon Falls Mills in South Berwick.

5. *a not very successful rendering of "Bonny Doon":* "The Banks of Doon" (1783), a popular song by the Scots poet Robert Burns (1759–96), begins "Ye banks and braes a' bonny Doon / How can ye bloom sae fresh and fair?"

6. *old Friend Meadows:* Members of the Society of Friends, or Quakers, began settling in Maine in the 1660s; the sizable Quaker community in Berwick dated back to the middle of the eighteenth century, when the Piscataqua region of Maine and New Hampshire became a center of Quakerism. Jewett briefly comments on the Quakers' presence in the area in "The Old Town of Berwick," *New England Magazine* 10 (July 1894): 605.

7. *gathered:* i.e., by God, into heaven, upon death.

CHAPTER XIII.
A STRAIGHT COURSE

1. *the young men who had wished to be his students:* In other words, as Dr. Leslie's apprentices, under the system of medical education described above (see chapter 10, note 19).

2. *certain traits of certain families . . . quickly proved fatal:* At the time, physicians often treated members of an entire family, on the assumption that knowledge of its constitutional peculiarities from one generation to the next was essential in delivering effective care to each family member.

3. *a haphazard way of doctoring . . . had stood like a lion in the way:* "The slothful man saith, There is a lion in the way; a lion is in the streets" (Proverbs 26:13). Dr. Leslie's sentiments reflect the well-known tension between clinical or empirical observation and experimental science—between "bedside" and laboratory—in American medicine at the time. With scientific inquiry on the rise, physicians in the United States nonetheless typically

distrusted experimental research and remained skeptical of its therapeutic value, or of its relevance to medical practice, until the end of the nineteenth century.

4. *so important to the sensitive medical mind:* Like the newly formed American Medical Association at its first meetings in 1847, medical societies in various parts of the country had recently begun formulating codes of ethics, which initially focused on matters of decorum, attempting to regulate the behavior and interaction of physicians in an effort to curtail the quarrels and rivalries that were so detrimental to the profession's public reputation in the United States for much of the nineteenth century.

5. *everybody had a specialty nowadays:* By the last third of the nineteenth century, specialization had become an increasingly widespread phenomenon in American medicine, with the number of different medical "specialties" rapidly multiplying.

6. *his Braithwaites and Lancets: The Retrospect of Practical Medicine and Surgery* (1840–45), continued by *The Retrospect of Medicine* (1846–1901), a twice-yearly overview of current literature in the field, was better known as *Braithwaite's Retrospect* after its editor, William Braithwaite (1807–85), an English physician and medical writer; for *The Lancet*, see chapter 9, note 11.

7. *with their clumsy blot of gilding:* The Sydenham Society (1843–58), followed by the New Sydenham Society (1859–1907), named after the esteemed seventeenth-century English physician Thomas Sydenham (see chapter 9, note 17), had been established in London for the purpose of republishing classics of medical literature, issued in volumes that carried the title in gilt on the spine and the Sydenham family arms and crest (replaced later by Sydenham's profile) in gilt on the cover.

8. *she must enter the medical school . . . its authority to practice her profession:* By this time, there were four orthodox or "regular" (as opposed to homeopathic or other "irregular") schools of medicine for women in the United States: the New England Female Medical College, the Woman's Medical College of Pennsylvania, the Woman's Medical College of the New York Infirmary for Women and Children, and the Woman's Hospital Medical College in Chicago. Despite the frequently noted vagueness of her description of the school and of Nan's training, internal evidence suggests that Jewett must have had in mind the earliest of those institutions, the New England Female Medical College (founded in 1848, and the only one of its kind in Boston, where

Dr. Leslie has already introduced her to his professional brethren during their earlier visit to the city). It has been argued, however, that "Jewett cannot place Nan at the New England because that medical school adopted the homeopathic method when it merged with Boston University in 1873," a conversion that would decidedly not have appealed to Jewett, whose father once announced, "I am no believer in Homœopathy; indeed, there is no such thing," and who presumably endorsed the orthodox or "allopathic" practice of medicine in which he had been trained (Barbara Bardes and Suzanne Gossett, *Declarations of Independence: Women and Political Power in Nineteenth-Century American Fiction* [New Brunswick, N.J.: Rutgers University Press, 1990], p. 144; Theodore H. Jewett, M.D., *President's Address to the Maine Medical Association, at its Annual Meeting in Portland, June 11, 1878* [Portland, Me.: Stephen Berry, 1878], p. 9). The chronology of events in the narrative is somewhat inexact, but if one assumes that Jewett (born in 1849) would have made her alter ego roughly the same age, and if Nan at the time is not yet twenty-five (as one of her aunt's friends later observes in chapter 18), then there is nothing anachronistic in having her enrolled at the New England Female Medical College, where she can plausibly be imagined attending shortly before its merger with Boston University.

9. *motives of expediency . . . the young men who study medicine:* Throughout much of the nineteenth century, it was commonly felt by the public and by faculty members even at the more respectable medical colleges that men who sought to become physicians tended to be interested in medicine as an easy way of gaining money, social station, or power.

10. *she found . . . the quality of the school:* Although the school managed to graduate a number of superior physicians, it had become well known that instruction at the New England Female Medical College, for all of its virtues as a pioneer in the training of women as doctors, suffered from deficient equipment and facilities as well as from an inferior curriculum, reflecting the financial difficulties that resulted in its aforementioned merger with Boston University.

11. *the examinations . . . Nan had been matriculated:* Applicants to the New England Female Medical College were not in fact administered qualifying examinations of the sort that Jewett seems to have in mind here; for that matter, entrance requirements were minimal, if they existed at all, at medical schools throughout the

United States until the last third of the nineteenth century, contributing to the popular image of (male) medical students—most of whom lacked a college education—as ill-prepared and subliterate.

12. *Not such doctors . . . an absence of high aim:* The obviously garbled phrasing has led some critics to argue that Jewett "revealed a surprising ambivalence about female physicians" as well as a "discomfort about women's medical education" in this passage (Bardes and Gossett, *Declarations of Independence*, p. 145). Its intended sense, however, is much clearer, and unambiguously affirmative, in Jewett's manuscript: "It was not such doctors as several of whom he reminded himself who were disgracing their sex, but those whose lives were ruled by a pettiness of detail, a lack of power and an absence of high aim" (Jewett, "A Country Doctor," ms., Sarah Orne Jewett Papers, bMS Am 1743.7, folder 25, p. 510, Houghton Library, Harvard University; quoted by permission of the Houghton Library, Harvard University).

CHAPTER XIV.
MISS PRINCE OF DUNPORT

1. *She never had been foolish . . . mistress of the finest house in town:* A round marble-topped center table would have become popular with the rise of mass-produced furnishings in the United States following the Civil War. By contrast, Miss Prince's mahogany is likely to have comprised elegant handmade furniture dating from the eighteenth century (as in Chippendale, for example) or earlier-nineteenth-century pieces in the Empire style.

2. *her first winter at the medical school:* Like virtually all medical schools located in urban areas of the United States during this era, the New England Female Medical College was typically in session for a single "winter" term that ran from November to March.

3. *it says in the Bible that children should obey their parents:* See Ephesians 6:1 and Colossians 3:20.

4. *as some old poet says of the whale:* "Strong against tide, th' enormous whale / Emerges, as he goes," concluding lines of stanza 76 from *A Song to David* (1763), by Christopher Smart (1722–71), English poet.

5. *on short commons:* Scant provisions; insufficient rations or fare.

6. *three dormer windows:* Vertical windows projected outward from a sloping roof.

7. *every inch a king:* See William Shakespeare, *King Lear*, act 4, scene 6.

8. *ship's husband:* In maritime law, the agent appointed by a ship's owner to be responsible for its management, outfitting, repairs, etc.

9. *made and mended her pens:* Until the introduction of metallic or steel point pens in the mid-nineteenth century, quills had remained the principal writing instrument, made by cutting back the plume of certain birds' feathers with a simple penknife, and then cut back further (or "mended") after growing worn.

CHAPTER XV.
HOSTESS AND GUEST

1. *a journey of several hours:* Unless Nan is understood to be traveling directly from Boston, Jewett evidently chose to imagine Dunport as much further from Oldfields than Portsmouth was from South Berwick, which would have been a short train ride away.

2. *gambrel-roofed house:* Topped by a roof with two sections sloping downward unequally from a central ridge.

3. *Prussian blue:* Prussian blue, an especially deep and powerful shade of that color, is thought to be the first modern pigment, created in Germany early in the eighteenth century.

4. *the collect:* Prayers uttered before the Epistle of the Mass or the Communion service in Anglican churches like the Protestant Episcopal Church in the United States.

5. *Apostle's Creed:* Standard enunciation of the basic tenets of the Western Christian faith, traditionally thought to have been composed by the original twelve apostles of Jesus Christ but dating rather from the early Middle Ages, and beginning "I believe in God the Father, Creator of heaven and earth."

6. *The letter s was made long:* In the "long" form in which it would have been commonly written and printed in English until the end of the eighteenth century, the letter *s* resembled a lowercase printed *f* with the crossbar only on the left side when appearing at the start or in the middle of a word.

7. *she had been confirmed while she was first at boarding-school:* In the American Episcopal Church, the rite of confirmation would have been ordinarily administered in early adolescence; Jewett herself, although raised a Congregationalist, was confirmed in the Episcopal faith at an older age in 1870.

CHAPTER XVI.
A JUNE SUNDAY

1. *old St. Ann's:* Some years after the publication of *A Country Doctor*, a local historian quoted the previous chapter's description of Miss Prince's church in identifying the structure as St. John's Church in Portsmouth, New Hampshire (Franklin Ware Davis, "Old St. John's Parish, Portsmouth," *New England Magazine* 17 [November 1894]: 331–32). It was at St. John's that Jewett had been confirmed as an Episcopalian in 1870.

2. *watch with him:* See chapter 2, note 5.

3. *with some of your red tape, I'm afraid:* The use of the term "red tape" in denoting undue bureaucratic or procedural delay originated in the eighteenth century, owing to the color of the tape once used in Great Britain to bind legal and official documents.

CHAPTER XVII.
BY THE RIVER

1. *yards:* horizontal spars from which sails are hung.

2. *main-to'gallant cross-trees:* Short horizontal spars affixed at right angles to the main-topgallant mast, the uppermost of three sections of the principal mast of a sailing vessel.

3. *gangway plank:* Bridge between shore or dock and the entrance in the side of a vessel.

4. *hawser:* Rope or cable used, for example, in mooring a ship.

5. *galley:* A ship's kitchen area.

6. *mizzen mast:* The last, and frequently the smallest, of the masts of a sailing vessel.

7. *square-rigged vessel:* The American square-rigger—usually a three-masted vessel with so-called square sails (more often rectangular in shape) hanging from yards, or horizontal spars, affixed at right angles to the mast—had been a familiar mercantile craft in various important trades since colonial times.

8. *sculler:* One who steers or propels a small boat forward from the back using a single oar.

9. *packet boats:* See chapter 2, note 16.

10. *high-peaked lateen sails:* Distinctive triangular sails, their name derived from *voile Latine* ("Latin sail"), originating in the ancient Mediterranean and typically found on gundalows, sailing vessels peculiar to Jewett's region, where they were used to transport produce and other goods down the Piscataqua River to

Portsmouth well into the nineteenth century. In her youth, as Jewett later recalled, "there was a picturesque fleet of twenty gundalows with lateen sails, sailing from the Landing wharves [in South Berwick] to Portsmouth. . . . The high peaked sail looks like a great bird's wing, and catches the flawy wind well in the river reaches" ("The Old Town of Berwick," *New England Magazine* 10 [July 1894]: 607).

CHAPTER XVIII.
A SERIOUS TEA-DRINKING

1. *field-corners:* On farms, the small uncultivated acreage that lies at a place where two fences join, creating a difficult corner in which to turn machinery, and thus often providing a habitat for wildlife.
2. *a monkey's wedding . . . old-fashioned expressions:* It is not clear what Miss Prince's housekeeper means by "a monkey's wedding" (more recently a colloquialism for "sunshower" in South Africa and in parts of northern New England) or by the second expression, which appears to be her coinage. Both terms are defined as indicating "[a] state of disorder or disarray," with these passages from *A Country Doctor* the sole illustrations offered, in the *Dictionary of American Regional English*, vol. III (Cambridge, Mass.: Harvard University Press, 1996), p. 647.
3. *the best blue teacups with their scalloped edges:* Cups and saucers made of white porcelain or china adorned with designs painted in blue, and with teacup rims segmented into four parts resembling a scallop shell, were commonly to be found in upper-middle-class and upper-class homes in nineteenth-century America.
4. *a work on ventilation . . . for a young woman:* Air quality in homes, schools, and workplaces had become one of the chief concerns of the public-health movement that arose in the United States by the middle of the nineteenth century, a movement with which many of the nation's early women physicians were associated.

CHAPTER XIX.
FRIEND AND LOVER

1. *square-rigged vessel:* See chapter 17, note 7.
2. *the world was still before him:* See John Milton, *Paradise Lost* (1667), Book XII, line 646.

3. *the broad aisle of St. Ann's church:* See chapter 16, note 1.

4. *the May term of court:* See chapter 3, note 12.

5. *the fair stranger within her gates:* See Exodus 20:10 and Deuteronomy 5:14.

6. *Dr. Leslie, unlike most physicians, was a man of fortune:* An oversupply of doctors, ruthless competition, problems in collecting fees, and other variables made the field of medicine largely unremunerative throughout the nineteenth century for all but the more successful practitioners in urban centers of the United States, or for those who also taught in medical schools. Rural and small-town physicians would have found it especially hard to earn a livelihood, and were often forced to supplement their income by operating a farm or some other small business. (Not unlike Dr. Leslie, Jewett's father was able to enjoy a career in medicine without such constraints thanks to her paternal grandfather, whose wealth as a prosperous shipowner left the family financially independent.)

7. *The old proverb . . . from a pebble to a diamond:* "Better a diamond with a flaw than a pebble without," adage often erroneously ascribed to the *Analects* of Confucius (c. 551–479 B.C.), ancient Chinese philosopher and sage.

8. *faint heart ne'er won fair lady:* The old saying, which first appeared in English in sixteenth-century verse, would have been perhaps most familiar from English translations of one of Sancho Panza's remarks in part 2, chapter 10, of *Don Quixote* (1605, 1615), by Miguel de Cervantes Saavedra (1547–1616).

9. *he had died of yellow fever at Key West:* Like other areas of Florida and throughout the South, Key West (where the United States had established a naval presence shortly after acquiring the island in 1822) suffered a number of yellow-fever epidemics in the nineteenth century.

10. *the Turnpike Company:* Turnpikes, unlike public roads and highways, were built or maintained in nineteenth-century New England by privately owned corporations chartered by the state legislature and authorized to charge travelers fees at a certain number of "toll-gates." Jewett would have to be referring here to the Milford and Princeton Turnpike Company (founded in 1863 and renamed the Granger Turnpike Company three years later), the only such corporation formed in Maine after its separation from Massachusetts as an independent state in 1820.

11. *its strait and narrow way where God had left no room for another:* Christ's words in the sermon on the mount: "Enter ye in at

the strait gate: for wide is the gate, and broad is the way, that leadeth to destruction, and many there be which go in thereat: / Because strait is the gate, and narrow is the way, which leadeth unto life, and few there be that find it" (Matthew 7:13–14).

12. *I must be about my business:* See Luke 2:49.

CHAPTER XX.
ASHORE AND AFLOAT

1. *a great price for ducklings . . . until Thanksgiving time:* See chapter 3, note 5.

2. *Captain Walter had tasted his wine . . . the rank and dignity of the contents:* Before it was brought to table and served at formal dinners in nineteenth-century America, wine would be poured from its bottle into glass decanters often carrying, attached to a chain, a silver plate with a generic word like "Wine" or "Madeira" engraved on the front.

3. *not to waste this in pudding-sauces:* Madeira wine and brandy were common ingedients of toppings on Christmas pudding.

4. *tiller ropes:* On small boats, ropes leading from the horizontal bar connected to the rudder and used to control the direction in which the vessel moves.

CHAPTER XXI.
AT HOME AGAIN

1. *her heroes were the great doctors:* Jewett later recalled this statement as uttered by Nan herself when she informed the prominent physician-writer S. Weir Mitchell of her own medical pedigree: "though I am a pen-holder myself I am child and grandchild of physicians and as I once made somebody else say, 'My heroes are the great doctors'" (quoted in John Eldridge Frost, *Sarah Orne Jewett* [Kittery Point, Me.: Gundalow Club, 1960], p. 66).

2. *The wielder of ideas . . . the other to men:* The familiar dichotomy that Jewett is rejecting here corresponds exactly to the contrast between the "deductive" and the "inductive" drawn in the Henry Thomas Buckle essay cited earlier by Dr. Ferris (see chapter 9, note 27). On the assumption that, "if [the scientific inquirer] begin with the facts his method is inductive," and that "if he begin with the ideas it is deductive," Buckle's essay argues that one of the reasons "women prefer the deductive" is that, "being more emotional and enthusiastic, they live in a more ideal world,

and therefore prefer a method of inquiry which proceeds from ideas to facts; leaving to men the opposite method of proceeding from facts to ideas." In alluding to the distinction on which he bases his praise of women's intellectual influence, even as she issues a much more unequivocally laudatory statement of her own, Jewett appears to be slyly exposing the belittlement at the heart of Buckle's claim that "women by encouraging in men deductive habits of thought, have rendered an immense, *though unconscious* service to the progress of knowledge" and "great *though unconscious* service to science" (emphasis added).

3. *at the children's hospitals:* Several alumnae of the New England Female Medical College continued their studies at the New England Hospital for Women and Children, the region's first hospital staffed entirely by women doctors, and founded in Boston in 1862 largely for the purpose of providing clinical instruction to women. (Comparable facilities elsewhere included the New York Infirmary for Women and Children, where a medical college for women had also been launched, and the Pacific Dispensary for Women and Children in San Francisco.) Since Children's Hospital and the Boston Lying-In Hospital, the city's only other institutions of the kind, did not yet appoint women to their staffs, however, it is not clear what other hospitals Jewett would have had in mind in imagining Nan's clinical training during her first term in medical school. In any event, at a time when most medical colleges in the United States were still unaffiliated with hospitals, Nan's experience would have reflected the advanced nature of the training American women often received in "orthodox" medicine, and its superiority to that of many of their male counterparts.

4. *checks:* As in baggage checks, to be handed to a porter on a train-station platform.

5. *as Christ came to his . . . to minister:* See Matthew 20:28 and Mark 10:45.

6. *The months went by swiftly . . . they had finished their studies:* Like nearly all medical schools in the United States before various curricular reforms began to be adopted in the last third of the nineteenth century, the New England Female Medical College administered a two-year course of study.

7. *Zurich held out a great temptation:* Many of America's early women physicians spent time in Europe to complete their clinical training, several of them attending the University of Zurich, which had become in 1867 the first institution to offer coeducation in the field of medicine.

8. *Nobody sees people . . . holds in his keeping:* Nineteenth-century physicians were encouraged to think of themselves as ministering to the souls as well as to the bodies of their patients, who often privately confided in them and sought their counsel on matters unrelated to health or illness. The notion that healers had a moral or spiritual as well as a therapeutic role to perform owed much of its authority to the enduring image of Christ as "the Great Physician."

9. *an offer of a fine position in Canada . . . best hospital experience and responsibility:* Since opportunities for work in hospitals north of the border did not become available to women until the founding in 1883 of Kingston Women's Medical College and the Toronto Woman's Medical College (the first such institutions in Canada), Jewett's reference to such an offer is probably anachronistic. Before the establishment of those two institutions, most of the few Canadian women who became doctors had themselves studied medicine and received their clinical training in the United States, where hospital posts (although still rare) would have been much easier to come by.

10. *likely:* See chapter 3, note 17.

11. *the Corners:* See chapter 2, note 18.

12. *a stubble-fire . . . into the still air:* Designed to burn off the stubble, or stalks, that remained after the harvesting of grain like wheat or barley, such a fire emitted a blue-colored smoke.

APPENDIX

"Theodore Herman Jewett, M.D., of South Berwick"

One year after Sarah Orne Jewett's father died, his obituary appeared in an issue of the Maine Medical Association's Transactions, *along with those of several other Maine physicians, as part of the "Report of the Committee on Necrology" compiled by association member J. W. Beede, who concludes his prefatory remarks with the assurance that "the following sketches . . . are presented precisely as they were furnished by the respective friends of the deceased." Largely on that basis, Richard Cary later attributed the obituary to Jewett herself, a conjecture authenticated by the existence of a manuscript, evidently unknown to Cary, of her father's obituary in Jewett's hand (Richard Cary, "Some Bibliographic Ghosts of Sarah Orne Jewett,"* Colby Library Quarterly *8 (September 1968): 140; Sarah Orne Jewett, "[Dr. Theodore Herman Jewett]," Sarah Orne Jewett Papers, bMS Am 1743.22 [28], Houghton Library, Harvard University). As Jewett's touching eulogy of a father who later served as the model for Dr. John Leslie in* A Country Doctor, *the obituary is reprinted below for the first time in book form.*

Dr. Theodore Herman Jewett was born at South Berwick, Maine, on the 24th of March, 1815.

His ancestors were English, of Danish descent on one side and French on the other, and he was the second son of Capt.

THEODORE F. JEWETT.[1] His childhood was spent in Portsmouth, N.H., the family returning later to South Berwick, when his father gave up, early in life, his business of following the sea.

He was a delicate boy, caring less for the active sports than for reading, and he soon showed his preference for the life of a student. He was fitted for college at Berwick Academy,[2] which, at that time, took very high rank, and entered Bowdoin College in 1830, at the age of fifteen. Professor PACKARD,[3] who was his life-long friend, remembers him at that time as "a handsome, red-cheeked boy, a most loveable young fellow, somewhat quiet and diffident, but very winning in his manner, and a very great favorite both with the faculty and his classmates." Early during his college course, he decided upon studying medicine, and, from that time until his death, he was always an eager, diligent, untiring student of the profession, which he loved with his whole heart, and to which he did as much honor as any man who ever followed it, if we believe such honor to be in having a rare and noble talent for his work, and a determination to cultivate and use this talent for the good of his fellow-men.

After his graduation, thinking himself too young to enter upon his medical course, he taught for a year or two at Limerick and at Derry, New Hampshire. He afterwards attended the medical lectures at Hanover and at Boston, studying for two years with Dr. WILLIAM PERRY,[4] of Exeter, N.H., who was a most eminent physician and surgeon, and who pronounces him to have been a most admirable student, of wonderful powers of mind and singularly close habits of observation and study. Dr. JEWETT was also, for some time, a student with Dr. WINSLOW LEWIS,[5] of Boston, who also recognized his ability and took the greatest interest in him. He spent a year at the U.S. Marine Hospital in Chelsea,[6] and was also for a time among the city charitable institutions of Boston. He took his degree at the Jefferson Medical College in Philadelphia, where he spent the winter of 1839.

After his graduation he had planned to go abroad for some time, to perfect himself in some specialty in the medical schools of Europe, and, on his return, to locate himself in one of our larger cities. But his health was at this time very delicate; he had had several alarming hæmorrhages from the lungs, and his brother had just died with consumption, which it was feared he also had inherited. His father, who was a man of considerable wealth, begged him so persistently not to leave home, that, to use Dr. JEWETT's own words, he stayed in Berwick merely to please him, always hoping that after a time the opposition would be removed. And there his life was, for the most part, spent. It could not help being, at times, somewhat a lonely life, for he was shut out from the larger circle of professional friends, with its pleasures and advantages, to which he would have belonged in a city. Not that his ambition ever needed more stimulus than it found, or that he ever felt that his skill had been thrown away, where it was not appreciated. The people in the village and on the lonely farms seldom realized what a man he was, though they put their confidence in him so fully as their doctor and their friend. How much of their care and trouble he helped them carry, how kind and how trustworthy he was in every way, one can never tell. There never was a man in all that region more deeply loved, and no man ever died there at whose loss more tears were shed. He wrought many most wonderful cures, which at times came to the knowledge of men who could appreciate them, but his victories over disease were oftener unheralded and unrecorded, and he was content to have it so, since his wish was not so much to be called great as to be useful, and the service done, he was glad, and there was an end of it. He was always busy, either about his active professional work or in his study, where he kept up with the time in his reading, though he had often anticipated, in his own thought and experience, what was paraded as a brilliant new idea or a novel success.

Dr. JOHN E. TYLER, late of the McLean Asylum for the Insane, who was one of his oldest and best friends, and who had known the medical men of his own country and Europe, said of Dr. JEWETT, that he was the best physician of his acquaintance; that his knowledge of therapeutics, and his tact in doing the right thing at the right time and in the right way was marvelous.[7]

One can only wish that the treasure of wisdom and experience which was his could have been left as an inheritance to some one who could go on with the exercise of its usefulness, but it is believed that such a legacy has been left in part, for he was pre-eminently a teacher; one could not talk with him for even a little while, without being the wiser for it. He was always willing and glad to impart his knowledge to his brother physicians, trying to learn himself and eager to help others whenever he could. In the course of his wide-spread practice as a consulting physician, he left the men whom he met always richer for the practical ideas and suggestions and excellent prescriptions of which his mind was always full. His enthusiasm for his profession was unfailing to the last day of his life. It was never a dull trade to him, and he ministered, as has been truly said, to the souls as well as to the bodies of his patients.

As a man, he won friends for himself everywhere; his genial, beautiful smile, and rare wit and humor, his unselfishness and kind-heartedness, made his presence seem like sunshine everywhere he went. There was something singularly attractive in his face. Even on a journey, or elsewhere, among entire strangers, he at once roused people's interest, and everybody seemed to recognize the true-hearted gentleman and charming companion at first sight. And the longer one was with him, the more one knew his nobleness and purity of mind, his wonderful insight into human nature, his perfect integrity and hatred of deceit, his great learning in his profession, his accomplished scholarship in general literature, and his unerring common sense. He never was tired of living, and never grew old; his heart was always young, and the thought of him brings to mind these words of the wise old doctor, Sir THOMAS BROWNE, "and since there is something of us that will still live on, join both lives together and live in one but for the other, He who thus ordereth the purpose of this life will never be far from the next."[8]

Whether one speaks of him as a gentleman, the hospitable, generous master of his own house, or the delighted guest, as the skillful, daring surgeon, or quick-sighted, ready, careful physician, as the faithful Christian, with his simplicity and loyalty and perfect trust, and his willing service to his best friend and Master, the Great Physician, it is hard to praise him enough; it is simply impossible to praise him too much.

Dr. JEWETT held for some years the Professorship of Obstetrics and Diseases of Women and Children at the Medical School of Maine,[9] and, during the war, he held the post of Surgeon of the Board of Enrollment for the first district of Maine, at Portland.[10] He was one of the Consulting Surgeons of the Maine General Hospital at Portland, an honorary member of several medical societies, and member of the Maine Historical Society, beside holding many other positions of trust and honor. He took the warmest interest in the welfare of this Association, of which he was, at one time, President, and his address, delivered at its meeting in 1878, has excited the attention it deserves, and has been considered, by the best judges, one of the ablest essays on the practice of medicine ever written.[11]

Dr. JEWETT contributed occasionally to the medical magazines, and presented most learned and valuable papers before this and other medical associations. It is much to be regretted, both that he wrote so little and that he did not keep his published articles together, as no list can be made of them.[12]

Dr. JEWETT died suddenly at the Crawford House, White Mountains,[13] on the 20th of September, 1878, from heart disease, the existence of which he carefully concealed from his family and friends, going bravely on with his work until a short time before his death, of which he showed no fear whatever. He dreaded an old age of enforced idleness, of failing health, and the gradual giving up of the duties of his profession, and it is a cause of gratitude to those who knew him best that he finished his work in this world and went away so quickly to a better one, since it was always his own wish and hope that it might be so.

He was married in 1842 to Miss PERRY,[14] of Exeter, New Hampshire, who survives him with three daughters.[15]

Transactions of the Maine
Medical Association 6 (1879): 680–84.

NOTES

1. Theodore Furber Jewett (1787–1860), the writer's paternal grandfather, established a lucrative shipowning enterprise after his time at sea, becoming one of the leading citizens of South Berwick, Maine.

2. Berwick Academy, founded in 1791, became a leading New England prep school and perhaps South Berwick's most prestigious institution, graduating a distinguished roster of students that included Jewett herself.

3. Altheus Spring Packard (1798–1884) taught classics, languages, and religion in a distinguished sixty-five-year career at Bowdoin College in Maine.

4. William Perry (1788–1887), prominent New Hampshire physician and surgeon, whose eldest daughter would later marry his apprentice and thus become Sarah Orne Jewett's mother.

5. Winslow Lewis (1799–1875) conducted a successful medical practice in Boston, serving as consulting physician at Massachusetts General Hospital and as Boston city physician in 1861.

6. Established in Massachusetts in 1799 to provide care for merchant-marine seamen, the U.S. Marine Hospital moved in 1827 from Charlestown to Chelsea, outside Boston.

7. John Eugene Tyler (1819–78), graduate of University of Pennsylvania Medical School, and formerly superintendent of the New Hampshire Insane Asylum, was superintendent of the McLean Asylum for the Insane (now the McLean Hospital), outside Boston, from 1858 to 1871. Jewett is paraphrasing remarks that Tyler made about her father in a September 1866 letter transcribed in one of her diaries (Sarah Orne Jewett Papers, bMS Am 1743.1 [341], Houghton Library, Harvard University).

8. "And since there is something in us that must still live on, join both Lives together; unite them in thy Thoughts and Actions, and live in one but for the other. He who thus ordereth the Purposes of this Life, will never be far from the next, and is in some manner already in it, by an happy Conformity, and close Apprehension of it": concluding lines of "A Letter to a Friend, Upon Occasion of the Death of his Intimate Friend" (1690), by Sir Thomas Browne (1605–82), English physician and writer. Some years after her mother died in 1891, Jewett cited the same lines in consoling Thomas Bailey Aldrich on his own mother's death: "When a larger life opens for those who are nearest and dearest it seems as if a larger life opened for us too. I sometimes remember

what Sir Thomas Browne said—about joining both lives together and living in one but for the other. 'For seeing there is something of us that must still live on,' he begins. I have not seen the page for a long time, but in such days the words come back" (quoted in Francis Otto Matthiessen, *Sarah Orne Jewett* [Boston: Houghton Mifflin, 1929], pp. 94–95). The passage remained a kind of funerary touchstone for Jewett as late as her short story "The Foreigner" (1900), in which the memory of a townswoman's death moves Mrs. Todd to insist, toward the end, "You know plain enough there's somethin' beyond this world; the doors stand wide open. 'There's somethin' of us that must still live on; we've got to join both worlds together an' live in one but for the other.' The doctor said that to me one day, an' I never could forget it; he said 't was in one o' his old doctor's books."

9. Founded in 1820, the Medical School of Maine was affiliated with Bowdoin College for a hundred years before closing in 1921.

10. With the passage of the Enrolment Act, which instituted the Civil War draft in 1863, each congressional district in the Union established an enrollment board that included a surgeon responsible for conducting physical examinations of draftees, volunteers, and substitutes.

11. Theodore H. Jewett, M.D., *President's Address to the Maine Medical Association, at its Annual Meeting in Portland, June 11, 1878* (Portland, Me.: Stephen Berry, 1878); for Jewett's extensive use of the address in *A Country Doctor*, see the explanatory notes especially to chapter IX.

12. Apart from his presidential address, as many as nine papers by Jewett's father—published between 1850–51 and 1876—are listed in the *Index-Catalogue of the Library of the Surgeon-General's Office, United States Army*, first series (1896).

13. Opened in 1859, Crawford House had become one of the most popular of the resort hotels in the White Mountains region of New Hampshire.

14. Caroline Frances Perry (1820–91), daughter of his medical preceptor (see note 4 above).

15. The writer and her two sisters, Mary Rice Jewett (1847–1930) and Caroline Augusta (Jewett) Eastman (1855–97).

FOR THE BEST IN PAPERBACKS, LOOK FOR THE Ⓟ

In every corner of the world, on every subject under the sun, Penguin represents quality and variety—the very best in publishing today.

For complete information about books available from Penguin—including Penguin Classics, Penguin Compass, and Puffins—and how to order them, write to us at the appropriate address below. Please note that for copyright reasons the selection of books varies from country to country.

In the United States: Please write to *Penguin Group (USA), P.O. Box 12289 Dept. B, Newark, New Jersey 07101-5289* or call 1-800-788-6262.

In the United Kingdom: Please write to *Dept. EP, Penguin Books Ltd, Bath Road, Harmondsworth, West Drayton, Middlesex UB7 0DA.*

In Canada: Please write to *Penguin Books Canada Ltd, 90 Eglinton Avenue East, Suite 700, Toronto, Ontario M4P 2Y3.*

In Australia: Please write to *Penguin Books Australia Ltd, P.O. Box 257, Ringwood, Victoria 3134.*

In New Zealand: Please write to *Penguin Books (NZ) Ltd, Private Bag 102902, North Shore Mail Centre, Auckland 10.*

In India: Please write to *Penguin Books India Pvt Ltd, 11 Panchsheel Shopping Centre, Panchsheel Park, New Delhi 110 017.*

In the Netherlands: Please write to *Penguin Books Netherlands bv, Postbus 3507, NL-1001 AH Amsterdam.*

In Germany: Please write to *Penguin Books Deutschland GmbH, Metzlerstrasse 26, 60594 Frankfurt am Main.*

In Spain: Please write to *Penguin Books S. A., Bravo Murillo 19, 1° B, 28015 Madrid.*

In Italy: Please write to *Penguin Italia s.r.l., Via Benedetto Croce 2, 20094 Corsico, Milano.*

In France: Please write to *Penguin France, Le Carré Wilson, 62 rue Benjamin Baillaud, 31500 Toulouse.*

In Japan: Please write to *Penguin Books Japan Ltd, Kaneko Building, 2-3-25 Koraku, Bunkyo-Ku, Tokyo 112.*

In South Africa: Please write to *Penguin Books South Africa (Pty) Ltd, Private Bag X14, Parkview, 2122 Johannesburg.*